Robert looked at Meleri. "You know, I have been thinking about your predicament. It has occurred to me that I may have the perfect way out for you."

Her face brightened. "Oh, that would be wonderful. I cannot thank you enough. What is your solution, pray tell?"

"I will marry you myself."

"Marry *you?*"

"Of course. Do you find the idea abhorrent?"

"I cannot marry you. We just met. You're a stranger."

"Which do you prefer?" Robert asked. "A stranger or Waverly? Because you will end up married to one of us. You are in a predicament, lass, and there is no easy way out. You have precious few choices, none of them good. What will you do when Waverly finds you? And he *will* find you. What then?"

ELAINE COFFMAN

THE BRIDE OF BLACK DOUGLAS

MIRA®

MIRA®

ISBN 0-7783-2388-9

THE BRIDE OF BLACK DOUGLAS

www.MIRABooks.com

Printed in U.S.A.

The Bride of Black Douglas is lovingly dedicated to the readers who patiently waited two years for the publication of this book. Thank you for your letters and e-mail, for your encouraging assurance that you would "wait as long as it takes," for the hilarious notes from Internet groups who searched used bookstores certain it had been published and they missed it, for your periodic notes just to keep in touch and make sure I was working, and lastly, for those like me, who will never forget a beloved Scots ghost.

ACKNOWLEDGMENTS

With appreciation to MIRA Books for bringing this book to life and believing in me, for giving me the freedom and support to write my best, for a wonderful cover and a hero with his shirt on, and for loving this book as much as I do. And very special thanks to all who made it possible—Isabel Swift, Dianne Moggy, my editor, Amy Moore-Benson, who has been a delight to work with, and my "hands-on" agent, Helen Breitwieser, for always being there.

Prologue

There are times
When substance seems shadow,
Shadow substance seems,
When the mark'd partition,
'Twixt that which is and is not seems dissolved,
As if the mental eye gain'd power to gaze
Beyond the limits of the existing world.
Such hours of shadowy dreams I better love
Than all the gross realities of life.

Anonymous

If you believed the legend, then you believed in ghosts.

It was said that only one spirit haunted Beloyn Castle. Over the centuries, he had been called many names, but most knew him simply as the ghost of Black Douglas.

He was their ancestor, their past and their future, a mystical being whose spirit dwelled in the hearts and minds of those who followed, because he left them with something more real and assuring than a bodily presence.

He gave them hope.

No one had ever seen the apparition, but that did not mean he did not exist. In this land of magic narrative and haunting folklore, they knew that what went before cast its shadow upon that which was to come. Fame can fade to nothingness. A great name can pass into the unknown. But the magic of a kindred spirit pervades the places through which it has passed, like the haunting scent of roses in December.

The ghost had been here long before they were born; before the Border raiders hid their rustled cattle in the Devil's Beef Tub; before the wolves and red deer disappeared from the Lowlands; before John Knox, the great reformer, preached his sermon against idolatry in 1559. He was here before Robert Bruce became King of Scotland in 1318.

Over the centuries, generations came and went, aware of his nearness as the seasons changed, for he was always present, quiet beneath a blanket of snow, reassuring in the green of spring, noble in the yellow and russet of autumn. With the haunting echoes of the Gaelic tongue, they sang of him along with ballads of empty dales and ruined keeps, of the clink and rattle of armored troops, of humbled pride. And they would continue to speak of him, through the ages, one to the other, telling of a time when he had lived and died, and a time when he would return.

"He will ride across the Lammermuirs, when the moon is silvering the heather and the wind is blowing thinly over the hills." Time had not dimmed their faith. They knew he would come.

He would reveal himself, a shadow cast long ago, who would step out of the mist of the past and into the present. No one knew who would be the one to see him, or what exact moment he would choose to appear. They only knew it would happen. Long years had not changed their belief that he existed.

It did not matter that they could not see him, for they could feel his presence. He called out to them in their dreams and spoke in a voice older than the moss-covered stones at the base of the castle. At night, the seeds were planted in the fertile soil of their minds, and they would awake to reflect upon all that was lost and what would be restored when he returned.

He was there, in the eerie silence of bleak landscapes, in the thunder and lightning that came before the rain. Heathery moors whispered and spoke his name at night. Whenever their bairns would cry out, they would gather them into their arms and sing,

Hush ye, hush ye,
The Black Douglas shall not get ye.

Yet, the little ones were not afraid, nor did they cry out. They felt his presence.

They believed.

PART ONE

True love is like ghosts, which everyone talks about but few have seen.
François, Duc de La Rochefaucauld (1613–80), French writer, moralist. Sentences et Maximes Morales, no. 76 (1678).

1

Northumberland, England, 1785

Most women would go to any lengths to be married to the son of a duke.

Lady Meleri Weatherby was not among them. Betrothed to Philip Ashton, the Marquess of Waverly, since birth, she would have done anything to get out of her engagement…*absolutely* anything.

As a child, she had adored Lord Waverly. Philip was ten years her senior and her idol. Tall, blond and handsome with a heart-thundering smile, he could do no wrong. Those were the days when she considered herself most fortunate.

But nothing remains the same. The years passed and she grew older. Things began to change. It was through a woman's eyes she viewed the world now, and not those of a child. What she had once adored was nothing more than a thin veneer, cracked and peeling away.

Thusly exposed, she saw the true man—one with a cruel side that he frequently exhibited toward animals and underlings. Now she realized Lord Waverly was not the man of her dreams. He was the last man in the universe she would want to marry.

The awareness was gradual, but the realization came to her quite suddenly one warm afternoon when she was on her way home after a long ride. She no more than crested a hill, when she came upon a horrifying sight that both shocked and filled her with revulsion.

Philip was holding the reins of his terrified horse and beating the poor beast unmercifully with his riding crop. Blood was everywhere.

Instinctively, she alighted and ran toward him, screaming, "Stop it! For the love of God, Philip, stop!"

When he turned toward her, with the crop drawn back, she thought for a moment he was going to strike her, and she stopped stock-still, her eyes wide at the sight of a side of him she had never before seen.

She saw the blood-rage in his eyes and the tightly clenched jaw. She knew he fought against the urge to use the crop on her. "Stay out of this, Meleri. It does not concern you."

"I beg to disagree with you, but cruelty of this magnitude not only concerns me, it concerns me gravely."

Never had she seen such raw fury in human eyes. It was only when Philip threw the crop to the ground and walked off that she noticed one of his groomsmen, a young lad they called Will, standing nearby. He clutched the reins of Philip's horse tightly in one hand, while the other hand held a kerchief to a bloody gash on his cheek.

"Will, what happened to your face?" she asked, although she feared she already knew the terrible answer.

"I…I hit a branch, milady."

Meleri went to him and pulled the kerchief back, then winced at the deep gash. "That wasn't done by a branch. He struck you, didn't he?"

Will looked down. "I hit a branch, milady."

"I understand," she said softly, then gave his arm a pat. "You need not worry that I will speak of this to Lord Waverly. Can you ride back by yourself?"

Will cast a fearful glance in the direction Philip had taken. "I must wait for his lordship."

"You need to have your face seen to before you lose too much blood. Go on home. I will explain to Lord Waverly that I was the one who told you to go."

"Milady, I thank you, but I cannot ask you to place yourself in harm's way for me. I think it best for both of us if I remain here."

She understood what Will was saying. It would be worse for him if he left, no matter what she told Philip. "As you wish. Wait here. I will see what I can do," she said, then walked off to find Philip.

She met him walking toward her. Apparently, he had recovered, for she saw that all signs of rage were gone. Remarkable though it was, he looked completely composed, as if nothing had happened. When he saw her, he smiled in his most charming and courtly fashion. "Meleri, my dear, I am sorry you had to see that, but things must be dealt with when they happen. It is more cruel to withhold punishment until later."

"Is that what you call it? Punishment?"

"You have a better term?"

"Punishment is one thing, Philip, brutality another."

"You think I was brutal? Well, I suppose it would appear so to a woman of such delicate sensibilities. It would serve no purpose to try and make you understand."

What Philip did not realize was that Meleri understood. She understood all too well. This one incident caused her not only to realize the significance of what she observed, but more important, what that incident revealed about his true nature.

After leaving Philip, she rushed home and found her father sitting in silence in the garden. "Hello, Papa," she said, and seated herself beside him. She picked up his hand and held it in hers as she gave a full accounting of the incident with Waverly. "I have never seen so much blood on a man or a horse."

Next to them, a bee droned in the lavender bush. From the kitchen came the sound of pots being banged about. From somewhere in the distance came the frantic bellow of a lost calf. The seconds ticked on, and still he did not respond.

Only when several minutes had passed, did he direct his attention to her. "Do you come here…to sit in the garden often?"

It was the first time he had looked at her as if she were a stranger, or spoke to her as if she were someone he did not know. Panic ripped through her, followed by a sense of dread. Of late, her father seemed to be changing, sometimes into someone she did not know. He was her beloved Papa, and then again, he was not. *Where do you go, Papa?*

She saw the expectant way he looked at her, and in spite of a heart that seemed too fatally cracked to live on, she managed to say, "Yes, I do come here frequently."

"So do I. Don't you find it odd that I have never seen you here before?"

"I…I am here earlier than usual."

"Aaah…that would explain it then. I prefer to come here late in the morning."

She felt as if her father had gone away somewhere—on a long trip, perhaps—for the man she saw seemed more shadow than substance. You are not my father! You are his shadow, she wanted to shout. Go away! I want my father back!

He was back, the next day, as brilliant and bright as he had ever been. Overjoyed, Meleri hovered about him until he retired for the evening, afraid his shadow would return if she so much as stepped away for a moment.

Time passed, and as she watched her father gradually slip away, she had ample time to fully grasp an even more detailed impression of what her recent encounter with Waverly meant. From that day forward, she was careful to note, with systematic observation, what she could not previously foresee. The result was, that in Philip, she discerned not a single defect, but many. This enabled her to note what her life would be like if she married him, and that led to her final conclusion that Lord Waverly was not only cruel and cunning. He was dangerous.

Although she knew she would not—could not—marry him, she was not so foolish to think there would be an easy way out. Next to impossible was more like it. He was, after all, the son of one of England's most powerful dukes—a man who was also a relative of the king. Impossible or not, though, she had to find a way out, which meant she would have to turn her back on her home, Humberly Hall, and the life she had here.

Her father was the only hindrance, the one consideration that prevented her from being completely free to flee to America, or Australia, or anywhere Lord Waverly would not find her. To even consider her father a burdening responsibility, or a drawback to her future happiness, was unthinkable. There were so few days, anymore, when his mind did not wander too far away to communicate with him. Poor Papa, she thought. So forgetful, so careless and inattentive, even of the daughter constantly before him. He had given her so much. It hurt now to realize he could not help her any more than he could understand.

Her maid, Betty, concurred when Meleri told her of her intention to escape marriage to Lord Waverly. She was readying Meleri's bed for the evening, fluffing the pillows with wild abandon when Meleri broke the news.

"Cry off? Break your engagement? Your father will not understand, milady. Even if he did, he would forget by the next morning what he understood the night before. You will get no help from that quarter, and without your father's support and help, I fear what you seek is beyond impossible."

"I am in a dilemma, truly. I must rely on myself and take action before Philip has the slightest suspicion. Yet, I am my father's child, and I cannot trample that in the dust of my hurried departure. I suppose the only consolation in all of this is, at least I won't have to suffer knowing I am a terrible disappointment, or that he will suffer humiliation over my action."

"You are right. Truly, milady, I do not know that your father would notice overmuch that you *were* gone. Don't be forgetting the doctor told you only a fortnight ago that it will get worse."

"Knowing was never a soothing balm."

"This is all too much to fall on your young shoulders. Have you written to your sister?"

"Yes, I wrote Elizabeth several weeks ago. Last week, I received a reply. She is coming here. She should arrive today or tomorrow."

"Did you mention your desire to put an end to the engagement?"

"No, I thought I would wait until she was here."

"It would be nice if she understood and offered you some help in that quarter."

"I cannot depend too strongly upon the chance of that happening. Although she is my favorite half sister, we were never really close—not because there was a problem, you see, but because of the vast difference in our ages."

Meleri's two half sisters, Mary and Elizabeth, were older than Meleri's mother. They were both married before Meleri was born. Of the two, Mary had always been distant and judgmental, but Elizabeth had managed to offset that somewhat by being more understanding and sympathetic, especially after Meleri's mother died. Her kindness extended so far as to invite Meleri to come to London and live.

But her papa had quickly dismissed that idea. "Live with you in London! I should say not! Melli is all I have left, now that her mother is gone. I cannot let her go to London with you, Liz' Beth. Whatever were you thinking, to extend such an invitation?"

"I was thinking of Meleri, Father. I was considering how lonely it is for a young girl her age to be reared in the country, to grow up without a mother or other children her age about. Humberly Hall is lovely, but it is remote."

"It is also her home and her inheritance." Sir William had turned to Meleri and said, "Well now, my little princess, do you want to go to live in London with Liz' Beth, or stay here with your poor old Papa?"

How vivid was the memory of the way she had thrown her plump little arms around her father's neck and hugged him fiercely. "I don't *ever* want to leave you, Papa. Never, never, never."

Little had she known then, that in the end, it would be her papa who left.

"Are you thinking about something sad, milady?" Betty interrupted her reverie.

"No, I was thinking about the past. It is the present I find sad.

How does one learn to accept all of this—to see those we love growing old; to watch them leave, little by little each day?"

"Keep thinking like that and you will find yourself married to Lord Waverly."

Betty was right. She could drown herself in sentimentality, or turn her thoughts to extracting herself from this ghastly betrothal. No one would do it for her. She would have to do it herself. The only thing certain was, she could not marry Waverly, no matter the cost. It would belie her truest sentiments if she did not at least try to save herself.

Betty had begun to pound the pillows harder with each word Meleri spoke, until so many goose feathers were floating about her head that she sneezed.

"Bless you."

"Thank you, milady. I've thought about what you said, and I know how you feel, but you cannot think to stop a betrothal that was made so long ago."

"You think that is a valid reason to marry?"

"I didn't say that, only that I don't see you have any choice. I was told betrothal contracts are binding. If that is so, being a woman, you have no more say about it than you have power to change it."

"That is true," Meleri answered, "but there is another side to everything, or at least another way around it."

Betty arranged the pillows, then opened the trunk at the foot of the bed. She withdrew a white cotton nightgown with a satin ribbon at the neck instead of buttons. "Will this one do, milady?"

Meleri half glanced at it and said, "Yes, it's fine." She turned around to give Betty better access to the row of tiny buttons that ran down the back, but her mind wasn't on getting undressed. "It isn't right for a woman to be treated so unfairly or so differently from a man. No one should be forced to marry, especially someone they cannot tolerate."

Betty handed the gown to Meleri, then turned back the bed while she dressed. By the time Meleri began brushing her hair, Betty was running her hand over the white cotton sheets, smoothing them until they were flawless. "I am sorry to say, milady, but the only choice you have is to do as countless other women before you, and that is to take it like a lady."

Meleri stopped brushing and wrinkled her nose at that disgusting recommendation. "That is the most unpalatable advice I have heard! Surely, you did not mean I should meekly surrender. You must know me better than to think I would blindly submit to nothing more than becoming a suffering saint. I could sooner drink vinegar."

"We do what we have to do, milady."

"I know," Meleri said sadly. She put down the brush and climbed into bed. Suddenly she doubled up her fists and struck the bed. "Oooh! So much anger, so few ways to vent it! I tell you, Betty, the unfairness of it all makes me quite desperate."

Betty's hands flew to her breast. "Oh, milady! It bodes ill for us whenever you feel desperate. Please don't do anything foolish."

"Hmm… Like you said, we do what we have to do," she answered, thinking upon the subject further.

After a few moments of consideration, she added, "I swear, by all that's holy, if it was the only way out, I *could* do something foolish." Meleri leaned forward and rested her chin in the upturned palms of her hands. "Faith! I am so desperate to dispense with this ridiculous betrothal, I would do anything to rid myself of it *and* Lord Waverly." She had a sudden flash of thought and her head popped up. "Have you ever known anyone who joined a convent?"

"Lud! Of course not! And pardon me for saying so, but that choice is not for you."

"Why not?"

"You are not Catholic, milady."

"Oh…yes, I suppose that does present a problem." She sighed deeply. "Perhaps I could simply disappear…mayhap, I could lose myself in a band of roving gypsies."

"*Lose* yourself? With all that red hair?"

"Hmm. What if I took up with a crew of pirates…or perhaps a clan of wild, uncivilized Scots?"

"Scots!" Betty gasped in a perfectly horrified manner. "Milady, I entreat you not to speak so, even in jest. Don't be forgetting the parson said we should always be very careful about what we ask for, because we might get it."

Meleri looked at Betty's round, trusting face and saw her maid felt none of the cynicism she felt. Why should she? I'm the one being forced to marry a man capable of almost anything, she thought.

Betty doused all the lamps, save the one by Meleri's bed. "Shall I leave this one burning?"

"Yes, leave it. I will take care of it later."

Betty gave Meleri a smile meant to be reassuring. "Do not fret, milady. I know something good will happen. You are too kind-hearted and clean spirited to have such unpleasantness befall you. Do try to get some sleep now."

"I shall try, Betty. Most of the time, I fall asleep easily enough. It is only later, when the dreams come that I awake, unable to sleep. The rest of the night, I lie abed thinking."

"Are they bad dreams, milady?"

"No…at least, I don't think they are. I cannot always remember much of what I dream. I only know it wakes me and then I think, and think, and think. I ask so many questions, yet I never find the answers."

"Perhaps it is better that you don't remember."

"If only I could forget everything connected with this wretched betrothal, or that beast, Lord Waverly. And then there's my circumstances—and the plight of all women back through the centuries."

"Through the centuries? You mean you spend time thinking about *all* the women who have ever lived, milady?"

"Of course."

"But they are dead, milady. What good does it do to dwell upon them?"

"Because we can learn from them, from their mistakes and servitude. How could I help my own situation without considering the wretchedness of all women who have been virtual prisoners of men since creation? Sometimes, I swear I can hear the clanking of their chains." Her mood took a downward turn when she said, "Soon I will be joining them, unless I find a way out of this betrothal. Oh, Betty, what am I going to do?"

"I wish I knew, milady. Faith, I cannot think of anything or anyone who could help you now, save the Almighty, of course. *He* is the only one who can help you now."

"You expect me to trust another man?"

"Why…" Completely flabbergasted, Betty's mouth snapped shut.

Meleri paid no mind. "In case you have forgotten, *He* happens to be the one responsible for all of this."

"It wasn't God, milady. It was our mother Eve who did this to us when she was deceived by Lucifer and partook of the apple."

"That's my point! Bah! Talk about unfair! All women punished, for thousands of years, for *one* woman taking *one* tiny bite of *one* apple? If that isn't a prime example of male logic, I don't know what is. Does that seem fair?"

"No, milady."

"Now, I ask you, how absurd can you get?"

"I don't know, milady."

"And why me? I don't even *like* apples!"

"You will have to trust. God's wisdom is not our wisdom. He is your only hope."

Meleri slid down farther into the bed, until she felt as if the world were growing larger and she, smaller. She released a long, wretched sigh. "It's not that I don't trust. It's just that I've been doing that for some time now, without even a hint of salvation, and now the time draws uncomfortably near. I am of marriageable age. Each morning I wonder if this will be the day the ax falls, the day Lord Waverly pays Papa a call to arrange the date of our wedding."

"Hold to your faith, milady. Do not give up. Pray as if everything relied on God, and work as if everything relied upon you."

Before Meleri could say anything more, Betty bid her a hasty "Good night, milady" and headed for the door.

"Good night, Betty," she said in an absentminded way. A moment later, she doused the candle.

As was her custom, Meleri fell asleep easily. It was much later, when she was in a deep slumber, that the dream came to her again, with the faintest glimmerings of enchantment. Vaguely aware of a sudden storm that blew fiercely and pelted her window, she bolted upright when the windows in her room were suddenly thrown apart. Stricken, she watched as the curtains billowed out and sent a chill down her spine. Then everything grew quiet and still.

He came into her room, a mere shadow at first—a dim, indistinct figure, nothing more than a swirling mist of green that began to take form. A moment later, he was standing in the frame of her window. She could see him clearly now, an imposing, queerly dressed figure of a man.

His clothes were in the quaint, old-fashioned style, with hose and a white ruff about the neck. A great black cape hung from his shoulders and flared about his feet.

I might be frightened, she thought, if he did not look so much like the king's jester. The thought no more than entered her mind when she noticed the immediate widening of his eyes. He did not speak, but the expression on his face told her he knew her every thought.

He stepped farther into the room and moved to one side, which left the window clear for her to see a black backdrop of dim starlight.

With a grand gesture and nary a word, he swept his hand in front of him as a sign that she should look beyond him. Through the window, she saw a long procession of women. Incalculable in number, the orderly succession did not end, but disappeared mysteriously into the vaporous illusion of moonlight.

Her thoughts clear and lucid now, Meleri saw a tiny pinprick of light glowing in the distance. It began to grow brighter the closer it came, until she saw it was a lamp, passed from woman to woman. It came closer, the light stronger and brighter, until the first woman took it and turned to face Meleri. The moment she extended her hand and offered the lamp to Meleri, a pureness of light washed over the woman's face, revealing all the beauty and whiteness of a pearl. Meleri gave a strangled cry, for she saw it was the face of her mother, dead these many years.

She tried to call out, to utter her mother's name, but her throat was frozen and the words came out nothing more than a whisper, papery and dry. With tears on her face, she saw the kind, soft look in her mother's eyes and felt her heart would break at the beauty of it.

Once again, she held the lamp toward Meleri, only this time she motioned her forward.

Meleri frowned, trying to understand the significance of the lamp or what would happen to her if she took it. Yet, she kept thinking, whom could you trust, if not your own mother? The thought propelled her forward, until she stopped a few feet away, prevented from going any farther by some invisible force.

Her mother smiled softly and offered her the lamp with outstretched hands. Meleri reached for it, and as she did, her hand brushed the hand of her mother. Suddenly, she knew what it all meant, but the moment she grasped the meaning and significance, the vision began to grow faint, until it vanished completely.

What had been so real was now obscure to her mind and senses, nothing more than the memory of indistinct figures in the distance.

Left with only a dim recollection, Meleri was engulfed with sadness and doubt. She was beginning to wonder if she had imagined it all, when she saw the transparent image of a lamp glowing in her hand. As she glimpsed the lamp, she saw into the ancient past, from generation to generation, and realized each woman in the chain was a part of the tradition. They were the keepers of heritage: the guards of the female legacy, the caretakers of the inheritance of feminine knowledge and instinct, the preservers of the ancient wisdom passed down from mother to daughter.

She knew that by taking the light, she was receptive to the

spirit of all those who had gone before, to the part of them that dwelled within the deepest part of her own spirit and soul—the place where instinct, inspiration, spirituality and reason meet. Tears came into her eyes, for she realized she had inherited more from her mother than she thought. She was a composition, for all of her ancestral grandmothers dwelled within her still, each of them contributing a distinct part in order to make her whole.

The will to survive… It had been there from the beginning. All along, she had the power and the will to carry on despite the hardships—the perceptive insight, the ingrained knowledge, the dyed-in-the-wool, bred-in-the-bone instinct to find her way out of the deep, dark forest and into the light.

It was there from the beginning, but she had not known it.

She went to the window and looked out, but she saw only the silver-leafed trees and a carpet of dew-spangled grass. Disappointed, she closed the window and returned to her bed.

Things would be different now.

She would follow her instinct and listen to her intuitive nature. She closed her eyes and fell into a deep, restful sleep, conscious of nothing, save the voice that said, "Follow what you know, what you feel to be right. Let your instinct show you the way. Do not be afraid."

The next morning, when she awoke, her head felt fuzzy, her memory blurred. Languishing in her thoughts, she was still abed when Betty came into the room with her breakfast tray, her voice tuneful as a whistling teapot.

"Good morning, milady." She put the tray on the bed beside Meleri, then gave her a questioning look. "Did you sleep well?"

"Part of me, part of the time." She said nothing about what happened to Betty, who busied herself with drawing back the curtains.

Brilliant sunshine flooded into the room, so dazzling that, when it struck Meleri full in the face, it made her blink. Blinded for a moment, she squinted at Betty. "How do you know if something really happened, or if you dreamed it?"

Betty moved about the room, pulling things out of drawers

and readying the clothes Meleri would wear that day. "I don't know, milady. Intuition, I suppose."

Now, *that* had a familiar ring to it. Almost immediately, Meleri felt wide awake. She reached for the breakfast tray and pulled it closer. "Mmm. Buttered scones." She picked one up and covered it with honey. It was warm, buttery and too sweet to resist, so she popped it in her mouth. Savoring each moment, she poured a little cream and added a spoonful of sugar to her tea.

"Did you have another dream last night, milady?"

With a mouthful of scone, all Meleri could do was nod. A swallow of tea later, she said, "Yes, at least I think it was a dream."

"You think? You mean you are not certain?"

"I'm certain. It's only that my mind tells me I think so because I *want* it to be real."

"Always do or believe the exact opposite of what your mind tells you—that's my adage."

"And it probably works nine times out of ten." Meleri sighed. "Oh, fiddle! If there were only some way to prove it truly happened."

Betty chuckled. "Nocturnal visitors rarely leave calling cards, milady."

Meleri could not help smiling at that. "No, I fear they do not."

Further conversation was cut short when the housekeeper, Mrs. Hadley, came into the room, stomach preceding, as if she were leading the grand march. She was the only person Meleri knew who could enter a room in such a manner that she looked like a complete procession. She was a stout woman, box-shaped and rather brusque, but she could be coddled into a smile now and then.

"Well, bless me," Mrs. Hadley said, standing on two stocky legs in the manner of a Sussex spaniel. "You're already up."

"At least part of the way," Meleri said. She finished the last of her tea and put it on the tray, then climbed out of bed.

Betty glanced at Mrs. Hadley, then picked up the breakfast tray. "I'll take this downstairs."

Mrs. Hadley nodded. She stood there with the commanding

confidence of a mountain, the way she rose up, considerable mass, steep sides and limited width at the summit. Her eyes were eagle-sharp and took in every detail, including the fact that Meleri was not dressed. "Will you be needing any help with your clothes?"

"No, thank you, Betty has laid almost everything out." Meleri opened the wardrobe doors and lifted the riding habit down from the hook where Betty placed it.

Mrs. Hadley nodded. "The color will be perfect with your brilliance. That shade of blue goes very well with red hair."

Meleri held the habit up in front of her and studied herself in the mirror. "Do you think so? It was most difficult to decide between this and the dark green. Betty liked the green. She thought it matched my eyes."

"You have several green dresses and only one blue, and it is a very pale color. I think this particular shade will be quite an unforgettable addition to your wardrobe."

"Unforgettable?" Meleri studied her reflection again. "Hmm. You know, I think you are right. This is quite a spectacular color. The seamstress said it was the latest rage in London. I suppose it's good we rarely go there, otherwise, I would look like everyone else in the ton when I took my morning ride through Hyde Park."

"I hope you aren't too disappointed that you never had the opportunity to reside awhile in London. You are young and so full of life, I know you would love going to parties and having a life filled with all the pleasures the other blue bloods your age are enjoying. Your father did not mean to slight you when he did not arrange for you to have a season or two. I am sure it slipped his mind."

"I know. His forgetfulness grows worse and worse. I find it a horrible reminder that he is growing old."

"I remember back before you were born, before he married your dear, sweet mother. He was the most loving and attentive father to Mary and Elizabeth, as he was with you…in the beginning."

Meleri was remembering the Christmas when he surprised her with her first pony. "I suppose that's what happens when a man takes a much younger wife." Meleri tried to imagine herself married to a man thirty years her senior or what it would be like to have a man over fifty father her first child.

Mrs. Hadley looked off for a moment and her eyes grew misty. "I only wish you could have known him all those years ago, when he was a young, strapping man, so full of life and always on the go. Parties, parties, all the time."

"All replaced with books and hounds, or cattle breeding and collecting fine wine." Meleri felt suddenly ashamed of speaking so of her father. "I shouldn't have said that. I am too strong-willed and have the bad habit of saying whatever jumps into my mouth."

"You are honest and that is to be appreciated. I admire a person who believes in calling a cowplop, cowplop!"

Meleri started to laugh, then clapped her hand over her mouth, but it was no use. The laughter would not be contained. At last, when she had control of herself, she said, "Mrs. Hadley, are you insinuating I called my father a meadow muffin?"

Mrs. Hadley seemed to gather her generous proportions and rearrange them to make her taller, which perfectly fit her righteous manner of speech. "I most certainly am not. I would never refer to my employer in such a manner." She then glanced down at the timepiece pinned to her bodice. "Lord save London! Look at the time, and here I stand, rattling on like I had good sense. I must be about my duties while there is still time to spare."

She rushed to the door and had no more than disappeared, when her head popped through the doorway. "The blue is definitely the right choice," she said, then she disappeared again—so quickly this time, Meleri was reminded of a turtle drawing its head back into its shell.

Meleri fussed over the new riding habit a bit before she stepped into it. She was preoccupied with the dream and took little notice of the gold trim so beautifully embroidered on the snug, fitted jacket. Once she was dressed, she spent some time in front of the mirror, trying to tuck an abundance of curly red hair beneath a small hat of the same dark blue, trimmed with iridescent black feathers that curved smartly around her head.

She was about to admit defeat and give it up as an impossible cause. She even considered throwing the entire outfit out the window.

By the time Betty returned, she was in the supreme of frustration.

"I came to see if you needed any help getting dressed," Betty said, then gasped. "Oooh, milady, don't you look as fine as flowers?"

Meleri forced a smile as easily as one would paste pictures in a book and gave her a nod. "Why, thank you, Betty. I do believe I feel as fine as flowers." She twirled around, forgetting about her earlier decision to stomp the hat beyond recognition. "It is lovely, is it not?"

"Oh, it is, milady. It truly is. I thought you should have gotten the green, but I can see now that the blue suits you ever so much better. It does wonderful things to your eyes."

Meleri was beginning to feel floral, in spite of herself. "If I look that stunning, I think I should go for a ride."

"'Tis only fitting the flowers in the meadow should see you."

Once she was outside, Meleri asked the groom to bring her horse. She sat down on the tree stump she used as a mounting block. While she waited, Mrs. Prolific, the barn cat, came around the corner, her tail straight above her back, the tip curled over like a shepherd's staff. Meleri picked her up and held her close, stroking her soft fur. At the first rattle of a purr, she wished happiness came so easily to her.

Inside the house, Betty and Mrs. Hadley stood at the kitchen window, watching Meleri.

Betty frowned. "She's been a bit melancholy of late, hasn't she?"

The expression on Mrs. Hadley's face softened. "Yes, she's lost some of her sparkle. And why not, with all this fretting over Sir William, and the worry of what to do about Lord Waverly. Poor puss, she reminds me of the way she was after her mother died."

"Lud! I do not remember those days, but I heard she was wild as a banshee. Cook said she never thought to see a time when she would turn out to be such a lady."

Mrs. Hadley nodded in agreement. "I remember those dark days for certain. Poor child, even now I cannot help feeling a bit sorry for her."

"Sorry?"

"Yes. She was a lonely little thing after her mother was gone. At times, I wonder if anything has changed. I suspect she is still lonely."

"How can she be lonely when there are so many of us about?"

Mrs. Hadley thought about that for a moment. "As an ant could be lonely in a beehive, I suppose."

"Not around their own kind, you mean?"

"Yes, poor child. She ought to be around people her own age, not sequestered off in some country estate with an absentminded old father and a house full of servants. And there is Lord Waverly to consider."

"Lud! Don't mention him. His very name I find frightening!"

"A love match is what she needs. Wouldn't that brighten her life? She would be well suited to marriage with the right man. She has all the qualities of a good wife and mother."

Betty sighed, fairly filled with romantic illusion. "'Tis true, every word you say. If only it were possible. She would be better off an old maid and nursing bunions, than married to that dandiprat, Waverly."

"Whenever you mention marriage, she looks as though she will burst into tears. I know it has been weighing heavily on her mind of late."

"It's a pity, sure enough," Betty said, stopping to lean on the broom and stare wistfully out the window."

"Something will happen," Mrs. Hadley said. "She has the kindest heart and deserves so much more. Just the other day she gave cook three dresses to give to her neighbor whose cottage burned. Last month she gave the Widow Peabody four months of her allowance to buy her daughter a wedding dress."

"What do you think Lord Waverly's reaction will be, when he learns how Meleri feels?"

"It's not Meleri he will miss, but her huge dowry."

"Huge?"

"Enormously so. After the death of Lady Seren, there were rumors that she wanted Meleri to have a dowry larger than those Sir William settled upon the daughters of his first marriage. You know she will also inherit quite a grand estate through entitlements from her mother and grandmother?"

"No, I didn't know. I cannot fathom why Lord Waverly isn't itching to get his hands on all that money. I've heard he has run up debts that are far larger than what he receives from the duke. It is said that he buys too many horses, and that he is a big gambler who frequents the gaming halls, when he isn't losing bets at White's." Betty shook her head in a puzzled manner. "The aristocracy is very peculiar. They never seem to look at things in the normal manner. My father always said a nobleman was like a turnip…best when underground."

Mrs. Hadley nodded in agreement. "Most of them are relics—things of the past. They have more wealth than power, which affords them nothing to do but cling to their vices. As for Lord Waverly, he runs up such debts—more than enough reason to cry off, if you ask me."

"Don't forget the mistress in London."

Mrs. Hadley sucked in her breath with a gasp. "A mistress! Where did you hear that?"

Betty's entire person seemed to swell with importance. "Why, I heard it from my sister in London. She has a close friend in the duke's employ."

Mrs. Hadley frowned. "Someone should tell Meleri."

"Yes, but who? Would you want such a dastardly task set before you?"

"Of course not, but *someone* should be up to the task." Mrs. Hadley gave Betty the eye.

"Oh no, I'm not going to tell her."

Mrs. Hadley fell silent, and when she could not think of anyone to undertake such a mission, she said, "I suppose she will find out on her own soon enough."

It was almost noon when Meleri returned from a long ride. As she dismounted, she was thinking she could have traipsed about the outlying terrain for the rest of the day. Every aspect of her jaunt through the countryside was pure joy, for today Mother Nature seemed bent upon putting her best foot forward, filling the hills and fields with colors only an artist could mix and splash about with such ease.

She did not change out of her riding habit, but went directly to the music room, where she sat down at the piano, her heart fairly bursting with the need to express with music nature's bounty she had so recently enjoyed. Soon she was lost in her playing. It was not until she was in the middle of Mozart's Piano Concerto Numer Five—which she played with a flourish—that Jarvis, the butler, came into the room.

He placed an envelope on the piano next to her. "Shall I wait for a reply, milady?"

Meleri nodded and said with a smile, "Yes, please wait a moment."

Jarvis nodded, then stood quietly beside the door.

She continued to the end of the piece, then stopped and picked up the creamy white envelope, which she opened. She withdrew a monogrammed note from her childhood friend Lady Rebecca Crandall.

Meleri had been so happy that Becky's marriage last year to Lord Crandall was a love match, but disappointment soon followed when she learned Becky would be moving to London. During the past year, they had tried to keep in touch by corresponding frequently, but even profuse letter writing was not the same as having her closest friend nearby. Becky's departure left an emptiness in Meleri that nothing had been able to fill—a great blank in her life that taught her the true meaning of the word *lonely*.

Fair to trembling with anticipation, her gaze swept quickly over her friend's note. As always, she was anxious to hear about the gay parties or the latest gossip, and certainly all about the most recent Paris fashions. She never dreamed that she would soon discover it was her very own name that was being bandied about by the ton, instead of the latest French styles.

Dearest Meleri,

I heard something at Lady Davenport's ball the other night that distressed me greatly. I did not write straightaway, because my dear David thought I should, as he put it, "mind my own business." However, after much consideration and further looking into the matter, I have decided to write you. After all, you were my dearest friend when we were growing up and running wild as two Highland ponies about the countryside—something that time, marriage and separation has not changed.

Dear, dear Melli, I know you better than anyone, and I know you will understand I am not telling you this to upset you, but rather because I feel it is something you should know before you set a date for your wedding. Lord Waverly has a mistress, a Lady Jane something-or-the-other. I am trying to find out the last name and will write you when I do. She has been his mistress for some time now. Apparently, he makes no effort to keep this liaison secret, or to keep his mistress sequestered, since they are frequently seen together. It is rumored that the reason he has not set a date for your wedding before now, is that he is has been hoping to find a way to marry Lady Jane instead of you.

Please forgive me for being the bearer of such tragic and disappointing news. I only wish there had been a way for me to deliver such disappointing news in person, or at least to console you. Do write back with the utmost urgency to let me know you do not hold it against me for having done what I thought best.

Always your loving friend,
Becky

Meleri's hands trembled as she felt the sudden surge of anger, white-hot and intense, that burned through her. To be humiliated in such a manner—it was as unspeakable as Waverly was despicable.

"Of all the… Oooh!" She sprang to her feet, fists clenched at her sides, and set the rosy coils of hair to bouncing as she began to pace the floor. "A mistress!" she said, reaching the windows and turning around. "In London, no less," she said when she reached the opposite wall and spun around. "I'm probably the only person in the whole of England who did not know!" She stopped sharply and pinned Jarvis with a look of inquiry. "Did you know about this?"

Jarvis, looking quite miserable, stared down at the toes of his shoes—a move that unerringly inferred he would rather be somewhere else. "I…that is…"

"I can see that means yes." She did not hear the gulp, but she saw his Adam's apple bob a time or two. "And the other servants? I assume they knew."

She heard the gulp this time. "I believe most of them have heard at one time or the other."

"Suffering saints! Am I the only one who did *not* know?" She was furious. "I am so angry with myself for being such a ninny! How could I have been so easily duped?" She knew she should maintain a levelheaded coolness in circumstances such as these, but knowing and doing were two different things. She was only human, and certainly not impervious to agitation, turmoil or any of the dozen other emotions that wrestled for dominion over her feelings.

She hated Waverly for doing this to her—for stealing her eagerness, her passion…yes, even her *joie de vivre!* From life, she got her fire, her enthusiasm and her almost rapturous outlook on life. The other aspects and emotions she could subdue, but not her appetite for life. Front and foremost, it was her greatest infatuation. That Waverly was capable of stealing even this sent her fury spiraling to new heights. She wanted to throw something. She wanted to scream, or stamp her feet until she set the church bells to clanging in the village. "Excuse me a moment, will you Jarvis?"

"Of course, milady," he replied in a voice that sounded as bewildered as he looked.

Calm as a grave, she directed her steps toward the front door.

Shrouded in mystery and the model of perfect temperance, she stepped out into the sunlight. With the most genteel demeanor, she closed the door behind her, walked to the edge of the steps and had her fit.

Fists doubled, fury bubbling forth, she paced back and forth, waving her arms and venting her anger. When she finished, she stamped her foot and let out a blood-curdling scream, its length equaled only by its volume.

Her anger tempered, she felt immensely better.

She was glad Becky broke the news. What better impetus to get her moving toward her final goal of extricating herself from Waverly's clutches and ending, once and for all, their farce of an engagement? No longer was she the romantic. She understood now that no one would ride up to her door on a white destrier, lance in hand, to save her, any more than she could rely upon her father to intervene on her behalf.

A deep frown arose from the state of careful consideration she immersed herself in. She was not angry over Philip's amorous liaisons. He could have a hundred such women and it would have no effect on her, since she did not give two tuppence for Philip, with or without a mistress. That was not the issue. Of greater importance and concern was his lack of respect and obvious disregard for propriety.

Having a mistress was one thing. Flaunting it publicly was another.

Thankful her father never gave her that season in London, she'd been spared the deeper humiliation, since most of the members of the ton she knew by name only. Humiliation before strangers was ever easier. She never wished more than she did at this moment for her father to be the strong, capable man he had once been—a discerning man of keen intellect and sharp understanding, so cleverly adroit in dealing with difficulty.

Wishing would not make it so, and even if it would, she was better off learning to care for herself. *Self-reliance* was the word of the day, she decided, with sudden remembrance of bygone days when her father always gave her a word to learn at the beginning of each day. *Self-reliance*—better to learn it now than to stumble and trip through life.

When she reentered the house, she saw Betty and Mrs. Hadley speaking softly at the bottom of the stairs. "Have you seen my father?"

"He was reading in the garden an hour or so ago," answered Mrs. Hadley.

Meleri's heart began to pound. "Alone?"

"No, milady, Geoffrey is with him," Betty said.

A relieved breath escaped her. "What would we do without the infinite patience and understanding of Geoffrey?"

"In your father, he has found his calling," Mrs. Hadley said.

Twice in the past year, Sir William had wandered off. The first time, they found him in the upper meadow, "pursuing butterflies," as he had put it, butterfly net in hand. The second time, he was discovered walking down the lane, some four miles from home. That time, he could not remember why he left, or where it was, exactly, that he was going.

"I know. I could search from here to Lisbon and never find anyone as dedicated or devoted to him as all of you," Meleri answered.

"Sir William was both generous and kind to us when we were in need," Mrs. Hadley said. "It is only right that the opposite be true."

Elizabeth arrived later that evening, alighting from the carriage in a hurry. With equal haste, she rushed into the house. Meleri, who was coming down the stairs about that time, could not keep the elation out of her voice. "Dear Elizabeth," she said, hurrying to embrace her. "I am ever so glad you are here."

"I wish I could have come immediately after I received your letter."

Meleri took in her sister's blond and fair English-rose coloring, so different from her own. "You are here now and a most welcome sight."

"It is good to see you, although you have grown into quite a lovely woman since I saw you last. Goodness, how long has it been?"

"Almost three years, I think, since you were here on Christmas."

Elizabeth shook her head. "Three years! I cannot believe it was so long ago. I do wish you had come to London when father came, although I know you did not want to miss your friend's wedding."

"No, I couldn't miss Becky's wedding. Do you ever see her?"

"Fairly frequently, actually. At the theater, or riding in Hyde Park. Once, I talked with her at some length at the ball Lady Primrose gave for the Countess Alexandria de Rubicoff." She paused and looked around. "It still looks the same. I do not know why, but I find that uplifting. Where is father?"

"Out walking his dogs with Geoffrey."

"Shall we go in search of him?"

"I would like to have a moment to speak with you first, if I may. "

"Of course."

"Why don't we go out into the garden? I'm certain that would be welcome, after being stuffed in a carriage for most of the day."

Elizabeth slipped her arm through Meleri's and the two of them strolled outside to sit on a stone bench that curved in front of a stately elm. "I remember you used to have a swing in this tree. What happened to it?"

Meleri smiled at the memory of the hours she spent in that swing. "It broke, and so did my arm when I fell."

"Oh, I do remember the broken arm. Please tell me about father. How bad is it?"

"Oh, Elizabeth, it is quite the most difficult and heartbreaking thing I have ever had to witness. How can I prepare you for something I don't understand?"

Elizabeth listened quietly, occasionally wiping tears from her eyes as Meleri told her about their father and how Sir William first began to exhibit isolated incidences of odd, sometimes bizarre behavior. She reported how everyone thought at first that Sir William was only demonstrating his own peculiar brand of eccentrics.

"What do you mean by eccentrics?"

Meleri told her about the time he came downstairs ready to be driven to church, still wearing his dressing gown, and when he began to address the members of the staff by different names.

"How sad."

"Yes, and sadder still was the time last year, while attending Squire Threadgill's Christmas party, he got into an argument with his longtime friend, Lord Peterby, after accusing Peterby of stealing his silver cigar holder. The holder was later found, on the table beside the chair where Papa sat most of the evening.

"This was about the time I began to realize he would never be the guardian a father should be," Meleri continued. "After that, my attitude toward him changed. I stopped becoming angry at his lack of involvement, or hurt over his seeming disinterest in my life. I even found myself regretting the times when I reached the point of exasperation with him."

When there was nothing more to say, Meleri waited patiently while Elizabeth stared off, reflective and silent. Meleri's heart ached for her, and she could not help wondering if life would not have been more pleasurable without so many plots and too much friction.

"You said there are times when he remembers who you are."

"Oh, yes, some days he is completely his old self, with no hint that his memory flagged the day before, or that it was gone completely the day before that. One moment we can be laughing about something that happened when I was a child, when, without notice, he suddenly stops talking and stares off in the distance. That's when I know it will be a stranger's eyes that I see when he turns back to look at me."

"So sudden."

"And so painful." Meleri stood. "Shall we go find him now?" she asked, and the two of them walked off in search of their father.

As they walked, she found Elizabeth was not very talkative, so Meleri took the opportunity to tell her about Philip. She was surprised to find herself wanting and needing the counsel of someone older and wiser in such matters. By the time she finished, the tight grip of anxiety that surrounded her had grown to a tight knot of dread.

"Nothing you have said comes as any real surprise," Elizabeth said. "Nor can I blame you for feeling as you do. Certainly I would feel the same if I were standing in your slippers. You know, I never cared for Lord Waverly, or for his father."

"I never realized that. I thought you were quite fond of him."

"No, that was Mary. There was always something about him, something I could not name, that made me uneasy. I remember seeing you as a child—so vivacious and full of spirit. You were quite a precocious little thing. Father was fond of saying you 'blossomed faster than spring tulips.' Whenever I looked at you, with your huge green eyes and red, bouncing curls, I could not help feeling so much pity for you and the future father sentenced you to when he signed that betrothal contract."

The sound of yapping dogs and male voices ended any further discussion, so Meleri and Elizabeth stopped to wait upon Sir William. Elizabeth was anxious to see the change in her father, while Meleri fretted anew over the problem of Waverly, namely what to do about it.

Later, after Elizabeth went to spend some time alone with Sir William, Meleri changed into a pale yellow dress of dimity, trimmed in green. As she subdued her hair with a length of green ribbon, she wondered if she chose this particular dress by accident, or because it had always been a favorite of her father's.

An hour later, she was working at her embroidery frame, her mind busily employed elsewhere. Her thoughts were not on Philip, but on the smattering of pity she felt for the unfortunate Lady Jane. It went beyond her, how anyone could voluntarily be Waverly's mistress. She decided the easy way out would be for Philip to marry the woman, but she knew he would never be so foolish as long as the duke was alive.

At the sound of footsteps, Meleri jabbed the needle back into the fabric and looked up to see Elizabeth come into the room, carrying a cup of tea.

When she sat down beside her, Meleri saw her half sister had been crying and felt compelled to soothe her as best she could.

"I'm so sorry. I know it isn't much consolation, but I know how you feel."

"I know you do, you poor child. And to think you have had to bear this, day in and day out, watching the gradual ebbing away of the man we loved so much, helpless to do anything about it." Elizabeth pulled a small linen handkerchief out from under her sleeve. "I don't think I could have done it. You are much stronger than I."

"I trust you are not upset that I did not write you sooner of his condition."

"No, if anything, I am happy you allotted me a grace period, time when I unknowingly thought all was well."

"How was he?"

A tear rolled down Elizabeth's cheek and she wiped it away. "He spoke to me as if I were a stranger. It broke my heart when he asked me if I was someone he knew."

Meleri and Elizabeth soon fell into a deep discussion, which lasted for more than an hour, which was about the time Sir William came tottering down the backstairs, looking for all the world like a man with a mission. He spotted Jarvis dusting a bronze statue and called out, "I say there, Jasper, have you seen…" He paused and frowned deeply as if trying to remember something. "Have you seen…"

"Are you looking for your daughters, Sir William?"

"By Jove, yes! I am looking for my daughter. Have you seen her?"

"I believe they are both in the sitting room."

Sir William started off, then stopped in front of the sitting room door. Meleri and Elizabeth both looked up, just as Sir William paused. They saw his quick glance toward Jarvis. "By the way, Jeremy, do you recall the way to the sitting room?"

"Yes, Sir William, I believe it is the door right in front of you."

"Dash it all," Sir William said, turning back to discover the door, "when did we put a door here?"

When Sir William entered the room, Meleri noticed the way his shadow raced ahead of him to stretch itself over the sunlit floor. She could not help wondering how long it would be before it was only the shadow of her father she would see, while her Papa was left permanently behind.

Meleri and Elizabeth both came to their feet. "Hello, Papa, how are you feeling today?" Meleri asked, noticing how the afternoon light gave added importance to his graying side-whiskers, and did nothing to soften the silver hair that was once so very black.

He stopped and fixed them with a look that said he was searching for the words that never followed. Meleri smiled at the dearness of him. "Would you like to join us?"

"Join you? Jolly time, to be sure. Dreadfully sorry to say, no. I'm off to Squire Tolliver's."

"Could you sit down for just a minute?"

"The squire is weaning the pups from his best hunting dog. I'm going over to pick one out."

"Elizabeth and I wanted to talk to you."

"Elizabeth? Oh, that must be the lady with you. Is she a new friend?"

Meleri sighed. "Papa, I wanted to talk to you about Lord Waverly."

Sir William frowned. "Can't talk about Lord Waverly."

"Why not?"

"Never met the chap." He took his watch out of his pocket and looked at it, then snapped the lid shut and put it back in his pocket.

At a loss for anything to say, yet needing to speak to prevent herself from crying, Meleri asked, "What time is it?"

"Time to see the dogs!" he said, and with that he headed toward the door.

Jarvis was still working in the hallway, busily employed with the feather duster, when Sir William saw him and said, "What luck! You are still here! Could you tell me which direction I was coming from when I spoke to you a moment ago?"

Jarvis, his face blank as paper, said, "You were coming from that direction, Sir William."

"Jolly good! That mean's I've had my lunch."

* * *

Elizabeth burst into tears before her father was gone.

Meleri immediately began trying to console her. After a few tries, she realized there was nothing she could do or say that would change the way Elizabeth felt, so she contented herself with simply patting her on the back in a way that let her know she was not going through this all alone.

"I'm s-s-sorry," Elizabeth managed to say.

Meleri patted her back again and offered what little encouragement she could. "Go ahead and cry. You will feel ever so much better for having done it."

When Elizabeth was all cried out and nothing but the hiccups remained, she expressed her apology again. "I cannot believe I was such a blubber puss! Me! A woman my age, crying like that."

"When it comes to tears, age doesn't matter."

Elizabeth folded her hands in her lap and stared down at them for a moment, as if considering something. "I have decided two things. The first is, I think you should be away from here with all due haste, if you still feel the same way about Lord Waverly."

"Leave Humberly Hall?"

"You cannot remain here any longer than necessary. Waverly could pop up at any time and demand to set a date."

"I'm not overly worried about that. He's been painfully slow to even put in an appearance here for ages."

"Yes, well that may have been true in the past, but I daresay that will all change the moment he hears of the state of decline our father has fallen into."

Meleri cringed at the thought. "I had not considered that."

"Have you decided where you will go? You know you are welcome to come to London."

"That is the first place Waverly would look."

Elizabeth patted Meleri's hand. "Do give it the utmost priority. Once Waverly knows and sets the date, your impossible task will only become more so."

"What was the second thing you decided?"

"I cannot return to London now that I know the full extent of

Father's decline, yet I cannot remain here. My dear husband will soon be pressing me to return home. And there are my children and grandchildren, most of whom are in London, at least for the biggest part of the year."

"You want to take Papa to London with you. Is that what you are saying?" Meleri asked, wondering how Elizabeth's soft gray eyes could possibly have turned softer.

"Yes, that is what I am saying. I can look after him there. If I leave him here, I shall do nothing but worry. There are many things in London to amuse him, and I think it will be stimulating for him to receive all the attention from his children, grandchildren and great-grandchildren." She smiled. "And that bloody puppy, too, I suppose."

Meleri laughed. "Knowing Papa, he would tuck the pup into his waistcoat if you so much as hinted at his leaving his new pup behind."

"I shall see to it that he has someone with him at all times."

"You must take Geoffrey. Papa adores Geoffrey and he is equally attached to Papa."

"I will speak with him when they return with that blasted puppy." She considered Meleri. "Tell me, how are you taking all of this?"

"I know you love your father, just as I know it is true that you would fret if he remained here. I am aware that is not the only reason you have decided to take him to London."

"No, it is not the only reason. You are young and have your future waiting out there for you. You will never find it if you remain here and marry Waverly. I am not so naive to think you would go traipsing off in pursuit of your own happiness and leave your father behind."

"And if I said I did not want you to take Papa to London?"

"I should take him, anyway. It is only a change, Meleri, not the end. Once you have secured yourself from any possibility of Waverly forcing you into marriage, you will be free to see your father whenever you like."

"Humberly Hall without Papa? It would never be the same."
Elizabeth shook her head and took Meleri's hand in hers.
"Humberly Hall isn't the same now. Your papa is already gone."

2

Beloyn Castle, the Scottish Lowlands

He was nurtured on the legend. Before he could walk, he knew the story by heart. His first words had been Black Douglas.

But that was a long time ago. He was older now, and wiser.

Robert Douglas did not believe in miracles. His hopes had been dashed too many times for that. He was tired of waiting for an old story, a legend to prove itself. This was not Camelot. He was no Merlin. He could not perform magic. God knows, if he could, he would have done so long before now. To his mind, in the dark, unfathomed past, the ghost of an ancestor who promised much and delivered naught offered no salvation and little hope—save to leave him brooding in sullen contemplation far into the night.

His had not been an easy lot. Born into strife, life had only gotten worse. He was restless now, filled with anger and bitter words, unable to sleep on his bed of sorrows, and he cursed the cause of it: England, a ravenous beast driven to dominate and destroy. England, who would not rest until the last living Scot was dead.

He damned the English for their reprehensible arrogance and secret deeds, for centuries of criminal behavior and for being at the root of all of Scotland's woes. He damned his father for dying too soon, for shifting the burden of tyranny to the shoulders of a son too young to understand or to assume the title of Earl of Douglas. Most of all, he damned the ghost of Black Douglas for giving his descendants hope for three hundred years, then abandoning them to an old enemy who would stop at nothing short of their complete elimination.

Driven to inhuman lengths, Robert was bowed by the weight of centuries, a man who faced the impossible task of making a choice between staying true to his beliefs, and the equal folly of becoming free of them. His heart swelled with sadness, regret and far too much cynicism for a man his age. He needed something to believe in, something to warm hopes grown cold, something to help him face a future so bleak that it closed around his throat, tight as gallows.

He wanted more belief than doubt, more hope than despair, more faith than distrust, more room in his heart for love than revenge. He needed a purpose, a reason to go on. Yet, there were times when he wondered if he was too far gone to believe in anything again.

Alone in the library, he waited for the day to end, for a time when darkness would envelop him. He was becoming a creature of the night, a man who found solace in the quiet, late hours, when everyone else was asleep.

During the day, his mind was occupied with the trials and tribulations of the present. It was only at night, when words faded and thoughts came alive, that he could put the misery of the day behind him. Only then, could he collect the fragments of his person and sit in still contemplation, as silent as a tree. Night pressed against him like a woman's breasts, soft and heavy with perfume, the hours marked by an unquiet soul always searching to find himself again.

When morning came, he would lift his head from beneath the thick tresses of darkness, to greet an old taste for vengeance that still lingered, warm and stirring, aromatic as wine. He did not know why the longing was always with him, why the thirst for revenge grew stronger now, or why it had been tormenting him so much of late. He only knew it gripped him and would not let go.

A noise in the hallway ended his silent contemplation, and he soon recognized the rustle of silk. His grandmother approached. Even before she entered the room, he had a vision of a chocolate silk gown. He saw each detail, from ruffles edged with Mechlin lace and gray hair combed back and rolled, to the cap of spotless cambric that closed around a beloved countenance. The cap was not the fashion of 1785, but a style peculiar to Gram.

In the thirty years since his birth, little had changed about her. She still sat before her wheel, other times knitting a stocking by the fire in winter or by the window during the warmer months. On occasion, she would venture as far as the garden, if it was late in summer and the evening was particularly fine. Her body, like some perfectly assembled piece of applied mathematics, still enabled her to accomplish her chores as she had always done. He found that both painful and pleasing. Painful to see the briskness and agility he remembered gradually diminish. Pleasing to see no indication that it would soon cease.

Of late, she wanted to speak of little save the days of Douglas glory, long past. He saw no purpose in this, for it had little relation to either the present or future. Not that it mattered. Gram had never been an easy sort to deter from a course of action, by either persuasion or exhortation. He had a feeling tonight would be no different.

"Ha!" she said upon entering the room and catching sight of him. "I thought I would find you in here, lurking in the gloom. Why don't you light the lamp?"

Her presence always warmed him, but tonight nothing could fill his voice with cheer. "All men should be entitled to an eclipse, now and then."

"*If* it doesn't become endless night. Daybreak and resurrection are kin, you know. The arrival of light each morning assures survival."

"Morning will come whether I light the lamp or not. As for tonight, I prefer it this way."

She lit the lamp on the desk and turned it low. "Weel, it's time to humor an old lady. I cannot talk to you if I can't see your face, now can I?"

She wanted to talk. He did not. He did not want to discuss the past. He did not want her to know the old torment was back. "You are always a welcome sight, Gram, although I fear I won't be very good company tonight."

"Aye, I suspected such. You have been distracted of late. What torments you?"

"It is nothing I want to worry you about." He was reminded that she had had more than her share of suffering and recalled those dark and terrifying days after his parents were robbed and murdered in London. Two years before their deaths, her husband was killed by a bolt of lightning. Robert's sister, Sorcha, had been the next to die, and then came his uncle Iain's wife, who died giving birth to twins.

So many losses. So much sorrow.

Yet, Gram remained steadfast. "Whatever it is, put it behind you. No good comes from pulling up old, painful memories."

"Now, that's a peculiar comment coming from someone who does a great deal of just that. I could as easily ask you to talk about that which is to come, or the here and now."

"Why would I want to talk about the future when mine is shrinking? We have so few pleasant things in our lives; I prefer not to think upon the present at all. Why should I, when we must concern ourselves with nothing but fallen fortunes and the declining importance of our family?"

She took a seat across from him and settled the chocolate silk about her. "The present and the future belong to you. The past suits me, I think. At my age, it is ever so much nicer to relive the glorious hours when we were abounding with wealth and prosperity, or to reflect upon times when our name was the mightiest in all of Scotland."

Cynicism gripped him. "I cannot relive something I have never known. The present is nothing but strife and woe, but that is, at least, familiar. Unlike you, I have no past abounding with wealth and prosperity to recall, or any hopes of such for the future. And that includes any thoughts of deliverance from an antiquated ghost."

"Hout! For the life of me, I cannot fathom where you have so recently come upon such derision. Of late, everything you say is delivered with mockery or sarcasm. You have no right to ridicule those of us who hold to the belief. The miserable have no balm but hope."

"My hope is that you will someday find someone else to quote besides that English bard."

She fluffed her skirts about her. "I did my best to disguise it."

"Next time, you should try harder, although a disguise cannot mask the words of that cursed Englishman."

"Shakespeare transcends England and the English. He belongs to everyone. Besides, he was right. You cannot take away a person's hope. It is all they have. A man without hope is nothing more than a beast."

"Ah, hope. Where would we be without it?" Suddenly his tone turned bitter. "Hope is for fools, for entertaining illusions. It is for the spiritually pompous. If hope is all you have, you are already lost."

"When you were a wee babe, I rocked you to sleep to the lullaby of Black Douglas. You were weaned on stories of his deeds. I never thought I would see the day you would turn against your upbringing and everything you were taught. It is a good thing your father is dead. To see you like this would break his heart. You are becoming a cold man, Robbie, and full of hate, although I know it is not your true nature to be so."

"I hate *only* the English, and you of all people know why." He came to his feet and turned away, not wanting her to see his pain.

She followed his lead and rose to her feet, as well. "You are bitter, and your hatred runs deeper than bone. You will never be happy until you learn to put it behind you."

"I have tried, but I cannot."

"I pray each night that it is only frustration and disappointment that shakes your faith. If all hope is truly lost, then I pity you, Robbie Douglas. I pity us all."

Frustration and disappointment? Aye, he had plenty of that. He was not yet thirty, and born into strife. The Battle of Culloden was history when he entered this world. Not that it mattered. As head of the family, he suffered the consequences as surely as if he had been there that fateful day.

He felt Gram's hand upon his shoulder. "All is not lost," she said, then kissed his cheek and walked quietly from the room.

He thought about what she said. Was all lost? Truly, he did not know. It had been so long since he felt anything that resembled faith, trust or conviction that he no longer knew what it felt like. If any hope remained, it was nothing more than a dying ember in a fire grown cold. It was not enough to restore trust in the ghost of Black Douglas, or the steadfast belief that he would return and be their salvation.

He leaned back wearily in his chair to stretch his long legs and gazed out the window. The sun was going down. Already the darkness that would soon settle over the ancient walls of Beloyn Castle was closing in. He made no effort to turn up the lamp. The light of a thousand lamps would not brighten his mood. Despair clung to him as tightly as his breeches. The castle was falling down around them. He barely had enough money to support them, or to pay the servants—even after he'd cut the staff to a fraction of what it had been, or what a castle this size required. He needed money, and soon. Money, or lose the only home the Douglases had known for centuries.

Born into the crushing grip of his own destiny, he was doomed to fail before he could start. Stamina, principles, moral convictions, even his resolve were of no consequence. He felt as if he were rolling, out of control, down a steep embankment. The only way he could go was down. With a ragged curse, he slammed his fist against the paneled wall.

If only he had Gram's optimism—and her belief that a longdead ancestor would save them.

Was she right? Was he here, lurking in the shadows of the

crumbling castle, silently waiting, patiently watching for the right moment to appear? Or had the ghost of Black Douglas truly abandoned them, after all?

Robert was running out of time. Already that English swine, the Earl of Drummond, had in his possession a note that would initiate the Douglas downfall. Drummond, long referred to as the greediest man in all of England, was on the verge of enlarging that claim to include Scotland. Robert cursed his name to perdition, unable to understand how such a man managed to wrest the Douglases' note from the bank in Edinburgh. Not only that of Beloyn Castle, but those of half a dozen farms and castles belonging to other Lowlanders, as well. If things continued along this vein, the deeds to half of the Border Country would be in Drummond's parsimonious hands by Christmas.

On the opposite wall, the faint glow of a lamp warmed the brooding portraits of his ancestors. He watched the light grow stronger, waiting to see who approached. With somber resignation and moody impatience, he watched his deerhounds, Corrie and Dram, amble into the room, circle and lie down at his feet. He gave them a pat and wondered how long he could afford to feed even them.

The dogs gave a whimper of recognition when his uncle, Iain Douglas, walked into the room. Of medium stature, he had iron-gray hair and lead-colored eyes that belied his amiable disposition. He was Robert's closest confidant, and his father's only living sibling. It was Iain who kept him from giving up, kept him from deep despair.

"God's bones! It's darker than a stack of black cats in here. Why are you sitting in the dark? You should light more lamps to chase away the gloom."

"Cheerful wretch! Penniless, yet happy, he speaks with music in his voice. I prefer the gloom."

"Och, lad. You have the look of a sacrificed sheep upon your face."

"Sacrificed…an exemplary way to describe the way I'm feeling right now. Any more rain and the crops will rot in the fields. A few more expenses and we are out of money. We have debt up to our eyebrows and servants to pay. Beloyn has fallen into utter ruin."

"You mean we don't have the coin to sustain us much longer?"

"Aye, if we are frugal, we've only enough to last until the end of the month. Everything I try seems cursed from the start." With closed eyes, he tilted back his head and kneaded the tightness in his shoulders. "I'm tired, Iain. My bones are weary. My heart is heavy. I feel like an old man."

"I wish I had the means, but like most Scots, I haven't two coins to rub together. What are you going to do?"

"I don't know. I often wondered what drove a man to ruin, what pushed him to seek consolation in whisky or opium. Did he seek the comfort to escape, or to simply live in a state of ecstasy? Perhaps both. In either case, it serves to free him from despair."

"You know what they say…the shortest way out of Edinburgh is a bottle of whisky. You could try turning to your faith for strength."

Robert leaned back in his chair and put his feet on the desk, then folded his hands behind his head. "Aye, I could. A good dose of John Knox is better than any opiate. What else would keep the beasts of burden so patient, while a few more weights are added to their load?"

Iain took a seat in the hard wooden chair across from him. "I know it isn't easy to be the head of such a family when you are so young."

"Careful, you are starting to sound like Gram."

He smiled. "Where do you think *I* got it?"

Robert pulled his feet from the desk and pressed his fingers against his eyes, as if he could rub away all his weariness. He heard Iain chuckle and could not resist asking, "What amuses you?"

"'Tis the odd look on your face. If I were a king, I would be worried about treason."

Robert gave him a half grin. "You are damnably close. I was thinking about the Chinese proverb that says, 'Of all the thirty-six alternatives, running away is best.'" His expression softened and he spoke with a tone of uplifting assurance. "Not to worry,

Uncle. I doubt anything will change. I have neither the heart to stay, nor the wit to run away."

He gave the globe standing nearby a spin. "My father saw to that with his persistent indoctrination, wanting me to be prepared for the burden of inheriting his title. It is all rather ironic, is it not? In the end, he has beaten me with noble blood. A lifetime of wants and desires drowned out by an aristocratic code, and the memory of my father's lectures on noble behavior." He shook his head sadly. "My defiance is brought to its knees by the discipline of optimism, hope and blind acceptance. All that I have turned my back on, everything I wanted to run away from, everything I denied, despised or ridiculed, has served to defeat me in the end. Being the Earl of Douglas is too firmly rooted within me." He looked at Iain. "'Train up a child in the way he should go, and when he is old, he will not depart from it.'"

Iain laughed. "Snared by proverbs, are you? Weel, if it makes you feel any better, your father and I had that one shoved down our throats along with our oatmeal from the time we were born. It does not surprise me that my brother fed you liberal doses of it, as well. You are not the first to question the role inheritance plays in the way we live. Most men struggle all their lives against the limits they are born to. The poor seek the wealth of the rich. The rich seek the freedom of the poor. The important thing is, do they learn something of the value of those limits?"

Robert shrugged. "I am learning to starve like a gentleman. It is part of the poetic training, I believe."

"There are always stultifying effects from being educated. What is it that you really want?"

"To be free as a fish."

Iain stepped toward him and clapped him on the back. "Weel now, don't look so dejected, lad. It could always be worse."

Worse? Robert looked around him and wondered how that could be. He saw the worn and threadbare appearance of a room that little resembled the finely furnished library he had seen in paintings of the castle—paintings dating back to the times before tragedy brought the Douglases to their knees. "I am backed into the corner, Iain. We need money and I have no idea where to get it."

"If you are meant to find it, you will. Faith and trust are all you have left, like it or not."

"Troth! That sounds remarkably like the way my life has been heretofore."

Iain chuckled. "Careful, or we'll end up back at proverbs again."

This time, Robert's full smile was followed by a soft chuckle.

"Now that you've stopped looking like the bleakest rock on the loneliest heath, I have something for you." Iain reached inside his doublet and pulled out a bit of parchment, which he handed to Robert. "This just came, delivered by the king's messenger."

Robert looked down at the parchment bearing the king's seal and felt the gnawing of dread.

"Go ahead and open it. Whatever it says, standing there staring at it won't change it."

"No, but it might delay the agony."

"Agony? Are you gifted with the sight? You *know* the contents before you open it? Perhaps it contains good news."

"Nothing from England is good, including news. If it comes from the king, it can only mean more suffering." He broke open the seal and began to read.

"Then take the suffering and learn from it."

Absorbed in the king's missive, Robert grunted, but said nothing until he finished. "Apparently the Douglases haven't paid enough, in spite of all we have endured or that we bleed from a dozen wounds."

"Then use the wounds to your advantage. Little by little they will make you receptive to wisdom, in spite of yourself."

"By all that's holy, you sound so much like my father—and knowing who educated the two of you, I think it is my grandfather I should be angry with."

"It would serve you better than being at odds with your king."

Robert snorted. "He is not *my* king, nor will he ever be."

"Tell me of the letter."

Robert thrust it toward him and turned toward the window. He clenched his jaw and thought over the king's decree.

"So he orders you to marry," Iain said after he had read the letter.

"Aye, marry an English witch, when I would sooner sup with the devil."

"It could have been worse."

"Every time you say that, things get worse, not that I see how that could happen."

"He could have picked the woman for you to marry. At least he has left that up to you."

"Surely you see through that bit of fake generosity. Three weeks to find a suitable wife among the daughters of the English aristocracy? Ha!"

"I admit three weeks isn't a very long time, but…"

"An impossible task and the king knows it. Why do you think he added that *he* would choose a wife for me, if I fail? We both know he won't go searching for the fairest flower in all of England, considering I am nothing but a lowly Scot who has been anything but a loyal subject."

"Yet, why go to such pains, when he could have ordered you to marry the woman he chose from the beginning?"

"Because this way, he will avoid any criticism. I may be a worrisome Scot, but I am still a peer of the realm, and as such, it would behoove him to at least *appear* to give me an opportunity to find my own wife."

"Like King Eurystheus and the twelve labors he set before Hercules…"

"He gives me an impossible task to perform."

Iain's laugh was gently teasing. "Hercules managed."

"I am not Hercules. I cannot fulfill this task in the allotted time, therefore I see no reason to waste my time with it."

"You mean to give up without a struggle?"

"It is what my head tells me to do, but my accursed Scots heart will not allow it. I have entered a fool's race, knowing I will be racing Atalanta."

"Then I pray you will be as fortunate as the suitor who tricked her and won the race."

"Not so much fortune as trickery. He knew she would stop to retrieve the apples he dropped. Unfortunately, I don't have three golden apples."

"I am confident you can work around that. First, you must ferret out a lass that you find suitable."

"If she is English, she is unsuitable. You, of all people, should know I would *never* find an English woman to my liking."

"Well, let's *suppose* for a moment that you did, then all you would need is something she desired enough to marry you for it."

"And what would that be? My wealth?"

"There are other things besides wealth that would appeal to a woman."

"Don't start preaching to me. It's as impossible as raising the dead, and you know it. The king has handed us a Gordian knot and no one can untie it. No one!"

"They said the same thing to Alexander the Great."

"Where do you get it, Uncle, that I am on equal footing with Hercules and Alexander the Great?"

Iain laughed. "Where do you get it that you are not? Cheer up, lad, you are disillusioned, but that will change. You were born to believe. It is in your bones as well as your blood."

Robert thought of his sister, Sorcha, and how he had believed in only one thing since her death. "Hating the English has replaced all of that."

"Have caution, Robbie. You cannot hate and be wise. Deal with the problem at hand. The king has ordered you to marry. Don't go complicating things by digging up ghosts from the past to stumble over."

"If it were only so easy."

"Sorcha's death hurt us all, but you it changed. I know you have always blamed yourself for her death, at least partly. I told you then, and I tell you now—there was nothing you could have done. You were a mere lad of sixteen and no match for the four men who held you."

"Held me and made me watch what they did to her."

He nodded and put his hand on his arm. "I know, lad, I know. It has long grieved me to know they made you watch. I know what that did to you."

Robert felt a stabbing pain to his heart as the guilt he carried for so many years gripped him. "I am at war with myself. Contrary to what you might think, I am capable of remorse. There are times I feel ashamed at what I feel in my heart. I take pride in the deeds done for those I care for. I feel with each sheep I shear, with each cattle I slaughter, that I am contributing something to Scotland, to the world. Yet, there are times when things happen that take us beyond what we once were. You cannot always offer the other cheek or turn and walk away."

"Your sister deserves a better memorial than that."

Aye, Robert thought, Sorcha did deserve more than being raped by an Englishman on English soil. He cursed the day his sister went to visit a friend's aunt who lived just over the English border. He cursed the day he went to bring her home, too young and foolish to take an escort. But, most of all, he cursed the day he let his grandmother and uncle persuade him to remain silent, when he wanted to bring charges against the bastard who caused her death.

"She was my sister, my twin, a part of me and dearer than life. I would have gladly died in her place. Tell me how does a man get over being forced to watch the rape of his sister? What will rid his mind of the memory of carrying her lifeless body from the loch after she drowned herself? How can he stop hating a man with such a capacity for dehumanizing another—one of his own kind? Dear God, she was the daughter of an earl and not fair game for anyone…not even an English lord."

"I know, lad, I know, but you cannot do justice to the dead. Sorcha is beyond all of that now, and at more peace than either of us. I know if she were here right now, she would tell you the same thing."

Bitterness filled him. "But she is not here and I will hate in my own way."

"Aye, and the king will intervene in his. Checkmate. No escape. No defense. The battle is over. You have lost."

"The battle has yet to be fought."

"You're wrong. It was over the moment the king entered into it. What better way to rid himself of an annoying dissenter and suppress all contradiction? Kings will be tyrants when subjects are rebels."

"I am a minor pestilence—insignificant as an ant bite, and nothing the mighty English king should be concerned with."

"He, obviously, does not see it that way. A rivulet, however small, is capable of becoming a river. You have crossed the king and his authority at every turn. I warned you before that it was only a matter of time until he found a way to bend you to submission."

"If he thinks taking an English wife will make me forget, or kiss his bloody boots…"

"It is my guess that the king, by forcing you to marry, is showing you he is in control. If you continue to challenge him, the next punishment will be worse."

"There is nothing worse than forcing me to wed an English whelp."

"Have a care, lad. You must avoid challenges that could further embroil us with the English. Look at it as a way to gain peace and equity between us. You must try to be fair."

"I am fair. I don't speak well of any Englishman."

Iain smiled. "Ah, Robbie, 'tis a pity sure enough that you were not fighting at Culloden. With such a stubborn lad about, the outcome might have been different. Try," he said. "The king expects…no, demands obedience."

"I would be a fool to obey a king who fights not with a sword, but by shuffling papers. He amuses himself by playing a game of human chess."

"Use this as an opportunity. Look at it as a fortuitous circumstance that shaped your destiny."

Robert thought about what Iain said as he lowered himself into a worn leather chair. He had to find a way to obey the king and have his revenge, too. "Worry not, Uncle. I shall do what is best for all of us," he said, his words drifting away as his mind began to flirt with the germ of an idea.

Iain studied him with a gaze that was eagle sharp with scrutiny. "You are up to something."

Robert gave him an innocent look. "Why, Uncle, I don't know what you mean."

"The devil you don't! Whenever you get that gleam in your eye, it bodes ill for the rest of us. You cannot disregard an order from the king. It is treason even to think it."

"You are in Glasgow and I am in Edinburgh. I was not thinking about disobeying at all. To the contrary, I have just come upon a most suitable reason for complying."

"You know I would not expect you to adhere to the doctrine of full obedience and total submission without reason. Nothing would give me greater pleasure than to see you find a lassie in Scotland to marry, someone you had feeling for."

"Aye, a Scottish lass without a boddle in her purse. When it comes to marriage, I must put responsibility first. Even if the king had not intervened, I could not marry a lass I fancied, unless she possessed a large dowry. Fate decrees I marry for money. The king stipulates an English wench for subjugation." He came to his feet and began to pace the room.

Iain spoke with loud conviction. "It would be a good time for the old earl's ghost to return."

"In spite of the volume, I doubt he heard you. In any case, I will not hang my hopes on that moldering legend. If my namesake did not wish us to be delivered into the hands of the English, he would have shown himself ere now."

Iain's entire countenance brightened. "Unless…unless that is exactly what he wants to happen. Not even God always gives what we ask for. Sometimes we are given what we need."

Robert stared at him in amazement. "I need an English wife? Are you daft?"

Iain smiled. "Perhaps, if her dowry was large enough."

"I have no need of English money."

"All right, be stubborn, then. Do nothing and let the king

solve the problem for you. Why waste your time going to England on such a fool's errand? Why bother with trying to find a wife in three weeks? Call the king's bluff and see if he follows through."

"Call his bluff? Not with my life at stake!"

Iain did his best to hide a smile. "Out of optimism as well as gunpowder! Then obey the king and take the easy way out."

"You forget that I am a good Presbie. If it is predestined that the dowry of an English lass will save our family, it will happen. As for me, I will do everything I can to rub salt in the king's wounds. Have no fear, Uncle. I will find my own English wife, and I'll do it in less than three weeks."

Iain groaned. "Shot with my own gun! I hoped to rally you to the cause, not send you off half-cocked. What are you going to do?"

"I don't know, but I'll have it figured out by the time I get there. Don't worry. I can always find a lass even if I have to kidnap one."

They were interrupted by a knock at the door. A young, dark-haired lad entered and handed Robert an envelope. "This just came for you."

"Another letter from Drummond. More bad news," Robert said as he removed the letter and read as far as Drummond's signature. "Three must be a magic number for the English. The king gives me three weeks to marry; Drummond, three months to redeem the note."

"You won't need three months. You'll be married before then."

You'll be married before then...

Sudden understanding hit Robert so swiftly he felt a gripping pain in his chest. Married in three weeks and he had yet to meet the unfortunate wench.

"I expect Drummond will mellow when he hears you've taken the daughter of an English lord to wife. When will you leave?"

"On the morrow. I'll take Hugh with me."

"Aye, your brother would be good company."

Robert scowled. "Are we speaking of the same Hugh?"

Iain laughed heartily. "Aye, Hugh, the instigator of mischief, the teller of jokes, the man with no worries, who thinks all the lassies were put on this earth for his sole pleasure." He paused to see how Robert was taking all of this, then said, "Cheer up, lad. Things are going to get better."

"When you are on the bottom, the only way is up."

Iain clapped him on the back. "'Tis a sad one ye are, Robbie Douglas. Thou art wedded to calamity."

"Aye, but not for a few more days," Robert said so morosely that Iain laughed.

3

Needing to think about things, Meleri went for a ride, which always helped to clear her mind. She was so preoccupied with distracting thoughts that she did not realize she had been traveling swiftly for some length of time.

She slowed her horse to a comfortable pace. About the only thing she had decided was she would have to speak with Lord Waverly.

It was not that much farther to Waverly's home, she thought, especially if she took a shortcut, so why not go now, and have it done?

She turned her horse off the main road and found herself greeted by a bright field of yellow-and-white buttercups. Now and then, she would catch a glimpse of the river threading its way through the trees clustered along the lower slope of the valley, or hear the noisy chatter of thrushes going about their daily search for food. Once, she was on the receiving end of a shrill scolding by a blackbird perched in the lofty branches of a sycamore tree.

Although it was warm enough to split rocks, the world about her was as splendid as any rendered by an artist's painting. The sun shone down with an almost liquid brilliance that made the trees in the distance a shimmering of great shadows and light, spangled with deeper contrasts. There was nothing like the colors one could see when riding in the summer, during the hours closest to noon.

She came to the end of the field and turned down the road, her attention still drawn to the vibrant splash of colors bursting with life in the countryside as she passed by. In a single glance, she could take in the bright white fence of a cottage, the tawny gold of a thatched roof, the glazed green of a chestnut tree and the sparkling blue of the river against the rich brown tones of the road that lay curled, like a lost riband, before her.

She passed a family out for a drive in their smart new carriage pulled by four beautifully matched bays. They waved, and Meleri smiled and waved back. As she watched them go by, she admired the smooth-gaited horses.

It occurred to her that she was able to appreciate the beauty about her, not because it was here, but because she had taken the initiative to ride this way. Was the same true of life? Would she only have the happiness she sought if she rode out to meet it, if she took the first step to be the initiator of her future?

Carpe diem...

She was a bit surprised to recall the words of Horace, memorized during her study of Latin. "*Carpe diem.* Seize the day." She said the words slowly, as if savoring them, and in a way, she was, for their flavor was as sweet and rich as the faintest suggestion of freedom. Sunday last, she recalled the parson spoke about life and how each of us is given a great opportunity, if we only seize it. He quoted something from Hippocrates about opportunity—that it was fleeting and judgment difficult.

"Turn obstacles into opportunities," he'd said.

Well, wasn't that what she was doing? It was satisfying to know that, for once in her life, she was in control of what happened. Wouldn't this be a nice habit to indulge? She continued on her way, and found her mood had changed somewhat. Getting away from Humberly Hall was a lot like Mrs. Hadley's tonics. It cleared her head and made the world seem a brighter place.

There was something about being out in the open—away from everything and everyone. With nothing but the feel of her horse beneath her and the wind in her face, everything seemed right and orderly. For the first time in her life, she felt at perfect balance with the world.

Overhead, the sun had passed its zenith and would be starting its descent. That and the gnawing in her stomach said it was well past the noon meal. There were few travelers out, for she had not met anyone since the family in the carriage, neither a gentleman on horseback, nor a farmer in a cart, not that she was surprised. This was not a heavily traveled area, and even when she reached the larger road, she knew it would be little used.

Not far from the village of Holystone, she entered the forest near Lady's Well, a place that was considered both ancient and holy. The shadows of the trees stretched out before her, long and thin across the grass. The woods became denser and darker, and she began to feel nervous and uncomfortable, for she had been afraid of the dark since she was a small child.

Thickets that were unfamiliar surrounded her. She regretted not paying close attention to where she was going. She feared she had lost her way, when suddenly, she rode out of the dense woods and into a clearing scattered with trees. Again, sunlight bathed her face, and she breathed a sigh of relief and rode on, happy and thankful for the assurance of the warm sun against her skin.

Just beyond the glade up ahead, she could see the smooth surface of the large well reflecting the sunlight. As she drew nearer, she spotted the Celtic cross that rose faithfully out of the center of the square wall that surrounded the well. As she knew it would, the medieval statue from Alnwick, of a bearded, long-robed man, seemed to stare back at her.

There was a quiet solitude about this place—creating a sense of peace deep inside, where all the turmoil she had felt earlier resided. Now she felt as if she didn't have a care in the world. Calmness descended upon her. Composed and completely relaxed, she rode along, listening to the steady breathing of her mare, the soft thud of hooves upon damp clumps of grass that lay thick and spongy beneath them. In the distance, a church bell rang. Someone was getting married.

She thought of her mother, about how young she was when she died from a fever that struck swiftly, leaving behind a grieving husband and a six-year-old daughter to live alone with nothing but the servants and too much time to wander the long, cavernous hallways of Humberly Hall. She thought of the massive rooms so silent and filled with pain, and the memories of happier days gone by.

There were moments when she longed for those bygone days, when the house was filled with people, and every room echoed with their shrieks of gay laughter. Those were the seasons of endless parties and weekend guests, of balls and hunts and long winter rides in the sleigh, where she snuggled against the warmth of her mother, the two of them buried beneath the fur of a great bear her father shot one summer in Russia.

As quickly as it had come, the memory passed, and with it, the return of reality. Her mother was dead. The sleigh was rusting behind the barn, and the hunting horses and dogs had all been sold a long time ago. For no one came to spend weekends at Humberly Hall anymore.

Suddenly, her mare reared, and she heard a loud thump, then a man's oath of surprise.

"Curse the devil!"

She sat stock-still, as if enchanted. Around her, a breeze stirred and ruffled the leathery leaves of the trees. Still she did not move. Transfixed, she was motionless with surprise. She was instantly happy she was riding over the site of an ancient priory dedicated to St. Mary the Virgin.

It was not until her chest began to ache that she realized she was holding her breath. She released a gasp of air, and saw a man lying on the ground. Dear God above, had she run him down? Was he dead? Had she killed him? Her heart thumped wildly, for he was as still as death. *Oh, Lord above, I've killed a man! What should I do? I can't run him down and simply ride away.* She looked down at the stranger, a man she had never seen before.

She may not have known him, but she rapidly learned one thing: he was quick. She barely had time to blink before he was on his feet. She no more than saw him standing in front of her horse, when a sinewy hand shot out, grabbed the bridle and gripped it tighter than a fat woman's corset.

"The devil take you! What are you trying to do? Run me down? Or was that your intention all along?"

She stared blankly at the black-hearted devil as he impaled her with a hard, unforgiving look. Unable to speak—which was something rare for her—she could not seem to move as she stared in a stunned manner at a stranger who was truly unlike anyone she had ever seen in her life. His hair was certainly longer than she was accustomed to—long and such a dark brown it was almost as black as the breeches and doublet he wore. She decided it was the eyes…definitely the eyes, that she found so mesmerizing. Piercing and brilliantly blue as a gemstone, they held her motionless.

He was not what she would call fall-into-a-swoon handsome, despite the power of attraction that fascinated and held her spellbound. Idiotic though it seemed, she was both frightened and intrigued. The sound of her own heart thundering in her ears was a new sensation—one she found not altogether unpleasant. As she sat there, looking down at him, only one thought penetrated the confusion of surprise and emotion in her brain: how dwarfed everything else seemed against him.

"Don't you watch where you are going, or is it your habit to run people down?" He spoke suddenly, with a tone so harsh and flinty, that instinctively she drew back and almost toppled from her horse.

"What is a lady like you doing riding alone in a place like this? Where are your escorts?"

Trembling in spite of herself, she was trapped by those eyes staring hotly at her. It unnerved her that he had the power to hold her spellbound, and she wondered if he was an apparition that stepped from the holy well, or an evil spirit that chose to haunt these hallowed grounds. Probably the latter, she decided. Judging from the dark, swarthy appearance of this creature of the netherworld, darkness was where he belonged.

A sudden stillness enveloped them, while a hushed silence seemed to settle over the holy ground where they stood. A vapory fog swirled up from the ground, surrounding her. Out of its midst, a crumbling old castle rose on a base of sharp, jutting stone, surrounded by darkness. There came a noise, like a strong wind blowing through a belfry, and she could feel it pushing against her back, as if someone had put his hands there and urged her toward the castle and into the darkness. Her stomach tightened at the thought of going alone into the dark.

From out of nowhere came the soft lilt of a man's voice, laced with entreaty…. *Follow your destiny… Step boldly into the darkness… Do not be afraid… 'Twas tragedy and grief that framed him thus… Follow your destiny… All is not lost…*

In the distance, a dog barked. The swirling fog began to lessen. It grew lighter and lighter, then disappeared altogether. When it was gone, and her senses returned to normal, she no longer felt another presence—save for the stranger she had just run over.

The dog stopped barking and the glen was as it had been, still and quiet. The vision of the castle disturbed her. She thought of the enchanted waterfall nearby, the holy well, the ancient priory built by the Augustinian nuns and felt neither fear nor wariness, nothing but a sense of complete peace. After all, she was standing on sanctioned, sacred ground.

Strangely, she felt an odd sort of curiosity about him, which she tried to quell by convincing herself that it was God's will that she encounter him. She even went so far as to envision him as part of some Divine Plan, which sent a cold shiver over her.

He did not look divine.

Whatever enchantment she thought she felt came to an abrupt end when the stone-cold grip of a hand encircled her wrist, and she heard the soft burr of a Scot's brogue as the ruffian said, "Do you speak English, or are you a complete simpleton?"

"A simpleton," she said, blinking at him.

He smiled beautifully, and she melted with relief when he said with an amused tone, "An English lass with a sense of humor. I did not expect to find that."

"There aren't many of us."

"Aye, I am aware of such."

"Do you know many Englishmen?"

"More than I care to, but you didn't answer my question. What are you doing riding in a place like this all alone?"

The dazed, bewildered feeling began to wear off, replaced by one infused with a shot of boldness. It would not do to let him think her weak or afraid. Some beasts only attacked those weaker than themselves, or those who made the unfortunate choice to run. "I don't see that it is any of your concern." She did not miss the spark of irritation that flared in his eyes. She wondered if, perhaps, she had been a bit hasty to confront him. She resigned herself to placating this backwoods ruffian, for she was most anxious to be on her way. "I always ride alone."

"And your family does not care?"

"They know I am an experienced rider."

"No one is experienced against accidents or ruffians lurking about."

She could not help the way her eyes widened as she asked, "Are you a ruffian, sir?"

He ignored her question. "Who are you?" he asked. "Why are you here, in these woods? Do you live nearby?"

"I'm not in the habit of giving my name to strangers, nor do I find my purpose for being here any of your concern."

"It's to be expected, I suppose."

"What is?"

"Your tartness…it probably comes from your hair, which is unusually red for an English lass. Are you part Irish?"

"What I am is none of your affair. I was born here. That makes me English to the core. That should suffice."

"You must be Irish. You've got the Irish temperament that goes with the hair." His blue eyes were wary, but in spite of that, he must have found something about her face that held his interest, for he seemed content to examine her at some length.

Meleri took advantage of that to do a little staring of her own.

"The way you stare, sir, makes me wonder if you plan to paint my portrait."

"Few artists could do you justice. You've a face that would be hard to forget, lass."

Lass... She didn't know why that irked her, but it did. "I would have known you for a Scot, even if you had not spoken. Your manner is only slightly above that of a barbarian."

"And you display all the coveted qualities of a true Englishman...you would rather be rude than polite."

The imprint of his features burned into her memory. His face was like a rugged mountain formed by ice and harsh winds, its summits forbidding, austere and brutal. But there were glimpses of verdant peaceful valleys hidden in the shadows of the mountain's raw and breathtaking presence. He was both frightening and mysterious, and at the same time, the most blatantly seductive man she had ever encountered, in spite of the emptiness in those frigid blue eyes. She felt drawn to him, yet baffled and unable to understand why. The last thing she needed in her life right now was this unruly Scot with eyes that missed nothing and promised much.

Just her luck! she mused. Here she was, on her way to rid herself of one ogre and she stumbles into another one. She did not need a replacement. But in spite of all the reasons why she should ride off, she found herself leaning toward him, her gaze on his mouth. It was this confusion, as well as her anger at feeling such an attraction for someone who was probably an outlaw, that she said harshly, "I have other things to do besides sit here and exchange barbs with you. I am long overdue at my destination. I'm certain they have sent out a party to search for me. If you would like to spare yourself the wrath of my family, release my horse at once. I must be on my way." She pulled on the reins to turn her horse and said, "I will leave you to your poetic quips."

He did not budge, nor did he release her horse. "They can send an entire regiment for all I care. If I can't outsmart a handful of Englishmen, I've no right to call myself a leader."

"And what do you lead, sir? A herd of Highland goats? Or is it sheep?"

"You've a sharp tongue, lass, but what surprises me is that you seem to take great pride in it."

"Will you release my horse so I can be on my way and you can return to your lair of meanness and mist? You are pushing me, and in a moment I am going to live up to the color of my hair."

"I like a lass with spirit."

"I promise you won't like me," she said, and, lifting her whip, she brought it down across his shoulder, while at the same time she planted her foot against his chest and shoved with all her might.

"Ooof!" he said, and relaxed his hold on the bridle as he took a step back, steadying himself before he fell.

It was all the advantage she needed. Instinctively, she kicked her horse and brought the whip down on her flanks. The mare bolted forward with a shrill whinny. Afraid he might follow her, she urged her horse into a run and kept her own head low, against the mare's mane, to avoid the slapping sting of low branches as they passed.

It was only when they left the last trees of the forest behind and rode out onto the open moor once again that she slowed their pace and turned to look behind her.

There was no sign of the Scot.

She laughed. He said she had a face that would be hard to forget. Well, she'd bet he had a good reason to remember her face now. Not that it would do him any good.

Their paths would never cross again.

4

Robert Douglas watched the mysterious woman ride off. He knew the hot and swift rush of blood through his veins was the cause of the furious pounding of his heart against his temples. What he did not know was why this woman had caused it.

She was English, was she not?

For several minutes after she left, he stood stock-still, looking toward the last place he had seen her. Filled with a brooding silence, he tried to recall the enchantment of her face…her *English* face. *Hout!* Something mysterious and extraordinary was going on here. He was feeling things—strange things, things he did not want to experience; things he had no explanation for.

The moment she was gone, he felt more than a twinge of disappointment, knowing he would never see her again, that he would never know more about her than he did now…never again to see the blessing of that face.

Why had he let her go?

What was it about her that nagged at him? Why her and not a hundred other beautiful lassies he had seen? Something about this one—but what, he did not know. He only knew it went deeper than beauty. His fierce attraction to her burned through him. He did not understand why his brief few minutes with her

haunted him so. And he did not understand why he had an inexplicable feeling that he would see her again.

Of course, he would see her…if it was his destiny.

Destiny… The word stole into his mind with such delicate
ease, he was not, at first, aware of it. *Destiny*… The word went
down as smooth as a glass of Drambuie. How could it not? He
was a Scot. It was natural that he would believe in the mysterious. He was also a good Presbyterian who believed in predesti-
nation. He closed his eyes and saw vivid red hair.

He kicked a clod of dirt, angry with himself for letting her go.
He had come here to find a lass to marry. A perfect choice almost ran him down and what did he do? Let her go, fool that he
was. He kicked another clod.

"Don't take it out on Mother Nature. Kicking dirt won't bring
your lassie back."

Robert stopped and turned to watch his younger brother,
Hugh, approach. "You saw what happened."

Hugh laughed. "Aye, I saw a wee lassie send you tumbling in
the dirt to land on yer arse. She was a pretty little thing, red hair,
and more than likely, green eyes. Quite a lass to send a man such
as you rolling in the dirt."

Robert forced a laugh and rubbed his backside. "I feel fortunate that's all she did. I could have broken my fool neck."

Hugh was looking at him strangely. "It's not like you to stand
there like a petrified forest and let a horse run over you. What
happened? Didn't you see her coming?"

"Aye," Robert said, still feeling dazed. "I saw her."

"Then why the devil didn't you move?"

"I didn't think she would run over me until it was too late."

"From where I stood, she looked determined to ride right
through you."

He dusted himself off. "Well, what is life, without conflict?"

Amazed, Hugh shook his head. "I can't get over it. I never
thought you were the kind to let anyone run over you, especially
a lass."

"I don't know why that would surprise you," he said. "She is an English lass. It has long been their favorite pastime to ride over *all* Scots, or have you forgotten?"

"How was I supposed to know she was English?"

"We are in England, are we not?"

"Aye, but we are not English."

"No, and come to think of it, she had no way of knowing I was a Scot."

Hugh laughed. "Maybe her horse did."

"It was probably the accent." Robert gave Hugh a stern look. "It must be nice to be the youngest and so free from responsibility that you can jest at a time like this."

"A time like this? What do you mean? You make it sound like we're at war or something."

"I came here to find a wife, remember?"

"Aye, and you might succeed if you didn't do your best to scare them off as fast as you meet them. Take my advice. You would have a better time of it if you would use a little humor yourself. Not many lassies want to spend the rest of their life with a man whose features look as if they're carved from Grampian stone."

"Thank you. I will try to remember that."

"Seriously, why *did* you let her go? We came here to find you a wife, did we not?"

"We came here to find a dowered lady."

"She could have been nothing but. Did you see her clothes? Her horse was of a superior bloodline. She was no ordinary homespun lass, some miller's daughter out for a dalliance. She had all the bearing of a woman of rank. I thought she was an opportunity from heaven, falling into your hands like manna. I do not think you will be able to do better. You must admit she was more than passing fair. If you had detained her long enough to show her your charming, captivating side, we could be on our way to Scotland by now, with your lass in tow."

"I don't have a charming, captivating side. I never had time for that. You are the younger, charming son. You're the one who had all the time to dally with the lassies."

"True, but you have a dark and mysterious side that women find both appealing and captivating. You just don't know it."

"I'm not interested in being appealing or captivating. I need a wife—one with a large dowry. It's as simple as that."

"And you are a Scot with nothing to offer but debt and a title. You had better start being interested in making yourself attractive to the lassies. You have little else to offer. You could have had her melting in your arms before the day was out. I saw the way she looked at you. You may come to regret letting her slip away so easily. She was unusually fair."

"Aye, she was fair…as for letting her go, I regret it already."

"Well, the milk is spilt. We will do better next time." Hugh chuckled and shook his head. "Don't think I've ever seen a lassie stand up to you like that one did. She sure got the best of you, didn't she?"

"She took me by surprise, that's all."

"Aye, she did at that. Not the ordinary English lass with a backbone of Yorkshire pudding."

"No, she was not," agreed Robert. "I think there must be some Celtic blood in there somewhere."

"Perhaps so. With that hair, she could be Irish."

"Aye, she could be."

Hugh studied his brother for a moment. "Want to go after her?"

Robert looked off in the direction she had taken and contemplated doing just that. "We'd have the devil's own time trying to track her over such a well-used trail, and our horses are tired."

"I suppose you're right…still, it's a shame. A lassie with so much spirit might survive the ordeal of being married to a Scot such as yourself."

"She might at that, but she is gone and I canna waste my time thinking about the one who got away. There are other lassies."

Hugh laughed and slapped his brother on the back. "Aye, there are other lassies. All we have to do is find one. Who knows? The perfect lass might ride into your arms when you least expect it."

"The probability of that happening a second time is remote."

"Well, a man can dream, can't he?"

Robert did not say anything more.

They reached their horses and mounted. The two of them rode on, Hugh talking as if he had an audience, Robert not listening to anything he said.

They rode for half an hour before they encountered a hunting party of well-mounted gentlemen and ladies. The party was large, with dogs, hawks and led-horses, and the air was filled with the barking, shouts and cheers from the hunters, and the occasional trumpeting of the horn. Robert and Hugh pulled up to watch the party pass across the heath.

"'Tis a pity they did not stop," Hugh said. "Lots of lassies in the hunt, but traveling too fast to see if any of them were fair of face."

"Fairness is not a primary concern. Her purse is."

"Be optimistic, brother. Why not try for both?"

"A lass will have either a large dowry or great beauty. One who possesses both is rarer than birds' milk." Signaling the end to their conversation, Robert turned his horse and rode on, not looking back to see if Hugh followed.

5

Once she was well away from the place where she left the Scot talking to himself, Meleri settled her mare into a slow walk to cool her down. The land about her was more open now, the terrain flat and uninteresting, which did little to keep her thoughts off the Scot. Why could she not put him out of her mind as easily as she had left him behind? Strange though it was, she did not find as much satisfaction in getting the best of him as she would have thought.

She was grateful when she left the bleak and barren landscape, interspersed with marshy pools of water, to ride over land that was more hospitable. Even so, she found her mind lingering on the same thoughts as before. He had claimed hers was a face that would be hard to forget. Would he not be amused to know she was thinking the same about him?

"Concentrate on what you are doing," she said aloud, and noticed the mare's ears pricked forward. She gave her a fond pat and, as she often did, fell into a one-way conversation with her horse. "If only you could talk, perhaps you could tell me why I keep seeing the face of a foreboding stranger, when I should keep my mind on the business at hand. Philip, the beast, should be at the forefront of my consciousness. Everything—my future, my happiness—depends upon it. Think, Meleri. Think about what you will say when you are standing face-to-face with him." That was a sobering thought, she decided, for it reminded her that she did not need a tall, slim-hipped distraction weaving in and out of her mind at will and spoiling her concentration.

Before she knew it, she was almost to the road that led to Heathwood Castle, the huge, impressive residence of Edward Ashton, the Duke of Heatherton and Philip's father.

Lord Waverly, golden-haired, tall and princely slim, she thought. Now, there was someone created in God's image. In fact, Meleri always thought of God sitting in judgment whenever she looked at him. He made her more nervous than King George. He was a hard, bitter man, and she doubted he had cared about anything for a long, long time—if he'd ever cared at all. In that regard, he was much like his father, Edward, who was aristocratic, aloof and more than likely lonely, having been a widower some twenty-odd years and not a man to gather friends.

In truth, Philip might be younger, but he was not any softer than his father, which made her wonder if Philip would be even more impossible than his father when he reached his age. She felt herself shudder at the thought of facing the duke. It was distressing to confront one of them. The thought of standing before them both, quaking, with her knees knocking together… It was simply too much. She found herself praying the duke would be off somewhere—anywhere, as long as he was not at home.

She turned up the long, tree-lined drive that led to Heathwood and saw the towers of the castle that poked over the top of the next hill. She had reached a decisive moment—a point when she must make a choice that she would live with for the rest of her life. The moment she had looked forward to for so long, and yet dreaded immensely, was at hand. She continued on her way, praying she would make the right decision. Dear God, if I'm doing the wrong thing, let me run smack into a tree…and let it knock some sense into my head, she thought. However, if I'm right, let me collide with my future the moment I leave here…and let the perfect opportunity drop, smack in my lap.

As soon as she rode down the long, graveled drive, saw the

grand angles and tiled roofs of Heathwood Castle, she knew she
had done the right thing by coming here.

She rode toward the stables, where a young, fair-haired groom
awaited. Another new one, she thought. I wonder how long he
will last. He helped her dismount and stood squinting against a
brilliant sun that seemed to be throwing out freckles as she
watched, most of them landing upon his face. She could almost
hear them exploding with a loud *pop* on impact.

"Will you be staying long, milady?"

"No, I shan't be here long at all." She handed him her whip,
then looked at the gleaming, wet coat of her horse, and added,
"Do cool her down a bit for me, please. You needn't unsaddle her."

The groom nodded. "As you wish, milady." He led the mare
away.

Meleri wasted no time in taking up a determined gait and covered the distance to the main entrance quickly. She was about to
go up the steps, when she stopped suddenly. She turned quickly,
just as the groom was about to disappear around the corner of
the stable. She called out, "I say there… Do you happen to know
if Lord Waverly is at home?"

The groom paused and began stroking the mare's nose. "Yes,
milady. He rode in a short while ago with two friends."

She knew it had to be Harry Wellsby and Tony Downley.
"Damn…damn…damn," she said, taking it upon herself to break
another taboo—one that forbade women to use words reserved
exclusively for men. Blame it on Harry and Tony, she thought.
Their being here was definitely not good news. Waverly did not
need reinforcements. They might be his closest friends—and
two of the most notorious libertines in London—but did that
mean they had to be joined at the hip? One rarely saw one without the others. She liked Harry and Tony. She really did, but this
was a very rare moment, when she would have preferred to be
with Philip alone. She neither needed nor wanted an audience.
How would she ever get Philip away from them?

She would not. She was certain of that.

She sighed. Having his friends here was a hindrance, but not a permanent setback. Undaunted and determined to see this thing through, she walked with quick confidence as far as the front door, then paused. Her heart and her head were embroiled in another skirmish of an ongoing war—a war between rebellious devotion to her plans for the future and steadfast loyalty to her upbringing and the ironbound codes of the aristocratic past.

She could feel her steely resolve melting faster than hasty pudding. If I go through with this, she thought, Papa will be terribly disappointed…but it will not last forever. On the other hand, if I do not go through with this, I will be miserable the rest of my life. Well, Meleri, what is it going to be? Are you going to obey your father, or yourself? What to do? What to do?

She recalled something her mother told her shortly before she died. "Believe in yourself. Trust yourself. Anyone who cannot obey himself will be commanded. Remember that. It isn't fair, but it is the very way human nature works. A gambler knows a horse named Obedience rarely gets out of the gate, but the nag named Independence always runs a good race."

She lifted the knocker and brought it down against the gleaming wood door with a loud, sure bang. Independence was out of the gate.

Chipping, the butler, answered the door in his customary annoyed manner. "Oh, it is you, Lady Weatherby."

"Yes, it is I," Meleri said, stepping through the door. She removed her gloves and slapped them against her palm. "I would like to see Philip…Lord Waverly, if you please. Would you tell him I am here?"

Chipping gave her a formal nod. "Straightaway. You may wait in here," he said, and opened the door to the receiving room.

Meleri stepped inside and heard Chipping close the door behind her.

When the great clock in the hall chimed the hour, she was surprised to hear it strike three times. The lateness of the hour, and her tightly wound nerves, made further sitting impossible. She began to pace across the room. Back and forth. Back and forth. As she walked, she practiced what she would say. She wanted to capitalize upon the element of surprise. Philip's rigid and unbending nature made things like discussion and reasoning completely out of the question. Surprise was the order of the day.

In spite of her confidence, there was a small quiver of dread that raced through her body. Philip was not as tall or as frightening as his father, certainly, but he was a commanding figure, nonetheless, and she was here on the most unpleasant business. The big question was how to approach it? Aim for the heart? Or, go for a more subtle approach, like a slow paddle around the lake, then shove him overboard?

She decided to leave it to fate, to allow the words to flow in a natural manner. Nothing rehearsed, but free and spontaneous. *How* was insignificant. The most essential element was to deliver her message, saying in a manner that was succinct, terse or pithy, that the idea of marriage between them was a ridiculous mistake. Of critical importance was to make her point forthwith. She must not dally, but be direct. *Simply behave in a dignified manner befitting a lady. Tell him in a gentle, yet firm way, that you came to cancel the betrothal contract. Concentrate and focus on diplomacy, control and finesse. Show good breeding.*

Any further self-instruction ended when the door opened and Philip strolled casually into the room, Harry and Tony trailing along in their customary jovial fashion, engaging in witty dialogue.

"My, my, look who we have here. Is this a *pleasant* surprise?"

Tony and Harry chuckled in response to the jab. Philip, only mildly amused, took a step closer, preparing to greet her with his usual perfunctory kiss. It was a stale, meaningless act, and one she chose to deflect with a clipped "Philip" and an outstretched hand, which prevented him from coming closer.

Taking the cue, Tony and Harry greeted her with a more formal bow.

With a wave of his hand, Philip indicated a place on the sofa for her to sit.

Meleri approached the sofa and stopped abruptly beside it. "I prefer to stand."

His only acknowledgement was a shrug. "My apologies for

keeping you waiting so long. I was not informed you were coming. Rest assured it will not happen again."

"No one is to blame. My visit was unannounced and planned at the last minute."

Philip stood beside a chair opposite her. Tony and Harry stood near the fireplace, between two chairs gilded in the rococo tradition.

"So, tell me, why are you here?" Philip said. "It is unlike you to pay a social call. I wasn't certain if Chipping was joking, or if his eyesight was failing him."

"His eyes are fine, but like everyone else here, Chipping is incapable of anything remotely connected with humor."

Obviously amused, Harry cut in with a compliment. "I daresay the country air agrees with you. You manage to get lovelier each time I see you."

Philip raised a questioning brow. "Do you really think so?"

"Of course I do!" he replied, breaking into a wide grin, apparently content to keep his gaze resting upon her face. "I say, Philip had a jolly bit of good fortune to have his betrothal to you under contract at such an early age. Looking as you do now, you wouldn't last half a season before someone snatched you away." He glanced at Tony. "Do you not agree?"

"'Pon my word, Harry! What do you take me for? I would have to be brainless as a feather duster not to." Tony followed Harry's lead and looked her over. "I'm beginning to wish I'd beat old Philip to the punch."

"But you didn't, and now I've got her all tied up with a neat betrothal ribbon. Lucky, lucky me. It's too late for you, I'm afraid," Philip said lightly, but Meleri saw through his banter. There wasn't a featherweight of humor in his flinty voice.

Harry slapped him on the back. "By Jove! You are positively oozing with overconfidence. I say, it is not a good idea to count eggs and call them chickens, especially when there is a fox about. Anything can happen, you know. A comely woman should never be taken for granted, before *or* after the wedding."

Philip ignored him. Meleri was aware of the furious beating of her heart, which grew stronger as her irritation began to rise and spill into outrage. Her breathing increased. Her skin felt flushed and warm. She knew her ire was erupting in splotches of heated color all over her.

She was both surprised and caught off guard when Philip took her hand, looped it through his and gave it a condescending pat. His smooth manner of provoking her was maddening, and directly related to the extreme dislike that grew stronger with each breath. Her body was becoming uncomfortably warm. She glanced down at her arm entwined in his and tasted the brassy bitterness of intense ill will. When she saw her skin slowly becoming a mottled red, she could no longer confine her feelings to her heart and her mind. With one swift yank, she snatched her hand back.

He lifted her chin with his palm and brushed his fingers across her fiery cheek. "A woman's face will turn this exact shade of red on three occasions. When she is intensely angry, withholding the truth, or after an afternoon spent in her lover's bed."

She was so horrified she could only gasp with outrage.

Still holding her chin firmly in his hand, he ran his fingers over her cheek in the same manner that he did before. "Tell me love, which one applies to you?"

She slapped his hand away. "Don't ever touch me again!" Not even an artfully polished manner or smooth sophistication could nullify something so reprehensible and intentional. She was shaking with fury. This time, he had gone beyond the bounds of insulting.

Before she could inhale, Harry tried to draw out the poison injected by Philip's humiliating words. "A woman can wear roses on her cheeks for a dozen reasons, but only an exhilarating ride over the moors can produce such cherry-cheeks on a country lass."

"She does not need you to defend her. She is quite capable of inflicting her own brand of lethal blows, and I have an inkling you will see a prime example of it before the day is out."

Tony leaped into the fray. "Upon my honor, Waverly! You are letting your tongue run amok! This is not London. Save your bearbaiting for the ton! Can't you see she isn't accustomed to this sort of thing?"

"Very well," he said glibly, then to Meleri he said, "Forgive me for the wickedness of my tongue. Would you care for tea? I can ring for Mrs. Plemmons."

Bristling with anger, she could only manage to say, "I did not come for tea. This is not a social call."

Philip raised his brows and tried to look surprised. "Not a social call? Then to what do I owe the pleasure of your visit?"

"I came to talk to you."

"By all means," he said, indicating a seat for her. "Please sit down and we'll talk to your heart's content."

She did not sit down. "I prefer to talk to you…alone, if you don't mind."

"Ah-hem!" Harry said. "By Jove! I do find myself in need of a little walk to stretch my legs. Care to join me?" he said to Tony.

"Delighted, old chap."

Tony and Harry headed off, but Philip stopped them. "There is no need to rush off," he said. "*Melli* and I have no secrets that we can't share with our closest friends." He turned to her and said, "Do we, my dear?"

It infuriated her that he used her childhood name, but she did not let it show. She knew why he did it. He wanted to have the advantage by getting her ruffled. She was determined that he was not going to succeed in bearbaiting her, as Tony put it. Initially, she wanted to spit back words as insulting as he hurled at her, but once she lost control of her temper, reason would go out the window. *Say what you came to say, and then you can bash a pot over his head.* "We don't have much of anything, Philip, and that includes an engagement."

He glanced at his friends. "Such dreadful news can mean only one thing. Do you suppose it's possible that another man has come between us, that she has allowed him to replace me in her affections?"

Tony and Harry had the wit to say nothing. As for Meleri, the anger that had been simmering suddenly came to a full, furious boil. Spitting mad now, she gave herself a mental scolding. *So much for holding your tongue and temper in check. Unleash the little devils and Waverly be damned! Say what you will. You can worry about the consequences tomorrow.* "When it comes to my affections, a termite could replace you."

"Fresh as paint, isn't she? I think she got a little kippered from being in the sun too long. Country maids sometimes forget their delicate side."

"Rubbish!" Meleri said. "Why don't you say what you are really thinking instead of so much pretense? I did not come here to quibble, giving tit for tat. I came to speak my mind."

"At least that will be brief."

"It couldn't be brief enough to suit me."

"Does Sir William know you came here and for what purpose?"

"Most of the time, my father doesn't know the time of day."

"Am I missing something here? Since when has it become customary for a woman to climb into the driver's seat and make demands as well as decisions?"

She walked the entire length of the room and then turned back to face him, trying not to let her anger show, but it was becoming quite difficult. He was looking at her with a challenge in his eye, and she had never been one to back down in the face of a challenge. If anything, it fired her will and hardened her resolve, both of which gave her added encouragement. "Think what you will. I am past caring. I have something to say, and I will say it…to you or to an empty room. I can tell it to half of London if need be."

"Really?"

"Invite King George. Include his court, too."

The corners of Philip's lips twitched and he gave his friends an amused look. "Quite a clever little actress, is she not?"

Seeing his glance, her fingers itched to pick up the stuffed parrot sitting on the perch beside her. She would have liked nothing more than to send it flying across the room. That, at least, would be a sign that she was not receptive to his sneering looks any more than she was to his disparaging words. However, she wanted nothing to sidetrack her. She had come this far, and she wanted to have this thing done. So many words were backed up in her head and throat, they created a jumble.

He smiled again, but this time it was forced. "Dear, dear, I don't think I've ever seen you with such a determined look on your face. Why, you look positively agitated. Has something happened to rile you to such irritating heights?"

"Oh, yes, you might say something has happened. Something remarkable…quite extraordinary, actually."

"Oh? And what might that be?"

"I have been enlightened."

"Enlightened?" Philip let out a low whistle. "An enlightened woman. That is impressive. I am honored that you went to so much trouble to ride all the way over here to share that little tid-bit with me."

"Don't be flattered. My coming here is not a complimentary social call. That isn't the purpose of my visit."

"I see," he said, with a tone so flat and so cold, it sent a shiver rippling over her.

"No, Philip, I don't think you see at all. You have never been able to see beyond yourself. Only I didn't realize it until recently."

"When did your kind regard turn so bitter?"

"I am not bitter. I am sick at heart over the years I squandered on someone so incapable of feeling, so capable at deceiving. Too many years lost, because our fathers were foolish enough to be-troth us as children, never taking into consideration that we might not suit each other when we were grown."

He brought his hands together and placed the extended fore-fingers against his lips. "I think I am beginning to see. You are concerned that I have not set a date. Is that it? You are anxious and ready to be married. That is it, is it not? Am I right?"

"You don't understand me at all. What I feel is in opposition to everything you said. If I have found anything pleasing about this betrothal, it is the delay in arranging a date for our wedding. Believe me when I say, I am truly happy you did not complete the arrangements. You might even say I am delighted."

"And why is that? Do you think taking this approach will prompt me to action, that I will leap to the challenge and make the arrangements posthaste?"

She felt suddenly weary and anxious to have done with all of this. "Oh, Philip, can we not be honest with one another for once in our lives? I do not want to set a date or make arrangements. I do not want a wedding. And I especially don't want to be married…at least not to you."

His entire countenance changed, and she saw beneath the facade he presented to the world. Now she understood what she faced. There would be no toying with her now, no more quips and sharply sent barbs. She saw blood in his eyes and knew the taste of fear.

"You poor, tiresome wretch. Are you trying to give me an ultimatum? Because if you are, I can save you the trouble."

Meleri was suddenly glad he had asked Tony and Harry to stay. She knew Philip well enough to know how he would react to what she planned to say next, and knew, too, that it would be markedly diminished in force and fury with his friends standing witness. He was no fool, and too proud by half. She counted on these to work against him.

"I came here today because I want to end our betrothal," she said simply.

The room fell silent. Not even the sound of the clock ticking could be heard. Almost giddy with relief, she took a deep breath, amazed that so few words could make her feel so light-headed.

A quick glance down to his hands revealed the tightly clenched fists. This doubled the relief she felt over Tony and Harry's presence. There was little cause to deny he was furious over his humiliation, nor was there any doubt that if not for his friends' presence, he might easily have struck her.

He went to great lengths to hide it, which was indicated by a tone of nonchalance. "By all means, let's end it, here and now. It might surprise you to know that it has been my intention for quite some time. Being a gentleman, I have waited, hoping to give you time to realize my utter dissatisfaction and dislike. I provided you the opportunity to take the initiative. You took so long. I was beginning to think you quite dense. I suppose that speaks volumes as far as female intellect. What a bother! And the waiting…such a dreadful bore."

Harry coughed and Tony shifted his position. Both of them were looking extremely uncomfortable as they stared fixedly at the floor.

She deflected every sharp comment he shot in her direction. She was so thrilled over the success of her adventure that she was more than willing to give him his chance to get even. "You have no idea how happy I am to hear that. There is something to be said for mutual agreement, for it does make everything so much easier, does it not?"

"It is always uplifting to have something one has waited for so long come to fruition. It was impossible to think I would ever stoop to marry a chit like you." He paused and gave her a chilling look of dismissal. "Is that it? Or was there something else?"

"No," she said, her relief tossed into a jumble of other emotions. She made it a point to look at Harry and Tony with firm resolve. "I would have your word as gentlemen and members of the titled nobility that you have witnessed the ending of this betrothal by mutual agreement. Do I have your word?"

Harry and Tony looked at each other.

"Do I have your word?" she asked again.

"Yes," Tony said at last. "You have my word."

"As a gentleman and a member of the nobility?"

"As a gentleman and a member of the nobility," he repeated.

"You have mine, as well," Harry said. "As a gentleman, et cetera."

"Very well. I do thank you both." She turned to Philip. "It would seem that we are all agreed, and now that the betrothal is called off to our mutual satisfaction, I have nothing further to discuss. If you will excuse me, I will be on my way…."

Philip cut in curtly. "Then you won't mind my not showing you to the door?"

"Of course not. I am accustomed to rudeness when around you. Good day, gentlemen."

Harry and Tony said, "Goodbye" in unison.

"And good riddance" was Waverly's contribution.

She was almost to the door when she heard Philip again, speaking in a loud voice this time. "A toast to my freedom, and a wager, gentlemen. A hundred pounds says I will be married long before my former betrothed."

"It's a bet," Harry said.

"I accept as well," said Tony. "Will you be accepting bets at White's?"

"All in due time. I find I have other pressing business in London that must come first. If we left today, we could be there by tomorrow. I am anxious to tell a certain *lady* that I am, at last, a free man."

That did it.

She whirled around, snatched that ghastly stuffed parrot from its perch and sent it hurling toward Philip. He reached for it, but it flew over his head and smashed into a brass chandelier. A shower of green and yellow feathers rained down upon Philip.

The sight of the princely and elegant Lord Waverly standing there like a molting bird, parrot feathers floating about him and clinging to his clothes and hair was too funny by half. She smiled sweetly and said, "You missed, but don't worry. If you cannot catch the bird of paradise, you can always settle for a wet hen. I do hope you like parrots. I understand the duke's daughter has five of them, all named for her former suitors. Philip the Parrot! It does have a nice ring."

Harry's laugh was immediate and bubbled up in an infectious manner that quickly prompted Tony to join in. "I say, that was a splendid reaction!" Harry managed to say. "And completely impromptu, no less! You're positively brilliant!"

Waverly, who was standing in a puddle of feathers looking like a defoliated tree, clenched his jaw until the lines around his mouth turned white. Anger, held tightly in check, was obvious in his voice. "Your performance exemplifies your country rusticity, which is one of the reasons I would have never considered going through with the asinine idea of marrying you. Our betrothal served a purpose, nothing more. Simply put, I used you, old girl! I used our betrothal to buy myself some time. Surely you knew you were never suitable for the wife of a duke."

"I knew I was never suited to be the wife of a certain *future* duke, but then, I'm not certain anyone is. You may be a marquess, but it is never befitting the daughter of a baronet to be used to one's advantage and then mocked and held up for ridicule. The peerage does not demean the peerage. You were foolish to ignore this. You are having your sport now, but you will soon understand how it feels. Once word of this reaches London—and it will—you will find yourself shunned and held up for ridicule by other members of the ton. I daresay it should delight your father. What a disappointment you have proven to be. It is truly a shame. You had so much potential. I do not know what happened, or what caused you to become a worthless example of a man. There was a time when I thought I loved you, a time when I knew I did not—and a time when I felt only pity. Now, I don't feel even that."

With nothing more to say to him, she quit the room and the gentlemen who stared after her. When she reached the entry, Chipping had the door open, and she stepped out into the sunlight, still shaking, but deliciously happy to have this dreaded event behind her. As she went down the steps, a shiver of relief traveled over her.

She was free of Philip at last.

The gravel drive crunched beneath her feet as she hurried toward the stables. She did not see the groom, but her horse was there, tied to a ring post. She hurried to untie the reins. When she finished, Philip was standing on the steps, talking to Harry and Tony. He saw her glance in their direction, and when he spoke, he almost shouted the words at her. "Now that you're in need of a husband, I hear the wainwright's son is looking for a wife. And so is the owner of the Wine Keg Inn."

He must enjoy the sound of his own laughter, she thought, for Harry and Tony barely laughed at all. Not that she cared. She was too busy ignoring them all the way to the mounting block. Once she was in the saddle, she gathered the reins and urged the mare forward.

She was almost even with them and thinking the worst was over, when Philip's voice rang out. "You would be wise to consider the wainwright's son, because that's about the best you'll be able to do. Mark my word, you will never find a husband among the gentry. I'll see to that."

She stopped and looked at him coldly. "Then you better hurry."

His amusement was obvious. "Hurry? Why should I? Who would want to marry a woman who was nothing more than a silly bit of fluff with too much confidence and no common sense?"

Silly bit of fluff?

The muscles in her body coiled spring-tight. Her scalp prickled. Her blood was flowing, swift, hot and full of scorn.

Silly bit of fluff?

She was so furious her anger replaced levelheaded thinking, and she turned on him. "You truly are what they say you are…the ultimate bastard."

"You poor, pathetic woman, do you really think you can find a husband before I dash all your chances, pitiful as they may be? It's impossible."

"Not if I marry the first man I meet."

"Not even you would dare go that far."

"To be free of you, I would dare that and more."

His mocking laugh ripped through the air. Meleri brought the crop down and her mare leaped forward and broke into a run. She did not glance back, not even once, but she did hear the sound of Harry and Tony's laughter blending in loudly with Philip's.

She would not let him win a victory over her again. Not this time. She swore that if she had only one thing left in life that she could do, it would be to do as she threatened. She would marry the first man she came upon.

Even if she had to ask him herself.

6

Before Meleri was out of sight Tony, who was looking rather pensive, said, "You realize, of course, what you have done."

Lord Waverly sighed in exasperation. He was tired of all of this. He needed time to collect himself after that disastrous encounter with Meleri. He did not want to discuss her, or anything connected with her. She was out of his life, and he preferred to leave her out of his thoughts and, particularly, out of any conversation. He did not want to discuss what happened. Truthfully, he did not want do discuss anything. He needed some time alone.

"I know precisely what I have done," he said, in a clipped, exacting manner. "I have let a minor source of irritation out of my life."

Harry and Tony exchanged looks before Harry said, "And let a major one into it, I'm afraid."

"A major one? Am I supposed to guess who this person is, or do you make it easy for me?"

"I don't know how easy it will be, considering it is your father I refer to," said Harry.

"My father won't be a problem. His main concern is that I marry, not so much who I marry."

Another glance passed between his friends.

After a moment, Tony said, "I think you may be underestimating your father. Are you forgetting how he feels about this marriage to Lady Weatherby, how he's refused to allow you to broach the subject of marriage to anyone else?"

"Only because he felt bound to honor a betrothal contract of such long standing. However, Meleri afforded me the perfect escape. I cannot be blamed for crying off."

"He may not see it that way," said Harry, "and the duke is the one in control here, not you. It was only a fortnight ago that we were all gathered here and witnessed that row between the two of you. Dreadful business, that."

"He gave you an ultimatum that night, in case you've forgotten," Tony said.

Philip's heartbeat began to escalate at the memory of that night and the furious direction things had taken. "He has made threats before."

"Not like that one," Tony said.

"What is your purpose?"

"We don't want to see you take such a risk with your future and your inheritance."

"What would you have me do? Go to the chit on my hands and knees and beg her to come back?"

"What you do is up to you," Tony replied. "We're your friends, not your barristers."

Philip felt a sinking sensation, but he refused to allow it to destroy his peace of mind. "Then remain my friends and change the subject. I grow weary of discussing Lady Weatherby and my father. Now, I say we all go inside and drink a toast to my newfound freedom."

7

Later that evening, when she returned to Humberly Hall, Meleri found Elizabeth waiting and proceeded to tell her of the meeting with Philip.

"Thank God it's over," her sister said, sounding supremely relieved. "I was on pins and needles. You were gone for such a long time."

"It was for a good cause. I still can't believe Waverly allowed his pride to get the best of his judgment. Before I knew what was happening, he was acting like the decision to go our separate ways was his idea."

"He could deny that, of course."

"I thought of that. Luckily, Tony and Harry were there, so I asked them to swear to what they had witnessed."

"And they did?"

Meleri could not hold back her smile. "They did."

Elizabeth fairly beamed with delight. "I was on my way to join Father for dinner. Will you join us?"

"I will, but first I must change out of these clothes."

"Don't be long. You know how impatient Father is."

The next morning, Meleri opened her eyes at daybreak. Her first thought was that she was free: free of Lord Waverly; free of her betrothal; free of marriage to such an undesirable man.

She was dressed by the time Betty came into her room with her breakfast. "Well lud! You are up early, milady…and dressed! Are you going somewhere?"

"No place other than downstairs. Is Elizabeth up?"

"Yes, milady, she is having tea in the garden."

"Lovely. I think I'll join her."

Meleri found Elizabeth in the garden, just as Betty said. Over a cup of tea, she explained her meeting with Philip in detail. "I cannot tell you how relieved I am to have this over with."

"I keep having a nagging feeling that it isn't as over as we think," Elizabeth said.

"There is little Philip can do about it now. He called the betrothal off and I have Harry and Tony as witnesses."

"I know, but still I worry."

"Don't worry. All will be well. Do come with me into the rose garden. I want to gather some roses for Mrs. Mayhew. I want to send them over with a sweater I knitted for her new baby."

"Goodness! Is Mrs. Mayhew still birthing babies? How many does that make?"

"Thirteen, I believe."

"Lord above, if I had half that number, I would insist upon separate bedrooms…no, separate floors!"

The sisters laughed, and arm in arm, made their way down to the rose garden.

After lunch, Meleri went for a short ride. When she returned, she ran into Mrs. Hadley. "There you are," Mrs. Hadley said. "I have been looking everywhere for you."

"I only this moment returned from my ride. Is something amiss?"

"Your father has been looking for you."

"Where is he?"

"He was taking some sun in the garden, but that was some time ago. I doubt he is still there now."

"I'll find him," Meleri said, and went in search of her father.

She found him easily, looking first in one of his favorite places, the library. He was sitting at the grand carved table that stood in an alcove, surrounded by mullioned windows on three sides. Stacked around him were volumes of old and ancient books, most of them quite rare. Two of them were considered priceless editions.

He was bent over one of his books with a magnifying glass when she came into the room. "Papa, may I talk to you?"

Sir William raised his head and pushed his glasses up from the place they had slipped, farther down his nose. "Melli, my child. Come in, come in!" he said. "I've something to show you."

She was so overcome to realize her father recognized her that she could not at first move. When she finally did, she approached the chair on the opposite side of the desk from him.

"No, no, don't sit there! Come over here, so you can better see."

She had no more than started around the desk, when Jarvis came into the room. Meleri turned toward him. "Pardon the intrusion, milady, but this just came for Sir William."

She took the letter and saw the crest of Lord Waverly. "Lord Waverly is here?"

"No milady. One of the Duke of Heatherton's grooms delivered it."

Meleri's heart beat violently. Why would Philip send a letter to her father? He was not the type to want to explain things. She barely had time to shove the letter into her pocket when her father asked, "Is something amiss?"

"No, everything is fine. It was only a messenger with a letter for Elizabeth," she said, feeling horrible and guilty for lying to her father, even though she knew it was necessary. "I must run the letter upstairs and give it to her. I'll be right back."

Sir William had already picked up his magnifying glass and returned to his scrutiny of the tome in front of him.

Meleri rushed up the stairs and found Elizabeth in her room. She explained about the letter.

"What does it say?" Elizabeth asked anxiously.

Meleri fished the envelope out of her pocket. "I haven't read it. It just this moment came."

She started to tear the envelope, then thought better of it, and handed the envelope to Elizabeth. "Here. You open it. I find I am too nervous."

Elizabeth's hands, she noticed, were shaking as she withdrew the note from Waverly and began to read.

Dear Sir William,

Meleri paid me a visit today. She was not in her best frame of mind. At any other time, this would have been of no import, but today I was feeling a bit under the weather, and I am afraid I allowed my irritation with her unruliness to get the best of me. When she said she wanted to cry off, I was in no mood to beleaguer the point. I felt it best to humor her, to play the indulgent father, until she was of a nature to see things differently.

When she left Heathwood, I fear she left with the mistaken impression that our engagement was ended. Nothing could be further from the truth. As I said, I only humored her to give her time to see the foolishness of her error. I send you this note, only to inform you of what happened. Knowing Meleri as I do, I am certain she will insist to you that I agreed most heartily.

It is my dearest hope that on the morrow she will awaken and find her delicate sensibilities have settled back to normal. I think I have been patient in waiting long enough for Meleri to mature. It is time to set a date for our wedding. In a day or so, I will ride over to visit with you before I speak with her.

I feel certain we can appease whatever it is that her weakened female mind has begun to imagine. Once we are married, I have every confidence that she will stop her foolishness and become the dutiful and obedient daughter and wife we have both so long desired.

Until tomorrow, I remain, your faithful and future son-in-law,

Philip

"Oh, the bounder!" Elizabeth said as she refolded the letter and returned it to the envelope. She handed it to Meleri, whose hands were trembling as she put it back into her pocket.

"I don't understand what happened to make Philip change his mind," Meleri said. "He certainly did not suddenly fall madly in love with me. It makes no sense."

"What does make sense is his comment that you will stop your foolishness and become a dutiful, obedient daughter and wife, once you are married," Elizabeth said. "That makes me think he means to beat you into submission, if need be."

"I don't doubt that is precisely what he meant."

Elizabeth took Meleri's face in her hands. "I know this will be difficult for you, but surely you see you must leave here as soon as possible. You must put as much distance between yourself and Lord Waverly as you can. I have already alerted the staff of my intention to take Father back to London. I shall hasten to see if they cannot have things ready for us to leave in the morning. I think it would be best if you left before us, at first light. That way, if Lord Waverly should arrive before we depart, I will do all I can here to stall him, or at least send him on a fool's errand."

She knew things were desperate, and listening to Elizabeth slapped her with reality. Elizabeth was right. She could no longer stay here. She was not naive enough to think she could persuade Philip a second time.

Her only problem was she had no destination in mind. There must be some place, she thought. Where can I go, where no one knows who I am?

"Where will you go?"

Meleri looked down at her hands. "I don't know. I thought I had more time to arrange things."

Elizabeth thought for a moment. "What about your former nanny? Don't you still correspond with her?"

"Agnes! Of course," Meleri said. "She would be perfect. She detests Lord Waverly, and she lives in Scotland, near Gretna Green."

Elizabeth closed her eyes and crossed her hands over her

breasts. "An answer to a prayer. Now, hurry and see to your packing, but remember to take no more than you can easily carry on horseback. I don't think it wise for you to take the carriage or anyone with you. It would make you easier to track. I'll ask Mrs. Hadley to pack you something to eat."

Without wasting another moment, Meleri hurried to her wardrobe and took down her letterbox. Inside, she found the last letter she had received from Agnes, written a few months after her husband died. She invited Meleri to come for a visit and gave directions to her cottage.

Meleri shoved that letter into her pocket, along with the one from Waverly. She would not bother to pack anything. She would be traveling at a fast pace and did not want to carry any extra weight that would only slow her down. Clothes could be bought. Her freedom could not.

After a night of restlessness and dreams, Meleri awoke as the first pale pink veins of dawn streaked the sky. Half an hour later, she rode hard, until she could no longer see her beloved Humberly Hall. She could not think about that now, she reminded herself. It occurred to her that she was past foolish to have left home without any money, save the small amount Elizabeth had given her. She shuddered to think what would happen if the mare foundered and went lame. She would never be able to escape Philip on foot.

She would not think upon it further. She would be well away by the time Philip arrived and that was the important thing. No matter what happened to her, it could not be as bad as going back to a life with Lord Waverly.

"Look to the future and Scotland," she told herself, and urged the mare ahead, trying not to think about the huge shadow the future cast upon the present.

8

"We have been riding all day, with nary a lass in sight," Hugh said. "It will be dark soon. Do you plan to continue your search in the dark, or do we make camp?"

"We make camp when we come upon a suitable place."

"If we can see it."

It was half an hour later when they came upon a brook, which issued from a narrow, wooded glen nestled among the hills. To one side of the brook lay a boggy marsh, impassable and dangerous. On the other side, the ground was comparatively sound. Nearby, where the ruins of an old castle lay scattered about, the ground was gently elevated above the marsh, which afforded them an esplanade of dry turf.

Part of the once-magnificent tower remained intact, with two remaining walls that formed an angle. They were of great thickness and would provide shelter to tether their horses.

"This looks like a good place to stop for the night," Robert said. "We'll make camp here."

He dismounted and tied his horse, but Hugh stared off wistfully in the distance. "And here I was thinking of a soft bed at an inn…with an even softer English lass to warm it."

"Always the dreamer. We don't need to spend the coin or draw attention to our presence."

Hugh shrugged and dismounted. "Aye. It's much more fun to camp in the wilds, so we can be run over by stray lassies."

"We? I didn't see any bumps on *your* head."

Hugh raised his brows in mock surprise. "You got a bump on the head?"

Robert rubbed the swelling knot at the back of his head. "Aye, a small one."

"To go with the bruise on yer arse."

"You are awfully cheerful when it is someone else's arse."

"Only when it's yours, big brother. God's love! I am truly amazed. Not many men who could knock you on your duffer. I am beginning to truly regret losing that lassie. Are you starting to regret letting her go?"

"Will you stop putting your oars in my boat? I regretted letting her go yesterday. Today, I have put her and the incident out of my mind."

Robert dismounted, then led his horse to where Hugh was standing. He slapped the reins in Hugh's hand. "Stop your chirping and see to the horses, while I see if I can find something with four legs to eat." He walked a few feet, stopped and turned around. "Try to have all thoughts of that lass out of your head by the time I get back."

Hugh laughed. "Aye, why don't you try doing the same thing?"

The sun was dropping low in the sky when Robert returned with a rabbit. He handed it to Hugh. "You can cook it."

Hugh tossed a few more sticks on the fire. "Why me? Why don't you cook it?"

"I killed it."

Hugh mumbled to himself and set about finding a green branch sturdy enough to hold the weight of the rabbit.

"I think I'll take a swim while you see to our dinner," Robert said as he rose to his feet. He stripped off his clothes and dropped them next to his saddle.

Hugh watched, grinning wildly. "'Tis a real pity yer lassie

didn't stay around long enough to see what you had to offer…one glimpse of that and she might have changed her mind." He whistled. "If she only knew what she was missing. I will wager these Englishmen don't have anything that will measure up to the likes of the Black Douglas himself. 'Tis a fine specimen of manhood ye are, Robbie my lad. Take care, or all the lassies hereabouts will come running and toss ye on yer duffer."

"The bigger the bait the bigger the catch," Robert said, then, naked as truth, he walked to the edge of the stream and left Hugh and the sound of his laughter behind.

When he stepped into the water, he was surprised to find it gooseflesh cold. He was accustomed to that at home, but did not expect to find it here. The water was waist deep and clear enough that he could see the smooth stones that covered the bottom, as well as a fish or two that darted past. One deep breath and he ducked his head beneath the water, then surfaced and swam with strong, swift strokes to warm his muscles and hold the numbing cold at bay.

Soon, not even vigorous swimming could hold back the penetrating chill of icy water. He tired quickly, slowing his stroke. When the numbness began to creep up his legs, he waded back to dry land. With cold, stiff steps, he headed back to camp and the clothes lying where he dropped them. The swim had been a good idea.

Cold water was exactly what he needed to get the lass out of his head.

As he made his way to camp, he was guided by the savory smell of roasting rabbit. He walked into the clearing and smiled. Hugh was hunkered down low on his haunches near the fire. The rabbit looked deliciously brown. "I hope that's ready."

"Looks ready to me," Hugh said, and took a sip of whisky from the bottle he was holding. "How was your swim?"

"Cold as MacDougal's feet the day they buried him."

Hugh chuckled and offered him a drink, holding up the bottle of whisky. "Here. Try this. One sip will have you as warm as a wee mousie in a churn."

"As soon as I get my clothes on."

"And here I'm just getting accustomed to you that way." He made a clucking noise. "Sure is a pity that flame-haired lassie couldn't see you now, with yer arse as bare as a baby."

"Can't you talk about something else?"

"Nope. I keep thinking about that poor lassie. She will never know just how close to Paradise she came."

Robert tossed a clod in Hugh's direction, but he easily ducked.

"Tsk, tsk, tsk. There is nothing like a missed opportunity with a lassie to make a man touchy!"

"I am not touchy." Robert was about to pick up his clothes when the thundering sound of an approaching horse caused him to go for his sword instead. He was lightning quick, but even then, he did not have time to reach the place where his sword lay before the horse and rider crashed through the trees and bore down on them at breakneck speed.

"Satan's spawn! The devil is going to run us down!" Hugh shouted.

The words had no more than left Hugh's mouth when the horse must have seen them and attempted to avoid running them over. It squealed and made a sudden, sharp turn to the left, just as Hugh took a dive to the right.

Hugh made the right choice.

Robert was not so fortunate.

The sudden turn of the horse unseated the rider, who came hurling out of the saddle like a projectile and struck Robert full in the middle. The force of the impact drove the air from his lungs and sent him reeling backward. He hit the ground with a hard blow to his shoulder and grunted in pain before he rolled a few feet, still entangled with the unseated rider.

Instinct guided him now, and he rolled on top of his adversary and pinned him to the ground. Immediately, his head was under attack with several weak jabs and punches that landed on his face and head. Robert did not bother to fight back, preferring instead to hold him down just enough to protect his face from the series of blows. Whoever his assailant was, he was nothing more than a lad, for he was slight and his punches, although well placed, were ineffective.

God's eyeballs! He was puny, even for an Englishman. He fought like a woman.

"Let go of me, you bloody fool! What are you trying to do? Kill me? Can't you see I'm a woman?" His adversary bucked beneath him. "Get off, you blithering idiot! Get off of me this instant!" Each word was backed up with more thumps and whacks, which Robert tried to deflect as best he could, considering he had an injured shoulder that pained him whenever he moved.

As he was preoccupied with protecting his shoulder, it took a bit longer for the words to soak into his brain. However, when they did, he exclaimed loudly, "You're a woman!"

"Of course I'm a woman, you idiot! Don't you have women where you come from? Now, get off me!"

He had no more than realized he had a woman beneath him, who was doing her best to rearrange his face, when he was conscious of the rumbling sound of Hugh's laughter. Leave it to his brother to laugh at a time like this.

Robert turned his head just for a moment and saw Hugh standing nearby. The next instant he felt a sharp, piercing pain to his other shoulder. "God's teeth! The wench has bitten me!"

Hugh was laughing so hard by now that he was shaking, making it a bit difficult to hold up the burning branch in his hand, but he managed somehow. The dull, golden light was enough to illuminate what was happening.

Robert yelped with pain again.

Hugh only laughed harder, but he did manage to say between breaths, "Instead of lying there, bleating like a sheep, I think I'd let the lassie go."

"I…am…trying…my…best," Robert said between pants.

The woman beneath him bucked again, then boxed him so soundly it left his ears ringing. "Let me up, you countrified rustic! I'll have you arrested for this!"

His body aching in a dozen places, Robert did manage to roll from her. A second later, he rose to his feet.

Hugh, with true courteous dispatch, went for the damsel on the ground and gave her a hand up.

She showed her appreciation by giving him a swift blow to the shin. "You took your own bloody time helping me up, you thick-witted clod!"

Robert noticed Hugh was looking down at the woman with a strange expression on his face. A second later, he saw why.

"Lord love us! You won't believe this!" Hugh grabbed the woman by the wrist and spun her around to face him. "Look what we've caught," he said. "It's your lass!"

"I'm not your lass!" she shouted, and landed a bruiser just beneath Hugh's eye. Two inches taller and she would have had him smack in the eye. As it was, Hugh yelped with pain.

Robert looked at the same moment she did. Their gazes locked. Hugh was right. It was the same lass—every redheaded inch of her. She must have recognized him, as well, for she stopped fighting the second their gazes met and stood staring at him with a disbelieving expression of frozen surprise on her face.

Apparently recovering from her shock, she gave Hugh an elbow to the ribs and shrieked, "Dear God in Heaven! Someone please help me!"

"We're trying our best to," Hugh said, "but you are making it difficult."

She was not listening to anything he had to say, however, for she whacked him again. "Have you no shame? I've been set upon by perverted lunatics and one of them is wearing no clothes!" She tore into Hugh with a new surge of vigor, kicking, biting, hitting and saying in a winded voice, "You depraved wretch!" She kicked him again. "He doesn't have a bloody stitch on!"

"Well, it isn't my fault!" Hugh said, doing his best to dodge her blows. "What are you hitting me for? I *have* clothes on. If you want to hit someone, hit him." Hugh was about to shove her toward Robert, when he realized what she said. Without thinking further, he yanked her fast against him and shoved her face against his chest, then mumbled a hasty apology. "Sorry, lass, I didn't realize…"

She plainly wanted nothing to do with Hugh or his apologies, for by the time he finished his sentence, she was struggling against him with all her might. Shouting and kicking, she tried to break loose from his hold. "Unhand me this instant! Let me go!"

"If you would only…"

She kicked him again and Hugh howled in pain.

Robert stood quietly watching with a mixture of incredulity and enjoyment on his face. It was hard to believe he had encountered her twice in so many days. It was also quite a sight to see such a lass get the best of his brother. He had never seen anything to compare with her. Where in the name of St. Andrew did she get that abominable temper? He had to admit it was a bit satisfying to watch her light into Hugh, deserving scoundrel that he was. Save him for a wretch, but he was damnably close to laughing.

"For the love of Scotland! Will you hurry up?" Hugh shouted, and then howled in pain. "Get your clothes on while I still have some hide left."

Robert took his time. Judging from the sound of things, Hugh was not faring too well. Robert had never felt better. He started whistling an old war ditty, "Jock on the Side."

"Robbie, by the Cross of St. Andrew, will you hurry up?"

Robert whistled louder. Eventually he finished dressing. He walked slowly back into the dim light of the campfire and quietly observed for a moment before he said in a calm, low voice, "Instead of howling my fool head off, I think I would simply let her go."

"It…is not…as easy as…it…looks," Hugh said, his breath coming in quick gasps between words. "Hanging on to her is like wrestling a wildcat. I can't hold on and I'm afraid to let go."

She bit his neck and Hugh let out one last yelp before he released her. He glared at Robert. "I was trying to give you time to get your arse covered," he said, rubbing his neck.

Free from Hugh's restraining grip, she turned angrily on Robert. "Listen, you bloody…"

"That will be enough," Robert said in a hard, masterful tone.

She snapped her mouth shut and stood glaring at him in a way that made him think she was not accustomed to being corrected.

"I think we've heard enough from you, lass. You have tossed me on my backside twice now. I am beginning to wonder if it was by accident, not that it matters. You have run roughshod over me for the last time. I would practice a little self-restraint, if I were you."

Her eyes widened and he saw a spark of anger flare in her eyes. He was right. She was definitely not familiar with the word *reprimand,* for she was clearly stunned into silence. He knew it would not last.

Just as he predicted, she came back at him with a barrage of insults. "Your insolence is boundless. How dare you insinuate I would throw myself at a country bumpkin like you! I don't know about Scotland, but here in England, naked barbarians are not well received."

Hugh looked from Robert to the lass, then back at the fire. He kicked a couple of coals into the flames and said, "This is starting to look like a marital spat, and I have never been one to go between bark and tree. If the two of you do not mind, I am going to eat my dinner, while I still have the strength to sit down. Does anyone want to join me? Or do I eat alone?"

"I'll join you," Robert said. "I'm so hungry I can hear my ribs clanking together."

"It's probably the rocks in your head you hear," she said.

Hugh's grin signaled his approval. "Would you like to join us? You're welcome to a share of rabbit."

"I…" She cast a quick glance in Robert's direction, apparently to see if the invitation met with his approval.

Robert remained expressionless, but Hugh held up the stick with a sizzling rabbit bobbing up and down on the end. "Have you eaten, lass?"

Clearly preoccupied with the rabbit, she licked her lips and said, "Not since this morning."

Hugh tried again. "You must be hungry, then. Would you care to share our meal?"

"Yes, I would like that."

"Well, that settles it, then," Hugh said cheerfully. Come here, lass." He motioned to her. "Over here. By the fire."

She looked at Robert warily and remained where she was.

"You are welcome to a bit of rabbit," Robert said. "As long as you behave yourself, you are perfectly safe here with us, even if you are English. I have never been known to ravish a woman on an empty stomach."

"Now, see what you've done. You're scaring her with your gruffness," Hugh said.

Robert saw she looked as if she was going to pitch camp right where she stood. Even after Hugh invited her again, it was apparent she was not going to budge. Someone ought to turn her over his knee, Robert thought, but he was too hungry and too tired to volunteer. Better to feed her and send her on her way. He held up his hand and motioned her forward with one word. "Come."

She closed her eyes and inhaled the scent of the rabbit, but she did not move.

Robert knew she was hungry. He now added *too stubborn to eat* to his list of observations about her. Foolish woman! There she stood, all decked out in her finest blue riding habit and feathered hat, looking down her aristocratic English nose at them. It made him wonder why this lady of rank, if not manner, was out—again—alone.

Still standing where she was, she obviously fought a battle between self-will and hunger. Hunger won out, for she started walking toward them, her steps hesitant, as one walking in the dark, drawn forward by insatiable curiosity, yet wary of what they might find.

Robert removed a plaid from his bags and spread it near the fire, then turned to her, indicating she should sit there.

She stopped and stared down at the plaid.

"If you are going to remind me that the plaid was outlawed after Culloden, I am aware of that," Robert said. "I am also in the habit of doing as I please, and that includes revolting against the English if I so choose."

He heard her draw in her breath in disbelief. "You are speaking treason."

"Fluently."

"I did not ask you to justify why you rebel against the law," she said, lifting her chin.

"Success is justification enough," he said. "Now, if you will sit down, Your Highness, we will eat. The rabbit grows cold."

If it was possible, she lifted her nose higher, sauntered over to the plaid and stopped looking down at it. "You should be more careful, you know. You are in England now. If someone sees you with this, you might not be so fortunate with it or your excuse."

"I will keep that in mind. Now, will you sit down or do I have to get up and see that you do?"

She sat down quickly.

"I like an obedient lass," he said, and handed her a piece of meat.

She took it hesitantly. "I am not obedient. I am hungry. There is a difference."

Robert began eating his rabbit, letting her know the conversation had ended. They ate in silence; each of them set upon devouring his or her small portion. At one point, Robert stopped and took a sip of whisky. He offered it to Hugh, who also drank.

She watched in silence, then after a few minutes, she said, "Might I have a drink?"

"I'll get you some water from the burn," Hugh said.

"I'll have what you're having."

Hugh grinned and eagerly offered her the bottle, in spite of Robert's scowl.

She took the bottle and was about to put it to her lips when Robert cautioned her. "That is usquebaugh."

She gazed down at the bottle, frowning. "Usquebaugh? What is that? Some sort of heathen potion? Or is it poison?"

"Scots whisky," Hugh said. "A few sips of that and you'll be ready to take on the devil."

She looked at Robert. "Well, since that already seems to be the case, I might as well do this right." She turned the bottle up and took a large swallow, followed quickly by a coughing fit.

"Might I suggest a smaller dose?" Robert said, looking at Hugh who was still grinning as if he had no good sense.

When she got her breath back, she spoke between gasps. "I didn't realize it was so strong."

"It's a man's drink," Hugh said and Robert wanted to punch him.

Instead, he gave his brother a look that said, *Don't open your fool mouth again.* He should have given Hugh that look sooner, for just as he suspected, Hugh's comment urged her on. With a defiant look, she took another sip—thankfully, smaller than the first. She held the bottle toward him and Robert put it down, wedging it into the dirt between them.

By the time they finished eating, the whisky had curbed her anger and loosened her tongue. Robert was trying to decide which was worse, as he listened to her telling Hugh about the holy well where they had first seen her. Since she was so talkative, he decided it was a good time to find out about her. "Who are you? Why out this late, and still without an escort?"

She mutely stared at the fire.

"I asked you a question, lass."

"Yes, the same question you asked before."

"You didn't answer it then, so I am asking again."

"It was daylight when I left, so I didn't need an escort. Normally, I don't ride this late."

"Why are you out this late now?"

She looked down at her hands folded in her lap. There was something about the way she did this that made Robert suspect hers was not going to be an easy story to tell—if they got it out of her, that is. "I asked you a question."

"I...I took a wrong turn and got lost."

"You don't live around here?"

Her head jerked around. "Why would you think that?"

"Your wrong turn."

She shrugged. "Oh, that. Well, I was upset when I left. I wasn't watching where I was going."

"Why were you upset?"

"I...I'm afraid of the dark."

Hugh said, "Being afraid of the dark is nothing to be ashamed of."

"That isn't the reason," Robert said. "Can't you tell she is lying?"

"I am not lying!"

"Let me see if I have this right. You did not need an escort because it was daylight when you left, yet you were upset because you are afraid of the dark, which caused you to make a wrong turn and get lost. Interesting, what you consider the truth here in England. *Do you take me for a fool?* What are you running from?"

"I am not in the habit of sharing private information with strangers."

Hugh laughed heartily. "Troth! She only shares rabbits and whisky with naked ones."

She glared at Hugh. "The whisky has sharpened your wit."

"Aye, but it doesn't seem to have the same effect upon you."

"I can be witty when I'm around those capable of understanding it."

Robert cut in. "You didn't tell us your name."

"You didn't tell me yours."

"Robert Douglas. This is my brother Hugh."

She did not say anything.

"I believe it's your turn."

"I am pleased to meet you."

"Give me your name, lass!"

"I don't give my name to strangers, either."

"It would take me two seconds to join you on that plaid, and another five minutes to toss your skirts and become better acquainted. Then we would not be strangers. Is that what you prefer?"

"Meleri," she said quickly. "My name is Meleri."

"And the rest of it?"

"Weatherby. Lady Meleri Weatherby."

"Now we are getting somewhere," Hugh said.

"Do you live nearby?" Robert asked.

"No."

"And your destination?"

"To visit my former nanny."

"Where does she live?"

"Not far from Gretna Green."

"That's in Scotland," Hugh said.

"Yes, since its inception, I believe," Robert said, not missing how great an effort it was for her not to smile. "Now, lass, I will have the rest of it, without any more witticism."

"The…the rest of it?"

"Aye. You have not told us your entire story, lass. I am not a fool. A lady does not travel at night without an escort, nor does she leave for a visit without taking any baggage. What are you running from?"

She drew her legs up and wrapped her arms around them, resting her chin on the top of her knees. She stared pensively into the fire. Robert was about to repeat his question, when she said softly, "Marriage."

"What did you say?"

"Marriage!" she shouted, and then, speaking softer, "I am running away from marriage."

"How far do you think you will get? Your father will obviously send someone after you."

She frowned in a way that made Robert think she was not going to respond, but she surprised him. "My father does not know."

"How can he not know his daughter is missing?"

"My father is unwell. My sister has taken him to London, where she can look after him."

There was more to it than what she was telling, but Robert let it ride for now. "And the man you were to marry? Will he not send someone to look for you?"

"I am certain he will, but he will not have any idea where I have gone."

"I think you should return home. You may stay the night here, with us, and in the morning we will take you back."

It had been a long time since Robert had seen such terror on a woman's face. Before he could inquire as to its cause, she shot to her feet, a wild expression filled with panic on her face. "No! I cannot go back. I will not marry him. I would rather…" She stopped there. Robert could not help admiring the way she quickly gained control of herself. She was a levelheaded lass, in spite of her temper. When she spoke again, she was calm, her voice soft. "What I do with my life is up to me. You have no interest in this matter, nor are you a relation. Consequently, you have no right to force me to return."

Hugh agreed. "She's right, Robbie. 'Tis none of our affair."

Robert agreed, but he still had one question. "What made you leave today? Is the wedding a few days off?"

That brought a mocking laugh from her. "A date has never been set."

"And what happened to change things?"

She stared at the fire again, then after some time, she sighed. "I suppose I might as well tell you the whole story."

"Start at the very beginning."

"I was born…"

Hugh burst out laughing.

"We can accept that assumption. When were you pledged to this man?"

"Shortly after my birth," she said, then went on to tell her story, which took some time—long enough that Hugh had to build up the fire, twice.

Once, about halfway through her story, Robert noticed Hugh was exhibiting signs of being deep in thought—something quite unusual for him.

Hugh, after maintaining his silent contemplation a bit longer, suddenly asked, "Why is this man so determined to marry you when he knows you do not want him? Is your dowry a large one?"

She nodded. "Extremely large." She continued with her story. When she reached the part about the letter her betrothed sent to her father, Robert stopped her. "And you still have the letter?"

"In my pocket," she said, and withdrew the letter. She offered it to him. "You may read it, if you like."

Robert glanced at Hugh.

With irritation in her voice, she said, "I assume you can read?"

"Only four-letter words," he said. "I don't need to read your private letter." He handed the letter back to her. "It would appear that you have gotten yourself into a rather precarious position. No matter which way you go, you're bound to bump into something unpleasant."

Hugh laughed. "Aye, she bumped into you."

Robert was about to say something, when Hugh interrupted. "I'd like a word with you in private."

Robert wondered what his brother was up to, but he remained silent.

"Would you would excuse us for a moment?" Hugh asked.

"Of course."

Robert accompanied Hugh to a place several yards away. "Why all the secrecy?"

"Keep your voice down. I have an idea and it involves the lass. I don't want her to hear."

"I have never gone along with one of your schemes, yet, that something didn't go wrong."

"This time will be the exception. It has occurred to me that marriage between you and the lass would serve you both well."

"Are you daft? Marry her? You have seen the way she lives up to that red hair. She is opinionated, too outspoken and obstinate as a headache. And on top of that, she's got the disposition of a sore-toothed bear."

"For a man who has less than three weeks to save himself, you sure are paying a lot of attention to trivial details. I say she is perfect. Just what we are looking for. She is English and titled. She is also well dowered. And better yet, she is in no position to refuse your offer. Why are you being so fussy? We came here for a wife, didn't we?"

"Then you marry her!"

"Great idea. I will marry her, and *you* explain it to the king." He glanced back at the lass. "What's wrong with her?"

"Nothing...everything! She isn't exactly what I had in mind."

"She's a woman and English. You do not have time to add anything else. You could do much worse, Robbie. She's comely enough, and I'll wager she would be grateful to you for helping her out of a terrible situation."

"What makes you think she would rather be married to me than that ogre her father chose?"

"I know your reputation, brother. I have heard firsthand what the lassies at home say about you. If there is anything you know, it's pleasing a lass…when it suits you, that is."

Robert looked back at her, crossed his arms, frowned and said, "She does not suit me. I've never been fond of red hair."

"Perhaps I could persuade her to shave her head," Hugh said, allowing his exasperation to show. "I'm sorry I tried to help you. If you don't find a willing lass to marry, and you end up married to some toothless old crone picked out by the king, don't say I didn't offer you a better way out."

"I won't. Now, was there anything else you wanted to talk about?"

"No. I prefer to remain silent from here on out and watch you hang yourself with all the slack you've cut." Hugh started walking back toward the fire, paused and said, "Are you coming?"

"Aye." Robert walked back slowly, contemplating what his brother said.

By the time Robert stopped by the fire, Hugh had her telling the rest of her story. He sat down and listened to her tale, until she mentioned again that she was going to Scotland, to the home of her former nanny. "You should have a care," Robert warned her. "It is not safe for a lass to be traveling alone and sleeping out in the open. Tomorrow you should take a coach to Gretna Green. It would be safer."

"I left in such haste, I did not take much money. I thought I would sell my horse tomorrow. That should provide me enough for the fare to Gretna."

"Our offer still stands. You are welcome to stay the night here," Hugh said.

"Well…I…"

"You haven't any other place to go, have you?" he asked.

"No…that is, no place they would not recognize me."

"Then it is settled." He looked around the camp. "You have your choice of rooms, milady."

Robert stared at Hugh, who was doing a stupendous job of making a fool of himself over this English lass. Five minutes ago, he was trying to pawn her off on him. Now it appeared he was going after her himself.

"Who is this man you detest to the point you are willing to leave your home and family?" Robert asked idly. "He must be abominable to take such risk with your life. Is he old?"

"He is about your age, nice-looking, and the son of one of the most powerful dukes in England, who is a relative of the king."

"My, my, and you are running away from all that?" Hugh said.

"Yes. I will go to America or Australia if I have to. Anything to keep from marrying Waverly."

Robert frowned, thinking it could not be. "Waverly?"

She nodded. "Philip Ashton, the Marquess of Waverly."

At the sound of that name, Robert's heart thumped wildly and then seemed to stop altogether. He closed his eyes, feeling as if the ground beneath his feet began to tremble and then give way. He could feel himself begin to sink slowly into a bog hole, its soft, muddy surface sucking and pulling him down, down, until he was engulfed in a shifting mass that turned his world dark and filled his lungs until he could not breathe. He felt suffocated. *Waverly*.... The name went through him like a white-hot brand, agonizing and searing. Surely it could not be. It was too much of a coincidence. Fate would not have been so foolish as to usher in the fiancée of the man he hated most in the world, right into his presence.

"Is something wrong?" Hugh asked.

Robert managed to focus on him through a blur. He realized both Hugh and the girl were looking at him strangely. A mask settled over him, a stone coldness that went deep within him and lodged in his heart. After all this time and so many years of grief, he may have found a way to lay his sister's ghost to rest. How fitting that it would take the sacrifice of an English lass to set him free. Without another thought, he knew she would be his wife, bound in a state of subjection to his power, his influence, his very will. Gaining control, he forced his voice to a normal tone. "Wrong? No, of course not."

"You're pale as a bleached bone."

"I'm fine."

Hugh continued to look at him for a minute longer, then with a shrug gave his attention to Meleri.

Robert rose to his feet. "I'd better check on the horses."

He left before Hugh had a chance to respond. He needed to get away, to be by himself. He needed some time to think, to clear his head of the residue left by such a shock. For over ten years, he had looked for a way to get even with the Marquess of Waverly. He remembered the day he learned the identity of the bastard who raped Sorcha, then turned her over to his three friends. Robert's first instinct had been to ride to England immediately and slit the bastard's throat, but his grandmother and Iain had cautioned him against it. "You want me to do nothing? You think I can simply pick up with my life where it was before and go on like all of this never happened?"

His grandmother wanted just that. "Aye, for the time being. In the end, he will get the justice he deserves. Evil never goes unpunished."

"He is the son of an English duke who is related to the king. He will never be punished, and you want me to leave him thinking he has gotten away with what he did, never to know even who she was?"

"Aye, to do otherwise could prove to be the downfall of all the Douglases."

In the end, Robert was persuaded. He realized a Scot would never receive any kind of justice against someone as powerful as the son of the Duke of Heatherton. He was convinced he would never have a chance to get even, or to see that Waverly paid for his sister's death. Now the impossible had happened. It absorbed Robert completely, for already he was devising the perfect plan, knowing even before he worked it all out, that this English lass was not only vital to his plan, but the crucial element necessary for its success.

It was perfect and so very simple. He would not marry the chit for himself, but he would marry her in a minute, in order to keep

Waverly from having her. He would steal her out from under Waverly's nose and then he would make certain Waverly heard about it.

He stared into the fire, unable to believe how remarkable it all was. To have such a key resource he could use at the opportune moment, dropped in his lap, had to be a gift from God.

A changed man, he looked at Meleri. "You know, I have been thinking about your predicament. It has occurred to me that I may have the perfect way out for you."

Her face brightened. "Oh, that would be so wonderful. I cannot thank you enough. What is your solution, pray tell?"

"I will marry you myself."

Hugh, who had just taken another drink of whisky, choked, spewing the drink, some of it going into the fire, which sent flames shooting upward.

Robert paid Hugh little notice. Meleri did as well. Her attention was all on Robert. "Marry *you?*"

"Of course. Do you find the idea abhorrent?"

"No, of course not…that is…I mean…" She put her hand on her head. "Oh, I don't know what I mean. Too much has happened in such a short time. I am so confused." She paused a moment as if what he said finally hit her. "I cannot marry you. We just met. You're a stranger."

"Which would you prefer? A stranger or Waverly, because you will end up married to one of us. You are in a predicament, lass, and there is no easy way out. You have precious few choices, none of them good. What will you do when Waverly finds you? And he *will* find you. What then?"

Once his choking fit subsided, Hugh looked ready to jump into the conversation. Robert directed a look at him that carried a warning, both cautionary and convincing. Hugh must have interpreted the look correctly, for he remained silent, although glowering a bit.

"So, what is it to be?" Robert asked.

"I…I don't know. Honestly. It's quite difficult to rush into marriage with a total stranger, you know."

"He isn't a complete stranger. You've already met him twice," Hugh said. "Besides, how can you call him a stranger, when you saw him without a stitch on? Naked as the truth, he was."

"I think we can leave off with that discussion for now," Robert said.

A hint of color still stained her cheeks as Meleri tried to explain herself. "Although I am in a fine predicament, as you correctly pointed out, I am finding it difficult to understand your reaction. Why would you want to involve yourself in my difficulties? And at so great a price. By marrying you, I have everything to gain. You, on the other hand, have nothing."

"That's where you're wrong. We came to England to find Robbie a wife," Hugh said. "A *rich* one."

Robert dropped his head in disbelief. The only thing worse Hugh could have done was to add he was ordered to do so by the king.

"Now, don't go thinking Robbie is the mercenary type, because he is not. It was an order, signed by the king himself."

Robert groaned. Hugh was worse than meddlesome Matty. For him, talk came first and thought last.

Stunned surprise registered on her face. "The king ordered you? Why would he do that?"

"Robbie is a powerful earl. The king knew if he took an English wife, it would go a long way in helping the relationship between the Scots and the English."

Robert was ready to throttle him. Was Hugh that dense? Didn't he know when to close that overproductive mouth of his?

"Yes, I can see that it would. Still, that is no reason to rush into marriage with a stranger."

Hugh was eager to reply. "Oh, yes, it is! The king only gave him three weeks to find a wife. After that, the king will find one for him. You see, now, that you would be doing Robbie as much of a favor as he would be doing you. You would be mutual benefactors, so to speak."

"Are you finished emptying your brain of every scrap that's in it?" Robert asked, his voice gruff and full of irritation. "If you don't mind, will you allow me the honor of doing my own proposing?" Robert decided then, that if Hugh so much as opened his mouth, he would punch him into silence.

He spoke to her, but his intention was to quell Hugh's bleating. "You must forgive my brother. His brain can only do one thing at a time. Think or speak. One or the other."

She smiled shyly. With a demure turn of her head, she looked Robert over again, this time with a spark of interest. "I suppose I could do worse."

"I don't see how." Hugh paused suddenly, apparently realizing what he said. "That is, I don't see how you could find any-. one better."

"Oh. Yes, I see," she said, frowning. "Well, I am certain that is true."

"What more can you ask for?"

"Silence." Robert wanted to muzzle Hugh. It was *his* offer of marriage, yet there was room for him to squeeze only one foot into this conversation. True to his nature, Hugh had taken the lead and jumped in with two.

Hugh ignored Robert's comment and went on babbling like a brook. "So, tell me if you agree that marriage is the best choice, and the only one completely foolproof?"

"I would have to agree that marriage would be impervious to any intervention on Waverly's part."

Hugh, beaming, slapped his hands against his thighs. "Well now! It sure looks like everything has worked out fine, Robbie. We can go to Gretna tomorrow and see the two of you wed."

"Don't publish the banns just yet. There are a few details that must be worked out." Robert wanted to slow things down. It had all gone so fast. Half an hour ago he was worried that his time would be up before he could find a bride, and now he had not only a willing prospect, but one that he could use to his advantage. It did not bother him in the least that she would be the means by which he would extract his revenge.

She shifted her position, which brought her directly into his line of view. He could not miss the restrained demeanor that brought out an almost haunting quality that hung about her like sadness. He hardened himself against that. She was a means to an end. He did not want to think of her as anything else.

Her skirts rustled as she came to her feet and stood looking down at him. "I have decided to accept your offer of marriage, my lord."

"As the saying goes, blest is the wooing that's not long a-doing," Hugh said, then leaned toward Robert, gave him a nudge in the ribs and whispered, "Tell her something, thickwit, without any more ado."

"You tell her. You've been doing all my bleating thus far."

Meleri said, "We can be wed as soon as you like, although I think it is always best to have at least a short time of wooing."

"Wooing should be done after the wedding," Hugh said.

"And what makes you an expert on the subject?" Robert asked.

"A man who has avoided matrimony as many times as I have has to know a great deal about it."

Robert turned to Meleri. "We won't have time for a big ceremony. We can be married in Gretna Green."

"Yes, that way I could still see my old nanny," she said.

Robert nodded. "We will leave for Gretna Green in the morning. Considering the secrecy that must be involved, I will postpone any correspondence with your father until after we are married."

The sad look washed over her face again. "That would be best," she agreed.

"Unless her father's search party finds us before then," said Hugh.

She almost laughed. "I doubt that will happen."

"Why not?" Hugh asked.

"There isn't anyone in my father's employ who could track a bleeding deer through three feet of snow." Her tone turned more serious as she told him the truth about her father.

When she finished, Robert said, "If his memory fails him, who makes the legal decisions for him?"

"My sister's husband. He is the Earl of Sheridan and a barrister. He came to Humberly Hall over a year ago to set my father's affairs in order. We were worried that my father might fall under the influence of someone capable of swindling him out of everything."

"So, your brother-in-law controls your dowry?"

"Yes."

"And does he know where you are going?"

"His wife…my sister, Elizabeth, knows. In fact, going to my old nanny's was her idea."

"Well, first things first. We have a long day ahead of us tomorrow. We will need a good night's sleep." Robert turned to Meleri. "You will probably feel safer if you spread your plaid down between the two of us."

Robert and Hugh tossed their bedding to the ground on each side of where she stood. As soon as that was done, Robert told Meleri he and Hugh would take a short walk to give her a "wee bit o' privacy."

"You have no tents?" she asked.

"Tents?" Hugh guffawed. "We are men, mistress, not English lambs."

As Hugh led the way down to the burn, Robert heard the soft, hesitant sound of Meleri's voice. "You won't…you won't go far, will you?"

"We won't leave you alone in the dark, if that is what you are worried about," Robert replied.

"I shan't take long. I need only to remove my shoes."

"Go to sleep, lass," Robert said, then followed the sound of swift flowing water tumbling over rocks, as it made its way down the hillside.

He found his brother and stopped next to him, each silently contemplating their own thoughts about what tomorrow might bring.

After a while, Hugh picked up a stone and flipped it into the burn. "You will be married before that water reaches the sea."

"Don't remind me."

"What happened to change your mind? One minute you were ready to take my suggestion to marry her and hit me with it. The next thing I know, you are proposing to her."

"I had a change of heart."

"I didn't know you had one."

"I changed my mind, then."

"I know, but something happened that made you change it. I saw your face, Robbie. You were looking like you had been shot in the back. Was it something she said?"

Robert figured Hugh would have to know, eventually, but he was not ready to tell him about Waverly just yet. "It was simply the right time. I had time to think about what you said. It made perfect sense to marry her and hie ourselves back to Scotland with all due haste."

"I'm glad you feel better about it."

"I don't feel better at all. If the truth were known, I feel remarkably like I went out for sheep and came home shorn."

The sound of Hugh's laughter danced out into the night, and like the gurgling water of the burn, made its way down the hillside.

9

Meleri drifted upon the quiet waters of a still lake. The air was heavy with a blossomy fragrance, sun-warmed and sweet. Tranquillity closed in, calm after the storm. Her eyes grew heavy and she slipped into the silence of sleep.

A bellowing barrage of terrifying noise shattered the serenity. Her eyes flew open and tried to focus, in spite of the confused sort of vagueness she felt, fully expecting to see a raging bull charging toward her.

She saw her husband-to-be. He nudged her with his foot. "Wake up! It is time to go."

"Mmm…"

He nudged her again. "Up, lass! If you stay here much longer, the sun will burn that fair English skin."

Meleri saw nothing but darkness. "What sun?" she asked, not caring that she sounded grumpy.

"You can be cross later. Up with you now."

She rolled over.

"I'll give you one minute, then I dump you in the burn."

She yawned and stared sleepily up at him. "It's still dark."

"That will change."

She shifted into a sitting position and moaned from the stiffness that greeted her. "Why must we be up so early?"

"It's your wedding day, or have you forgotten?"

She rubbed her eyes and yawned again. "I daresay it will still be my wedding day if I sleep another hour."

"We've a lot of traveling ahead of us. It is best to start now."

"It isn't that far to Gretna Green."

When that did not seem to work, she tried a different approach. "How about a little more sleep…for my wedding gift?"

"I don't make bargains about such as that."

She did not know why his harsh tone surprised her. Scots were barbarians. Everyone knew that. Shouting was probably the only way they could communicate. "Why?"

"It's against the rules."

"Sleeping longer?"

"Aye. You must be an early riser."

"On my wedding day?"

"Aye. It's an old Scottish custom."

"I am not Scottish."

"You soon will be."

"How can I be a Scot when I am English?"

"You will come to your senses soon enough."

"Are you saying you will make me to give up everything English?"

"I won't have to. You will decide to do it of your own accord."

"You are very confident."

"I know what I know."

Talking to this man was like solving a riddle. She knew the answer was in there somewhere. All she had to do was find it. She glanced around the campsite, trying to make out the terrain in the dim light. Nothing looked familiar or hospitable.

Including the man she would marry a few hours hence.

He made a move to pick her up, and she felt the icy reminder of the burn. "All right! All right! I am getting up! You don't have to be so grim about it."

"You don't know what grim is until you get to Scotland."

She came to her feet, because she knew he would harry her until they both grew beards. "So, now I'm up." She fished around in her mind for something positive to think. This was her wedding day, and he was a tall, warm-bodied man with a harshly handsome face and a not-so-handsome disposition. More important, however, was the fact that he was willing to marry her, to take her off to Scotland, to protect her and keep her safe from Waverly's harm. It was enough for her to feel a gratefulness that was genuine. She stole a glance at the tall, dark stranger and felt something she had not for a long, long time: protected and safe. She supposed she could well afford to put up with a little of his gruffness in return.

A split-second later, she found herself hoisted into the air and onto her horse. He handed her the reins. "What about breakfast?" she asked.

"You slept through it."

"Don't I get something to eat?"

"Aye, you get breakfast…when you rise early enough to eat it," he said.

While she searched for the proper verbiage to throw at him, he mounted, kicked his horse and left her staring after him.

Her stomach growled, but she would starve before she let a man or a Scot get the best of her. She caught up to him and heard his soft chuckle when she slowed her horse to keep pace with his. They rode on without speaking, and she found the silence a welcome repose—soon shattered when Hugh rode up babbling like a brook.

"How is the bride to be?"

"Tolerable, considering I had no breakfast and no sleep."

"The starving fox sleeps," he said. "If you want to eat…"

"You must be up earlier," she finished. "I've had that bit of wisdom shoved at me already this morning. If you want to beat Robert, you must be up a little earlier yourself. You must have many rules in Scotland. Is there one for everything?"

"Aye, and if there isn't, we can always find one that will apply."

"Or make one up."

"You don't care for rules?"

"I will add 'perceptive' to my list of qualities you possess."

"What do you have against rules?"

"They were invented by men."

Hugh raised his brows in amusement. "How do you know?"

"Because they are generally for women, and there are too many of them."

"I guess I never gave the matter much thought."

"That's because you're a man."

He laughed again and she decided she liked him, this man to whom laughter came so easily. She found herself comparing his sunny nature with his brother's dark and brooding one. He was nothing like Robert. They were opposites in every way.

"Don't overly concern yourself with rules, lass. We don't have so many of them in Scotland."

"Truly?"

Robert, who had remained mysteriously silent up to now, said, "Careful about the kind of stories you put into her head."

"Does it make you nervous to talk about rules?" she asked.

"Not particularly. Scots are given one rule the day they are born, and they live with it all their life."

"What rule is that?"

"Hate the English," he said shortly before he picked up his pace and rode on ahead.

She watched him. "He seems to have taken that rule to heart."

"Aye, it was bitterness that caused it."

"Bitterness? Over what?"

Hugh opened his mouth as if to tell her, but something must have changed his mind, for he said, "I think it would be better to let Robbie tell."

"He may never do that. He isn't very talkative."

"Don't worry, lass. He will tell you…when the time is right."

She shuddered, feeling a cold chill sweep over her. "Hate the English. That is not a very encouraging note on which to begin one's marriage. It does seem rather unfair to me, as if I am being punished for something I did not do."

"The way I see it, you English have the same rule concerning the Scots, so the two cancel each other out. That puts you back to the starting point, with your marriage on even ground."

She drew her brows together and thought about that. The English were very prejudiced toward the Scots, that was true, for she remembered Philip was a man who felt an inordinate amount of hatred toward Scots, although she never understood why. "I suppose the English are a bit intolerant and biased when it comes to Scotland, but it was not something I noticed in our household. My father was never the kind to pick up the standard that bore another's flag. He preferred to form his own opinion and make his own judgments."

He was quiet for a while and she wondered what he was thinking. Probably that she talked too much. Well, it was his own fault. He should not be so cheerful, so adept at making her feel comfortable. She felt as if she had known him for a long time. It made her sad to think these attributes did not describe the man she was to marry, but his brother.

"Your life hasn't been an easy one, has it?"

His question surprised her. He was such a happy, good-humored man, that it was easy to overlook the fact that he had a deeper side. He was obviously well educated and quite perceptive. "My father is very wealthy, so I have been blessed with all the creature comforts. In other areas, I was not so fortunate."

"Such as?"

"My mother died when I was young. My father, although a dearer man you will never find, is old enough to be my grandfather. I have no brothers or sisters, only two half sisters who were married before I was born. Creature comforts are not everything."

"How old were you when you lost your mother?"

"Almost seven."

"That's a difficult age to lose a parent. I'm thankful I was much older when I lost mine."

"Both of your parents are dead?"

"Aye. Now all I have is a doting grandmother, an understanding uncle, one troublesome brother and two nieces."

Her heart leaped at the thought of marriage into such a family. "Oh, I should have loved to have a doting grandmother! I never knew either of mine. The closest I have is our housekeeper, Mrs. Hadley, and a well-meaning staff who always doted on me. My nanny came the closest to understanding how much I missed my mother and how deeply losing her affected me."

"Do you look like her?"

"Everyone says I do, right down to the red hair."

"She must have been a very beautiful woman."

"I never understood how anyone could say I favored her. Whenever I looked at myself in the mirror, I would see carroty red hair and freckles. I wondered how anyone not in their cups could see any resemblance between us."

After so much talk about her mother, the world seemed to close in around her and Meleri looked off. She found her thoughts going backward, and she remembered the tired expression that had come over Lady Seren's face the day she spoke her last words to Meleri.

"I wish you were older so you could understand what I am telling you. I wish I had more time before I have to leave."

"Where are you going? Can I come with you?"

"No. I am going on a long journey. You cannot come with me. No one can. I must go alone."

"Why? Why can't I come?" She hugged her mother fiercely, as if by doing so she could prevent her going away. "Don't leave me! Please don't leave me!"

"Shh. Do not cry, child of mine. Although I must go away, I will never leave you, my sweet. Remember that. No matter what happens. No matter how long I am gone. I will never leave you. Are you listening to what I am saying?"

A tear slipped down Meleri's face as she remembered the way she had wrinkled up her nose and looked at her mother in a per-plexed way. "I think I understand…but how can you go away and not leave me?"

"Because there will always be a part of me that remains be-hind. You are a part of me, Meleri. I will not fail you. Listen care-fully, and try to remember what I say. No matter how long I am gone, I will not leave you unguided. You will be watched over, but you must be strong. You must listen to your heart and search for the answers. Promise me you won't forget that."

"I promise."

"And promise me you will never give up your thirst for learning, your love of books."

"I promise."

"Books will set you free. They hold the answer to so many things. Read, lambkin, for that is when you will feel the closest to me. Promise me you will always read."

"I do promise, Mother. Truly, I do."

"Give me a kiss and a hug before you leave. I am weary now." Then her mother had turned her head to gaze toward the window where the rain-spattered glass dimmed the view to a world outside that was cold and dreary. She let out a long and steady sigh. "How I long to see one more summer…the brilliant colors of spring…the scent of flowers. Aaah, to feel the sun warm my face one last time."

Meleri hugged her mother fiercely and covered her face with kisses. "I will go and paint you a beautiful picture," she said. "It will have sunshine and green grass…lots and lots of *bee-u-tee-ful* flowers. When I am finished, I will bring it in here and put it on your wall. Then you will have summer all the time."

Her mother stroked her face. "You are my summer, my sunshine and my flowers. In you, I see all the beautiful colors of life. Now, go. Go paint me a picture."

She went, but when she returned with her picture, she tiptoed up to her mother's bed. She did not realize at that moment that her mother was dead. She only knew that the light was absent from her mother's lovely green eyes, that Lady Seren was no longer there. Her mother had gone on her journey, as she had said, and left her behind.

Meleri swallowed and took a deep breath. Some small remnant of her sadness must have reached Hugh, for he said, "Would you like to walk awhile? We could stop and lead the horses."

"I would love the opportunity to stretch. I feel as if I've had far too strong a dose of equine backbone."

They crested a ridge and paused to take in the vast sweep of open terrain. "There is an untouched wildness about this place that reminds me of Scotland," Hugh said.

She looked out over the bleak barrenness of the Borderlands and saw beauty in the newborn colors of the day. She glanced toward the ragged notch of a hill and noticed Robert astride his horse, sitting as still as they. He was nothing more than a silhouette, dark against the sun that rose behind him—an image that seduced as well as intrigued.

As if he knew she watched, he shifted his position and looked in their direction. Her heart leaped in response and began to pound, anticipating her desire to have him ride back to accompany her, in the manner his brother had done. Expectant, her heart filled with newfound hope, for she knew he could see they had stopped. Now, she thought, now he will ride back to me.

Expectation slowly gave way to frustration when he made no move to ride toward them. Instead he spun his horse around and disappeared over the hill, and she felt the stabbing bite of disappointment. She understood the meaning of the act and what it represented. It was a new sensation to be discarded as something useless. She decided inexperience is neither remedy, excuse, nor solvent, and it did naught to counteract her hurt or the damage done to her pride.

She had no doubt that she had been rejected. What she did not know was why.

PART TWO

This looks not like a nuptial

Shakespeare, *Much Ado About Nothing*

10

The wind in her face, English soil falling away beneath her feet, Meleri wondered what her intended thought about her—other than the exasperation he expressed. Did he wonder what kind of woman would ride off to marry a complete stranger?

On and on they rode, through dark woods and along winding, country roads, across open moorland, with the horses eating up the miles that lay between her past and her future. Faint, and yet surprisingly persistent were the voices that kept repeating in the back of her mind, *Are you certain you are doing the right thing?*

In spite of that reminder, she found it exciting to embark upon such an adventure, to be free as the wind that chased the clouds overhead. She could not help thinking the future held much promise, in spite of the fact that beside her rode the most complex and forbidding man she ever hoped to meet.

A fine mist rolled in and it looked like rain. Robert offered her his plaid, telling her, "It will keep you dry and warm," but she refused it.

What was a little rain, when you were weary enough that you did not feel it? She was so tired. There were times when she felt as if she would topple right out of the saddle if she so much as closed her eyes. Everywhere she looked the land about them was dreary and depressing, and she tried not to think about the bleak and cheerless prospect that faced her—and the future she had so impetuously chosen for herself.

She felt as if she were going crazy. One minute she was feeling close to Robert and desirous of his touch. The next moment she was wary and reserved, afraid she was making a terrible mistake. Why could she not settle down with one feeling? That was all she asked, but even as she did, she could not help thinking that it was, indeed, a wild and foolish undertaking.

They crossed over the border from England into Scotland. A short while later, they rode into Gretna Green, which lay among the marshes near Solway Firth. It was the first town over the border, which must have been the reason it was sought by many young English couples who chose to elope, for the town itself was a sad, ominous place surrounded by barren land and full of poverty. The small houses were dull and beggarly, so smoke-filled it was difficult to see the faces of those who stared out at them as they passed.

Hugh studied Robert for a bit, then, with a wink at Meleri, he said, "You are not a very talkative bridegroom."

"Why talk? I have nothing to say."

"Och, mon! You don't have to look so miserable in your silence."

"I am about to be married. I will soon be filled with the misery of a man in the pursuit of happiness. Let me enjoy it in my own way."

"Be of good cheer, brother. Marriage does have its advantages. Soon you will have your very own Scots warming pan."

Unable to keep her curiosity at bay, Meleri asked, "What is a Scots warming pan?"

"A wench," Robert said sourly.

"Humph! I might have known."

Not even the sudden sprinkle of rain could dampen the cheerful tones of Hugh's laughter.

As for Robert, he did not look as though he saw anything humorous. Meleri was in complete agreement with that.

Almost in unison, they both shot Hugh an ill-humored look, which only served to make him laugh all the harder. "Och! There is nothing so uplifting as the dawn of a brother's wedding day."

It was raining very hard by the time they came upon an old, mahogany-faced woman covered in a coarse wrap, her bare, stockingless feet thrust inside crude, heavy shoes. Robert asked the way to the blacksmith.

She guided them along the streets until they were close enough for her to point the way. Robert nodded and thanked her after giving her two coins. The woman nodded and said something Meleri could not understand.

They rode past a few houses when Robert said, "Well, lass, here we are."

Meleri looked about her and wondered if this was Robert's way of teasing her, or if it truly was their destination, depressing as it was. Everywhere she looked, she saw nothing but gray sheets of rain and little rivers of water running down the muddy streets. Directly in front of them stood a dank and dark smithy's shop—certainly not the best place for a wedding. She gave him a puzzled look. "What do you mean here we are? What is this place?"

"Why, it's Gretna Green. You do remember we were to be married here?"

She nodded.

"Then, this is the place where it will happen," he said, throwing his leg over the saddle and sliding to the ground, before coming for her.

"This is it?" she asked, looking at the crudely constructed building, which served as a place of work for the local blacksmith. "We are going to be married here? In a smithy's shop?" She could not hide the sadness, the self-pity in her voice. Desolation and misery closed tightly about her. She had agreed to marriage, but not in a smithy's shop.

She would marry only once in her lifetime. She wanted a true wedding, the kind normal people had. She wanted a lovely dress, and the presence of family, and a parson to say the words. Everything about this place was dismal and unfortunate. Her spirits sank about as low as they could go. However, she was not about to tell Robert that.

Hugh, who was talking to her again, dismounted and she looked pleadingly at him. "Is this truly Gretna Green?"

"Of course. Are you disappointed?"

Disappointed? Surely, he could offer a worse, more descriptive word. How about devastated? Or, heartbroken? Even filled with dread? She shrugged. "A little. I had no idea it would look so…like this."

"I know it doesn't look like much, but this is truly Gretna Green, where so many come to marry. I am surprised you haven't heard it was a gloomy and somber place where life was dreary and difficult."

Faith! She could find little encouragement in those words, or anything to fill her voice with lightheartedness. "I have never known anyone who married here, so I had no way of knowing. I had only heard it was a place couples could be married without parental permission. Naturally, I thought that meant in a church, or at least a nice parsonage."

She felt acutely disappointed, for there was nothing of the mystical feeling of romance she expected. Why had the stories of elopements to this place always seemed so magical and idyllic? How could she have thought something so childish and so foolish? She ignored a small voice inside her head that answered, *Because you wanted it to be.*

"Well, you know now," Hugh said. "Once you are married, you will forget all about the unpleasant parts of it."

"I doubt I will ever forget this place," she said. She was tired, wet and cold. She looked around at her bleak surroundings once more. "I suppose one must always try to make the most of every situation, regardless of how grim."

Hugh laughed. "Aye, 'tis a grim place, no doubt."

Robert merely said, "If you're in a hurry for a wedding with no banns and few witnesses, this is the only choice."

She looked all about her and saw no altar or anything that resembled one. Her trampled spirits fell with a soggy *squish* into the mud. "But...but where will we stand?"

"Before the anvil."

Shock and dismay swept over her. She felt like crying. She eyed the cold, impersonal structure. "An anvil for an altar. It seems a sacrilege."

"I'm certain you have been guilty of worse irreverence," Robert said.

She expected to hear the sound of Hugh's boisterous laughter, but for once, his expression was almost sympathetic. "Like Robbie said, being married without banns and few witnesses reduces your choices somewhat."

"Yes," she said, "it does...*somewhat.*"

Robert was suddenly beside her, and he put his hands at her waist. He lifted her down from her horse. "I imagine God will understand your improvising. The marriage will be legal and that is what's important."

It seemed incredible to her that Robert and Hugh could be so disrespectful toward an event that was not only a sacrament, but also a huge step into the unknown, at least for her. How composed her bridegroom looked, how indifferent. She supposed her only recourse was to strike a pose of similar nonchalance.

With a shiver of dread and anticipation, she wondered if she was doing the right thing, then reminded herself that it was too late now for such questions. Better to pray for a blessing upon her future, than to question what was already done.

As she walked along, she wished she could shrivel up into nothing more than one of the insignificant stones that lay scattered about under her feet. She had no more time to make wishes, for she was further horrified when Robert said they were not only going to wed before an anvil in a smithy's shop, but that their wedding ceremony was going to be performed by...

"I'm sorry. I must have misunderstood you. Who did you say would perform the wedding ceremony?"

"A blacksmith," Robert repeated.

"Oh."

"Do you have a problem with that?"

She would have liked to tell him a resounding yes. She would like to say she had not objected to being married without a bath. She had not objected to being married in a wet, mud-soaked dress. She had not even objected to being married in front of a smithy's anvil. How she would love to tell him she could not accept this, that a blacksmith would not, under any circumstances, marry her.

What she did say was quite different, however. With a deep, fortifying breath, she looked around her and gathered up her sodden skirts. "Well, if it's to be an anvil wedding presided over by a smithy and witnessed by unshod ponies, I suppose we had best be getting on with it."

Robert and Hugh exchanged glances, but said nothing.

A few minutes later, Meleri and Robert stood before the blacksmith—a burly, bushy-browed fellow with arms as big as tree trunks, who wore a dirty leather apron. As for Meleri, she was still wearing her mud-trimmed riding habit. She almost cried when she looked down, no longer able to see it had once been a lovely shade of blue. It was appropriate, she supposed, that her wedding dress, like her groom, was not chosen by any tender regard, but out of necessity. She did manage to straighten her hair a bit, before replacing her dripping hat.

They were just taking their places before the smithy when Hugh came running in with a damp handful of sodden heather, mud clinging to the roots. "A wedding bouquet," he said, trying to pull the roots off, but the stems were wet and tough.

Meleri reached out, took the heather from him, muddy roots and all, and held it in front of her. It wasn't Hugh's fault that there was nothing better available, she reasoned. At least he had tried to make it proper in that regard. She thanked him in a muted voice that trembled as she tried to hold back tears.

She clutched the lavender-hued heather to her bosom, as a beggar would hoard the purple robes of an emperor, and stood woodenly beside Robert, her heart broken, her mind blank. Then, she turned toward Robert, gave him a weak smile and said, "I am ready, milord."

Robert caught her by surprise when he handed the smithy two gold coins, then took her by the arm and said, "Come lass. Let us be away from this place."

Puzzled, she looked around her. "What? What is it? What has happened? Are we not to wed?"

Suddenly, powerful hands locked on her shoulders and she was spun around to look into what she expected to be the frightening countenance of the man she was about to marry, but instead, his expression was softer, his words kinder. "Aye, lass, we will wed sure enough, but we will not marry here. Let us continue on our way."

"I don't understand. What made you change your mind?"

He stood looking down at her, a tall, formidable man, frightening even, but in spite of these things, she knew he would never strike her. "You did."

"I? I changed your mind?"

"Aye, you did, lass."

"How?"

"By your willingness. I never intended us to marry here. It was a test, nothing more."

She eyed him suspiciously. "A test? What kind of test?"

"If we Scots have learned anything about you English over the years, it's that you cannot be trusted. I wanted to know, before we reached Beloyn Castle, if you were of a mind to go through with this marriage. Or, was this all an act, a sham?"

"Sham? You think I would stoop to such?" She was trembling with fury. "Of all the mean—" she hit him on the arm with her flowers "—despicable—" she whacked him again, on the shoulder this time "—calculating—" she hit him again, but did not get to say anything more, for his arms went around her, tightly, and he held her fast against him.

"I may have been cheated out of my marriage, but I will have my wedding kiss."

His mouth came down on hers, hard at first, but when she did not resist him, he softened the kiss and gathered her more deeply in his arms. Instinctively, she brought her hands up against him to push him away, but she was too shocked and surprised to do anything but surrender.

The kiss ravaged her mouth in a way that dominated and lay siege to any denial that lodged in her breast, and she was unable to gather enough strength or will to deny him. It was overpowering and seductive. It was wonderful, and she felt the fight go right out of her.

As I live and learn, she thought. No wonder the housemaids were sneaking out of the house at night and ministers were pounding the pulpit on Sunday morning.

So this is a kiss, she thought. *I should like to practice this more often…*

If he had wanted to consummate their union, right there on the soggy ground and in front of the smithy, the anvil, his brother, even God, she would not have been able to resist him.

At last, when he ended the kiss and released her, she stumbled against him, her muscles weak and lacking control, and her mind confused and in need of a sense of direction. Her mouth burned where his lips had touched hers. Her body still cried out for more. "Why are you staring at me so?"

"You are a woman with mettle," Robert said. "It is something I am pleased to see. A strong woman who can prevail in the face of disappointment and surmount obstacles is a necessity in Scotland. It is also a rare find."

"It is?"

"Aye, it is. I admire a woman with a powerful spirit and great strength of character. It is not always easy to overcome disappointment. I like the way you manage to persevere when all seems harsh and hopeless."

"I like the way you kiss," she said, lost in a dreamy state induced by delicious kissing, an understanding groom-to-be and compliments as golden as her future seemed to be. It was only when the boisterous sound of their laughter penetrated her trancelike state that she realized she had spoken the words she meant to keep private. Well, she told herself, it is a little late for mortification, so instead, she said, "If you two are finished, let us be on our way. Good as the sound of laughter is, it will not get us a mile farther down the road."

Hugh clapped Robert on the back. "Seems like you've got yourself a sensible lass, after all. You can add that one to your list."

"What list?"

"The list of things you like about your lass. She is alert enough to spot an opportunity when it comes, and to respond appropriately when it does not."

"You seem to be the one collecting tidbits. Why don't you add it to your list?" Robert spoke to Hugh, but it was Meleri he kept in his line of vision.

Afraid he could see the confusion, the desire that she knew was still in her eyes, she looked down and saw he had stepped on the bouquet of heather she dropped.

She studied the flowers lying as abandoned as her hope, when suddenly he leaned down and caught them up in his hand. When he offered them to her, she took them. Unable to think of anything to say, she gave her attention to the bouquet, which was horribly crushed. "You have trod upon my bouquet," she said, unable to look at him.

"Aye, lass, your bouquet is smashed, but not your hopes, I think."

11

Far as the eye could see, everything looked gray and grumpy, nothing but miles and miles of bleak landscape and angry gray clouds that were determined to drop their wet burden on anyone foolish enough to be out on such a drizzly day. *Well, what is a little rain after all I've been through?* wondered Meleri.

After leaving the smithy's shop, Meleri found she was having more difficulty walking through the deep mire than she did when they arrived. She was relieved when Hugh appeared beside her and took her arm. "Hurry along, lass. The sooner we are off, the sooner we will arrive."

A deep and insightful thought, she decided, trying her best not to laugh, but there was no way to keep the corners of her mouth from turning up. She continued to walk beside him through the puddles and muck, holding on to his arm, praying she did not fall, as she trudged along. By this point, she did not bother trying to hold up her skirts. As wet as they were, they were far too heavy and her arms too tired for her to care about a little more mud. Her lovely new riding habit was ruined, but as Robert said, not her spirits. She glanced down at the ragged edge of her hem and the torn piping that banded it, unable to tell that it had once been shiny and gold.

Pomp and circumstance! What she would not give for a hot

bath and one of the lovely dresses she had at home. While she was wishing, she might as well add the rest of her desires—a warm meal, the wet shoes and stockings off her feet and a soft, sweet-smelling nightgown to roll up in before she went to sleep.

Ahead of her, Robert walked through mire and over puddles, as easily as if he were crossing dry ground. She studied the way he moved, deciding she liked the fluid way the parts of his body were inclined to cooperate with one another. He looked every bit as good from the back as he did from the front. In fact, he was equally pleasing to the eye from any direction. He was a striking figure, tall, strong, imposing, and she was suddenly reminded that she was more than a little angry with him for charging off and leaving her to Hugh, once again.

She saw her horse waiting patiently just ahead and dreaded, more than she could ever imagine, the very thought of having to mount and ride endlessly over more rough, inhospitable terrain. She was tired, sore, and she felt horribly unattractive, none of which did anything for her disposition. How she wished they would stop at an inn, where she could do more than simply flex the tired muscles in her cramped legs.

She said nothing, of course. After all, Robert thought she had mettle, moral strength and a host of other fine attributes, and she did not want to do anything to change his opinion of her.

Unable to help herself, she stole one more furtive look in Robert's direction and found him watching her. Their gazes locked and she could feel the searing intensity of attraction that ran between them.

"Where do you plan to meet up with us?" Hugh asked.

"I haven't decided."

"How far is it to your home, to Beloyn Castle?" Meleri asked.

"We could make it in less than four hours," Hugh answered. "But, with you along, it will take closer to five."

She stopped stiffly and said to Hugh, "Don't alter your pace for me. I can ride hard and fast, if need be. Proceed as you normally would and don't be surprised if I pass you by. My father always said I could ride as well as any man."

"A statement that had you overflowing with confidence, I would imagine."

She glanced around at the sound of Robert's voice. It was a surprise when he appeared quite suddenly beside her and took her by the arm. When they reached their horses, he turned her toward him and put his hands at her waist. When he was about to lift her into the saddle, she placed a detaining hand against his chest. "I would ask a favor of you before you depart."

Robert searched her face for a moment. She thought him far too arrogant and self-assured. She knew he was aware he made her uncomfortable, and still he would not look away. At last, when she did not think she could stand another minute of his scrutiny, he said, "And what favor would that be, lass?"

"I would like to stop by the home of my former nanny, Agnes Milbank. She is a widow and it is my hope to convince her to accompany me to Scotland."

Hugh whistled. "A lass with her own reinforcements. I like the sound of that. Ought to make things more interesting."

"No," Robert said.

"Aw, Robbie, don't be so quick to decide. Can't you see your lass is in need of a little moral support? I think she is afraid of you."

The vivid blue eyes darkened and narrowed on her. "As she should be."

Meleri swallowed hard and, with a defiant lift of her head, returned his stare with a narrow one of her own, which brought a hearty chuckle from Hugh, who said, "A lass who gives as good as she gets. Bless my weary bones, but I am actually beginning to enjoy this little jaunt of ours."

Without further comment, Robert lifted her high in the air and placed her on her horse. While she settled herself, he mounted his great black beast, who showed no signs of tiring after so long a ride.

Meleri wondered if his slowness to respond was another test. Not that it mattered. She knew now was the time to stand her ground, to match him, meet him, or even beat him, if and whenever she could. If she did not establish this feeling of equality before they were married, she would never gain it once she said "I do."

Hugh kept prodding his brother. "What can it hurt? It can't be more than an hour's ride or so to her nanny's home."

"I would be careful if I were you," Robert warned his brother. "Keep applying liniment to my raw places and I'll give her over to your care…indefinitely."

Hugh shrugged. "Can't see how I could do any worse than you."

Meleri watched Robert as Hugh spoke on her behalf. A wide range of emotion showed on his face—irritation, puzzlement and frustration—they were all present, and she could not help but wonder why.

She decided to try again. With confident ease, she guided her mare to the place where he sat upon his horse like a great black hawk ready to swoop down upon the nearest thing that moved. She stopped close beside him and tilted her head back, so she could look him in the eye. "I know how you must feel, what you must be thinking."

His eyes narrowed, and she felt the frozen shaft of accusation stab into her. "You cannot possibly know. If you did, you would hie yourself away from me and the fate that awaits you."

A wave of loneliness swept over her at the thought of leaving, and not because she had no place to go, although that was certainly true. She was convinced now that Philip would find her before long, even if she went to stay with Agnes. Robert's home was the only place she could hide and be safe. Besides, she reminded herself, she and this grim Scot had made a bargain, and she intended to see that they stood by it.

Both of them.

"Let her bring her nanny with her," Hugh said, "or we will be here all night, while the two of you butt heads like two Highland sheep. If you think she is such a pain in the arse, let her have her nanny. That way, she can annoy someone of her own kind, and she won't be getting under your feet all the time, cute as a speckled pup with a fondness for shoe-chewing."

"You are fairly brimming with hope and confidence."

Hugh stuffed his hands deep into his pockets and put on an innocent look that Meleri bet he worked on a great deal in order to perfect it as he had. "Hope and confidence is about all a second son is entitled to."

Robert did not say anything. Meleri had never been more conscious of how he towered over her. He was an impressive figure of a man, the rain running down his face, the residue of doubt still apparent in his expression that looked as bleak as granite. She found it odd, but there was something sustaining about him—in the way the rain darkened his skin and ran in rivulets along the wet skeins of his hair—as a mountain is substantial: strong, solid, stable. She did not know how she knew, but she was convinced this man was everything she would ever want in a husband. And to think she had stumbled upon him…or over him, if one wanted to be precise. Well, she thought, if he won't give way and come to me, then I will go to him. "If you don't want to grant me a favor, how about we strike a bargain?"

"Aside from your horse and your dress, you don't have anything to bargain with."

"Oh, I wouldn't go so far as to say that," Hugh said. "Take away her horse and her dress, and I'd say she would have plenty."

"Enough!" Then with a dismissing wave of his hand, Robert turned his horse away and said, "Take her to find her nanny if it pleases you. Be forewarned, however, that if you do, I hold you responsible. Once you have located the nanny, bring both of them with you, and you better pray to whatever deity you have influence with that you arrive with her in tow."

Hugh was grinning at Meleri when he asked Robert, "Where shall we meet you?"

"I'll make camp near the fork in the river and wait for you there."

As he rode off, Meleri watched him go, feeling as if she had just been handed a victory.

"Come, lass, we had best be off."

The rain was coming down harder now, pelting them with drops that seemed to come faster and harder as time progressed.

It showed no signs of letting up. The sky overhead was dark, and the air carried a chill that blew down from the gaunt hills in the distance.

They stopped once to ask directions to the home of Agnes Milbank and discovered she lived farther away than they expected. They had to cross back over the border into England again, but thankfully, the cottage was a short ride after that. As they rode, Meleri's mind was aflutter. She could not stop worrying. It was certainly possible that Philip could be behind them—and he would stay clear of the main roads, riding through dripping trees and along swiftly flowing streams, fed by the runoff from the rain, just as they were doing.

Meleri stroked the neck of her horse. Poor beast, she had never been ridden so hard or so far, and certainly not through terrain such as this. Both of their horses were tired from trudging forward at such a difficult pace. The soggy turf sucked at their hooves and drained what little energy that remained in overworked muscles. After going to such lengths, what if Agnes was not at home, or chose not to accompany them?

As it turned out, her luck had improved over the way it began the day, for Agnes was not only at home, she was elated at the prospect of going with them.

"An answer to prayer delivered in person!" she exclaimed. "Oh, milady, I cannot think of anything that would give me more pleasure. Since my husband died, 'tis been beyond dull here."

Agnes packed up a few of her belongings to bring with her, then put the rest out to pack in her big trunk to send with a driver and wagon to Beloyn Castle. While Agnes packed, Hugh made arrangements with a neighbor, who agreed to deliver her trunk.

Once everything was in order, Agnes and Meleri waited on the small porch, while Hugh fetched a horse for Agnes to ride. He soon came trotting around the corner of the house, leading a small mare. After dismounting, he helped Agnes into the saddle.

"I assume you know how to ride."

She nodded and took the reins. "My father was a groom. I grew up with my own pony, although that was a long time ago. Still, I think I am up to the challenge."

Apparently, that satisfied Hugh, for he gave her a boost into the saddle. When he saw Meleri was already sitting astride her horse, he swung up onto the back of his and the three of them set off.

Meleri turned quite talkative and began to tell Agnes about everything that had happened. She did not care if Hugh listened, boring though it would be, since he already knew all the details. Once she started talking, however, Hugh appeared to have all the woman's talk he wanted for one day, and he urged his horse forward to ride just ahead. They watched him for a moment before Meleri picked up where she left off with her story. When she reached the part about her "near marriage" at Gretna Green, she could not help asking, "Why do you suppose he felt it necessary to test me? Don't you find that a bit odd?"

"Not at all, milady. He was simply being cautious. After all, he is taking you home with him. You can imagine, can you not, how he would feel if he discovered you never intended to marry him, that you only wanted safe passage out of England?"

"You're right. I never thought of it that way. Of course he had to be certain. He is a very proud man."

"I am sure he figured if you would marry him in Gretna Green, you would marry him anywhere."

"Faith! 'Tis true, Agnes. I would gladly marry him anywhere, save Gretna. I have never seen a more wretched spot in my life— certainly no woman's dream of the place she would choose for her wedding. The best part about it was leaving. I am truly thankful to him for sparing me the indignity of being married there."

"He seems to be a wise and just man. He must have known such a wedding would not be every woman's dream. However, you must admit, it would have been easiest for him."

"I do wish I knew when he planned for us to marry."

Agnes smiled. "So anxious to marry a stranger? He must be quite a man."

Meleri's face lit up. "Oh, he is that, but you know I would never be so forward if it were not for a good reason."

"And that good reason has united us once again and we are on our way to live in Scotland."

At that reminder, Meleri took a long, surveying look around her. "I can tell we are no longer in England. Even the land here seems harsher and more unforgiving." She felt a chill ripple along her spine. "The closer we get to where we are supposed to meet, the less accepting I become. I am filled with both a sense of awe and horrifying dread, at the merest thought of facing him again. He is a wild Scot, you must remember. He does not have the centuries of culture and refinement bred into him as does an English lord."

Agnes laughed. "Good! I cannot imagine you married to a stuffy English lord who dresses like a dandy and has no more difficult decisions facing him each day than the choosing of his snuffbox. However, you should be optimistic, milady. Any man can be domesticated by a zealous woman."

"Not if she has red hair," Meleri said woefully. "You, of all people, should remember how easily my zeal can turn to anger." Meleri took a deep breath. "However, you will notice that I am determined to remain cheerful and optimistic."

After a pace the Roman army would have found exhausting, they slowed the horses enough to ride, single file, across a narrow stream. Riding just ahead of her, on a much smaller mount, Agnes bounced around a bit, but it was obvious she was quite adept at riding, in spite of not having done it for some time. Once they were on the other side, she turned to see how Agnes was faring and found her nanny was smiling brightly, her head bobbing with each step, obviously enjoying herself and making the most of her adventure.

Hugh slowed his pace and they caught up to him. "We need to liven our step a bit if we are to meet Robert on schedule."

"What will happen if we don't?" Meleri asked.

He answered with a laugh. "Whatever happens, he will stop short of murder."

"If you are trying to frighten me, it isn't working."

"You're an independent lass, opinionated and of strong disposition."

"I happen to like my disposition."

"I would hope so. I'd hate to think anyone went to such lengths to be stubborn when they didn't like being that way."

They came to a fork in the stream and her heart gave a thudding lurch, for she could see Robert had made camp a short distance away, in a glen divided by a narrow trickle that fed into the larger stream. A stand of trees crowded down to the water's edge on the far side, but on the camp's side it was all clear land.

The men spread plaids for the women near an outcropping of rocks. Robert had already gathered wood and built up a fire by the time they arrived. While he and Hugh talked, Agnes and Meleri went down to the stream to wash, but after poking a finger in the frigid water, they decided to forgo cleanliness for warmth.

They returned to camp, sat on their plaids and waited to see what would happen next. They were sitting a short distance away, content to observe the brothers quietly. "He is a handsome devil, milady," Agnes said, after watching Robert for some time.

"I don't find him terribly handsome in that slick English way, but he is very appealing to me, and all man. I have heard tell that the blood of dragons flows in their veins, and we have both heard dozens of stories about Hadrian's Wall and why it was built to keep those barbarians out of England."

"That was a long time ago, milady."

"Blood will tell."

"I find Hugh is pleasing to look upon, as well."

"Hugh is charming and obviously fond of the ladies, but he does not have the strength of purpose or the leadership qualities that Robert possesses. You can see by Robert's bearing that there is something different about him, something that has tempered him like the finest steel. They are both handsome, but I can fairly give Hugh the edge there. However, I believe a man's appearance is the least part of him. I would rather have a man who understood me than one who possessed all the attributes of a Greek god. I do so despair that there will never be a man who understands me, Agnes."

"Hmm," Agnes said. "He reminds me a bit of my grandfather. He was a Scot, you know, and a more superstitious man never lived. His name was Seamus MacDougal. I spent many an evening on his knee, hearing tales of bogles and kelpies, monsters, ghosts and second sight."

"That shows what a foolish lot they are," Meleri said, and had the strangest feeling that someone, somewhere heard her say it, for she would have sworn she heard a man's eerie laugh. The thought had no more than occurred to her when a thick, greenish mist suddenly surrounded her. She blinked, and when her eyes focused, she saw a sturdily built man of medium height, with dark hair and a stern countenance. He was also very familiar. However, it was his eyes that mesmerized her, eyes that were blue—darkly, deeply, beautifully blue.

They were Robert's eyes.

However, this man was not Robert. Who are you, she wanted to ask, but the words jammed in her throat and she could not make herself speak. Her heart began to hammer and she felt herself growing warm. She was afraid she was going to faint, and she closed her eyes briefly. When she opened them the man, and the mist, were gone.

"Milady? Are you all right?"

"What? Yes, I am fine. I had a spell of dizziness, nothing more. What were we talking about?"

"Monsters, kelpies and ghosts, milady."

"Ghosts," she repeated, feeling a sudden chill of drafty cold blow over her. She dismissed it. She was tired. That is all it was. She rubbed her head, feeling quite dazed. For some strange reason, she felt as if someone were watching her. "Yes, I remember I said the Scots were foolish for believing in such…"

"Not so foolish. It is not only the Scots who believe. Don't be forgetting that there are many in Northumberland who still believe in brownies."

"Yes," she said slowly, "and a lot of good it did me to believe in brownies, or anything else."

Agnes smiled. "Your life is far from over milady. You are still quite young. Your life is only beginning."

"Oh, Agnes, I have never felt so old, so old and weary—truly

I feel as if my life is over," Meleri said, not caring that she was the picture of abject misery.

"It is understandable. Your life is changing in a multitude of ways. You are apprehensive and uncertain. I think you will be much better when you reach your new home. You will feel more secure. I, for one, am looking forward to our new life. And I cannot thank you enough for bringing me along with you."

Meleri barely heard. Inside, she was at sixes and sevens, terrified to go through with everything that was happening, yet at the same time, just as terrified to set foot on English soil, ever again. She saw the look of apprehension on Agnes's face and she forced a smile. "Don't worry, Agnes. Everything will be fine, I am certain."

Agnes cast a glance in Robert's direction. "If you were going to marry a stranger, you certainly lucked upon a good one. However did you find him?"

"We ran into each other."

Agnes smiled. "Knowing you, milady, I imagine that means you ran him down."

12

Robert sat on a rock in silent regard of all that was going on around him and thought about the woman he would soon marry, the woman who was English to the core.

He was already past caring. He was damned, for he had tasted the aromatic wine of retribution. Now it was time to drink the rest of it, to savor it, warm and tangy, never thinking of its bitter aftertaste. He had chosen this woman. She was the victim he would prepare for sacrifice, although he knew he would sacrifice his own happiness along with it.

She had been willing to marry him in Gretna, he was certain of that. Still, it did not mean he trusted her, it simply meant she wanted a husband. It would only be a matter of time until her English breeding won out. He was glad that it would. There were too many times he felt himself softening toward her. He knew that would spell disaster for him.

From here on, he would plan carefully, minutely, for he had to allay the fire that burned in his belly, the pain that swelled in his heart. He would adhere to his plan carefully and thus would he be indifferent in his deception, callous in his vengeance, tenacious of purpose, unscrupulous in method, always driven forward by profound and deep-rooted hatred for English injustice. He would not care, nor would he feel. There was room for only cold-blooded calculation in his heart and a two-edged sword in his hand—to execute vengeance and punishment. He had no choice. He no longer controlled his destiny any more than he knew himself. Some unseen force guided him now, and he wondered, dear God in heaven, he wondered if he had been abandoned by God himself and handed over to the devil.

He drew his brows together, watching Meleri, while considering his feelings. At that moment, she turned her head and looked straight at him, and then she smiled. For a blinding moment, a brilliant flash of light—one that seemed to radiate from her—stunned him. He wondered if some charm had taken hold. Was she an English witch, sent to seduce him? Was that why he suffered such disturbing and lustful thoughts? Even now, when he looked at her, he thought only of the way she would look turning toward him, her naked body draped in an incredible length of red hair.

His body reacted to the image, but he checked it. He could not afford the luxury of giving in to passion or his emotions. It was another burden heaped upon him along with his inheritance and his title. He was a master at control, and he was glad of it, for he knew already that where she was concerned, he would need it. Damn unsettling woman. Around her, he was as vulnerable as an open wound.

"My, my, that was a hungry look," Hugh said, joining him. "I guess that means you still intend to marry her."

"Like it or not, I will have to marry her. We need money and I still have the king's edict hanging over my head. I have neither the time nor the inclination to find another. I must marry her and quickly, and settle the matter of her dowry, if we are to keep a roof over our heads. Otherwise, we lose everything at the end of three months."

"You realize how fortunate you are to have found a lass so easily, and to have found one who looks as she does, and with a wealthy father and a sizeable dowry…quite remarkable!"

"I would like to see the expression on King George's face when he hears I have beat him at his own game. I not only found a titled English lass, but I did it my first day in England."

Hugh laughed. "That won't endear you to him."

"As if I care. The man's mind is like the sky: full of air. He bends his ear too often to those foppish advisors that surround him."

"Speaking of the king, don't let your pride force you into waiting too long. If anything should happen to change her mind, we lose it all. To tarry any longer than necessary is to take a great risk."

"Aye, I know that."

Hugh changed the subject. "I have a feeling they will be surprised when we return home. I don't think anyone will be expecting us back so soon."

Robert did not respond. He glanced heavenward and said, "It will be dark soon. The sun has almost gone down."

Hugh looked back at where the women sat. "I know they must be tired."

"Good. A tired woman is a quiet woman."

Hugh laughed. "I wouldn't bet on it. Your lass is a talker. What do you plan on feeding them?"

"Whatever we eat."

"Fine. What are we going to eat?"

"Whatever you find to shoot."

"Me?"

"I furnished the last meal, if my memory serves me right."

"You call that tiny rabbit a meal?"

"We'll discuss that after we see what you come up with."

Hugh grumbled a bit, then made a few halfhearted attempts to talk Robert into hunting their dinner. He might as well have saved his breath, for in the end, Hugh ambled off in search of food.

While he was gone, Robert unsaddled the horses and led them down to the stream to drink, then tethered them nearby. When Hugh came walking into camp some time later, he offered his excuse before showing the meager results of his hunt. "This area has been hunted overmuch."

Robert took in the two squirrels he held up. "That's it?"

"Aye. This will have to suffice. It was this, or a couple of scrawny birds." He must have noticed the critical way Robert was looking at him, for he said, "Do you think you could have done better?"

"Aye. With a slingshot."

Sitting on their plaids, Agnes and Meleri watched the two brothers skewer their dinner on two green branches, then roast it over the fire. Meleri had been occupying herself with watching them…or rather, watching Robert. Every time she looked at him, something strange happened, something that began innocently enough, nothing more than a gradual warming sensation in her stomach. Soon the warming gave way to a fluttering of her heart and perspiring palms. She did not want to be so determined to watch him, but she could not seem to help it. She would have loved it, if at that very moment, he would turn to look directly at her, and smile.

"Oh, I do hope they have it ready soon. It must be all that riding that has made me so hungry," Agnes said.

"Did you see what Hugh brought back?"

"No, milady, I saw him carrying something, but I could not make out what it was. He was too far away."

Meleri put her elbows on her drawn-up knees and rested her chin in her palms. "Perhaps it is just as well we don't know. It does seem to be taking a dreadfully long time to cook." She did not know what they were having, but whatever it was, it was not big. It should have been easy to cook—and quick. Her stomach growled, and she closed her eyes and inhaled the savory smell of cooking meat. "I'm so hungry, my stomach does nothing but growl."

"Faith! I don't think I have enough strength for mine to growl."

Meleri began to drum her fingers against her cheek. "You know how much I love to wait."

Agnes smiled in remembrance. "I remember you were never one to enjoy being idle, unless you had something to do."

"Well, where is the fun in doing nothing when you have nothing to do? Mother of humanity! What is taking so long? If they do not hurry up, I'm going to say something I'll regret. I'm about at the end of my patience." Meleri made a move to stand up.

Agnes put her hand on Meleri's arm. "Don't say anything just yet. I think they're finished."

With mouthwatering anticipation, Meleri watched Hugh hungrily as he picked up one of the sticks and carried it out to them. He thrust it toward them. "It isn't much," he said, "but it's hot and filling."

She looked down at the roasted meat skewered on a branch, swaying mere inches from her nose. "You are right. It isn't much." Even at this distance, she still could not make out what it was. It smelled delicious, but it did not look appetizing in the least, for there it was, bobbing up and down, legs sprawled and impaled. "A rather ignoble end, isn't it?"

Hugh swung the stick around and looked at it. He grinned and said, "Aye, I suppose it is."

"What is it?"

Hugh did not answer.

"What's the matter? Don't you know?"

"I know."

"Then tell me."

"What difference does it make to you? If it's good, eat it. If it isn't, leave it alone. It's as simple as that."

"But I want to know what it is that I'm eating."

"Squirrel."

Her stomach lurched. Squirrel? Those darling little bushy-tailed creatures that sat back on their haunches on her windowsill and took nuts from her hand? They had personalities and families. Some, she knew so well she had given them names. They were like friends. How could he expect her to eat something that was like an acquaintance? She turned her head away, unable to look at the distressing circumstances that had befallen this unfortunate little creature. "Take it away."

Hugh looked down at the roasted meat. "Take it away? Why? You haven't tasted it."

"I could never taste it, because I could never eat a squirrel. I can't believe anyone would."

He looked down at the squirrel again, as if he expected it to change. "Why not?"

"If you had ever played with them as a child, you could never eat one."

"Even if I had, it wouldn't bother me to eat one."

"I don't expect a Scot to understand. The English are a people of delicate sensitivity. We could never eat something we watched scampering about our yard."

This time, he held the limb up to eye level and looked the meat over with critical appraisal. "Those were English squirrels," he said. He shoved the splayed squirrel toward her. "This one is a Scot." When that did not seem to work, he added, "It isn't as if you knew this squirrel personally."

"All squirrels, like people, are related," she said with haughty presence. "If I knew one, I knew them all."

Hugh's boisterous laughter shattered the stillness.

She gave him a disapproving look and said, "A loud laugh, a vacant mind."

"Loud laughs and vacant minds aside, this is the only choice for dinner, I'm afraid. It's squirrel or nothing." He thrust it back at her.

She drew back. "I'll have nothing," she said softly.

"This is perfectly good meat. You need to eat. Try a little bite." He shoved it toward her again.

She turned her head away. "I don't like squirrel."

"Have you ever eaten squirrel?"

She looked offended. "No! Of course not."

"Then how do you know you don't like it?"

"I simply know. I can tell by looking at it." She turned her head and waved him off. "Please. Take it away. I can't eat a squirrel."

"I can!" Agnes said, cheerfully scooting to the edge of her plaid. She must have seen Meleri's horrified look and thought better of it, for she straightened and said in a dignified manner, "However, I don't think I'm in the mood for squirrel tonight." She gave the squirrel a fond look and scooted back.

Hugh was determined. "I understand your tender feelings, but once it's in your stomach, you won't know the difference."

"I would know," Meleri replied.

"You need to eat. We've a long day tomorrow."

In spite of her determination to remain cheerful, optimistic and pleasant, she was finding it difficult. She was tired of this bantering back and forth. "I...do not...eat...squirrel," she said slowly, enunciating each word. "I am speaking perfect English. Now, what part of that do you not understand?"

"Only the part that prompted you to be so stubborn. You will eat when you are hungry enough."

"I am hungry now."

"But not so hungry that you can't get your dander up. You are being foolish. If you would try being reasonable—"

"I have slept on the ground without complaining. I have ridden when I was wet and tired and covered with mud. I have gone without a bath and slept on hard ground. I have eaten rabbit and fish, neither of which was very tasty, but I cannot—and will not—eat a squirrel. It would be like eating a friend."

Hugh shrugged and offered the squirrel to Agnes. "Is this a friend of yours?"

Agnes looked longingly at the meat and shook her head. "No...I mean, yes...that is...I think so."

"I suggest you eat now and make up your mind later," he said.

Agnes looked indecisive for a moment, but hunger must have gotten the best of her for she reached for the squirrel. She probably would have taken it, too, if she had not taken a quick glance in Meleri's direction and seen the disapproving frown. "No, thank you," she said at last, never lifting her hungry gaze from the morsel of meat.

"That will be enough!" Robert's voice boomed out so suddenly Meleri gave a start. "If they prefer to be hungry, so be it," he said. "Bring the squirrel here! We will eat."

Hugh gave Meleri one last look. "It isn't my fault if you go hungry. I tried."

Meleri paid him no mind. Anger was burning inside of her,

tingling like an itch in the palm that needs scratching. She took in completely the cynical and hard mouth, the way Robert's very stance said he had not forgotten that she was English—as if she could do something about it.

Shaking his head, Hugh walked back to where Robert sat on a rock near the fire. "Looks like we get a bigger meal than we thought." He handed one squirrel to Robert. "You take this one and I'll have this one."

They began eating and talking softly, until Hugh suddenly said, "You know, this tastes just like roast pheasant to me." His voice was extraordinarily loud, and Meleri knew it was for her benefit.

From where Meleri sat, it looked to her like Robert almost choked on his food, but he managed to recover enough to maintain the same dark unsmiling countenance she had observed since leaving the smithy's.

"Yes, it is definitely like roast pheasant," Hugh continued, "but this is a bit more succulent, I think. I'm truly surprised it's so juicy."

"Are you?" Robert asked.

"Aye. Fair to dripping off my fingers, it is." He turned toward Meleri. "Change your mind?"

"Leave them to choke on their own hunger," Robert said.

Hugh shrugged and continued eating. "I've decided I don't understand women."

"Why would you want to? When it comes to understanding women, it is rarely worthwhile going through so much, to learn so little."

She doubled her hands into fists and had to bite her tongue to keep from lashing out with her opinion of that comment. Meleri knew Robert was baiting her, testing her temperament. Keep this up, she thought, and you may be testing my aim, when I decide to pick up this rock next to me. Men could be such children.

She knew she was too smart to be caught in so obvious a trap. She would give him his pound of flesh, if for no other reason than the fact that he had saved her from Philip.

In apparent high spirits, Hugh zealously finished off the last of his meal, licked his fingers with flamboyant drama and tossed the remains in the fire. Robert tossed his in as well. Meleri barely noticed. She was busy trying to reason how everything had gotten so far off track. As for Agnes, she sat there as if she didn't have a care in the world, or an inkling as to what was going on. In some ways, Meleri envied her. It was ever so much easier to go through life, floating like a bubble, drifting hither and yon and never lighting anywhere.

Dear, sweet Agnes. Sincere ignorance was her chief asset— and more than likely the mother of her devotion. Whenever she looked at people, she saw only good. It was one of the reasons Meleri had always been so fond of her, and protective.

Finished with his squirrel, Hugh took four oatcakes out of his bags. He put two down for himself and handed two to Robert. "Perhaps the ladies would like an oatcake," he said, and fished out two more and handed them to Robert.

Robert took the oatcakes. He looked them over, as if he were weighing something in his mind, then he handed them back to Hugh. "Where are your brains, Hugh? These humble oatcakes are not fine enough for two such ladies. It would be insulting to offer lowly oatcakes to ladies of such refinement and gentle birth."

Hugh looked puzzled. "But I thought…"

Robert did not let him finish. "As your older brother, it is my responsibility to instruct you in the areas I find lacking. I can see that you are obviously ignorant of the ways of a true lady. You must understand that she is a paragon of well-bred refinement with obvious and delicate sensibilities. Such a noblewoman should never be offered anything but true feminine subsistence, such as lobster and champagne. Small wonder that such discriminating and dainty fragility could not only refuse, but would be repulsed at the mere mention of eating something so base as squirrel."

Hugh was looking a bit puzzled, but managed to go along with whatever it was his brother was setting up. "Why, thank you for pointing out such a shortcoming. I don't know what I would do without your wise, brotherly instruction."

"You must also understand that a woman of refined taste would be similarly repulsed at the insulting thought of partaking of such peasant's fare as an oatcake."

Meleri rolled her eyes and said, "Oatcakes would be lovely. I am quite fond of oatcakes. Aren't you, Agnes?"

Agnes sat there mutely staring at the squirrel remains crackling in the fire, until Meleri elbowed her and she blurted out, "Oh, yes, I love oatcakes. I eat them all the time."

Robert went on talking, as if he had not heard a word she said. "I am glad you have seen the error of your ways. I hope you never forget that English ladies are tender, discriminating creatures made with a fragile constitution. I do hope you never forget your manners in such a way again."

Hugh slapped himself on the forehead and exclaimed with great drama, "For the love of St. Andrew! When I think how close I came to being so rude to such flowers of femininity. Well, I can tell you I am shamed to think I almost offered them these…these…ignoble oatcakes." He tossed the oatcakes into the fire.

"Don't overdo it," Robert whispered, then they went on calmly eating their oatcakes as if nothing out of the ordinary was going on.

Meleri grabbed a stick and began pawing and stabbing at the burning oatcakes, berating Robert as she did. "Of all the thickwitted numskulls! What do you use for ears? Didn't you hear me? I said I like oatcakes! So did Agnes."

"I do apologize for my brother," Robert said.

"Stuff your apology. We are hungry!" she said, wondering what was happening to her. She was frustrated beyond measure. She felt as if he had poured water on her fuse, reducing her outburst to a sputter, which was quite humiliating for one who had never been guilty of sputtering in her life. To make matters worse, she was speechless.

He was not.

"Alas," he said so dramatically that Hugh, who had been munching on his oatcake, stopped eating and sat there grinning like a fool. "I must beg your forgiveness again. I have nothing else to offer you. Be assured I shall rectify this on the morrow. Go to sleep and dream of your forthcoming wedding night."

"Don't think I don't know what you are doing," said Meleri angrily. "I did not just fall off the hay wagon. I am a very astute person."

"Are you, now?"

"I hope you are enjoying yourself." She kicked at the fire, more from a lack of direction than any real anger.

"Go to sleep and you won't know you are hungry," Hugh offered.

"Blast you! I can't sleep when my ribs are clanking together." She made another halfhearted attempt to paw through the coals. This time, she managed to get the two oatcakes out, but by then, they were nothing more than two smoldering charcoal circles. She gazed forlornly at the smoking rounds, saying more to herself than him, "I said we wanted the oatcakes and you threw them in the fire. I cannot believe anyone would throw away perfectly good food."

She threw the stick in the fire. "Well, there is nothing to be done about it now." Without giving either of them another look, she walked back to where Agnes was waiting.

As Meleri sat down, she said, "If you expected a change of circumstance, I'm afraid you're going to be disappointed. Sleeping with our hunger is the only offer we've had."

"What shall we do now, milady?"

"We do as they said. We go to bed hungry."

"Good night, milady."

"Good night, Agnes. I am truly glad you are here and sorry you must go to bed hungry on your first night."

"Do not worry overmuch. I have had a most enjoyable day." Without another word, Agnes lay down. Meleri did likewise; only she made certain she gave the men her back before she pulled the plaid over her shoulders.

* * *

Robert stared at Meleri's back for a few minutes, then pulled two oatcakes out of his bags.

Hugh leaned back, looked at the oatcakes and raised his brows in an interested manner.

Robert put his hand to his mouth, indicating Hugh should be quiet, something he should have known was impossible.

"Can't play the beast overlong, can you?" Hugh whispered. "I knew it was only a matter of time until you showed your soft side. This was another test, wasn't it?"

"And if it was?"

"I am dying to learn what you discovered."

"You should be more observant and you would learn it for yourself."

"Does that mean you aren't going to tell me?"

"For the time being."

"What are you going to do now? Give them the oatcakes, or toss them in the fire like the others?"

"What do you think?"

"I'm going to content myself with silent observation, so I can learn." Still leaning back, he folded his arms over his middle, locked his fingers together and began drumming them against his chest. "My, my, I'm certainly going to enjoy watching this."

"Really?" Robert brought the oatcakes closer and looked them over. "What do you suggest I do with them?"

"You aren't going to eat them, are you? Surely you're going to give them to the women."

Robert shook his head and whispered, "No, you're wrong. I am not going to give them to anyone. You are."

Hugh shot upright. "Me? Why is it always me?"

"Because you're the youngest."

"Well, it isn't my fault. I didn't choose to be youngest. Why don't you let me be the oldest once in a while?"

"Because I would have to act young and pampered, without a care in the world or a serious thought in my head."

"You make me sound positively infantile."

"Take the oatcakes."

"You never miss an opportunity, do you?"

"I try not to."

Hugh snatched the oatcakes and, mumbling to himself, said, "There are times when I think I understand you."

"Really?"

"Aye, but this is not one of them."

13

They arrived at their destination late the next afternoon.

It was shortly before sunset and a most flattering time of day, but not even favorable light could make Beloyn Castle look promising. Upon seeing its stout walls for the first time, Meleri said to Agnes, "The Scots must have a deep reverence for stone. It's everywhere."

That much was true. Poised high on a hill capped by a huge rock, it rose out of the ground, looking part kirk, part fortress and part God knows what. At some point in history, it must have been quite an impressive sight—a stalwart fortress with its crow-stepped gable, baronial turrets and its odd combination of aloofness and warmth. Now it was horribly neglected and partially roofless, one wing nothing more than a pile of tumbled-down stones where crenellated parapets and pavilions once existed.

The rest of it did not fare much better, for it was a heap of crumbling griffins and grotesque carvings that rose majestically from its base of sharp, jutting stone. Yet, there was something almost noble in its desolation. Meleri could almost feel the past calling out to her. There it stood, a crumbling castle built upon a rocky outcrop in the midst of a fair meadow. In spite of that, she could almost smell the rushes, scented with meadowsweet and flowers that must have graced its floors, in the years gone by.

She closed her eyes long enough to see it as it must have been, with its walls covered with fine tapestries and silken arras, set with fine glass windows. She found it strange that she felt so drawn to it, more from feeling a tangible link to its romantic and tragic past, than any curiosity as to why parts of it lay in ruins. Even in its roofless grandeur, it seemed deserving of such a past.

"I think this place must look a fright in the dark," Agnes said.

"It looks a fright now," Meleri replied, and rightly so. Even the gardens look tattered.

"We are almost there," Hugh said.

At the sound of his voice, Meleri could not help feeling a dull sense of disappointment that Robert was not with them. Last night, when she had gone to sleep, she had lain on his plaid that still carried his scent and watched him staring moodily into the fire, until her eyes would no longer stay open and she drifted off to sleep. This morning, when she awakened, the fire was gone, and so was Robert.

"He had business to attend to" was Hugh's only explanation. "Did you need something?"

"No." Meleri had tried to smile, but her heart was not in it. "When will he return?"

"When he is finished."

She wondered if she would ever become accustomed to the Scots' way of abruptness, like Robert's unannounced departure. She tried to put herself in his place, to see things through his eyes, but it was no use. Try as she might, she could never catch sight of the devils that drove him. Her only compensation was in knowing they would soon marry, and then perhaps one day, she would understand this complicated man.

With Hugh now leading the way, they drew closer to the castle. She saw signs of a rich and noble past as they rode by terraces and mounds, where orchards and beds of flowers once grew. The gardens were divided by towering yew hedges, each garden having been distinctively different at some point in time, but now horribly neglected and overgrown. However, she did catch sight of some lovely statuary, both upright and knocked down, and a fountain that held no water. From the looks of it, it had not held water for quite some time. The most breathtaking sight of all, however, was a tranquil swan pond, surrounded by a field of lavender.

As they approached, she was aware of the haunting sound of a bagpipe, so faint and melancholy that she wondered where it was coming from. "I wonder who is playing."

"Playing what?"

"The pipes. Don't you hear them?"

Agnes turned her head slightly, as if to listen. "No, I don't hear anything, milady."

"You can't hear the bagpipes?"

"No, milady. I hear nothing—not even the sound of wind. It is frightfully still and quiet here, like a graveyard." Agnes shuddered and rubbed her arms, then mumbled something about it being colder in Scotland.

Meleri was about to ask Hugh if he could hear the pipes, but before she could ask, the melody grew fainter and eventually died away. Perhaps it was her imagination, she thought. It had been a long trip and she was apprehensive, apt to hear anything.

Once they arrived, she dismounted with Hugh's assistance. "Careful of your legs," he said. "They have a way of giving out beneath you when you first use them after so long a ride. Do you think you can walk alone, or would you like to lean on me?"

She lifted her chin and said, "If you can walk, I can walk."

Listening to his rocking laughter, she prayed that was true. Thankfully, she did manage—with stiff legs and knees that tended to buckle as she climbed the steep steps, trying to make it look as if she did so without any great difficulty. When she reached the top of the steps, she paused, watching Agnes accept Hugh's offer of help.

Agnes glanced in her direction once, blushed and looked down.

Shameless, Meleri thought with amusement. Agnes was as strong as an ox, and if the truth were known, she probably could carry Hugh up the steps with no help. However, Hugh was young, robust and pleasing to gaze upon. She could not blame Agnes.

There were only so many pleasures in life.

"This way," Hugh said, and led them to a large door, heavily carved and studded with brass, with a lion's-head knocker large enough to wake the dead. He opened the door and stood aside, bidding them to enter.

Inside, the entry was dark. Not one single candle burned. Meleri hesitated, but when she heard Hugh's chuckle, she stepped through the door to greet her future.

And stepped into complete darkness.

Everywhere it was pitch-black. She could not see the hand she lifted in front of her. Maybe she would wait and greet her future tomorrow.

Hugh went on, as if bumbling around in a dark entry was commonplace. "I know you must be hungry."

"I am afraid to respond to that. The last time I did, I went to bed with nothing to eat. However, I wouldn't be against a bit of light."

Hugh said nothing as he drew back the heavy draperies on two windows and sunlight washed across the stone floors, illuminating the cavernous hall. "Your wish is my command. Come along, lass," he said, and led them into a rather forbidding medieval banquet hall.

The room was huge—drafty, cold, with thick walls and deep-set windows. It was quite gloomy and lacking cheer. Meleri shivered, not knowing if it was more from the chill in the room or the oppressive gloom.

The fireplace looked as if it had not been lit for years. The stone floors were bare and quite dirty. The walls were grimy and dark from an accumulation of centuries of wood smoke. Gone were the rushes and scent of meadowsweet, the tapestries and the silken arras she had imagined earlier. She surmised the place to be a pathetic heap. Certainly nothing like they had in England, and definitely nothing like she imagined living in for the rest of her life.

She looked around her forlornly and discovered, much to her delight, the far wall of the banquet hall possessed a lovely rood screen. She also discovered an old tapestry, which miraculously seemed to have escaped the ravages of fireplace smoke that covered everything else.

On the verge of wondering if anyone even lived here, she jumped when Hugh's voice suddenly boomed out, "Where is everyone?"

He gave Meleri a sheepish grin. "Robbie would have told them we were coming. I expected them to have a meal ready."

"I am not so confident as you. Eating does not seem to be as necessary to Scot survival as it is to the English. Don't you ever get hungry?"

"Sometimes." He walked up to a long trestle table. "Hello? Is anyone here?" He banged his fist.

A cloud of dust arose.

Meleri turned her head aside and covered her nose, but still she coughed.

Hugh joined in with a bit of his own coughing.

Meleri was incredulous. A castle this size, and no one to greet them? Surely, this was some sort of jest. She looked around at the abysmal surroundings. She had heard Scotland was a backward country, but this went beyond that. In England, the horses had finer stables. This shabby, soot-filled place could not be the home of the Earl of Douglas.

Agnes wrinkled up her nose. "Faith! It reeks of a barnyard, yet looks like bedlam. What kind of place is this, milady?"

"I know not, Agnes. I am too shocked to speak." Meleri searched the room for Hugh and received a jolt, for she spied Robert standing next to Hugh near the fireplace. They were talking to a tall man, rather distinguished with graying hair. Robert acted as if nothing out of the ordinary was going on. In fact, he was looking relaxed and quite jovial.

"Perhaps we should join them," she said to Agnes.

"Oh, milady, let us wait right here."

Meleri looked around her. "I am not certain how long I can respect anyone who lives like this. Why, our pigs had it better than this at Humberly Hall."

Agnes looked around as well. "It is a sight. Now I believe everything I ever heard about the Scots. Alas, but your poor earl appears to be very poor indeed. Poor as a parson, it seems."

"I hear all Scots are too frugal to part with any of their coins." Like Agnes, Meleri was truly shocked at her future husband's lack of wealth. It would appear he did not have two sixpence to rub together. She reminded herself that she should always try to find something positive about every situation, so she surveyed the great hall once more, seeing many signs that said the near-destitute state that surrounded the Douglases had not always been with them.

The castle had, without doubt, been a remarkable fortress at one time, with gardens that were equally magnificent—enough to rival any in France or England. Even the rood screen and the fine Flemish tapestry on the far wall bespoke of a wealthier time. Were they frugal, or had something drastic happened to change their fortune?

"Whatever the state of his finances, I am confident it will not matter. He is of strong character and that is more important than high birth or wealth," Agnes said.

"I suppose that is true. Yet, when I look around me, I find myself agreeing with you, or worse. Judging from the looks of this place, they should be dressed in wolf pelts." She rubbed her neck. "Zounds! I am weary to the bone…more tired than hungry, I think."

"Would you like to sit down, milady?" Agnes asked, indicating a nearby chair.

Meleri eyed the rickety chair, covered with dust.

Agnes looked apologetic. "I know living here seems a poor choice, but it's the only one we have at the moment."

Meleri reflected on that for a time. "There is only one other choice that I can think of."

"What is that?"

"Change."

"Change what, milady?"

She drew her shoulders up as she looked at the disorder that lay all about. "Whatever we find that is in disarray or unpleasant."

Agnes looked as if Meleri had asked her to drink poison. "Why would we want to do that?"

"Because it is impossible to live like this, and what we cannot tolerate, we must change. Everything changes, Agnes. What doesn't, will die. Do you not agree?"

"I don't know, milady. It seems to me it would be easier to change the way we feel than to change what we find disagreeable."

"Agnes Milbank! Complacency is not an admirable trait! I could never submit to follow the course of destiny meekly. I would rather make an energetic effort to set things right. You are like a wheel rolling always in the same rut."

"Aye, but at least I know where the road leads and that I will get there."

"What boredom!"

"As for this place," Agnes said, looking around her, "it is too far gone, milady."

"I have always believed in the impossible. I am not happy unless I have done at least one impossible thing each day, before I go to bed. It has been neglected, that is all. It only needs someone interested in putting it to order."

"I don't know. I have not seen much of this place, milady, but judging what little I have seen, it would appear there is more ailing it than simply neglect. What do you know of his finances? You will need a great deal of money to make enough changes to be of much benefit."

As if someone opened the spigot and drained out all the ale, Meleri felt the thrill of excitement flow out of her. No, she was not going to be glum. Think cheerful, Meleri, she reminded herself. "I know nothing, but even if I did, it would not matter. My dowry is large enough to set this place to order and have plenty left over." Meleri looked around. "Hmm… What shall we do first?"

"Tear it down."

"Oh, Agnes, this is no time to jest."

"'Twas no jest, milady." Agnes looked as lost as a lamb. "I am without any other suggestion. You are the one with all the energy."

"I fear I haven't much inspiration, either, at the moment. Night will be upon us soon. We need a place to sleep."

"We are only two women…and English to boot. Judging from the looks of them, they will not be taking too kindly to any interference from us. Heaven help me, but I fear if we merely mention the word *bath,* we may find ourselves dumped in a vat by our heels."

Meleri did not have an opportunity to respond, for Robert suddenly was beside her, thumbs hooked in a brown leather belt, feet planted wide apart, looking at her as if he was trying to decide what was going on in her head. "Forgive my rudeness for leaving you to wait so long after such a journey. I know you must be tired. I should have seen that you were shown to your rooms before I stopped to speak with my uncle."

"Your uncle?"

"Iain. You will like him, I know."

She was caught completely by surprise. A man who apologized was unheard of. She did not know what to say. She felt her cheeks go as red as her hair.

"Your face is turning red."

"Better a red face than a black heart," she said, feeling she had one of the blackest hearts about for thinking such terrible thoughts about his home. "When are you leaving?"

"Cheer up, lass. I changed my mind about leaving a certain lass behind. I am here now. Things will look better on the morrow."

Her face grew warmer. Her blush, caused by the way he looked at her, as well as the words he had spoken, suddenly embarrassed her. It was as if the redness of her skin indicated the depth of her vulnerability. Something she did not like. "I can't say I am as optimistic as you, nor am I overly impressed with anything I've seen thus far. Truthfully, this place is in shambles."

He was smiling, as if shambles were not an issue with him. "Aye, 'tis that."

"We are, as you said, tired. We are also hungry and desire a bath. So far, no one has been inclined to offer us as much as a sip of water. My first instinct was to think perhaps you brought me here to settle some centuries-old grudge against the English."

The grin disappeared, replaced by a cautious look. "Why would you think that?"

"I have spent my life in Northumberland. I know all about the Border wars and the Scots deeply rooted hatred of the English."

"If you were so well versed, why did you agree to marry me?"

"Because I felt I was supposed to," she said, surprised she did not refer to Lord Waverly.

He raised his brows and gave her an odd look. "You think it was your fate?"

She shrugged. "Something close to that, I suppose. I cannot explain it, really. It was simply that everything seemed to come together. I broke my engagement and left home with no place to go. Then like magic, you and your brother appeared…."

"Ordered by an English king to find an English wife…and there you were."

"Yes, and I cannot shake the feeling that all of this has been something that was meant to happen."

He was looking at her in the oddest manner, as if she had suddenly given him something and he didn't know what to do with it. "You are quite unusual, you know—interesting and nothing like what I imagined an English lass to be." He stopped. "All this talk doesn't do anything for your hunger. Come along. I will see my lass well fed…and her nanny as well."

They followed him to the end of the table, Robert barking orders as they went, which sent a motley crew of servants scampering into the hall and running in a dozen different directions. Soon the table was cleaned.

"This looks like a good place," Robert said. He stopped at the end of the table and pulled out a chair. By the time Meleri and Agnes sat down, several servants returned with bowls of food, which they placed before them.

"Humble fare, but hot and filling," Robert said. "Eat your fill. I will return in a moment."

Meleri and Agnes went after the roast capon, following it

with rosemary potatoes and warm bread, which they generously topped with honey, since there was no butter about. As she ate, Meleri kept up with Robert's whereabouts, pausing in wonder when she heard his thunderous voice explode at the opposite end of the hall.

"What in the devil is going on here?" he asked.

He grabbed a young boy by the ears as he passed. "By the robes of St. Columba! What is happening here? I bring my intended home for a feast and you have nothing ready? Where is Fiona? Why isn't this place cleaned up and a fire going? Has no one done anything while we have been gone?"

"I don't know," the lad replied.

He gave the lad a push. "Get someone to help you and have this hall cleaned."

"Fiona!" Robert shouted.

A slim, gray-haired woman came rushing into the room, drying her hands in her apron and looking as guilty as Judas with his hands full of silver. "You called me?"

"You bet your claymore, I called you. What is the meaning of all this? You dare to serve our guests in such an unkempt place?"

The woman glanced toward the place where Agnes and Meleri were quietly eating. "You arrived earlier than we expected. We didn't have time to prepare..."

He cut her off.

"I want this hall cleaned. Understand?"

"Aye, my lord," Fiona said quickly, and dashed from the room.

Meleri took advantage of the opportunity to watch Robert as he spoke to the woman. She did not pay so much attention to what he said, preferring to simply observe him in detail. He was a complicated man, and more interesting because of it—in the way a three-dimensional figure is interesting when compared to a flat plane. She found his many dimensions, characteristics and contrasts most attractive.

He was compelling and fascinating, appealing and disturbing. Serious, unsmiling, mysterious one moment, he could change

without notice into a man who was warm, teasing and straight-
forward. She took in the manner in which his breeches and doublet hugged a body that was deceptively muscled for such a
slender build. In him lay the pride of the past, the hope of the future. Whenever she looked at him, she thought of the heroes of
Arthurian legend, of Sir Lancelot, or Sir Tristram, or perhaps the
Green Knight. One glance brought to life the lure of stories of
old. Stories of highwaymen and knights in shining armor, of
Norman conquerors and legions of Romans, of seafaring Vikings
and warring Celts, of naked Highlanders and ancient Britons
painted blue.

By the time Robert returned to them, Meleri and Agnes had
finished their meal.

"Where is your grandmother?" Meleri asked.

"She isn't here."

"Yes, I can see that. Does she always have such a strange way
of welcoming guests?"

"My grandmother is not fond of anything English, except
Shakespeare."

"You mean I must prove myself worthy…slay dragons, and
all of that?"

"Gram has her own way of determining a man's value."

"And what way is that?"

"Scots are slow to judge or form an opinion, and do so only
after careful consideration. Gram holds we can judge a man's
merit by testing his resiliency and character; that and the way
we handle trials and tribulations demonstrate who and what
we are."

"And you think she is right?"

"In principle, if not method."

"It's also a good way to see that you aren't very well liked.
No one enjoys being ignored."

"No," he said slowly, never taking his gaze from her face, "no
one does."

Meleri felt as if something passed between them, some slender thread of connection that held them one to the other. She

could not deny her attraction to him and counted herself most fortunate in that regard.

She thought about what he told her about his grandmother and her peculiar way of forming an opinion, and how quick she had been to discount it. But now that she thought about Robert and the things she discovered about him that helped her to form an opinion, she realized they came to her through careful observation of the way he handled himself in the face of difficulty. Sometimes we criticize in others what we are quick to overlook in ourselves, she thought.

He was a man with a proud history; a man of deep and dark mystery, the inheritor of a legacy of desperation and mistreatment, of treason and treachery. Little could she blame him if he did not trust her or the English. Centuries of betrayal had taught him that to trust was to be betrayed. She found she was intrigued with his past and filled with the desire to know more about the history of his people. Perhaps then, in knowing the past, she would understand the present and the man she was to marry.

"If you are ready to put this day behind you, I will show you to your rooms."

He walked beside her, Agnes having fallen a discreet distance behind. This afforded her the opportunity to speak with him alone—something she had little opportunity to do before now. She asked a few questions about Beloyn and learned there were thirteen bedchambers on the second floor, five of them located in the wing that lay in ruins.

They reached the second floor and walked down a long, dark corridor and stopped at the last room. Robert opened the door and they followed him inside. Meleri felt that when she passed across the threshold, she was stepping not only into her bedchamber, but into her future, as well.

It was a large room, with an adjoining dressing room, which they decided would be the perfect place for Agnes to sleep that night. Upon entering the room, Agnes approached the bed, where the belongings she brought with her had been placed. "I shall stay in here and unpack, milady."

Meleri saw that the bedchamber had been handsome in its day, but it, like the rest of the castle she had seen, had fallen into disrepair. Now all she noticed were the large dimensions, the many windows and the dark wainscot that covered the walls.

It was cold, inhospitable and meagerly furnished. In front of a trio of smaller windows stood a magnificently carved table, its leg broken, and a tattered chair, its seat covered with worn, gilded leather. Another chair, smaller than the first, stood beneath the largest window, its cushion of brocade faded and horribly worn. The fireplace was as bare as the rest of the room. Meleri almost dreaded to look at the bed. It was lumpy in the places it did not sag and covered with green silk, also faded.

She thought of her beautiful room at home. For one feel-sorry-for-herself moment, she felt as if she might cry, but she detested women with no more resource than the ability to shed tears. Besides, why should she cry?

The room, like Robert, had possibilities.

This was her home now, and she would make it into something beautiful. She would be happy here, simply because she was determined to be. Think happy thoughts before you go to bed, she reminded herself.

She was suddenly aware that Robert was standing next to her, observing her reaction. "I did not thank you for showing us to our rooms," she said. "I am aware you could have sent someone else to do it."

"Why do you suppose I chose not to do so?"

She searched his face. "Perhaps for the same reason you did not leave for Edinburgh as you had planned."

"Aye, 'tis possible they were the same." He took one of her curls in his hand and rubbed it between his fingers. "Perhaps I found I had a fondness for red hair."

"Is that all?"

A hint of a smile gave slight lift to the corners of his mouth. "No, it isn't all, but it is all I am going to tell you for the moment."

"It is dreadfully mean of you to leave me in wonder." She looked into the intense blue eyes almost hidden beneath craggy brows. She wished her heart would stay calm. "Can you not tell me?"

"Nay, lass, 'tis certain to fill your head with ideas."

"What kind of ideas?"

"This kind." He leaned toward her and brought his face to the side of her cheek, before he touched her lips softly with his own. The kiss was light and lingering, making her yearn for even more. "Some things are much simpler than words."

"Is…is that all you are going to say?"

His chuckle rumbled up from deep within him. He placed another kiss upon her lips. One that was softer and shorter than the first. "Aye, lass, it is for now."

She felt suddenly awkward, and for diversion, she glanced around the room.

He looked around as well. "I know it isn't much…"

"No, it isn't."

"In time, I trust you will find it comfortable."

"I am sure I will…in time."

"I realize you must make some changes."

"Yes, if I live long enough to see them done."

He chuckled. "You are young and I am full of optimism." He looked as if he might kiss her again, but the look passed, and he said, "I shall leave you to ready yourself for bed. If you have any further need of me, send Agnes. Later, I will send someone up to see how you are faring."

As she watched him go, she vowed she would make an effort to be more tolerant and accepting, less critical and quick to condemn. She would do better. She would! She would because something about him touched her, and touched her in a way no one ever had.

"Has he gone, milady?" Agnes came fully into the room, then stopped. "Are you unwell, milady?"

"No, only disappointed. Oh, Agnes, why is everything in my life turning upside down? I was so optimistic about my future here, about a husband who would come to love me. What if that is not to be?"

"You must be patient, milady. There will come a time when you will realize it is possible for you to have both. Give yourself time. Be patient. Rome wasn't built in a day."

"No, but a day is all it took for it to burn."

"You will have a wonderful future here. You have no way of knowing what will happen. I do not think you should worry. I feel very confident that things will work out well for you."

Meleri sat down on the bed. "Keep talking. I am on the verge of feeling better."

Agnes sat down beside her and patted her hand. "You are too hard on yourself."

"Think of something else. That isn't very reassuring."

"Well, you know life comes with a certain number of mistakes we all have to make. It's not the mistakes that are important, but how we handle them." Agnes shifted her position and the bed creaked like a warning. She sprang to her feet. "Faith and super-stition! This bed must go back to Moses."

Meleri smiled. "Farther than that, I think." She bounced a time or two. "I swear it feels like it's stuffed with old bones."

Agnes shuddered. "Don't say such things. I am having a hard enough time thinking I must close my eyes in this place, and now you are talking like that. It's enough to give a body the shudders."

"Surely you aren't worried that some harm will come to you?"

"No. I don't think even a ghost would want to stay in this place long enough to do that."

"Agnes Milbank! I had no idea you were such a milquetoast."

"It is not so much that, as it is the place. It is touched with melancholy. I don't yet feel a part of it."

"I, of all people, understand that," Meleri said glumly. "I don't exactly feel part of anything here, either—especially the man I am supposed to marry." She let out a long, mournful sigh. "Oh, Agnes, I have never felt more undecided. I do not know if I am more miserable, or expectant. This place is shoddy and creepy, and yet, I have such high hopes. I do not want to go home, but like you, I do not yet feel comfortable. I don't know what's wrong with me. I feel so…up and down…so out of place. I'm like a crumpet on a plate of raisin scones."

"I am certain we will feel differently after a good night's sleep," Agnes said, sounding semicheerful. "Good night, milady."

Meleri nodded and patted Agnes on the arm before she turned away. "I am glad you're here, Agnes."

"So am I. Will you be needing my help to undress?"

"No, go to bed. I can manage…although…"

"Although what?"

She looked down at her riding habit. "I haven't anything to sleep in. In fact, I have nothing to wear, save this pathetic rag I've worn so long it's beginning to feel like my skin."

"I saw a gown lying on the end of the bed. Perhaps someone put it there for you. Once my trunk comes, I can make your dresses. I packed several lengths of fabric."

"I can't take your fabric."

"Of course you can. You need dresses."

Meleri walked back to the bed and picked up the white cotton gown. The fabric was worn and thin, but someone had lovingly embroidered it and the workmanship was quite fine. "I wonder who put this here?"

"Perhaps it was someone who wanted to feel better before they went to sleep."

Meleri smiled. "Good night, Agnes."

"Good night, milady."

Meleri undressed quickly and climbed into bed. She found a comfortable position and settled down, thankful for the opportunity to sleep in a bed again.

Not long after she had closed her eyes, she heard a strange sound.

Her eyes flew open. She held her breath and listened.

From somewhere deep within in the castle, she could hear music. As she lay there, listening, she recognized the ghostly music of a bagpipe, the same melody that she heard earlier. She lay as if frozen, afraid to take even a deep breath for quite some time.

The sound of the bagpipe grew louder, as if the piper was

coming closer. Strangely, the louder it became, the more relaxed she felt. She pulled the covers up over her nose and whispered, "I'm not afraid of you. No one who plays anything so lovely could be bad."

A sweet fragrance drifted over the room. She sighed, feeling suddenly relaxed and so terribly sleepy. She closed her eyes, listening to the melodious sound that struck her as both heartfelt and melancholy. Tomorrow she would try to find out where it was coming from and who could play with such bewitching sentiment.

"Tomorrow," she whispered, then drifted off, to dream of a silent heath where bloody battles had been fought and druids old were said to walk.

14

Philip was sound asleep in the arms of his mistress when his father, Edward, the Duke of Heatherton, kicked in the bedroom door and strode furiously into the room.

"Father!"

"Get out of that whore's bed and get your clothes on."

"How dare you…" When Lady Jane Middleton raised her head and saw the duke's face, her words froze in her throat.

"Your services are no longer needed," the duke said, tossing an envelope on the table. "This should compensate you for any embarrassment you feel you might have suffered."

Meekly, Jane lay back down.

Having already leaped from the bed, hastening to do as his father demanded, Philip felt his heart race. He had never seen his father so furious, and he was at a loss as to why. His father knew he had a mistress. Jane was a frequent visitor to their country estate. He could not understand what caused this sudden change. "What is the meaning of this?"

"In the carriage," the duke said. "Now, if you please."

"My shoes…"

"You've other shoes." His Grace turned and left the room in the same manner that he had entered, only this time, Philip ran behind him, tugging on his coat in his bare feet.

By the time he reached the carriage, his father was waiting inside. Without saying a word, he climbed inside. The moment the coachman closed the door, the duke turned on him with dreaded intensity. "I have waited for you to amount to something until I am out of patience. I have provided you with every opportunity, the finest education, the benefit of my wisest counselors, as well as my own guidance and a bloody fortune. What do I get in return? A wastrel! A good-for-nothing, fornicating wastrel who thinks his father is too stupid to realize he is being played the fool."

"I never…"

"You never intended to marry Lady Weatherby, did you? It was all a ruse, a way to placate me. Somewhere in that tightly drawn mind of yours, you thought your father was old and stupid, a relic from the past that you could outwit and outwait. How I must have disappointed you when I continued to enjoy supremely good health, instead of dying and leaving everything for you to squander."

"That isn't…"

"Don't lie to me! Spare me that indignity, at least! I have been on to you for some time now, but out of respect for your mother and a reluctance to humiliate myself by disowning my own son, I allowed it to go on. Well, my boy, you took it one step too far when you broke your engagement with Sir William's daughter."

"She's the one who wanted to cry off."

The duke slapped Philip in the face with his leather gloves. "Do you think I am a fool? I have all the details. I have talked to your friends, whose fathers managed to extract the truth in a manner similar to this. It would serve you well to remember the reason you were betrothed to Lady Weatherby in the first place. In case you have forgotten, let me refresh your memory. We are a very wealthy family, but in land only. When it comes to money, I am afraid that is another matter entirely. Our fortune has dwindled over the years. There is only enough left to cover the expenses for your mother and I, and to provide you with your monthly allowance…an allowance that you squander. Lose the lands we hold, and you have nothing. However, if you have any interest in holding on to what we now own, so that you will some day inherit, it is imperative that you marry a wealthy woman. Do I make myself clear?"

"Explicitly so."

"Good. I want no misunderstanding on the graveness of this matter. Now, should you foolishly choose otherwise and decide you want to fritter away our holdings by lavish misuse, I will be forced to start selling off property you would have inherited. In other words, the longer I live, the less you receive. That should be all the motivation you need. You bumbled the whole affair, and badly. When she came to you, it was your place to satisfy her, to set a date for your wedding."

"But I... She did not want the wedding date set. She—"

"I know you did not lift a finger to put things right, so don't insult me by trying to say you did. I have already met with my solicitor to change my will. You better pray my good health continues, because when I die, my boy, you are left without a sixpence."

Philip realized he was caught, that there was no way out of this thing except by begging mercy and asking for one more opportunity to prove himself. He knew his only chance to save himself was by bending to his father's will. He had to lower himself to whatever level his father required. The duke could not prevent his inheriting the title. It was his right by birth. However, his father could sell off the lands he would inherit, just as he said, and he could do it as easily as he could disinherit him. Philip knew that would leave him with nothing more than the title and the clothes on his back. He would be ruined. Not even the lowliest of titled persons would allow his daughter to marry someone so disgraced.

"What can I do? I had no idea you felt as you do, or that things looked so bleak. I think I deserve another chance, before you disown me. Give me a chance to prove myself."

"You have one month to convince Lady Weatherby to forgive you and set the date. After that, you have one month to see yourself wed and the marriage consummated. Once I am satisfied, I will change my will, but even then, you will receive only a small pension from my estate as your inheritance in yearly sums that gradually increase, as long as I am pleased with your progress."

They had reached the duke's London town house, and the carriage stopped. The Duke of Heatherton climbed out. "Charles will drive you home. Remember, two months is all you have to set things right and marry the chit. After that, you are no longer my son and all financial assistance to you will terminate."

15

Early the next morning, the jubilant song of a bird outside her window shattered her sleep, and for a moment, Meleri thought she was back home. She climbed sleepily out of bed, curious and anxious to see what the day looked like. She went to the window, threw open the shutters and greeted the beautiful setting before her.

Below her window, a lush expanse of lovely green lawn seemed to go on forever. Overhead, a golden eagle soared above clumps of sturdy violets that grew along the edge of a small wood. A herd of sheep grazed in the distance, while up close, a gaggle of geese went honking across the gardens, obviously on a snoop. Everything seemed set to music, perfumed with the wonderful fragrance of bog myrtle.

Meleri turned and thrust her arms up in a luxurious stretch before wiggling her toes and taking a deep breath, vowing to have a fine, glorious day. With no clean clothes, she had no choice but to remain in her gown until Agnes cleaned her riding habit.

Suddenly, the door was thrown open and a huge dog came loping into the room. It jumped upon the bed and off the other side, faster than Meleri could blink an eye. While she stared in slack-jawed silence, the great beast reared up on its hind legs and gave her face a good washing. Never having had a pet of her own, Meleri was not sure what she should do, but a couple of licks later, she did what came natural. She put her arms around the dog's neck and fell over laughing.

Agnes came running into the room, breathless, clutching a breakfast tray in her hands. "Oh, milady, I am so sorry! That vile, wiry-haired creature has hounded my every step. I tripped over her every inch of the way. I was petrified, afraid I would drop your breakfast before I made it up the stairs. I did nothing but bump into her no matter which way I turned."

Meleri, who was enjoying all the attention, even if it was wet, and from a dog, said, "It's all right, Agnes." She barely managed to speak between gasping for breath and giving in to a fit of laughter. "She is a friendly dog, although I've never seen one quite like her." She managed to extract herself from the playful creature. "She certainly is big."

"The other one is a male and even larger."

"Two of them? Oh, how wonderful!"

"For now, two is all I have seen, but one never knows. There could be *puppies,*" she whispered, as if whispering might not make it so.

"Puppies! Wouldn't that be wonderful?"

"Humph! Puppies are just little dogs, and like babies, they grow up."

"Oh, Agnes, they aren't just little dogs. They are something else entirely. And this is the sweetest dog ever!" Meleri had her hands on each side of the great dog's head, stroking the silky hair as she studied her dark, blue-gray coloring. "You are a strange-looking creature indeed. I've never seen anything like you." She stroked beneath her chin. "I wish I knew what breed you are."

"I was told they were Scottish deerhounds."

"Deerhounds? For hunting deer?"

"I don't know for certain, but that would be my guess."

The dog had a long head, with small black ears folded back like a greyhound's. However, it was not a greyhound. Or, if it was, it was a rough-coated greyhound and much larger than any Meleri had ever seen. The black nose was aquiline, and she had a delightful silver beard that was much lighter than the black muzzle. When Meleri released her head, the dog sat down and watched her with large, dark eyes, her long, curved tail thumping the floor madly. Meleri stroked her back. "Oh!" she said, jerking her hand back and laughing. "Her hair is so coarse and wiry." She laughed again at the almost whimsical expression on the dog's face.

She ruffled the dog's fur. "She is a dear, isn't she? Do you know her name?"

"Corrie. Corrie Linn. The male is called Dram, for Drambuie."

"Corrie and Dram. Don't you think she is quite the loveliest dog you have ever seen? We shall have such pleasant company, shall we not?"

"As long as they remain friendly…and stay out from under my feet."

"I cannot see such a sweet dog being anything but friendly. What a darling." Meleri leaned down and gave the dog one last hug, before returning to Agnes, who was still holding the tray and eyeing the dog suspiciously. "Just put the tray on the bed," she said.

Agnes put the tray down, but before Meleri could get to it, Corrie sprang into action. In the squeezing of a lemon, the dog was on her feet. Two long strides and a leap later, she landed in the middle of the bed. In a blur of confusion, Meleri did not see exactly what happened next. She heard Agnes scream. She saw Corrie with her front paws on the breakfast tray. Then she saw the tray sliding like a sleigh toward the edge of the bed.

Agnes screamed again. Meleri made a dive for the tray. Just as she reached the bed, she tripped on the carpet and went sprawling over the top of the bed. She and the tray—which went airborne when Meleri hit the bed—collided. China and glassware fell to the floor and shattered. Silverware clanked and clattered across the floor. The tray took off like a sled and shot across the room. Meleri, who had too much momentum to stop, sailed over the edge of the bed and landed on the floor with a loud thump. "Ooof!"

"Oh, my heavenly stars!" Agnes exclaimed. "Are you hurt, milady?"

A giggling reply came from the vicinity of the bed. "Only my dignity."

"I'll go after something to clean up the mess."

Meleri took one look at Corrie, sitting majestically in the middle of the bed, a link of three sausages dangling from her mouth, and burst into laughter. When she got control of herself at last, she was so weak from laughing that she could only lie there, on the floor with great globs of oatmeal in her hair, her nightgown splashed with tea and dotted with clotted cream. Corrie walked over to the edge of the bed, looked down at her and dropped the sausages on her chest, then sat down next to her, as if standing guard.

While all of this was going on, Agnes was still standing near the door, looking as lost as one mitten. Curious as to what turned her to a pillar of stone, Meleri was about to inquire, when Robert stepped into the room.

Over the years, she imagined many reasons why she would one day find herself fiercely attracted to a man. It never occurred to her that he might not be equally attracted to her. Whenever she looked at Robert, she was aware of a compelling sense of remoteness. What would one have to do, she wondered, to get close to him? She was not the person to answer that, but the thought of being close to him, of being the object of his attentions as well as his affections, warmed her. One day, you will walk into the room and see me, she thought, your eyes will light up and your heart will fill with pride. One day, you will not be able to stand so far apart. One day, you will love me, only you don't know it yet.

She fell immobile beneath the scrutiny of his gaze. In spite of what was going on about him, not one spark of mirthfulness emitted from that rigid face. A fierce tension strained the atmosphere, caused by some unknown element that passed between them. She knew at that moment it was all or nothing. She believed with all her heart that was true. It had to be true. Either this man would come to love her until his dying day, or he would destroy her. They would not—could not—ever be mere friends, any more than they could be a married couple who found contentment instead of love.

One look from him and Agnes shot from the room, faster than an arrow from a string.

"You did not tell me about your dogs," Meleri said.

"I haven't told you about a lot of things."

Corrie grabbed the sausages, jumped back onto the bed and sat down. She looked from Meleri to Robert with such interest that Meleri laughed with relief and said, "Corrie has a fondness for sausages."

"She has a fondness for anything she doesn't have to run down. You look a fright."

The cool tone and lack of interest in his voice stung, but she was determined to maintain her cheerfulness. She deemed it necessary to show him there was another side of her, one that was not always critical, or quick to anger. She rolled over onto her side, propped her head in her hand and looked down at her gown. "You're right. I cannot argue with you on that point. I am a holy mess. I seem to be wearing my breakfast."

"And seem remarkably content to do so."

Her laugh was immediate. "Why not? There is precious little I can do about it, so I might as well be content."

"And are you content?"

The look she remembered from the night before was back, warm and curious in a way that made her conscious of him as a man, and herself as a woman. She called up the memory of his kiss, the contrast between a hard man and his gentle touch. "As content as rum and religion, milord."

He said nothing, and nothing, coming from Robert, spoke volumes. It was apparent that he was holding back, keeping her tense and apprehensive on purpose, while he remained calm and wary, waiting for her to do or say something foolish. Corrie, bless her, provided the diversion Meleri prayed for, when she leaped off the bed and sailed over Meleri's head, graceful as you please. With a silent tread, she walked to

Robert, stuck her nose in his hand, then slipped quietly from the room.

"How did she come to be in here?"

Meleri was not going to implicate Agnes, so she simply said, "I have no idea. One minute I was standing here alone. The next, a great gray beast came charging into my chamber."

He glanced back toward the door. "Someone must have left the gate open. The dogs know they are not supposed to come up here. We don't allow them above stairs."

"Maybe no one told them that." She saw his dark scowl and, with a more cheerful tone, added, "I'm glad you didn't tell me about the dogs. It was ever so much nicer to meet them this way, although I haven't met Dram yet." She paused. "Where is he?"

"Hunting with Hugh and Iain," he said.

Meleri was still lying on the floor, feeling her insides humming with delight from simply watching him, when she suddenly recalled she was not yet dressed. Horribly abashed at the thought of wearing her nightgown, she scrambled to her feet and looked quickly about, searching for something to put around her.

He must have thought she needed covering as well, for he gave a muffled curse and crossed the room in a few long strides. Without slowing down, he yanked the coverlet from the chair. "Here," he said, almost throwing it at her. "Cover yourself." She saw it coming but had no time to react. The next thing she knew, it landed on top of her head and fell over her, tent fashion, covering her face.

She attempted to fight her way out, but the coverlet was heavy and progress slow. Getting it off her head at last, she tried to work it around her, but it was difficult to do. She did manage to get it over one shoulder, but it promptly slid off the other. Unfortunately, when it fell, it took the shoulder of her gown with it, exposing her breast. Stunned horror sent a hot wave of red color splashing across her face. She drew in a gasp of air and yanked the gown back in place.

"For the love of God!" Robert said, and jerked the coverlet from her. "Are you completely helpless?"

She stared up into his face, unable to move, as he wrapped it around her. "Only around you," she said, never taking her eyes off his face.

"English witch!" He let the coverlet fall to the floor and pulled her against him. Her hands were trapped between them in such a way that she could not move. The sudden staccato of her heart sent a wave of warm languor washing over her, while the hand that caressed her neck was as sobering as a pan of cold water. "You will ruin…"

The rest of her words froze, for his lips moved like softly whispered words over her cheek, her ear and lower to her neck and shoulder. She gasped at the intense knotting of her stomach and exhaled the words trapped there and finished her sentence… "your shirt."

He released her quickly. Her mind was numb, her thoughts jumbled.

"This wasn't supposed to happen," he said. "One of us should have their head examined."

"I don't feel like I have much left to examine, at the moment."

"That is because you are a woman."

Yes, she thought, but you do not seem to realize it yet. She closed her eyes and clenched her mouth against the words she wanted to hurl at him. *Think, Meleri. Think before you speak.* She had seen him at his best. She understood what gentleness he was capable of. She did not understand why he was not being kind or gentle now.

The only reason she could find for his continued coolness toward her was the suspicion that he had changed his mind—perhaps even as far back as the day they stood before the smithy's anvil in Gretna. Since that time, he appeared to have a great deal of difficulty deciding if he wanted her or not. She might not have a place to go, but she did have feelings and pride. She was above groveling. She was also tired of trying to please someone who was beyond pleasing.

"Apparently you think this was a mistake," she said. "I am sorry I was so oak-witted that I did not realize that fact until now.

No more cold looks or harsh words are necessary. I will find Agnes and we will be on our way." She smiled, feeling it was either that or cry. "I do not hold it against you. One cannot change the way they feel. You either want someone, or you do not. It is not the sort of thing that can be forced."

"You have precious few options. *Leaving* is not among them."

She was ready to throw up her hands and go down to defeat. "I don't know what it is that you want. I only know I am not the one to give it to you." She crossed her arms in front of her and looked off. "Oh, I don't know why I bother! Talking to you is like talking to the wind. Everything I say blows back into my face. You ask me to marry you, and then you do not go through with it. You bring me to your home, and then go out of your way to show you want nothing to do with me. I offer to leave, you tell me I cannot go. And you think *I* am difficult? Well, milord, I may be difficult, but you are *impossible!* You cannot have it both ways. I can go. I can stay. I cannot do both. I can be your wife, or I cannot. What is impossible is trying to be something in between."

"I have asked you to do nothing."

"No, you haven't. In fact, you have not said much of anything. About all I get from you are cold words, cold stares or a cold shoulder. Pray tell, why are you being so cold and indifferent?"

"I am a cold and indifferent man."

"Bah! You are about as cold as the tropics. I seem to be the agitator here—the thing that chills your words and freezes your response."

"I agree with your conclusion, but not your reason. That is the difference between men and women."

"Then you tell me, milord. You offer me a bouquet, but it is filled with strange flowers of reason that I cannot comprehend."

"There are times when we must be ruled by design and not our passions."

"I have no way of knowing the sentiment of your heart, the motives behind your behavior, or the dictates of your mind. I only know that when you are cold, associations are unfruitful. What do you want, milord?"

"I wanted a wife."

"And now you don't?"

He did not answer. Once again, he let his silence speak for him. Meleri stood quietly, feeling the despair of disappointment. She was back where she started, with no place to go and fearful that wherever she went, Waverly would find her. She had known from the first that Robert was a stubborn, obdurate man, full of hatred for her country and bitterness for what hardship fate had tossed his way. He was like a windstorm, threatening, fierce and convincing, ready to come against her with a driving force, to toss her about like last year's leaf and send her on her way.

There was nothing else to be done about it. She had tried to set things to right, and he came along and knocked them flat again. If he wanted to spend his life in brooding loneliness, she was powerless. If he was determined to wallow in the pain life had tossed him, so be it. If he wanted to dwell in the hatred of the past, she would not stand in his way. She wanted more from life than that. She deserved more. "Very well, don't answer. Your silence speaks plainly enough."

His silence persisted, and she was aware only of his continued scrutiny and thoughtful observation. She laughed dryly. "Well, I seem to be doing all the talking, and now I have run out of words." She blinked back tears and called upon an iron will to hold them at bay. She looked down at her hands and started across the room.

"You are leaving?"

"I must find Agnes."

"Why?"

"I believe you know why."

"You are angry?"

"No, I simply know my limits, and I have reached them. Now I will find Agnes and tell her not to unpack the rest of her trunk, that we are leaving."

"What about yourself?"

She paused. "I am fortunate in that regard. No trunk, and no belongings. What comes easily goes easily."

"Bitterness does not become you."

"Nor you, milord."

"You judge what you do not know."

"Just like you."

"You talk too much."

"And you don't talk enough."

"You are a woman who does not know her place."

"I am a woman without a place to know."

Silent and watchful again, she thought.

She stared at the hard mouth and would have given anything to know what he was thinking, not that it mattered. He was probably thinking she was like a leech, a woman who found a man to attach herself to—a woman who would drain the life from him. She almost laughed. How wrong he was, how very far from the truth.

He knew nothing about her, nothing about the way she yearned to belong to a man, to love him and only him, to bear his children and stand by his side. He had no inkling of her loyalty, her pain, her passion, her loneliness, her fear that she would not measure up to the women he had known before her.

He would never know the desire she felt for him; the way his nearness warmed her; how the sound of his voice made her mouth go dry; the way the most indifferent look could set her heart to fluttering wildly; the way she would lie in bed at night, trying to imagine what it would be like if he loved her. Poor, foolish man. He had no idea what he was throwing away. He was sending her back, like a coat one decides is the wrong color, or a gold bauble that does not shine. He had considered her and found her lacking. Now even his gaze made her uncomfortable.

"Why are you looking at me like that?" she asked.

"I am curious to know what you were thinking."

"Would you prefer something clever, or the truth?"

"The truth, if you or any other Englishman know how to tell it."

"You cannot forget that, can you? No matter what I do, or say, or where I go, I am, first and foremost, English. You cannot forget that one fact any more than you can forgive or overlook it. It is a weed growing out of control in your mind. It supersedes everything and clouds your judgment. Unfortunately, it is the one thing I cannot change. I am what I am."

Once again, he remained silent.

"I must be after Agnes. She has probably unpacked and will be sorely vexed to hear she must put everything back." She turned away, wishing with all her soul that he would ask her to stay, knowing at the same time how impossible that was, how foolish it was of her to even consider it.

"I wouldn't go out that door, if I were you."

Her heart stilled. She held her breath, afraid to breathe, afraid to say anything for fear it would be the wrong thing to say. At last, when she could stand it no longer, she turned and asked, "Am I to go, or to stay? If I remain here, am I to be your wife, or your hated English prisoner?"

"You are to remain here…whether as my prisoner or my wife—that is up to you."

"But, you said…"

"I *know* what I said, and I know what you assumed."

She was confused. She had never known anyone to talk around things as he did. Why wouldn't he simply come out and say he wanted her to stay? Confounded, complex, stubborn man! Why could he not say he wanted her? She brought her hand to her head and rubbed the tightness there. She was uncertain as to what she should do. "You will have to do better than that, I'm afraid, Robbie Douglas. I am through guessing and trying to read your mind. If you want me to stay, you are going to have to say so."

"I said you were to remain here."

"That isn't good enough."

"All right, damn you! I want you to stay!"

"Why?" When he did not answer, she felt suddenly tired. She rested her head in her hand, her fingers covering her eyes. She needed to think, and she could not do it with him in her line of vision. Would she ever be able to make him love her? She began to fear she could not. There was too much bitterness, too much history that lay between them. "It is almost laughable…two strangers who couldn't agree on the color of the sky, who think they can marry and live out the rest of their lives in harmony. You could never come to care for me…not if I learned to spin gold from straw. It isn't *who* I am, it's *what* I am. I'm sorry—for both of us—but I cannot settle for that any more than you can forgive my being born in England."

"Damn your English eyes!" Suddenly, he took her in his arms. She could feel his body trembling against her. His mouth closed over hers, and her arms went around him as his lips moved over hers slowly; then with brutal tenderness, his arms tightened around her and he kissed her deeply, soundly. He was seducing her, drawing her into him with his wildness, his brooding remoteness, as surely as water would rise to cover her when she stepped into a warm bath.

His fingers began a slow, rhythmic search in a lock of raspberry-hued hair that curled like a question mark about the smooth skin of her throat. His hand moved lower, slipping from the softly rounded shoulders, down the slender length of arm until his fingers brushed against her breast and she gasped.

"I want you, you little witch," he whispered.

Suddenly, the door opened and a woman entered the room. Blindfolded, Meleri would have discerned Lady Douglas, Robert's grandmother.

Dark gray silk, fashioned in a style from another era, dared not rustle as she entered the room, as silent and alert as a cat. She was small, but the power her presence commanded made her tower above even her grandson. Lady Douglas was a woman who eclipsed everything, including him—as the moon passes in silvered silence over the fiery violence of the sun.

So, Meleri thought, this is what a grandmother is: hair the color of gunpowder pulled back in a neat coil, eyes that missed nothing, capable of complete devotion, formidable as any bird of prey.

When Lady Douglas stepped into the room, Meleri knew she was anxious to have a look at the woman Robert had brought with him from England. It had to be quite a jolt to her tired, old heart to hear the news of the sudden appearance of a soon-to-be-bride, especially an English one, even if the king did order it.

The moment she thought about the king, Meleri wondered how much Lady Douglas knew. For some reason, she seemed quite perplexed and filled with curiosity—something she might not be if she knew about the king's decree. Moreover, if that were true, and she did not know of it, then she must be wondering what happened to spur Robert's sudden quest for a wife. Meleri knew the heart and mind of women. If Lady Douglas was not informed, she would be trying to find a way to arrive at the answers, without showing her astonishment. It was Meleri's guess that she had been the matriarch of this family long enough to know the best way to win information was to appear as if you already had it.

Meleri did not miss the way Robert's face seemed to light up the moment he saw her. "Gram," he whispered, and kissed her cheek.

"Back almost a full day, and I have yet to see you, you scoundrel."

"You know you are always foremost in my mind. I dropped by last evening, but you had retired already. I did not want to disturb you."

"So many answers, and I believe them all." She tapped his arm with her cane. "You could talk the leathern boot off a Tartar horseman, if you set your mind to it," she said. "Your trip was obviously a success, and expeditious, for you were hardly gone before you were back."

Without any change in expression or tone, Meleri knew the moment her sharp gaze focused upon her. "And this, I assume, is your English lass, soon to be your wife?"

"Aye," he said, hesitating a bit too long before he looked briefly at Meleri. "This is Lady Meleri Weatherby." He turned to Meleri. "This is my grandmother, Lady Douglas."

"Pleased to make your acquaintance, Lady Douglas."

Lady Douglas nodded. "Lady Weatherby."

Robert gave his attention back to his grandmother. "What brings you sallying forth from your quarters at this early hour?"

"I came to see if you had murdered her. Never have I heard

such commotion." She looked about, taking in the condition of the room. "This place is a holy fright. What happened?"

"Corrie came above stairs, leaped in the bed and scattered the breakfast tray."

She pointed to Meleri with her cane. "She is a frightful-looking thing. It is obvious you did not choose her for her looks. I've never seen such carroty hair, nor did I know you had such a fondness for it."

"I don't know that I do have a fondness for it…or that I dislike it, either. I never took the time to give it much consideration."

"Well, you have time now…you will spend the rest of your life considering it. Does she have the temper to go with it?"

Lady Douglas did not miss the exchange of uncomfortable glances between Robert and Meleri as Robert said, "You might say she has shown a tendency for it on occasion."

Apparently satisfied, Lady Douglas turned her attention back to Meleri. "I recall hearing your father was a man of noble birth, but the formal title escapes me at the moment."

"He is a baron, milady."

"Yes, I recall now, a nobleman of the lowest designation."

Meleri wondered what bit of information the woman would try to ferret out next. Meleri assumed it would be obvious to her that she did not have the polish or the ease of execution one her age would have, if she had lived in or spent a great deal of time in London, or if she had gone through a Season or two. She knew there was an element of the country in her, but nothing to identify what part of the English countryside that would be.

"I am certain you must find comfort in knowing you are still in the Border country," Gram said.

Meleri smiled inwardly and played into Lady Douglas's hands. "Yes, I find little similarity between Northumberland and the Lowlands, milady."

Lady Douglas looked positively fortified. She must love a good quest, Meleri thought.

"Specifically, how are they dissimilar?" Lady Douglas asked.

"Scotland is…more bleak."

"Bleak, is it? Well, I daresay you will come to have a new understanding of the word, ere long."

In spite of knowing what Lady Douglas was about, Meleri was relieved when she directed her next question to Robert. "Did you also bring us a fat side of venison to gnaw on?"

"Not this trip. We saw nary a deer the entire time."

"'Tis a pity the red deer are mostly gone from the Lowlands. In my young days," she said, dropping back to the old way of talking, "a man wad hae been ashamed to come back frae the hill without a buck hanging on each side o' his horse, like a cadger carrying calves."

As Meleri listened, she realized she was truly overwhelmed by the commanding presence of Lady Douglas. She was also fascinated by the reciprocal warm feelings so obvious between her and her grandson. Never had Meleri heard so much adoration, gratitude, love and admiration packed into one word as she heard when he said "Gram."

Meleri was not a person to envy anything, but oh, she did covet the look that accompanied it. Would that she could hang a lifetime of hope upon one wish—that there would come a time when he conveyed, with look or words, such passion for her.

She saw the way Robert held his grandmother at arm's length, to better look her over. Transfixed, Meleri had watched him conduct a thorough investigation—from pearl combs holding pewter hair, to ancient sterling buckles upon out-of-fashion shoes—his proud eyes searching with all the scrutiny of an inspector hunting for clues. Aside from the way his eyes sparkled as he looked upon Lady Douglas with fondness and respect, Meleri had the distinct feeling that he owed this woman a great deal, that she occupied a very special place in his heart.

The quiet atmosphere of enlightenment disappeared quickly, and holding up as best she could, Meleri stood quietly, wondering what Lady Douglas thought of her, yet terrified to find out. She knew how important it was to her future that this stately old matriarch accept her. At the same time, she knew deep down that no one's grandmother would be overly impressed by someone

with wild, uncombed, *carroty* hair, wearing a nightgown deco-
rated with eggs and jam.

Struck with mute silence, she watched as the curtains at the
window billowed, although no one else seemed to notice. She did
not sense any sort of presence in the room, but she was certain
she heard a voice close by. The words were softly spoken, the
lilting brogue thick and not the sort spoken by the Scots today.

*"Come lass, forget and forgie. Dinna be vexed, for it serves
naething to strive wi' the old—they are aye cankered. Her bark
is waur than her bite. Ye will gain a muckle more if ye mind yer
tongue till the blast blaw by. 'Twas no ill luck that hae brought
ye sae far frae hame. When the hirdie girdie comes, ye maun trow
yer braw lad. Binna afraid, bide yer time, and gowd will come
to ye. Believe, an ye can, dinna kilt awa' afoor ye ken the troth."*

The room grew still. The curtains dropped back into place.

Neither Robert nor his grandmother appeared to have heard or
seen anything, and Meleri was determined she was going to do
the same. Besides, it was probably her imagination, her mind's
way of finding a diversion from an otherwise unpleasant situation.

She did not believe in ghosts, anyway.

"Come, Lady Weatherby," said Lady Douglas. "Let me have
a closer look at you."

"I am not yet dressed to receive guests, as you can see."

"Well, I have seen the state of your affairs already, so your
point is a moot one."

"All the same, I prefer to stay here."

"Rebellious and outspoken. Dear me, I fear you have picked
quite a stubborn one, Robbie. Willful, too, would be my guess."

Lady Douglas rapped her cane on the wooden floor with a
loud bang. Meleri flinched at the sound. "Show your respect for
your elders. Come stand over here, so I can see what mischief is
at work in those eyes."

Meleri was in no mood to be cleverly dissected by this
woman, grandmother or not. She eyed the distance to the door,
ready to dash for her life.

"Close the door, Robbie. Your bride-to-be looks ready to bolt."

At the sound of his amused chuckle, Meleri branded Robert a traitor of the vilest sort. When she heard the door click shut, she swore to get even with him for his betrayal. With her prospects for escaping this horrid ritual nonexistent, she took a fortifying gulp of air and went to stand before Lady Douglas, where she endured a scrutinizing going-over that no horse being sold at a country fair would be put through. *If she asks to see my teeth, I am leaving here, if I have to climb out the window.*

"She is not nearly as bad as I first thought, although she does smell frightfully like a poached egg."

"There is a good reason for that, thanks to Corrie," Robert said.

"She doesn't look as fierce as I first thought, either, but then, the English are more known for bluster than steadfastness."

Meleri was beginning to feel about as low as she could feel, for she was certain now that she had ruined whatever chances she might have had to favorably impress Lady Douglas. She meant to be kind and polite. Truly, she did, but that was more difficult to achieve than it was to plan. What amazed her was that Robert could not see what a rude, impolite and mean-spirited woman his grandmother was.

It was obvious to Meleri that Lady Douglas was a descendant of a Border family who acquired its lands by robbery and violence. When she had first walked into the room, Meleri was reminded of a Scottish deerhound, very distinguished and regal. She was wrong. Now she saw this descendant of horse thieves differently. Beneath the wizened features, something else had emerged, something Scottish, something prickly and unbending.

"I grow weary," said Lady Douglas. "It is past time for my morning tea. Bring your lass to see me when she is cleaned up. I will have a closer look at her then."

Stately as a Scotch pine, she left the room. As she went, the last thing Meleri thought was that Lady Douglas might be an inheritor of blood feud and cattle raid, but she both admired and envied the way she walked with a proud and noble stride.

"You didn't care for my grandmother, did you?" Robert asked her after she'd left.

Meleri was too cross and tired to pick and choose her words. "It's not so much that I did not care for her, but more that she did not fit the description I have long held. I thought grandmothers were nice old ladies, who made aprons and knitted shawls. I thought they read you stories and gave you pieces of old jewelry and taught you things about life."

"That is what they do," he said.

"Then what happened to yours?"

Robert never got the chance to answer that, for Agnes came into the room with a length of yellow fabric looped over her arm. "This will make a lovely dress for you, I think, milady. Oh, my I did not realize…"

"It is all right," Robert said, "I was just leaving."

16

After the bitter confrontation with his father, Philip paid a visit to Humberly Hall.

When he rang the bell, Jarvis answered the door. "Good afternoon, your lordship."

"Tell Sir William that Lord Waverly is here to see him."

"I am sorry, but Sir William is not at home, your lordship."

"When do you expect him to return?"

"Due to Sir William's declining health, I don't think he will be returning to Humberly Hall. His daughter Elizabeth has taken him to reside with her, so that she might look after him. We are, at the moment, packing everything in readiness for closing the house."

Taken completely by surprise, Philip was too stunned to respond. He could not think. He could not breathe. He was already overwhelmed and infuriated over the recent turn of events, and now this? Gone to London? Closing down the house? "I will have a word with Lady Weatherby then, if you will tell her I am here."

"I regret to inform your lordship that Lady Weatherby is not here, either. There is no one here, save myself and the other servants."

Philip could think of nothing he loathed more than his father for putting him through this. "If you will give me Lady Elizabeth's address in London, I will pay Lady Weatherby a call when I arrive there tomorrow."

"Lady Weatherby did not go to London, your lordship."

"All right, if she is not here, and she is not in London, then where is she? Come, come, my good man. Tell me where I might find her."

"I do not know, your lordship. No one knows. She has simply disappeared. Vanished into thin air, she has."

"Don't be a fool! People do not vaporize and leave no trace, no clue as to where they have gone. Tell me what you know of this!"

"I only know Lady Meleri went to her room after dinner, and the next morning when Betty took her breakfast tray up to her room, she wasn't there."

"And her things? Were they missing as well?"

"According to Mrs. Hadley and Betty, nothing was missing. She must have left with only the clothes she was wearing."

"And her horse?"

"Missing as well."

"Was her sister here when all of this occurred?"

"I believe she disappeared the night before Lady Elizabeth and Sir William left. Or it might have been the night after."

"Then give me Lady Elizabeth's address, and be quick about it."

Once he had the address, Philip returned home. Of all the things he expected, he never considered this. He was dazed by the backlash that whipped through him. Desperation burned like a brand in his brain until the reality of what she had done forced him to think.

She was gone…and his hopes for a future along with her.

That there would be consequences ripped into his consciousness and filled him with a new hatred. Thanks to Meleri, his life was no longer his. His mind was clouded with rage, and he knew she was to blame for all of his misery. His hands curled into fists as he thought about what he would do to her when he found her. And he would find her. When he did, he promised himself that she would never, ever do something as foolish as to run from him again.

Without her, his future was ruined. The knowledge that he was in imminent danger of losing everything made him desperate. She had to be found. Time was working against him.

He called for a fresh horse to be saddled, after deciding he would leave for London as soon as he changed clothes. As he dressed, he cursed his ill fortune. Damnation! He had just come from London. He did not need to waste more time—time that he did not have.

As he rode away from Humberly Hall, Philip was no longer thinking about his irritation over having to return to London. He was thinking about all the ways he could avenge himself upon Meleri for what she had put him through. Whatever he decided upon, it must be severe enough to prevent her from ever considering such actions again.

Once they were married, she would be completely under his control.

That was exactly where he wanted her.

17

As a child, Robert was taught the Copernican theory and shown how the world revolved around the sun. As a man, he learned it revolved around money.

Everyone needed money, only a few possessed it, and no one ever had enough. In between lay varying degrees of desperation. Money was the most important thing in the world, the center of the universe. Men were valued for their money, and they married for it. Life was judged, built up and torn down for money. It was the source of a man's hope, his joy, his peace and his aspirations. He lived for it, and he died for it.

Money was the answer to all things. It was a goal everyone wanted to attain—and the primary cause of evil. No matter who you were, what you did, or how hard you tried, in the end, all that truly mattered was money. You could not change that, and you could never escape it.

Money was everything.

And it was something the Douglases did not have.

Robert thought about that as he sat behind his desk. He had been paying the servants, until he handed out the last boddle and plack in his leather pouch. He leaned back in his chair and sighed wearily. It could be worse, he supposed. At least every servant had been paid—not what he was due, but enough to keep the wolves away from the door.

Head back, eyes closed, he kneaded the tenseness that gathered in tight knots along his neck and shoulders. It always got to him, having to pay the servants when there was naught to pay them with, and he wondered if it would always be like this—always destitute, forever desperate, perpetually with too many mouths to feed.

He thought of Meleri and the money that would soon be his, providing her dowry was as large as she said. Dear God, it has to be large, he thought. Without it, there is no hope. Hope was all he had now. Hope and his stoicism, he thought. He realized at that point, that it had all come back to money. There was no escape.

The sturdy oak chair was tilted back on two legs, affording Robert a better view of the world outside. He considered his circumstances as he gazed through the tall, arched window opposite him.

A few minutes later, when Meleri wandered into his line of vision, he found himself distracted momentarily by the sight of her, her flaming hair loose, her manner playful and childlike, as she was being chased by Corrie and Dram. Each time he saw her, it became more difficult to remember the reason he'd brought her here, the purpose she was to serve. Desire for her kept getting in the way.

He watched her take something out of the pocket of her dark gray dress and give it to the dogs, who swallowed it eagerly. His attention went back to the dress. Where did she find it? he wondered. He recalled Gram telling him of the dresses lying unworn in her trunk, and how she had given them to Agnes. "They can be altered for something passable for Meleri to wear, until she can have her things sent from Northumberland."

The leather-bound ledger in front of him beckoned, and he pulled it closer. He winced at the long rows of expenditures that glowered up at him in defiance, as if they somehow knew that on the opposite page, beneath the word *income,* there was only one very short column.

Near the ledger stood a silver inkwell, engraved with the crest of King James. The king had given it to the first Earl of Douglas. He picked up the writing pen and plunged it into the reservoir, then began to tally the last row of figures. When he finished, he made the usual notations. In time, the faint smell of ink and the rhythmic scratch of the quill moving over foolscap began to work its magic. He began to relax, soothed by the calmative of movement.

"Robbie, are you in here?" Iain called out.

Robert put the quill down and closed the lid to the well. "Aye. I was just finishing my calculations."

Iain came into the room, followed by a sturdy fellow, obviously a farmer, judging from his dreadnought overalls.

"This is Charlie Armstrong," Iain said. "He lost his farm and is looking for work. I told him we had plenty of work, with the lambing and all. I thought perhaps you might be able to put him on."

"We've plenty of work, Iain, and no coin," Robert replied.

"I've told him that. He's willing to work for a place to stay and food for his wife and bairn."

Robert hated times such as this. It was not easy to turn away a hardworking man who was down on his luck and hungry. But Robert could do nothing. He would have to turn him away. He would say he was sorry, there was nothing he could do to help, that when it came to food, they were scraping the barrel and getting by on what they were able to raise in the garden. He noticed the man's work-roughened hands that held a hat covered with wax cloth. In his eyes, he saw hunger and desperation. "How old is your bairn?" Robert asked.

"Twa years."

Two years was too young to go hungry. "Do you know anything about sheep?"

"Aye, ye have lang sheep, or short sheep?"

"Both, and a few black-faces."

"My father often tauld me about the time o' the black-faces."

"Do you think you can care for all of them?"

"Aye, troth I ken ye maun hae turnips for the lang sheep, and 'tis muckle hard wark to get them, baith wi' the pleugh and the howe."

Robert smiled in agreement and nodded his head slowly.

"Aye, it's much hard work, even with the plow and hoe, just as you said."

Hugh came into the room. "Plow? That sounds remarkably like work. I don't know if I want to come in or not."

Robert picked up a mutchkin of whisky and poured a splash into three glasses. He glanced at Hugh, then poured a fourth. "And how would you be knowing anything about work?"

Hugh grinned. "I know enough to stay away from it."

"Aye, you've managed to do that well enough." He offered a glass to Charlie, who hesitated.

"Hout, Charlie," Iain said, falling back to use the speech Charlie used, "take ye that dram the landlord's offering ye, and never fash your head about it."

"Wussing your health, sirs," Charlie said, lifting his glass to them. He took a drink.

Hugh took the glass Robert offered. "Long sheep and short sheep! In spite of all my father tried to show me, I could never see any difference in the point of longitude, between one sheep and another."

Robert, Iain and Charlie laughed, then Charlie said, "It's the woo', man…it's the wool, and not the beasts themselves that makes them be called long or short."

"I remember my father always said, short sheep had short rents," Iain said.

"Aye, I ken that is very true," Charlie said.

Robert told Charlie to come to work the next morning. "Since Hugh is so interested in plows, he will meet you at the stables in the morning at six and take you to where the sheep are pastured."

"Troth! I am thankful, I'll never deny it," Charlie said. "Bless you, your lordship. You have brought good to us in a time o' trouble."

After everyone had gone, Robert went to the open window and stared out. He did not see Meleri, but he could hear her shouts to the dogs and the sound of Dram's hoarse bark. It had rained during the night, but now the sun shone down on the swells of gently sloping grounds lying snugly cloaked in a mantle of green, beneath a clear blue sky. The heath was in deep bloom, and the bees were on the wing, filling the air with murmurs of their industry. The world looked back at him in serene contentment. Everything was as it should be, orderly and in place. At least that was true on the outside.

Inside, within the thick walls of Beloyn Castle, things were different. Nothing was as it should be. All was indecision and turmoil. He knew what he wanted. He just had difficulty accomplishing it. Nothing had been right with him since that English sorceress ran over him with her horse. God help him, he did not know what to do about her.

He left his study and went to find Gram. He had known for some time they needed to talk and now the time was right. He would have to tread carefully. He could not let her know the real reason he wanted to wed Meleri, for he knew not even Gram would look kindly upon his using her as a way to lay Sorcha's ghost to rest. Once they were married, it would no longer matter. He did not care if she found out then. He would tell her himself, if need be. He would tell them all, Meleri included, but for now, he would keep his own council and keep the secret unto himself.

He found Gram in the library, one of the few rooms in the castle that retained its classical decoration and fine plasterwork. But not even this room had escaped the tragedy that befell the Douglas clan. The marble busts by Roubiliac were all gone, as were the Van Dyck paintings. Only one family portrait remained in this room, a painting of the wife of a long-ago ancestor. He stopped and stared at the portrait, contemplating the woman's solemn and composed face. He could see nothing of hardship in her face—the wars, the famine, and stillborn children.

He could not help wondering if his own portrait would deal as kindly with him.

Lady Douglas was leafing through a book, and he took in the sight of her with a fondness that stretched back as far as he could remember. He knew she heard him enter, but she did not look up. She was a lover of books, and he had her to thank for his devotion to them as well. He remembered how fond she was of telling the story of how many of the Douglases' books were rescued by a young girl named Margaret, back lang syne, when the castle was in its youth and under siege. Perhaps that was why the library was a favorite room of hers, or maybe it was because the books were old and rare, the majority of them being a fine collection of Middle English texts.

He would never forget the severe tongue-lashing he had received not so long ago, when he'd had "the audacity" to suggest selling what was not his to sell. "These books are a Douglas legacy," she'd said, "and irreplaceable."

In his mind's eye, selling rare books that would fetch a princely sum was a sound and logical thing to do. Gram did not see it as either sound or logical, for as she put it, "A man who would sell family treasures ought to lose a *treasure* or two of his own, if you get what I mean."

He got it, and he never mentioned selling the books again.

"I knew I would find you here, soothed by *The Townley Plays* or *The Tretis of the Twa Mariit Women and the Wedo*."

She held a slim volume up for him to see. "Wrong on both accounts. This is *The Siege of Jerusalem*."

"I remember when I was a lad I would come in here at night, after everyone had gone to bed. My young boy's mind was taken with a book written by the Chinese general Sun Tzu, in the sixth century B.C. called *The Art of War*. I do not remember much of what I read, I only remember his wisdom was remarkable. Do you know the one I mean?"

"'If you know the enemy and know yourself, you need not fear the result of a hundred battles. If you know yourself but not the enemy, for every victory gained you will also suffer a defeat. If you know neither the enemy nor yourself, you will succumb in every battle.'"

He smiled. "Aye, that is the one." His fondness for her glowed as a lamp lit from within. "I have always admired your remarkable memory. Tell me, what did you think of Lady Weatherby?"

"I look forward to knowing her better. It will be like reading a book. You find yourself anxious to discover what is on the next page—and praying you live long enough to reach the end."

"I knew you would be quick to make your assessments and tabulate the results. I look forward to the time when you have learned something about her."

"I can tell you a great deal already. She is clever, resolute and a survivor. She will yield when she must. She will bend with the wind. But she will never break. Although I would never have chosen an English lass, I must admit I am glad to see my successor is strong, bendable, canny and capable."

He noticed there was no sadness in her voice, only resignation, as if she had been expecting the day when a new Lady Douglas would come along. "No one can take your place."

"She will not have to. She will bring her own knowledge, her own ways and the youthful fire to move mountains. That is as it should be."

"Don't concern yourself with it now, Gram. If I go through with this marriage, there will be plenty of time for concern then."

"*If* you go through with it? What kind of talk is that? You brought her here, and you are not certain if you are going to marry her? Her father is a baron."

"I know what you are going to say. As she is a baron's daughter, I cannot take liberties with her reputation."

"Aye, that is precisely what I was going to say. You must marry her and stop this nonsense," she said, her voice as strong and powerful as a young lass's. "What are you waiting for?"

"Am I waiting?"

She narrowed her eyes and stared at him with hard suspect. "Now is not the time for jest. Have you bedded her?"

"No."

"Then, take her to wife and do not waste any more time. Wait too long and she may change her mind—you would be in a fine fix, then, wouldn't you, my laddie? I know about the king's letter to you."

"I knew it was only a matter of time. Who told you? Was it Hugh or Iain?"

"A good spy never reveals his sources."

He picked up a thin volume of sonnets and flipped through the pages. "I don't think she will change her mind. Our circumstances are mutually advantageous. She cannot go home any more than I can send her back. Our marriage will benefit her as much as it will me."

He saw she was about to question him further, so he continued on, explaining in more depth what he meant. He brought her up to date on Meleri's circumstances at home, about her father, the long-standing betrothal, of Meleri's action to end it. He did not identify her former betrothed as the Marquess of Waverly, or tell her that he was the one responsible for Sorcha's death. He had never told Gram the identity of Sorcha's murderer. He wanted to keep it that way.

"Poor lass," said Gram when he finished. "How could I fault her? We all want to be happy, but few of us will risk everything to have it. It took a great deal of courage to do what she did. Courage and fortitude—they are things I admire. She may have the face of an angel, but she has the heart of a gladiator. With a little help and encouragement, she will do you proud."

"I knew you would take her under your tutelage, England be damned."

"Surprisingly, I find I do not hold that against her. She cannot help the fact that she was born English, but there will be those who will not be so understanding or approving. How she is accepted will depend largely on her attitude. If she flaunts her English ways and snubs ours, it will not go well with her."

"It may not go well with her when she discovers she has landed in the midst of a family of dour Scots with peculiar ways, odd speech and strange food."

"With our help, she will withstand even that onslaught." Lady Douglas stopped to consider him with those blue, penetrating eyes that made him turn his head and look off. "Concerning this matter of marriage, you must not dally. The longer you wait, the more opportunity for something to go wrong. What if she should change her mind? The king will only be appeased if the marriage takes place within the allotted time. I would think you would feel a need to press ahead."

"I do."

"Well, I am relieved to hear that. I will rest easier when you are married and the king is no longer treading on our coattails. We have less than two weeks, and there is the matter of her clothes…and a wedding dress." Lady Douglas put her hand to her head. "Pomp and circumstance! I feel as if I have opened a trunk of bats and they are flying out faster than I can count. There is so much to do. The minister…the church…the guest list… Blast that king and his meddling ways! Three weeks indeed! I doubt he could get his wig powdered in three weeks, and yet he expects you to be wedded and bedded."

His brows shot up in surprise. "Why Gram, did I hear you say the word *bedded*—for a second time?"

"You did, and I pray you can practice restraint in that regard, until after the wedding. It is one thing to snitch her out from under the nose of her betrothed and quite another to take her virginity without the sanction of marriage. Don't be giving the king of England any more reason to hate us."

"I can behave myself when I have to. You have no worry in that regard. As for the wedding, the important thing is to keep it small and be frugal. I have yet to settle the matter of dowry."

"Have you written to her father…her family?"

"Aye, I've posted a letter to her sister's husband. According to Meleri, he assumed responsibility for managing the family holdings some time ago. This was due to her father's decline. His memory is failing, and his behavior is often quite eccentric."

"Aye, I have seen such afflictions. They only worsen with age. I assume you mentioned her dowry in the letter."

"Aye, I mentioned we could make arrangements regarding her dowry, and that I felt it would be best to have my barrister contact him. I also told him how to contact us, in case there was any change in her father's condition, with a reminder that it was imperative that no one else know of it, for Meleri's safety. I also expressed my regret that they would not be able to attend the wedding, but Meleri felt it best for her father not to travel—not to mention the need to keep our whereabouts a secret until we are wed."

"You have contacted your solicitor, then?"

"Aye, I dispatched a letter to John Sinclair the day we arrived."

"You haven't forgotten a thing."

"Aye, and I trust you won't forget what I said about the wedding plans. Frugal and small."

"My middle names are Prudence and Restraint. I hold that a small wedding is wisest, not only for us, but for her as well. She needs time to adapt, to make her place here, to feel a part of who we are, what we are and what we are about. A large wedding on short notice would not be wise. It is too early to put her on public display. And then, there is the matter of that lethargic ancestor of ours."

"What has *he* got to do with anything? It's *my* wedding."

"Ghosts appear when you least expect them."

"Then, where has he been?" Robert asked. "I haven't expected him for years."

"My point is, we will have to tell her about him at some point."

"Why? None of us have ever seen him."

"That does not mean he does not exist."

"She will think us light-minded."

"She probably thinks that already. Still, I wouldn't put it past him to show himself the day of your marriage."

"That's easy to prevent."

"Robbie Douglas, are ye daft? How can you prevent a *ghost* from coming to a wedding…or anything else if he should so choose?"

He laughed. "Don't invite him."

She punched him lightly on the arm. "'Tis a joyful thing to hear you laugh again."

He gave her a peck on the cheek. "Don't fash yourself over all this, Gram. I am not concerned, and I don't want you to worry yourself into a stupor over this ghostly relative…*if* there is one."

He could tell by the rapturous expression on her face that she was only half listening. There was nothing that entranced Gram like the mere mention of that absent apparition.

"You are saying that to get me riled," she said. "Although, I must say that for a ghost, he is remarkably inactive. Leave it to this family to inherit a sluggish ghost who doesn't know the first thing about ghosting."

"If that's all .that's keeping him from coming to our rescue, why don't you volunteer to teach him?"

"You know what I mean. He should be doing *something*. Ghosts are not slothful."

Robert laughed again. "Ours is."

Meleri ran down the path after Corrie and Dram, until they burst into a small meadow dotted with daffodils. To catch her breath, she slowed her pace and began to wander aimlessly through the grass, where the daffodils bobbed and fluttered in gusts of wind, as if they were looking for a place to hide. She gathered an armful and carried them to a stone fence that had fallen into ruin.

Scattered stones lay about—some of them partially covered with enough soil for violets to give root. She stepped over these and chose a grassy mound that lay flat against a part of the fence that still stood. She sat down and leaned her back against the uneven stones, hugging the daffodils to her. She watched Corrie and Dram loping in a zigzag fashion across the meadow, laughing when they began snapping at bees and biting at the heads of flowers.

She saw the way the daffodils turned their faces toward the sun, and following their lead, she leaned her head back and felt the result, warm upon her face.

Even with her eyes closed, she knew when a shadow moved over her face and thought at first the sun had gone behind a cloud. She opened her eyes and saw Robert standing there, tall as a pine, eclipsing the sun. About them, the gusts of wind died down, and everything was suddenly still as an odd sort of quietness settled over the meadow. Not even the dogs could be heard barking. Even the trees seemed to stand guard, silent as sentinels.

She tilted her head back, to better see his face, and squinted against the shaft of sun that escaped around him and warmed her.

"You've been busy," he said.

She glanced down at the daffodils in her arms. "I gathered these for your grandmother. I saw her looking at them through the window this morning."

"She will like that. I remember her saying a house could never have enough flowers. Yellow is her favorite color."

"Were you looking for me, or did you just happen upon us?"

He looked around as if trying to decide who *us* was. She looked around as well, and saw no sign of the dogs. "Corrie and Dram were here only a moment ago."

"They are large dogs and can cover quite a distance in their roamings. It is their habit to slip off by themselves whenever the opportunity arises."

She put her face into the yellow blossoms. "They don't have much of a scent—just a faint trace of something… *tarish*."

"Tarish?"

"As in smelling like tar."

"Hmm. Is that a word?"

She wrinkled her nose and said, "It is now."

Nearby, Corrie and Dram shot out of the brush, circled the meadow, snapped at a few flowers and disappeared again. "I always wanted a big dog."

"Why didn't you have one? I would think your father would have given you anything you wanted."

"He was a very loving man, but he did not believe in spoiling. I suppose he must have thought that since he had so many dogs I did not need one of my own. You see, my father raised his own hunting hounds, but I was not allowed to play with them. It was not as black as I am painting it. He did buy me quite the loveliest dapple-gray pony. To this day, I have not seen her equal."

He sat down next to her. "I would have a word with you about the wedding."

She hugged the flowers closer against her. She did not know why she felt so nervous. "Yes, I was thinking you would be bringing that up before long."

"Have you any thoughts on the matter?"

She considered for a moment, searching her feelings, her sentiments. There had been a time, of course, when she visualized an enormous wedding, but now practicality was more the order of the day. "Something small, I would think."

"My sentiments also."

"I have one request, milord. I know you are pressed to meet the king's deadline, but I should like to wait as long as possible, if we may."

"For what purpose?"

She felt suddenly shy and uncomfortable. "I…I do not know you well. It is my hope that we might have more time to become acquainted with each other if we did not marry straightaway."

"And we cannot become acquainted *after* we marry?"

She could feel the splotches of color dappling her face from embarrassment. "Once we have married, there are certain…that is, you will be expected to…" She was dying inside. How could she possibly mention something as intimate as consummating a marriage to him?

He leaned forward and kissed her with surprising gentleness. She sat motionless as he took the daffodils from her and placed them on the ground. With his hands against her cheeks, he kissed her again, holding her face up to his.

She felt the rippling awareness of something inside her responding, wanting to kiss him as he was kissing her, but she was new at this, and shy. As if understanding the way she felt, he held her close, giving her time to adjust to the feel and nearness of him, of the scent she was coming to know as his alone. She had never felt so alive, so aware of the magnetic pull of a man's body. She relaxed against him and followed his lead, until she felt as if he touched all her secret places. She shuddered in response and pushed him away. "I think that should be all the lessons for today," she said, breathlessly trying to control her breathing.

"Is that what it was? A lesson?"

"Not for you, certainly, but for someone unschooled in such matters." She paused, debating with herself. Honesty or coyness? she asked herself. Which shall it be? "You must understand what you are dealing with here, milord. When it comes to matters of the heart, I am a novice. I have nothing to guide me save my own romantic notions, which I fear are terribly out of date, inadequate and ill-formed, when compared to the reality. I have not had a Season in London, and because of my early betrothal, I never had a beau." She stopped speaking. This was not coming out the way she wanted. She doubled her fists in frustration. "Oh, blast it all! I am trying to tell you…"

He drew her back to lean against him and put his arms around her. She felt the weight of his chin as it rested on the top of her head. "It is nothing to be ashamed or embarrassed about," he said, and she could feel the vibration of his words. "Time is critical for both of us, however I will grant you as much time as possible. I have contacted the minister, but I have not set a date. Perhaps we can do that in a few more days."

"Yes," she agreed, "after all, what can happen to change things in such a short time?"

His only response was to turn her, so that she lay in his arms, gathered close against him. Her eyes fluttered shut, and she sighed deeply. There was security here. She liked that. She also liked the strength in his arms, the heat and the hardness of his body, so close to hers.

A long-held moan vibrated from low in her throat when his mouth closed over hers. His kiss was hard and seeking, almost brutally erotic, his lips moving over hers, again and again. He kissed her cheeks, her throat, her ear, tugging on the lobe. Her heart pounded painfully and the blood pulsed into her starved lungs.

She tucked her face into the folds of his soft linen shirt, feeling the weight of him against her. His mouth moved over the pulse in her throat, and he whispered, "Don't be frightened, lass."

She could not help smiling. Among his many talents, she discovered a gift for the absurd.

Hot, confused and trembling with anticipation, she wanted him to…she had no name for it, and no knowledge, either, but the desire was there. The need for him burned brightly and she yearned for him to take her where she had not been before. All rational thought evaporated under the heat of his kiss and the fiery burn of words whispered against her bare throat—words that told her what he wanted to do to her, what he would do, because he knew she wanted it. And she did.

She felt intoxicated, as if her blood had turned to brandy, flowing hot and burning, touching every part of her, searing, then smoldering, and finally leaving her weak and languorous, the heat having burned away any thought of stopping him. It was not until his hand covered her breast that she realized her dress was open. She was powerless, lost in the stamp of desire branded across his face, the passion-filled eyes, the longing that became heavier with each breath.

His hand left her breast. His mouth quickly took its place, while he pushed her gown down farther, lower, across the flat plane of her stomach, lower, until it found safe harbor and came to a melting stop. She moaned and moved against him, lost in a world that she did not know existed, where every consciousness fell away into oblivion and she was surrounded by a stark silence.

Nothing existed but him. She felt the magic of his hands and wondered how he knew what to do so well—and just how to do it. It did not matter that others had shown him, or had lain beneath him as she did now, burning with need, opening beneath the quest of his mouth, his hands. Untold numbers had taught him this, but it was she who gathered the fruit.

He might not be hers now, but he would be.

Soon, he would know she was his, that she had belonged to him since before she was born, not by forfeit, or seizure, or even a gift, but because it was meant to be. She wondered how she could have felt so shy with him a moment ago, and so brazenly open to him now. It was what they both wanted. She could not deny that, any more than she could caution herself with the reminder to stop him now, while she still could. In a moment, she told herself, and then realized all too late that the moment had come and gone.

He knew where to touch her, how to touch her in a way that called forth her wildness, her untamed spirit that so perfectly matched his. She yielded to him, knowing he wanted her as much as she wanted him, when she heard his groan and felt the power in his fingers threaded through her long hair.

When he took what she gave him, she knew instinctively that it was good and perfect. She would never even consider he had taken advantage of her inexperience, or that he seduced her. She knew what she was about as surely as she had known what he wanted—what she wanted, and had wanted since she first encountered him. At last, the unknown mystery was solved. He had shown her the way of it, and she was glad. She would never have enough of him—even a lifetime was too short.

She lay beneath him, as spent as he, her hands moving absently in his sweat-dampened hair. His scent floated over her, a fresh, wind-whipped smell of the out-of-doors, of grasses and flowers, of wild things and the harshness of spring—the very essence of life. She yearned to tell him of her feelings, of the newborn love that she nurtured deep inside. She was afraid the time was not yet right to speak to him of love, and she knew she would have to hold the secret unto herself for a little longer, tucked away in the center of her heart.

She needed to know he belonged to her and no other, but she could not claim him any more than wax can hold feathers fast too near the sun. He did not have her openness, her desire to share all she felt inside. He hid what was within him in the darkest shadows, forming a dungeon unto himself, fearful to trust, too stubborn to love, doubtful of loyalty, too cautious to reveal himself and walk in the brightness of the sun.

She looked up at him, his proud, dark head hovering like a bird of prey over her. He regarded her silently, searching her face. She wanted to tell him he would not find the answers to his questions there. She saw his expression change, and disappointment swept over her. He was detached, separate from her now, impenetrable and resistant, for he had closed himself and sealed his heart against her. It was too late to tell him anything, for the mask had slipped back into place.

"Forgive me," he said at last. "That is not what I meant to happen. I knew better. I should not have allowed it to go so far."

She pulled her dress up to cover herself and said nothing. She lay in mute silence and watched him dress, not moving to dress herself until he offered to walk her back. She sent him on, to walk back alone. They had gone full circle, and now that passion was spent, they were back where they had started—the Scottish thistle and the English rose—and a million miles apart in everything, except in the memory of close proximity where two entwined bodies had lain.

With a heavy heart, she realized he was her knight in shining armor, but she would never be his lady-fair.

18

Philip left for London at a frenzied pace. He rode like a lunatic, with little rest for himself or his horse, until the poor animal could go no farther.

In spite of his push to arrive early, he lost three hours trying to procure a fresh horse midway through his journey. By the time he arrived at the home of Meleri's sister Elizabeth, he was greeted with the news that she was not at home.

"When do you expect her?"

"The entire family is on a holiday in Italy," the butler replied. "They will return in a fortnight."

"Did Sir William accompany them?"

"Most certainly he did, your lordship."

Philip was about to consider going to Italy, when he remembered Meleri had another sister living in London. "Would you happen to know where Lady Elizabeth's sister lives?"

"I do, indeed, your lordship, but Lady Mary is not in London at the moment. She is at their country home in Kent. Would you like me to write the address down for you?"

"If you please."

Once he had the address, Philip set off for Kent. After a mad dash to get there, he arrived too late to call upon Lady Mary and had to take a room at a nearby inn. At ten o'clock the next morning, he presented himself at her house, only to be told she was out riding. He had run into nothing but snags, detours and disappointment since becoming entangled in this jumble of a farce, trying to locate the whereabouts of his missing fiancée, then her father and now her sister. It was a quest filled with impediments, hindrances and obstacles that continued to mount up and cost him precious time. Upsetting though it was, however, there was nothing he could do about any of it. Even now, he had no choice but to accept the butler's invitation to sit in the parlor and wait for the return of Meleri's sister.

And what a wait it was… Three bloody hours he had to sit, listening to some great-aunt in her dotage babble on about everything from aardvarks to zucchini, until he was actually wondering if anyone had ever actually died from acute boredom.

By the time Mary arrived with her daughter, Grace, and her gaggle of honking children, he was almost praying she would not return at all, and he would be spared the drama of marrying into this family of lunatics.

Mary was bouncing a fat baby, which she identified as her latest grandchild, in her arms. "Heavens, I have no idea where Meleri might have gone. We were never very close, you know. Elizabeth is the one who was always more *tolerant* of her. But, Elizabeth is in Italy at the moment."

"Yes, I was so informed. That is my reason for coming here," said Philip. "You cannot think of anyone Meleri might turn to in a time of need? She is *your* sister."

"She is my half sister and she is *your* fiancée, so why don't you think of someone?"

"Like you, I was never very close to Meleri. However, it is of the gravest nature that I find out where she is."

"Lord Waverly, I am doing my best and trying to think of someone," she said. She paced back and forth in front of him, patting and cooing at the baby until he was insane with anxiety.

"Surely there is someone. An old friend, a distant relative, minister…"

"Her nanny! I believe her name was Agnes. Yes, I am sure it

was Agnes. She would be as likely a choice as anyone, I think. Father was always talking about how devoted she was, how Meleri was so very fond of her. I'm sure you remember." She paused and gave him a considering look. "Well, perhaps you don't remember."

"Do you know her last name, where she lives?"

"Goodness me, I haven't the remotest idea. I did have her name in a letter my father wrote, but I think I tossed that letter out years ago."

"Would you mind checking?"

His words obviously startled her. "Here," she said, thrusting the overweight consumer of too much food at him.

She left the room and Philip looked down at the burden of deadweight in his arms. He had never held a baby in his life—had not, in fact, come within ten feet of one—but he bounced the baby as he had seen her do, until his arms were aching from the baby's weight.

"Here it is," she said, coming into the room and waving the letter. "Faris. Her last name was Faris, but I'm afraid it won't do you a bit of good. I happen to remember that Agnes married several years ago, so her name would no longer be Faris."

"Can you think of anyone I could ask?"

"My best guess would be to ask someone at Humberly Hall. The servants there all knew Agnes. Perhaps one of them kept in touch with her.

"Would you like…oof!" she said, when Philip thrust the baby at her and bolted from the room.

"Well, I never!"

19

It was raining when Meleri paused from her sewing to look toward the window and frown. "It doesn't seem to be letting up."

"No, milady," Agnes said, "it is raining steady, sure enough. That does not mean it will continue to do so. The rains here can go as quickly as they come."

Agnes returned her attention to putting a hem on Meleri's new yellow dress, while Meleri sat across from her, sewing buttons on the bodice. For the past few minutes, she had stopped sewing to gaze out the window, observing the patterns left on the windowpanes by rivulets of running water. She could not keep her mind on anything for very long before thoughts of Robert superseded all others. The memory of being held in his arms, the power and force of his passion, the depth of emotion she saw on his face all lingered in her mind.

Whatever he felt for her, she knew it was not indifference. That measured up poorly next to the love bursting into full blossom in her own heart. Before, she felt intrigued by him, but things were different now. She was falling in love with him, and that made her vulnerable. She knew she must tread carefully. It was not a feeling she liked, nor was it one she could do anything about. Being vulnerable meant she could be hurt, and the probability of that happening with a man like Robert was greater than she liked to admit.

"There," Agnes said, and bit the thread in two. "All done!" She glanced down at the bodice, as if searching for any buttons left undone. "Are you finished, milady?"

"No, but this is the last one." She quickly took a few more loops with the needle and tied the knot. "All done."

She held the dress against her and looked at herself in the mirror. "Such a lovely soft color." She wondered what Robert would think about the dress. Did he care for this shade of yellow? Would he like it with her red hair?

"Why don't you wear it today?"

Meleri agreed that was a grand idea and soon had the dress on. Agnes was ready with a compliment. "Milady, you look so lovely in that color."

Meleri picked up her apron and tied it around her waist as she went downstairs. Just as she came off the last step, Robert appeared and she almost ran into him. Instinctively, his hands came up to grasp her upper arms.

"Whoa, there!" He looked her over with thorough regard, but made no comment about the way she looked. Disappointment came like a flood drowning out all her former elation. She had taken great care with her appearance, and yet he hardly seemed to notice anything.

"I'm glad I ran into you," he said. "I will be spending most of my time working in the fields for the next several days. I leave quite early. I doubt you will be up before I go. If you should have need of me, send one of the servants to find me."

"Oh, I did not realize you…that is, I didn't know…"

"You didn't know that I work?"

She immediately felt like a moron for phrasing the statement so. She knew men worked, of course, but she ignorantly assumed all landed gentry worked like her father, by spending a few hours in their study each day, going over figures, or discussing the running of their day-to-day affairs with their overseer. She blushed. "Yes, but I did not mean it to sound that way."

"I don't have the luxury of being the kind of earl you have in England. You might say I am a working earl. This time of year we have more work than the few men in our service can deal with. We are humble farmers. We grow and raise everything we eat on the land that surrounds us. It takes everyone working together to get it all done."

"I find it gratifying to hear you put being sensible and pragmatic before arrogance and pride."

"Do you?"

"Yes, I do. What one can do, two can do faster."

"A good point."

"And a valid one. I do thank you for taking the time to enlighten me as to your whereabouts. If I should have need of you, I will send for you."

With nothing more than a curt nod, Robert left.

Meleri wondered how he could go from lovemaking to being scarcely civil in such a short period. And they said women had a changeable nature? In the end, she decided it was pointless trying to figure him out. The best idea would be to give him plenty of room and let him work things out for himself. In time, he would come to realize he needed her. Time would mark her worth. As for her, calm forbearance would be the key. She would need patience, and a great deal of it, before they both had what they wanted.

Not long after he left, she reached a decision. If her husband-to-be had to work, she was not about to loll around in lazy repose. "If he works, I will do the same," she said to Agnes.

Agnes set to work on altering another dress, but Meleri stopped her. "Leave the sewing for now. I want you to come with me." Meleri explained they would begin working today, telling her what they would be doing. "Although everyone had been more than kind, I know there must be those who feel some resentment toward me because I am English. I want them to see me as willing to do my part."

"And I'll stay here and sew."

"I need your help, Agnes, as well as your support. No one wants to ride into battle alone."

With a regretful look, Agnes dropped the fabric. "Where is the first battle, milady?"

"I think we should start with the great hall. Come along, Agnes. Don't be weak at a time like this."

Agnes closed her eyes and prayed, "Lord, help thou my force-less nature to be strong."

"Will you stop trembling like you've swallowed shiver pills? Be firm. Be strong. 'I think, therefore I am,'" she quoted. "You must act brave and you will find that you are. In the meantime, you cannot let them think you are weak."

Agnes shook her head slowly. "I'm afraid thinking wouldn't do me any good. I am certain they already know I have no back-bone, milady. Pure gelatin, it is."

"Then you must pretend you are made of sterner stuff than you are. Head up. Shoulders back. Stand tall. Learn to look them square in the eye when you speak. If there is anything they admire, it is courage and fortitude! We must show backbone or these Scots will run slapdash over us and make our lives miserable while they are about it."

Agnes still had her reservations. "The cook…the one called Fiona. Have you seen how large she is? She has arms like oak limbs. She isn't going to like our interfering."

"Oh, fie! Fiona will not be a problem once she learns we mean her no harm. It's the unknown that people distrust." Seeing that Agnes looked almost ill at the thought of accompanying her, Meleri said, "Agnes Milbank! You are hopeless. I daresay you could not say boo to a goose! I would have never taken you for such a pusillanimous mouse. Where is your spirit?"

"Gone, milady."

"Agnes, be forceful. Be spirited. You break easier than a biscuit."

"I know, milady, I truly am sorry. I am not a brave person. My mother said I crumbled like an old ruin. I fear she was right. I was born with the heart of a chicken. Peace at any price! That is my motto."

"Nonsense."

"It's true! I believe the best way to deal with aggression is to yield to it." Agnes stopped what she was doing, then looked toward the door. She heaved a great sigh, looking so dejected Meleri had to fight back the urge to laugh. "Maybe I'll be feeling braver by the time we get downstairs."

Grim as a gravedigger, Agnes followed her mistress, and the two of them set off. They stopped by the kitchen and found Fiona and three young women working. The four of them immediately stopped what they were doing and turned to stare when Meleri and Agnes entered the room.

"Good morning," Meleri said. "It's looking like it is going to be a lovely sunny day, and very welcome after so much rain, don't you think?"

The women looked at one another but said nothing. Meleri did not let that disturb her as she began to take mental stock of the room. She was becoming accustomed to the ways of Scots and their tendency toward silent regard.

Her first thought was, how could anyone work in a kitchen such as this? She had never seen such disarray. Why, she would not have been surprised to find a dirty sock or two, stuffed behind a pot that had boiled over.

The dried herbs hanging overhead must have been hung there during the Crusades, for they were pale and powdery, positively cracking with age. Next, her gaze traveled to the bucket of ashes sitting by the fireplace, then to the tarnished tongs and rusty grate, and lastly, to the grimy pots that hung overhead, her eyes lingering for a moment on the festoons of cobwebs that draped and ran from pot to pot. There was an appalling layer of dust, which covered everything not in use.

Fiona and the other help gaped in an openmouthed fashion as Meleri made her visual inspections, occasionally dragging a finger over a bowl, pot or a piece of crockery, to check for grime—and finding plenty. No one said a word, but Meleri did not let that bother her. "I would like you to show me around the kitchen, so I can familiarize myself with everything here."

"Why? Was there something wrong with your breakfast?" Fiona asked.

Meleri was distracted for a moment by the long wooden table where two girls were chopping vegetables. A mound of dirty crockery almost covered the table between them. She could not help but wonder how they could work under such cluttered circumstances.

About that time, she noticed Fiona was looking at her strangely, and she realized she had asked her a question. "Wrong? Oh, no, there was nothing wrong with my breakfast. It was very good, actually. I do hope there will be time for you to show me how you made the scones. They were quite the tastiest I've had."

"Then why would you want to look about the kitchen?"

Fiona's large, flowerlike face was looking quite perplexed. "I know the castle is understaffed," Meleri said. "If you could show us about, I am certain we can manage on our own. I will need a few things…soap, brushes, sponges and plenty of hot water."

"You will have to speak to Effie about that."

"Why?"

"Because Effie is the housekeeper."

"But you are the cook and therefore the kitchen is your domain, is it not?"

"Aye, it is, but you must speak to Effie about the things you need for your bath. We've never had anyone take a bath in the kitchen."

"I don't want to take a bath."

Fiona had a face that went beyond plain. The skin was thin and as tightly drawn as a lady's corset. Her eyes were a lovely shade of dark gray that matched her hair, but they bulged a bit too much to be called pretty, especially when she focused them narrowly, as she did now. "If you don't want a bath, then why would you be wanting the supplies?"

Pomp and circumstance! Was the woman always going to be so inquisitive about every little thing? She was soon to be the lady of the house, was she not? If she wanted a pear tree planted in the middle of the great hall, it should be done without any further adieu. One look at Fiona told Meleri she was settling in, like a winter storm.

She would be hard to budge.

"I want the supplies because Agnes and I wish to help with the cleaning."

Meleri was thankful she knew how to work, having done it frequently at home. At first it had been out of boredom, but soon she found a certain amount of satisfaction in it. She turned to Agnes, who stood there looking as indecisive as a weathercock. "Let us familiarize ourselves with the kitchen, then we will move to the great hall. It is sorely in need of a thorough cleaning."

"Waste of time," Fiona said.

"Why is that?" Meleri asked.

"We don't use the great hall very much."

"You used it the evening I arrived."

"That was a special occasion. Truth is, I do not have any help to spare, your ladyship. These girls are needed here in the kitchen to help with the evening meal."

"I am not asking for any help, Fiona. I know you need all the help you can find. Truly, I do not know how you manage with just three girls to help you. I would not dream of taking you or your help from your duties. All I want are some cleaning supplies. If you would be so kind as to show me where I can find them, Agnes and I will do the rest."

"In that cupboard," she said, pointing out the location, then she returned her attention to the pot she was stirring.

"Come along, Agnes. Let us see what we can find." Meleri walked with sure, determined steps to the cupboard and threw open the doors. She began to take stock of the things they could use—bits of flannel, a scrubbing brush with most of its boar bristles missing, half a bar of yellow soap and a broom that appeared to have been made from the missing boar bristles.

She began heaping Agnes's arms full of the things she would need. When Agnes could hold no more, Meleri dropped the bar of soap into a bucket, then hooked it on her arm and closed the cupboard. She stopped to add some water to the bucket from the water barrel. Next, she added a couple of dips from a pot of hot water boiling over the fire.

Pushing Agnes through the door ahead of her, Meleri was soon out of the kitchen and in the great hall. Once Agnes had deposited her supplies on the long banquet table, Meleri handed her an empty bucket and the small broom. "Here. Take these and sweep out the fireplace."

Agnes took the bucket and trudged toward the fireplace as if she were going to her own execution. However, she got into the spirit of things before long and even managed to hum a melody or two as she worked. From time to time, Meleri joined in, but for the most part, she was concentrating too hard on what she was doing to think about the words to a song. She was surprised when more hot water arrived, lugged into the room in a large cauldron by two young boys, whose names she learned were Fingal and Gowan.

"Well, Fingal and Gowan, you look like very strong, young men."

"Aye, milady, we are the strongest in these parts."

"That is good to hear, for I have need of a couple of strong arms to assist us."

They dropped the cauldron with a cavernous, hollow sound that echoed throughout the empty hall and made a dash for the door. They were not fast enough, for Meleri stopped them before they made good their exit, catching each of them by the ear. "Not so fast, my laddies," she said, guiding them back to where they'd left the cauldron.

"We are needed to muck out the stables, milady."

"I think the mucking out of your lord's hall is more important than his stables. Now, put some hot water in that bucket and toss in a bar of soap. I want you to scrub every stone on the floor. You may start over there, where Agnes has already swept."

"But we are supposed to clean the stables!" Gowan wailed.

"Cleaning the hall will be much more fun, and when we are through, you will be proud to have had a hand in it. Besides, you have no choice. The earl has gone to the fields, and that leaves me in charge. Now, do as I say or I'll pin your ears to that far wall and leave you there for everyone in the castle to see."

They exchanged glances, and she knew they were trying to decide if she meant what she said. They grumbled to themselves a bit, whispering and looking in her direction, but in the end, they did as she asked.

It was midafternoon before Agnes swore she was starving and went to the kitchen. Meleri stayed behind to finish cleaning the chandeliers that hung over the long eating table. Once she'd removed the dust, she rubbed everything down with oil and replaced the candles. When finished, she gave the signal for Gowan to pull on the rope that would raise the huge iron chandelier back to its rightful place, below the heavily carved beams overhead. This was quite a task, since the great hall was two stories high.

Meleri and Fingal cleaned the iron candlesticks, which stood on tripod bases, and afterward, impaled new candles on the vertical spikes. Agnes returned in better spirits after her lunch and began to fill the oil lamps on tall stands that were scattered along the walls. Meleri turned to Fingal and Gowan. "Take down the paintings and stack them against the wall. When you finish, move the tapestries lying on the end of the table into the yard. Beat them carefully, until there is no more dust."

Their next chore was to clean the ornately carved wood paneling and replace the tapestries, which were in very poor condition. Meleri thought how splendid the tapestries she had in her chest at home would look hanging here. She made a note to discuss sending for them and all the other things she'd inherited from her mother and grandmother.

When everything was cleaned to her liking, the long table was covered with white cloths, which Meleri found to be remarkably clean and in good condition—a most welcome surprise she discovered in a cupboard hidden in the paneling. Next, she carried the iron candlesticks to the table and placed all six of them in the center, at intervals of several feet. Satisfied with the way they looked, she stepped back to survey the results and found she was more than pleased. Now it was a table fit to eat upon, one she would not be humiliated to seat a guest before.

It was almost dark when they finished cleaning. As Gowan and Fingal lit the candles, Meleri and Agnes stood proudly at the end of the room to admire their work. Meleri had not realized before now what a truly magnificent hall it was. Its proportions made it fit for royalty, and the wainscoting on the walls rivaled that found in the king's own castles. She had never realized what a difference cleaning made, but that alone would not have created such a room. It was more than apparent that in spite of what the Douglases were now, they had, at one time, been very, very rich. The next question looming large and unanswered in her mind was, What had happened to all that wealth?

"You were right, your ladyship," Gowan said as he approached, a wide, pleasure-filled grin on his face, "this was more fun than mucking out the stables."

"And it does make me feel proud," Fingal said as he joined them. "You will tell the earl we helped, won't you?"

"That won't be necessary."

The four of them turned at the sound of the voice to see Robert walk into the hall accompanied by Hugh and Iain and two young girls who looked identical. Robert, she noticed, was going over the room with a critical eye. "Have you had everyone in the castle working in here all day and not on their regular chores?"

Hugh, always the buffer between the two of them, laughed and said, "If she got any work out of the help around here, you ought to congratulate her. I wonder what she used to persuade them. I have never seen anyone here that was capable of getting two thoughts together, let alone completing a task to this degree. Mostly they resemble a swarm of bees without a queen." He gave Meleri a teasing grin. "What did you do? How did you get them organized? Gram gave up two years ago and threatened never to leave her room again." He walked around the hall, taking in all the changes. "This is remarkable."

Meleri smiled at Hugh and gave a curtsy as she said, "Why, thank you, Hugh."

"What about these two scoundrels?" Iain asked, indicating Gowan and Fingal. "Did you have to threaten them with severe measures?"

"She showed us what to do," Gowan said proudly.

Fingal added, "And we did it all by ourselves. No one helped us, did they, milady?"

"Gowan and Fingal worked most diligently. We couldn't have done it without their strong arms."

"I hardly recognize the place," Hugh said.

"Nor I," Iain agreed. "It has been years since the hall looked this good. It's amazing, isn't it?" he said to Robert.

"Oh, yes, it's absolutely, positively amazing."

If he had slapped her in the face, it would not have hurt her any more than his sarcastic reply. She waited a minute longer for him to say something equally complimentary, but he never did. To hide her disappointment, she looked down at her hands and was appalled at their appearance. She put a hand to her hair, fearing she looked a fright with a kerchief that must be dusty and feathered with cobwebs and her white apron carrying a great deal of what she'd removed from the hall. Well, she told herself, there is nothing to be ashamed of. It was good, honest work, and she was every bit as proud as Gowan and Fingal for the doing of it. She lifted her head proudly.

No compliment was coming. Instead, Robert introduced her to Iain. "This is my uncle, Iain."

"I believe we met the day you arrived, Lady Weatherby."

"I am loath to admit I was more concerned with my own comforts than being gracious. I hope you will forgive me."

"No need to explain," Iain said in a manner that reflected his good nature. "I was married for several years. I also have two daughters, so I have some understanding of how the female mind works."

"Explain it to me when you have the time," Robert said, and everyone laughed, except Robert.

Meleri joined in the laughter, and when it was over, graced Iain with a warm, heartfelt smile. From the moment she saw the acceptance in his eyes, she was completely won over by this tall, distinguished man with eyes bluer than a robin's egg.

Iain turned to the two young girls standing beside him. "These two bonnie lassies are my daughters, Catriona and Ciorstag.

"Twins?" she asked.

"Aye," Iain said, "and twice the trouble. Whatever mischief they find is doubled."

"And redoubled," Hugh added. "They never do anything alone. Always together, aren't you, my lassies?"

The girls went to stand on each side of Hugh and hugged him with obvious affection.

"I cannot believe girls so lovely could be a bit of trouble," said Meleri. "What are your ages?"

They gave her a quick curtsy in unison and answered at the same time, "Twelve, milady."

"So, now you have met everyone in the family," Iain said.

"Yes, everyone Gram has to fret over," Hugh added.

"That is what grandmothers do best," Meleri replied.

Ciorstag said shyly, "Gram says a home without a grandmother is like a loch without water."

Iain laughed. "My mother has a vested interest in her opinions. They are never wrong."

Meleri hardly noticed when the laughter died down, for she was too busy studying Robert's face as he looked around the hall. She thought for a second that she caught a semblance of pride in that look, and it filled her with so much warmth, she felt dizzy. But then it disappeared so quickly, she began to wonder if she had seen it at all. Well, there was one way to find out. She turned and placed her hand upon his sleeve—something that was difficult for her to do. "And what about you, milord? Does the hall meet with your approval?"

"Aye, you have done a fine day's work," he said, looking around. "It is something you should be proud of."

"I am proud of all the help I had."

Robert was studying the slight forms of Gowan and Fingal. "I am glad to see someone found a way to inspire these two ruffians to do an honest day's work."

"It was both honest and of long duration," she said, giving the boys a bright smile. "I couldn't have accomplished half so much without them."

To Gowan and Fingal he said, "I am placing you under my lady's direction for as long as she has need of you. You will report to her each evening for your assignments for the following day. You will be wholly devoted to her slightest whim, her every command. Whatever she asks, I expect it to be done. If it is not, you will answer to me. Is that understood?"

"Aye," they said, grinning like the gargoyles on the parapets of the oldest wing of the castle.

Robert must have seen her troubled expression, for he said, "Does this not please you?"

"It isn't that. There is much to be done here, and I need their help, 'tis true, but I do not wish to usurp your grandmother by being placed in charge. I am perfectly willing to work under Lady Douglas's direction."

"Don't worry about my mother," Iain said. "Although her mind is sharp, her eyesight isn't what it once was. She also has an overwhelming tendency to catnap whenever she sits down. She has neither the inclination nor the stamina to perform such tasks as you have done today. The servants long ago realized that, and they have used her age to their advantage. What this household has needed for some time is someone younger, with a healthy Presbyterian bias against idleness."

"I suppose I have detained you overlong," Meleri said, "and I have much to do if I am going to appear for the evening meal looking better than I do now."

"Lady Weatherby?" Catriona asked.

"Yes?"

"Might we, Ciorstag and myself, help you with your chores and cleaning?"

"We do not know a great deal about cleaning, milady, but we would like to learn, and we are most eager and willing," Ciorstag added.

Meleri glanced toward Iain, who smiled at his daughters and said, "I know a little work never hurt anyone. I have long wished they had a woman closer to their age to instruct them. I would consider it a great service if you would take them under your wing."

"I can think of nothing that would give me greater pleasure." To the twins, she said, "I am delighted to have your help. But please, you must call me Meleri. How about we start tomorrow, right after breakfast? Do not forget to bring an apron—and wear something old. Can you do that?"

The girls looked at each other and giggled. "Aye, old is all we have," Catriona said.

20

Late that afternoon, with Agnes following closer than a shadow, Meleri stopped by the kitchen to speak briefly with Fiona, then continued on to the great hall. She was puzzled to see Robert lingering in the hall.

"Good evening, milord."

"You seem shocked to see me here."

"Yes, I am quite surprised. I would not think you would tarry here any longer than necessary."

"I was waiting for you."

"For me? Why?"

"So I could walk you to your chamber."

"If you have no further need of me, milady, I will go to my room now." Agnes barely finished the words before she was through the door.

Robert watched her go. "That woman is all sail and no anchor."

"Only around you."

"Why?"

"Because you frighten her, milord."

"Frighten her? How? I did not say a word to her. I think she is terrified of anything that moves."

"Only if it growls."

"I did not growl."

"Perhaps she did not see it that way."

"I merely said I would walk you to your room. You consider *that* a growl?"

"It was the inflection, your tone of voice. If you will pardon me for saying so, you are a bit of a growler, milord. Instead of pronouncing your words clearly and distinctly, you have a tendency to sound like you are snarling."

"A growler, you say?"

She nodded. "Most definitely."

He laughed and they continued on their way, out of the hall and into the long gallery, which contained what she called the great curved stairway, for it was massive and wide, as large as any she had seen in the grandest castles in England.

Ahead of them, she noticed Corrie and Dram, lying in their customary place at the base of the stairs. When the dogs heard them coming, they turned their large heads to watch. It was apparent the moment they recognized Robert, for their tails began to thump madly against the stone floor. "Your dogs happily await you," she said. "Unlike Agnes, they do not fear you."

"And you?" he asked, taking her arm and drawing her around to face him. The intensity of his gaze searching hers caused her to feel the heat rising to her face. "Do you fear me?"

"I have a healthy respect for you," she said, and saw immediately that her response pleased him.

"You have a healthy respect, do you? Well, lass, I suggest you keep it." He gave the dogs a quick glance. "They are not so particular as you would think. They await anyone who will open the gate so they can bound upstairs and find a place to hide while they sleep."

"Yes, I remember my first meeting with Corrie." She glanced at the gate across the stairway. "Who plays the bagpipes?" she asked suddenly.

"Bagpipes? No one plays, at least not anymore. At one time, Iain was quite a deft hand at it, but he has not played for several years. Now I am the only one who plays, although it is not something I do often. I cannot remember the last time."

She frowned, wondering who had been playing the day they arrived.

"Why do you ask?"

"On more than one occasion I have heard someone playing the pipes. The first time was the day we arrived."

"It must have been the wind you heard."

"No, it was bagpipes. I am certain of it. Each time, the melody has been the same."

"Hmm" was all he said, and she did not mention it again, preferring to change the subject. "This is a quite the loveliest staircase," she said, admiring the massive forms carved in the oak balustrades.

"Aye, it was quite grand at one time, but it is in need of repair, and the molded plasterwork on the ceiling is crumbling. The wood on the staircase is dented and chipped from falling plaster."

She tilted her head back and looked at the ceiling. "Water has leaked in through the roof. I shall add that to my list," she said.

"You have a list?"

She pulled a small piece of foolscap from her pocket and smiled up at him. "With me at all times." Her attention was suddenly taken by a huge painting in the gallery as they passed. She was puzzled why she had not noticed it before.

It was quite large, at least five feet wide and eight feet tall, by her estimation. She paused and stared intently at the painting, and as she did, she tried to decide what it was about this particular piece of art that disturbed her.

She recognized Beloyn Castle in the background, but the two deerhounds portrayed there were not Corrie and Dram. That was when it occurred to her that her attention was held, not by what she could see, but by what she could not see. It was obvious, even to her untrained eye, that there had once been a figure portrayed there—a figure that was now missing.

Finding this most peculiar, she turned to Robert. "This painting appears to have something missing. Was there a figure, or an object that was painted over?"

"No, it was not painted over…but neither is it as it was first painted."

"You mean something is missing." She studied the painting again. "Is it a person?"

"Aye. William, the first Earl of Douglas."

"So, it was painted over."

She could not miss the way his eyes seemed to light up in a humorous fashion as he said, "Not exactly."

"What do you mean, not exactly? It was either painted over, or it was not."

"Was not," he said, looking down at her with a teasing look. "Have you not heard Beloyn Castle is haunted?"

"Haunted? No, I had not heard that particular bit of news. Is it one ghost, or several?"

"Only one that we know of."

"One…you mean the ghost of the earl that is missing from the portrait?"

"Aye."

She waited a moment, mulling over what he had said and waiting for him to finish the story. When he did not, she ran out of patience. "Are you going to tell me what happened?"

"Aye, I will tell you because I can see you won't rest until you know the way of it."

"Aye," she said, mimicking him, "I won't rest until I have the whole of it."

He went on to tell her the story of the ill-fated Douglas clan and how they came into the title, how they lost it and regained it again. He began with Sir James Douglas, called the Good, who was one of the captains of Robert the Bruce. "After Bruce died in 1329 at Cardross, he was buried in Dunfermline, without his heart."

"Without his heart?" She shuddered. "Why would they do that?"

"His heart was removed and entrusted to Sir James, who had been instructed by Bruce to take it on a Crusade in fulfillment of a vow and to bury it in Jerusalem. At the time of his death, when he made Sir James take the vow, Bruce gave Sir James his sword, where the words *And Thair Bury My Hart* were inscribed upon it."

"You mean Bruce's heart is actually buried in Jerusalem?"

"No. It never reached Jerusalem. Sir James was killed in 1330, fighting the Moors in Spain. Bruce's heart was brought back to Scotland and buried at Melrose Abbey."

"How sad to think his heart traveled so far only to be brought back to where it came from. Is that when the Douglases were given the title?"

"Aye, it was because of Sir James's loyalty that Bruce's son, King David II, bestowed the earldom on the Douglas family, and the heart became the principal emblem of the Black Douglases. After Sir James's death, his brother, Archibald, drove Edward III out of Scotland, wearing only his shirt and one boot. Edward returned to Scotland in 1333 and marched on Berwick, capturing the Lowlands. In 1355, Berwick was recaptured and the English beaten by William Douglas, the nephew of Sir James, at Nesbit Muir." He paused and looked at her. "Are you certain you want to hear all of this? Family history can go beyond boring."

Not your family history, she wanted to say, but what she answered was "Yes, every single, solitary word. Leave nothing out."

"This is quite trying on my memory of Scottish history. I have been out of the schoolroom for some time now."

She cuffed him on the arm, feeling relaxed and enjoying his lighter mood. If only he were like this more often. "For shame! This is your family history we are talking about. You should have every small detail permanently etched in your mind. Now, on with the rest of the story, if you please."

"Are you that anxious?"

"Of course. If I'm going to be haunted by ghosts and forced to believe in them, I have a right to know as much about them as I can."

"As you wish," he said as he lifted her hand and brought it to his lips. "By the time Sir James won glory as one of Bruce's captains, the Douglas power rivaled that of the crown. Sir James's son, Archibald, was made Lord of Galloway and Warden of the West March. He was also given Threave Castle, which is a mile to the west of Castle Douglas and not far from Beloyn. In 1357, my ancestor, William, was made Earl of Douglas and became the Earl of Mar by his marriage with Margaret, sister of the thirteenth Earl of Mar."

"So, he was the first Earl of Douglas and the man missing from the portrait?"

He nodded and continued with his tale. "William's son, James, the second earl, was killed at Otterburn in 1388, in a battle between the Douglases and the Percys. The Queensbury branch of the Red Douglases are descended from James, the second Earl of Douglas. His half brother, George, became the Earl of Angus in 1389. The Douglases, as I said, were a powerful family. Too powerful, and when King James II was six years old, he was placed under the care of a regent, who was immensely powerful and the next heir to the throne."

"It was the Earl of Douglas?"

"Aye, but Douglas died in 1439, leaving two young sons, so the regency passed to Sir William Crichton, who feared the Douglases and their power. In 1440, he summoned William Douglas, the sixth earl, who was a mere lad of fourteen, to dinner with the little king in the great hall of Edinburgh Castle. The earl's younger brother and a friend accompanied him there. Once they were seated, Crichton had a plate carried into the hall that bore the symbolic Black Bull's Head, which was a token of death. He then murdered the earl, his brother and the friend."

"Oh, how awful. They were just children."

"But not too young to be a threat, or too young to die."

"What happened then? Did the Douglas clan retaliate?"

"Not right away. The vast Douglas estates were divided up, and for a time their power was diminished. After William was murdered, he was succeeded by his great-uncle, James Douglas, known as James the Gross. James, who was the seventh earl, was thought by some to have connived at his nephew's murder. In 1443 his son, William, the eighth earl, succeeded James. He was negotiating with the English, the Earl of Crawford and John of the Isles—three extremely powerful men negotiating with the enemy. King James made some effort to conciliate

Douglas, but his advances were rejected. It is said that William, the eighth earl, went out of his way to provoke the king, while his allies, the Islesmen, seized Inverness. In 1452, the king, perhaps recalling the incident that happened when he was six, invited the Earl of Douglas to dine with him at Stirling Castle. Douglas went and during dinner he was stabbed by the king himself."

"They could do nothing to him, of course."

"Aye. He was the king. It was the tactful judgment of Parliament that the earl was guilty of his own death by resisting the king's gentle persuasion. For a time it seemed the dead earl's four brothers might, with English help, successfully defy the king. In the end, the king won out, and James Douglas, the murdered man's heir, fled to the Isles and then to England. At the Battle of Arkinholm, his three brothers were defeated and killed. The power of the Black Douglases was finally broken and Parliament agreed to the forfeiture of their vast estates.

"Immediately, King James began the systematic destruction of all the Douglas strongholds, which included a two-month siege on Threave Castle in the summer of 1455. The castle resisted and was not taken by force, but it surrendered eventually and was made uninhabitable. Beloyn Castle was next on the list."

"That was when the ruined wing was destroyed?"

"Aye, and after that, our family never regained their powerful position or their wealth. All that remained was their honor and their pride, along with a few scattered remnants of the glory that was: family portraits, suits of armor, some furniture and books."

"I hope the king paid for what he did."

"He did. A bomb burst at Roxburgh in 1460, killing James. By 1474, Archibald Douglas, Earl of Angus, head of the Red Douglases—who rose upon the ruins of the Black—had replaced the Black Earls as the chief menace to the crown. Archibald, who was known as Bell the Cat, rose up against King James III, at Lauder, and hung many of his favorites from the bridge. Later, Douglas and his men returned to Edinburgh, taking the king with them. In 1488 Archibald managed to capture the king's young son and proclaimed him king in his father's place. Later that year, they met the king at Sauchieburn, south of Stirling.

"It was during that fight that King James's horse bolted and threw him. He was badly injured and called for a priest. A passerby, who claimed to be a priest, stabbed him to death as he lay helpless in the kitchen of a mill. His son, James IV, was crowned, and for a time, Archibald was his regent. The king married Margaret Tudor, sister of Henry VIII. In 1513, the king was killed at the Battle of Flodden Field, which killed the flower of Scottish chivalry."

"What do you mean, 'the flower of Scottish chivalry'?"

"Nine earls, fourteen lords, many clan chiefs and hundreds of their followers were killed. James V was just a baby when he became king. His mother, Margaret, assumed the regency. In 1514, Margaret married the Earl of Angus, the powerful Red Douglas, and the young king was a virtual prisoner. In 1528, he escaped and vowed Scotland would not hold the two of them. He was true to his word, and the Earl of Angus was driven across the border into England."

"Strange as it sounds, my grandfather was of Tudor blood. It is ironic, is it not?"

"Scottish thistle and the English rose," he said, stepping closer to her.

"The Thistle and the Rose," she said, looking up into his face and feeling disappointed when he did not kiss her.

"So, now you know the whole story."

"Not all of it. You never said what happened to the first earl. The one in the portrait."

"He left."

For an instant she stared at him, not grasping what he said. "He left?"

"Aye."

"What do you mean he left? Painted figures do not leave portraits."

"This one did."

"You are telling me he came to life and walked out of the painting."

"He did not come to life, per se, but simply disappeared. Actually, it was a hundred years later when he left."

"Then, how could he up and leave, unless he was…"

"A ghost," Robert finished. "It is his ghost that haunts the castle."

"Have you seen him?"

"No one has."

"Then how do you know he exists?"

"We know."

"Well, I don't know and I don't believe it."

"You may not believe, but some things you will have to accept, and one of them is the fact that the Earl of Douglas was in this painting…and now he is not. Explain it any way you like."

"All right, if I should accept that, then tell me why he waited over a hundred years to leave."

"You remember I said the Douglases lost the title in 1452?"

"Yes, you said King James had William murdered, along with his brother and a friend."

"Actually, King James is the one who drew his dagger and stabbed the earl first. Then his courtiers joined in and soon William was dead. Immediately after his death, the ninth earl sprang into action and proclaimed the king a murderer. The Douglases were defeated at Arkinholm and the earl was exiled. King James, although only twenty-one, resented the power of the Douglas clan, and he ordered the systematic destruction of all the Douglas strongholds. Threave Castle, which lies not more than a few miles from here, was under siege for over two months. The king attended the siege, having left his residence at Tongland Abbey to reside in a field tent he had erected on the grounds of Threave. Even though Threave was bombarded with heavy shots from a bombard…"

"Wait a minute! What is a bombard?"

"It was a legendary siege gun of gigantic proportions. Although they used it in the siege, Threave remained intact. It surrendered only after the garrison commanders were paid off and offered safe conduct. Threave was annexed to the crown until it was given to Lord Maxwell in 1640."

"And Beloyn? What of it, milord?"

"Beloyn Castle was not so fortunate. Its garrison commanders refused to surrender at first, and this so angered King James that, when they did eventually surrender, he ordered the castle to be slighted."

"Slighted? You mean destroyed?"

"Aye, it was partially destroyed and made uninhabitable."

She looked back at the painting and found herself thinking about the ruined wing. "That is when he left," she said, her voice barely above a whisper.

"Aye. Before the castle was surrendered, they only had time to remove the furnishings and paintings you see here. They were hidden away in the dungeon. What was saved was only a small fragment of the Douglas wealth. The other paintings and furnishings were removed before the castle was slighted."

"And moved to the king's residence, more than likely."

"Probably, at least most of it showed up in his possession within a few years. However, there was one painting, a Van Dyck portrait of the Countess of Sussex, which has never been found."

Meleri could not hold back the burst of laughter that bubbled forth with her next words. "Perhaps the first earl decided he preferred to spend eternity with the countess instead of two dogs."

He smiled down at her. She was warmed by this gentler side of him and found herself hoping he would come to trust her enough to show this side more and more. He had such a beautiful smile. What a pity he did not show it more often.

"I take it your theory is that when we find the painting of the Countess of Sussex…" he started.

"We will find the earl is with her," she finished. "It is as good an explanation as any, don't you agree?"

"Aye, I understand he had an eye for the lassies."

"Especially the Countess of Sussex."

Suddenly—*bam!*—one of the paintings in the gallery fell and went crashing to the floor.

Corrie and Dram sprang to their feet and began howling and pacing back and forth.

Robert laughed. "On second thought, perhaps I was wrong."

It was her turn to laugh. "Fie! I really think you believe all of this ghostly talk."

"I believe it, but I have lost faith in it," he said seriously. "Have I convinced you?"

She shook her head. "No. I do not believe in ghosts and nothing could make me change my mind."

Bam!

Another painting crashed to the floor.

Corrie and Dram were truly agitated now, and their pacing became more frantic. Up and down the gallery they went, pausing frequently to stare up at the painting with the missing earl.

"If I were you, I might consider changing my mind," he said.

"Why?"

He laughed. "Because if you don't, every painting in the gallery will end up on the floor."

Her heart fluttered. "If no one has ever seen him, how do you know he is living here?"

"There are signs…"

"What do you mean, signs?"

"There are times when the servants say they hear strange noises and feel a cold chill enter the room. Other times, the dogs will start acting strange, and we will get an uncanny feeling that someone is in the room with us, although we cannot see anything. From time to time, things will disappear around the castle, only to reappear somewhere else."

"Humph! That is not much to convince a person to believe in ghosts." Meleri saw his expression and said, "I know, you don't have to see something to believe in it." She thought about that for a moment. "Well, perhaps *you* don't." She turned to go on up the stairs. "If that is all there is to the story, I will bid you good-night."

She started up the stairs, having climbed two steps before his next words caused her to jerk to a halt.

"That is not all there is to the tale."

She whirled around quickly and noticed that going up two steps made her the same height as he. His face was only a few inches away from hers. Memories of their lovemaking darted into her consciousness, and she had an overwhelming urge to step closer. She found it strange that she was feeling such a power-ful attraction toward him while standing here in the midst of the stairwell, discussing ghosts. In spite of where they were, how-ever, she felt drawn to him and could feel herself tilting forward. His lips were quite close now. Close enough to kiss. "There is more?" she whispered, her mouth brushing his lightly.

"Aye," he whispered, bringing his mouth closer to hers. "A bit more."

He drew her against him, and her arms found their way around his neck. "Tell me the rest of it," she whispered against his lips. "Tell me everything."

He held her more tightly, his mouth covering hers in a kiss that was intimately questioning, hard, then demanding. It was also long, but when he broke the kiss, she found herself think-ing it was not nearly long enough.

"Tell me," she whispered, "tell me the rest of the tale."

He closed his eyes, as if to settle his brain and regain some of his earlier composure. It gave her no small satisfaction to think he found her unsettling. He released her and she was sorry she had asked for the rest of the story. Why had she insisted upon talking about a man dead almost three hundred years, when she had a very living, breathing and more than willing man right here in her arms?

He kissed her nose and eased his hold on her. "It was not only the Douglas power that the king envied. It was also their immense wealth. Their jewels alone were said to be worth more than those in the possession of the king himself. In fact, they were said to rival the crown jewels of England."

"And the king ended up with them?"

"No. Like the Van Dyck of the countess, the jewels have never been seen again."

"Were they hidden in the dungeon with the other things?"

"No one knows. The castle was being slighted. We know the paintings and furniture were hidden in the dungeon because they were found later, but the jewels simply disappeared."

"They must have been stolen by some of the king's men during the siege."

"I don't think so. They would have shown up somewhere by now. They were not the kind of jewels to remain hidden, and some of the stones were well known—the kind that would be easily identified."

"Then, they must still be hidden here."

"I've always thought so, but the big question is, where? If they haven't been found by now, they probably never will be."

"So they have disappeared without a clue," she said, finding she was becoming quite entranced by this ghostly tale—in spite of her determination to remain impassive.

"Aye, but tradition says they will be returned when the one with the heart of the truest Scot is living here at Beloyn. At that time, according to the legend, the earl will reveal the location of the family jewels, then he will return to his rightful place in the painting."

She rolled her eyes. "This story is getting more unbelievable by the minute. How can you believe all that poppycock?"

"Let me show you something."

He took her arm and walked her down the length of the gallery, pointing out many of the portraits of the Douglas women, drawing her attention to the exquisite jewels they wore. Majestic and dazzling, though they were, one stood out over all the others— a magnificent ruby necklace with stones as big as a falcon's egg.

"Beautiful, isn't it?"

"Yes," she whispered. "Extraordinary. Quite the most exquisite thing I have ever seen."

"They are called pigeon's blood rubies. They are reported to have been taken in Spain during the Crusades."

"It is breathtaking. I can't believe such lovely gems may never be found."

"That is the way of things sometimes."

"Has anyone ever looked for the jewels or searched the castle? I mean really, really looked?"

"There have been numerous searches, and many of them on

quite a grand scale, not to mention dozens of smaller ones over the centuries. I would think it a fair estimation to say every stone in the castle has been looked at as a possible place of hiding."

"Then perhaps they aren't here. The earl could have hidden them anywhere… England, even."

"No, they are here. Supposedly, the earl left a note that said the jewels would never be taken from Beloyn. It was also said the note contained a riddle that, if solved, would reveal the location of the jewels. Unfortunately, the note has never been found."

"Naturally." She felt the surprisingly gentle stroke of his fingers against her cheek before she realized his hand had moved.

"Perhaps it has been found," he said softly. "It pleases me to discover there is more to you than I first thought."

Her face grew warm. "You discovered quite a bit of it the other day," she said, then shyly ducked her head.

He drew her face up to his, and as she looked into his eyes, she saw so many things—including humor; something reinforced by the slight uplift of the corners of his mouth.

She turned her head and looked off, gazing down at the place where the dogs lay. She did not say anything more, for at that moment Corrie came to stand beside her. The dog poked her nose against the palm of Meleri's hand. "I think I have been accepted by your dogs."

"It is not a bad beginning," he said, watching her stroke Corrie's head.

Meleri started up the steps again and he fell into step beside her. Neither of them said anything for some time. She thought of this threadbare castle, and how its very walls were radiant with a happy spirit. She had the feeling that here, in this place, she could be anything, do anything, say anything. She could love or be indifferent. She could even hate. She was unfettered, at liberty to stay the same, to change or to be a chameleon if she so chose.

"You are fortunate to have such a family," she said after a moment.

"I consider myself fortunate to have you." He stepped toward her and took her in his arms, not in a manner of passion, but as a brother would comfort a sister. She released a long, quivering sigh and said to herself three times, *I will not cry.* With an acute sense of peace, she lay her head against his chest and listened to the steady assurance of a strong heart.

21

Robert held her for quite a long time, feeling his heart pound, saying nothing. He was disturbed and distracted, unable to think of much beyond the yearning he felt for her. His thoughts were all directed toward one thought. She was his. He had thought of little else since the taking of her virginity. Even now, he wished to make love to her again.

He was surprised, when at that moment she lifted her head and stared up at him, turning those unbelievable eyes upon him. *You are so lovely, so innocent, looking at me with heavy-lidded desire,* he thought. *I want you so much I ache. But, you are English and not to be trusted. Because of the man you were to wed, my sister is dead.*

An eye for an eye…

Sweet little English witch, if you knew the truth, would you still want me? He could feel the soft weight of her in his arms, the firmness of her breasts pressing against him. His heart thudded with desire and left him dizzy from the effect of it. He saw she was looking at him in a way that was watchful and wary. Did she know what he was thinking, that he ached to take that yellow dress and rip it from her body, so he could see again what she was like beneath it? He threaded his hands into the red hair he found so intriguing, the memory of her sweet breasts burning into him.

His body hard and trembling, he had no control over himself now. He was unable to stop the arms that tightened around her, just as he was powerless to resist kissing the mouth that parted with breathless surprise. He kissed her hard, wanting to hurt her as she was hurting him, but it had the opposite effect, and he heard her moan as her arms went around him.

He broke the kiss long enough to open the door to her bedroom and close it behind him. He swept her into his arms and carried her to the bed. Without taking his gaze from her face, he began to unbutton the yellow dress, pushing it from her shoulders, until it fell in a buttery puff on the floor. Her undergarments fell away next, until she was bare and beautiful, the lines of her body gleaming smooth and pale in the moonlight. He took a small step backward to get a better look at the full swell of breasts, unable to stop his hand that came up to take the full weight in his palm.

He kissed her with shattering intensity, tenderly and long, sensing her weakness to resist her overpowering desire to mate with him once again. He pushed her back to the bed, covering her with his body, knowing just how to kiss her and where to touch her to make her moan with wanting. Everywhere he put his mouth, she was smooth, fragrant skin and tightly coiled muscle, and she fitted against him perfectly, the sharp outline of him cradled against her belly.

Breath mingling with breath, his senses were dulled to inaction as if drugged with an opiate. The silky coolness of her hair fell away from her face and brushed against the heat of his arms, surrounding him with the scent of roses.

"I want you," he whispered. "I want you, and I know you want me back."

"Yes," she whispered, "'tis true. I do want you."

His lips skimmed over the softness of her throat as he whispered, "I have thought of little else," and was surprised to discover what he said was true.

He had been called many things when it came to women—everything from a seducer to a magician—because he could bend their will to his so easily, but he found no pleasure in magic or in seducing her. He wanted to possess her, but not at the cost of her destruction. He knew now, that he could not punish her for what another had done. That was why he had not been able to bring himself to marry her before now. His motive was wrong, and something within him knew it.

Suddenly she was undoing his clothes and he helped her push them from his body. He groaned as her hand touched him and slid down, across his ribs, her touch fire and ice. When her hand reached out to take him, her eyes were intense and brilliant. He could not stop now any more than he could halt the cascade of water over a fall.

He kissed her one last time and stepped into warm, blessed peace.

He would remember forever the feel of her, the sharp rise and fall of her breasts, the deep, shuddering breath as she closed her eyes and went over the edge with him.

God only knew he had performed such dozens of times, with an equal number of women. So, why did he mark this time as different? There had been many before her, he could not deny that, but there had been none like her, and no one had left him feeling as he did now.

A pure and perfect peace settled over him, a quiet stillness that put to rest the turmoil and hatred that had lain so deep inside him. From the darkest center of his person, Robert could feel all-consuming peace, glowing like a red-hot coal at first, then growing hotter and hotter until it burst into a white and purifying flame. A feeling for Meleri he had never felt before settled deep within his innermost being, and he felt inhumanly close to her, as if he could not tell where one of them ended and the other began.

He had not meant this to happen, and yet it had, again. She was his now. He would marry her and soon. He would not have his sons born bastards. He would send word to the minister to set the date.

Soon, he thought and closed his eyes. Soon she will be mine, completely.

He slept for some time before he stirred and opened his eyes. He looked at the window where the last remains of the fading day filtered into the room, a murky gray haze, both stingy and sparse, barely enough to afford him enough light to study the woman sleeping quietly beside him.

The pale, faded hue of evening light worshiped her skin. She was so lovely, lying in blameless nudity, the softly rounded contours of long, luscious legs entwined in a spiraling curl of damp sheets. Even now, the lingering smell of ripe, mellow roses filled him with a longing to take her in his arms and make love to her again. Exquisitely lovely, even in repose, she lay in a tangle of rosy hair, one hand curled beneath her chin as she slept. The still-moist curve of full lips brought back a pleasure-flushed memory of what it was like to kiss her. He leaned down, his face so close to hers that the slight rush of his breath stirred the sweat-dampened hair that edged her face, and he wondered for a moment if he would be able to make himself leave her. Every slumbering inch of her called out to him, and he burned with a need to respond.

Enveloped in the gossamer hues of an indigo twilight, he searched his feelings, his motives, even the logic of what had passed between them, looking for answers, afraid of what he would do if he found them. He had never afforded himself the luxury of looking at the world with undefiled eyes. Everything he saw was edited by a definite set of rules, the cultivation of a lifetime of intolerance, bias and bitter hatred. Her innocence called out to him for protection, when he knew he would be wiser to guard himself against it. Emotion came in a painful flood, leaving him raw with the reality of how easily he could lose what he had so recently found. Life was tenuous at best, where every day's blessing hung by the slimmest gossamer thread, as silken as a spider's snare and equally entangling.

Gently, slowly, so as not to wake her, he leaned forward and kissed the dewy texture of her cheek, cursing himself as he did for his newfound benevolence that tempered the fire within.

He arose and dressed quietly, then drew the covers over her

with great reluctance. Unable still to leave, he looked down at her, waiting for a calming of inner disquiet. He could not use her for his own shameful purposes and now even the thought that he had once been capable of such caused a burdening weight that sank like a cannon ball in an ocean of guilt.

He turned and left the room.

The dogs were waiting for him at the bottom of the staircase, gazing at the painting with the missing earl with a comprehension and knowledge he could not discern. What was it they sensed about this painting? What drew them to this same spot, time after time, and held their attention? Always, this painting, he thought, and none of the others. He paused and looked up at the portrait, studying it in detail. He had grown up with this painting and could vividly remember staring up at it as a young boy. He could remember, too, listening to his father and Iain as they repeated the legend of the Good Douglas, the first earl, the Black Douglas and Douglas the Red.

He had never been afraid of the ghost and had, for many years as a youth, anxiously looked forward to his return, but over the years he had become disillusioned. Although, he knew that in spite of his anger at the old earl for not returning and giving them the Douglas jewels, somewhere deep within him he still did believe.

"Staring at the painting won't tell you where the jewels are. I know, because I tried it. I also tried talking to it. That didn't work, either."

He turned to see Iain and the twins approaching.

Iain stopped beside him and the two of them stood gazing at the painting, but when Iain looked back at his daughters and saw their large, round eyes, he laughed and said, "I'm not going to tell you any ghost stories today, so don't get your hopes up."

"But…"

Catriona got out only that one word, before Iain told them to "run along and change for dinner."

The twins giggled at something only they knew the truth of, then hitched their skirts and charged up the stairs.

"I'll wait for you down here," he called after them. They giggled again and kept on going. "I wonder if I'll ever be able to make ladies out of them."

"When the time is right." Like Iain, Robert had watched them race up the stairs, never tiring of the sound of their girlish laughter. "They have brought many smiles to our dour faces. I never thought I would admit it, but I have truly enjoyed watching them grow up."

"I don't know how I would have survived Anne's death if she had not gifted me with our daughters. Like you, I have enjoyed each moment I have had with them. Already, I begin to worry about what I will do when it comes time for them to marry."

"That time will come sooner than either of us suspect. They are at an interesting age, no longer girls and not quite women."

"Have you made love to her?"

Iain's directness startled Robert, but he did not answer.

Apparently, he did not need to. "Have you taken leave of your senses? To use her this way is abominable! How long do you intend to allow this to go on without the union of marriage?"

"I intend to marry her," Robert said simply.

"It better be soon. Have you thought about the possibility that you could get her with child? Is that what you want…for your son to be born a bastard?"

"Why don't you shout, so everyone in the castle can hear you?"

"They will know soon enough, whether I shout or not. I am surprised at you, Robbie. I thought you capable of more self-control. I also thought you a man of more breeding than to use a woman for revenge. Your father would have never considered such."

"What good is high moral standing, if it causes you to lose your life before your time? And what about Sorcha? Did her high moral standing serve her well in the end?"

Anger held Iain's jaw in its grip. "Then consider this. She is English and titled to boot. While I have as much reason as you to despise them, I am a respecter of those in power. If the king gets wind of this, your goose is cooked and the rest of us will be tossed in to baste in the same pot along with you. You should put more thought into what you are about. Your casual fornicating could cost us all dearly."

"I never fornicate without a reason," he said with a ruthless disregard of his uncle's position of respect. "I also have more to lose than anyone here, therefore I would suggest you follow your own advice and put more thought into what you are about. While we are at it, I will add that I have had about all of the interfering and meddling in my life that I intend to have. I can follow only so many dictates without losing my sanity."

Iain lowered his voice. "I don't mean to be overly dramatic…."

"A goal you have fallen short of."

"In spite of what you may think, my purpose was well-meaning and…"

"Aye, like the streets of hell…paved with good intentions." Robert made a move to leave, then checked himself and turned back to Iain. "Tell me something, Uncle, did you sleep with Anne before you were married?"

It was apparent that his words struck Iain with unexpected intensity and caught him off guard. "No. I didn't make love to Anne until two months after our wedding."

Robert regarded him in a new light. "Now, that must be some sort of record. Care to elaborate?"

"No," he said, letting his feeling show in his choice of words. "One thing about love is that you can really make an ass of yourself."

"You're calling yourself an ass? For you, that is a milestone."

"I'm saying I was foolish. I was a young lad, you see… younger than you. I was inexperienced, and a wee bit overeager. I went after her with so much enthusiasm I frightened her and she kicked me out of the bed."

"And you waited two months because of that?"

"No, I waited two months because I broke my leg."

When Robert stopped laughing, Iain said, "Seriously, I would not wait overly long to marry. Even the best-kept secrets have a way of surfacing. If Meleri should get even the slightest inkling as to the depth of your feelings about Sorcha's death, it could mean the end of it. No lass, no matter how much she cared, would want to be on the receiving end of a marriage for the sole purpose of revenge. If that happened, there would be no way you could force her to marry you. English or not, there is not a minister in Scotland who would perform a wedding when the lass did not want to be married. You are running a great risk by waiting."

"You underestimate me, Uncle. I have everything under control. There is nothing to worry about."

"For your sake I hope you are right."

Dinner that night was not bad, but it might as well have been for all the food Meleri ate. In Robert's opinion, food was food. You ate what was in front of you and you were thankful that it did not bite you back. After watching her pick and poke at her meal, putting nothing more than a few sips of wine to her lips, he looked down at his plate with a more critical eye. Was he missing something? There was brown meat—possibly venison or jugged hare, judging from the vegetables around it. He decided it looked more like jugged hare…but even then, he was not certain. There was a white blob of something that might have been potatoes, and then again, it might not be.

The oatcakes were easy to recognize, though, and for that matter, so was the crannachan. He was not certain how it was made, but he remembered his mother mixing oatmeal, crowdie and raspberries together with a little whisky and honey, which she then left to steep overnight.

He looked down again and frowned. Crannachan was pudding, but it looked as though it had been left to steep for a month or so, and there seemed to be a scarcity of raspberries and an overabundance of oatmeal. He supposed Meleri was accustomed to grander fare, and he stared with rueful apology at her sitting next to him, quietly giving the food in front of her a bewildered stare.

"What is it?" she whispered, looking down at her plate and giving it a poke before she turned a questioning face in his direction.

He looked at the brown lump on her plate. "It's probably jugged hare."

"Probably? You mean you aren't sure?"

"Not completely, but don't let that discourage you. The good news is I have narrowed it down to three or four possibilities. Beyond that, I'm afraid I'm no help."

"Jugged hare," she repeated as she picked up her fork and gave it another stab or two. "Why would anyone want to jug something that looks like this?"

"I don't know."

"You were never interested in finding out?"

"I was never that curious about what I ate, apparently. For whatever reason, I never asked about it. Maybe you jug it so you don't have to look at it."

She shook her head. "It's amazing what one can do to a piece of meat when one wants to disguise it."

"Why don't you try the oatcake?"

She wrinkled up her nose, not bothering to give the oatcake a glance. "I've eaten too many oatcakes lately."

A short eruption of laughter distracted him and Robert looked off. When he returned his attention to Meleri, he saw her cast a quick and furtive glance about the table and saw, too, the hand that came up to snatch the oatcake from her plate, then disappear somewhere in the vicinity of her lap.

Beneath the table a few seconds later, the mad thumping of a dog's tail told him she had passed the oatcake to Corrie or Dram. Obviously hearing the sound, she turned her head and stared up at him through curious eyes, a guilty expression on her face. Amused, in spite of himself, he feigned innocence and stared back at her in a guileless manner. Somehow, she made it through the rest of the meal, but she did not eat much or ask any more questions.

After dinner, the family members went their own ways, and Robert walked with Meleri to her room. When he opened her door, he chuckled at the sight of the dog lying on the floor beside her bed. He pushed the door closed and placed a caressing hand on her shoulder and lifted her chin, holding it in place between his thumb and forefinger. Her eyes widened as he then turned her face up to his. He kissed her cheek, where the delicate curls fluttered with his breath, working his way over the smooth expanse of forehead, over the brow and down her small, perfect nose. He kissed her soundly, her lips firm and trembling beneath his. When he broke the kiss, he saw her eyes were closed, the curve of deliciously long, dark lashes folded like a fan to rest against high cheekbones. Even before she opened her eyes, he saw the stain of red stealing over her cheeks.

"You aren't embarrassed by all of this, are you?" he asked.

Her eyes flew open. "I am not exactly accustomed to this sort of thing, you know."

It was said with such crossness that he wondered what he had done to upset her. "You aren't worried about what happened, are you?"

"Oh, no, I am delighted. I have longed for the day I could be gainfully employed at the Lost Maidenhead pub."

He started to tell her he would send for a minister on the morrow, but decided against it. It would be better to surprise her. He held her against him. "I wouldn't report to work just yet, if I were you."

She did not look at him but gazed into her room, where Dram sat looking at them, his head tilted to one side, as if trying to decide if they were going to enter or not.

"Dram seems to have formed a fondness for you."

"Yes, he hangs around like a heavy meal."

"You should be honored. He is not as easily swayed as Corrie. He does not take up with everyone." He pulled her closer, pressing her lightly against him. "Your betrothed. Did he ever kiss you?"

"Once, but not the way you do."

"Once? That was all? You were engaged for your entire life and he kissed you once?"

"Yes, when I was twelve or thirteen."

"He was a fool."

She looked down at her feet and spoke so softly he barely heard what she said. "No, I think he was afraid."

"Afraid of you?"

"Yes."

"Why?"

"Because the day he kissed me, I shoved him away so hard, he fell off the boat landing and into the water."

"Why did you push him?"

"I didn't like his kiss."

"What was it about his kiss that you did not enjoy?"

She threw up her arms and walked away from him, giving him her back. "I don't remember whether I enjoyed it or not. All I remember is that it made my heart sad."

"A kiss made your heart sad?" he asked, trying to understand.

"Yes. I was sad because his kiss was not so wonderful as all the dreams I had. I was given disappointment, when I so desperately wanted something to recall."

His heart seemed to light up from within. "Come here," he said softly. "Come here and let us see if we can make a memory."

22

Not in the best of moods when he rode up to Heathwood Castle on a well-lathered horse, Philip was in a panic. He hoped he would find Meleri in Gretna Green and not end up on another pointless trip. He was nearing exhaustion and desperately in need of sleep. He jumped down from his horse and dropped the reins. "Saddle Wellington for me," he called to the groom before he turned to race up the steps. When he reached the top, he hurried through the front door and took the stairs three at a time, cursing Meleri Weatherby to perdition with each furious step.

He ordered his valet out of the room. "Out, damn you! Out! If there is anything I have learned to do, it is dress myself!"

He finished dressing and went downstairs to discover his friends, Harry Wellsby and Tony Downley, waiting for him. Surprising though it was to him, he was glad to see them. He needed to talk to someone before he exploded with rage. "I did not know you two had returned to the country."

"We never left," Tony said. "Been here the entire time."

"Not by choice, you understand," Harry said.

Philip gave him a brief glance. "What does that mean?"

"It means your father had a talk with our fathers, and as a consequence, we've been banned from London for the rest of the year," Harry said.

"Damnably unfair consequence, if you ask me," said Tony.

"Well, don't think I'll forgive you for passing information to them that they passed on to my father," Philip said. "As it now stands, I could lose my inheritance."

"We came an inch away from losing ours," Tony said. "Bloody unpleasant mess, it was."

Philip was not moved. "Whatever happened to the two of you, it was nothing compared to what my father did." The story of his father's visit flowed with furious energy from him.

When he finished, Tony said, "I cannot believe he actually came into the room while you were in bed with Jane."

Philip made himself a drink and brought them up-to-date on the most recent happenings. He explained how he'd been fortunate to find even a stablehand at Humberly Hall, since all the other servants had already gone. It had been his good fortune that this man knew Agnes Milbank and where she lived. "It was my first break, and long overdue." He looked at his friends. "Now, you can appease me for telling your fathers what you did. Come with me to Gretna Green."

"I don't think I should get involved in this," Harry said.

"I second that," Tony agreed. "This is something you need to settle alone, and if my father finds out…"

"I'll settle it alone, but I'd like a little company on the way, and you owe me. The two of you can wait nearby while I pay a visit to the nanny's cottage. I assure you, I want nothing more than your presence during the journey."

Reluctantly, Harry and Tony agreed, and the three of them set off, riding at a breakneck pace. They had to change horses once more before they reached the border. By that time, it was dark, so the three of them stabled the fresh mounts and spent the night at an inn. The next morning, when they went to the stables for their horses, they discovered all three had been stolen during the night. "I can't help wondering if this isn't some kind of omen for me to mind my own business," Tony said.

"Right you are, old chap," Harry said. "I've got the same sinking feeling."

"Stop complaining," Philip said. "Horses are easily replaced."

The three of them found new mounts and rode on, until they were less than a mile from where Agnes Milbank resided. "Tony and I will ride on into Gretna," Harry said. "We'll wait for you there."

Philip nodded. "Just make sure you're still there when I return."

By the time he reached the road that led to the cottage he had been searching for so diligently, Philip was fair to loathing the name Agnes Milbank. He dismounted and knocked on the door. A man answered. "Agnes is not here," he said.

"Are you her husband?"

"No, her brother."

Philip asked question after question, but the man was tight-lipped and frugal with his answers. Having had enough, Philip grabbed him by the shirt and slammed him against the wall. "I want to know where Agnes went…in detail, and I want to know if Lady Meleri Weatherby accompanied her. Do you understand?"

"I was in Edinburgh when my sister left. All I know is what she left in her note, which wasn't much."

"Then show me the bloody note!"

"I threw it away."

Philip drew his knife and pressed it to the man's throat. "You've got five seconds before I use this."

"They…they've gone to Beloyn Castle."

With fate's clock ticking against him and his father's words ringing in his ears, Philip had no time to rest. He had to find out where this Beloyn Castle was, since Agnes's brother managed to get inside the door and close it before Philip could get directions.

Philip rode back to Gretna and met up with Harry and Tony, who were about to have something to eat at an inn. Philip joined them, and they ordered salmon pies, the only fare on the menu. Over the course of the meal, Philip told them what he found out from the brother of Agnes Milbank. "The task before me is to find out where this Beloyn Castle is."

The innkeeper brought them a tankard of ale and Philip gave him a generous tip. "I say, we are looking for a place called Beloyn Castle. Have you heard of it?"

"Aye, Beloyn Castle is the home of the Earl of Douglas."

"You wouldn't happen to know where it is, or how to get there, by any chance, would you?"

"It's no more than a couple of hours ride from here."

After the innkeeper left, Philip turned to look from Tony to Harry. "Any ideas on how I go about extracting her from a bloody Scot?"

"You don't suppose there is any chance she has up and married him, do you?" Harry asked. "She did say that day that she would marry the first man she met."

Philip had not considered that possibility. "I would not put it past Meleri to marry the first nodkin she met, but I have to believe an earl—even a Scottish one—would not rush into marriage with a chit he barely knew. But, you haven't answered my question. How do I get her away from him?"

"Well, let's see," Tony said, sounding lighthearted. "You could murder the Scot and take her...but then they would put you in prison for that. Or, you could kidnap her, which would solve the first part of your dilemma, but it would be damnably difficult traveling with her thrown over your saddle and fighting you every step of the way. So, I guess that means you should appeal to her softer side and convince her you made a terrible mistake in letting her go."

"What if she doesn't buy it? What if she doesn't believe a word I say?" Philip asked.

Harry shrugged. "If she doesn't, you better start saving your coins."

Philip finished his ale and ordered another, his brow furrowed in thought, until he suddenly said, "I think I like your other idea."

Harry and Tony looked at each other blankly. Harry grinned a moment later and asked rather jovially, "Which one? Murder the Scot?"

"Exactly," Philip said.

The humor drained away from both their faces as Harry and Tony exchanged glances. "By heavens! You're serious," Harry said, his face turning pale.

"Of course I'm serious," Philip said. "Why wouldn't I be?"

"I'm sorry," Tony said, rising to his feet, "but you'll have to count me out of this. Lying and kidnapping is one thing, but murder…I may be a rogue of the first water, but not even I can go that far. I am sorry, Philip, but I cannot be a party to something like that."

"Neither can I," Harry said as he, too, rose to his feet. "I encourage you to think about what you are doing. This is not the sixteenth century. An Englishman, especially a titled one, cannot go across the border to murder a member of the peerage without expecting some sort of justice."

Philip did not say anything more, but he was thinking his friends had shown their true colors. There was no point in trying to convince them. They were fools, both of them. They did not understand how desperate his situation was. This had to work, simply because it was the only thing he could do in order to save himself. "Go on. Get out of here. I don't need your help or your advice."

PART THREE

you want to know
whether i believe in ghosts
of course i do not believe in them
if you had known
as many of them as i have
you would not
believe in them either

Don Marquis (1878–1937), U.S. humorist, journalist.
ghosts in archy and mehitabel (1927).

23

Meleri continued to anguish over the disquiet that intruded upon her customary feeling of well-being. Something was not right, and it nagged at her until she was ready to face anything in order to put an end to it. She could not concentrate. Her appetite ceased to exist. She had never been so on edge. There was no explanation, no cause and no cure. It was simply an intuitive feeling—one strong enough that she pleaded a headache and excused herself from dinner that night.

It was her habit, whenever she walked the length of the gallery, to keep close to the windows that looked out upon the heathery moor. Often, she would pause to look upon the ruined wing of the castle that called out to her in a way that was both tragic and sad. It must have been quite magnificent, back when the king's army lay siege, but now it was nothing more than a pile of rubble, burned beams and moss-covered stones. How enormous it must have been, for to her mind, Beloyn was a huge fortress now, without the added rooms that were once housed in that ravaged wing.

Meleri was disappointed to see she had missed the sunset, for the sun had already disappeared behind the remains of the ruined wing. It was almost dark, and she was reminded that the days were starting to grow a bit shorter. Fall came a bit earlier in this part of Scotland than it did in Northumberland. Before long, it would be winter—a time for roaring fires, roasted chestnuts and long walks along pathways brilliantly colored with an array of leathery leaves.

Thinking of her first winter in Scotland, she felt a bit odd, for she was not certain of their customs and traditions here. Anticipation of the unknown made her acutely aware of the silent stillness, which surrounded her, and how very far she was from the warm company of those in the hall. She admonished herself and tried to shake off the eerie feeling of foreboding that left her spirits sagging. Why was she plagued with the sense that something was going to happen?

She caught another glimpse of the ruined wing and thought it was such a pitiful thing to be laid to waste and forgotten. How sad to have once been proud and majestic, only to fall into decay, a victim of the tall grass that springs up and the wild vines and briars that slowly creep over the ancient foundation—a place where no one walked anymore. A place once beloved now lost beneath the destruction of years.

The sound of wind that swirled around the eaves and the tall chimneys reached her ears. She quickened her step, until she realized it was not the wind she heard, and she paused to listen. Suddenly, from somewhere deep in the bowels of the great fortress came a mournful sound, a sad lamenting. The sound grew louder, the eerie, mellow tone hauntingly familiar. Someone played the pipes again—someone who knew a great deal about suffering.

With her mind concentrating on the melancholy sound, she gazed absently out the long, narrow windows. A man was standing on the tumbled stones of the ruined wing, surrounded by a swirling mist. She could not see his face, but he was close enough for her to tell he was wrapped in a plaid and playing the pipes. Behind him, the phantom specter of a great sailing ship rose up; black sails and a rotting flag hanging from her mast…a flag that carried the symbol of death.

Heart pounding fearfully, she moistened her dry lips, then

glanced in the direction from which she had just come, as if by doing so she could connect with the living and those she had left in the great hall only moments before.

By the time she looked toward the ruined wing again, the sound of the pipes began to fade, and she saw the piper and the ship were gone, with nothing left behind but the memory and the mist. With a shake of her head, she dismissed the whole episode as something imaginary. Where it came from or why she had imagined it, she did not know. Perhaps she was allowing herself to be carried away by the mood of Scotland itself.

She had the most extraordinary compulsion to turn around and rush back to the great hall. Yet, at the same time, she felt as though some force was pushing her along, forcing her to continue on her way.

The gallery was growing dim. Shadows absorbed the light. She stopped and lit a lamp, wondering as she did if anyone had ever become truly lost in this great wilderness of a castle. Her natural instinct told her to return to the others, where she would be wrapped in the warm conversation in the great hall. Only the logical part of her seemed to be functioning normally, allowing her to put everything in its place with proper perspective.

High overhead, the ornamental ceiling arched gracefully over the dark, carved wood of the curving staircase. At the foot of the stairs, she was relieved to see the dogs. Only today, they did not thump their tails madly against the stone floor, nor did they stand to greet her. Still and tense, they remained in place, gazing along the row of pictures in the gallery as if they descried a presence she could not perceive.

She gazed upon the sober faces of Robert's ancestors, eternally staring at the generations that passed. Today, they appeared no different than they had before, although this time, not even the ornate carvings of fruit and flowers that adorned the black wainscoting could counter the oppressive mood that hung over the gallery. She had the strangest feeling as she continued on her way—a feeling they were all watching her. Watching and waiting, but for what?

"Hello, my loves," she said, stopping to pat Corrie and Dram.

Since coming to Beloyn, she had heard nothing but ghost stories and haunting legends that impregnated her mind. Hearing bagpipes and seeing visions was nothing more than some supernatural humbuggery she had allowed to affect her reason. A dilettante interest in their superstitions had overridden her sound judgment and common sense. What she needed was a good dose of rationality, and she prayed for a return to some sort of mental normalcy. This is the sort of fancy that put people in Bedlam, she thought. She had to get control of herself.

First, she thought she heard bagpipes. Now she had the notion that she had seen a spirit tromping upon a pile of stones in a drizzling mist, while playing the pipes. Dear Lord above, what if these delusions persisted? After the piper, what would be next? Conversations with them?

She hesitated, waiting to see if one of the paintings crashed to the floor as it had the other day, but everything remained as it had been. Behind her, the dogs began to whimper. She turned around quickly. They were on their feet now, pacing back and forth, looking toward the gallery, where the family portraits hung, then back at her.

"Poor dogs," she crooned, "I'm passing my distress on to you." She went down the steps again and opened the gate that blocked the dogs from the stairs. "Come on up, then. You can sleep in my room tonight."

It was obvious they wanted to come, but they were agitated and began to pace a step or two in one direction, then whimper and turn away, as if they were afraid to go above stairs—something she could understand, since she was becoming a bit nervous about going up the stairs herself. She gave them another pat. "Good dogs. Robert has trained you well. You know better than to go above stairs, don't you?"

She started up the stairs, repeating softly to herself, "I do not believe in ghosts. Do not…do not…do not…"

For a moment, she thought she heard something and she stopped. The castle was eerily quiet. She stood very still, listening. She could hear nothing, but in spite of that, she felt a presence nearby.

The idea was absurd, of course. Everyone except Agnes was in the great hall or in the kitchen. She was almost angry for being so foolish as to frighten herself. This will not do, she thought, and continued on her way, in spite of the renewed agitation of the dogs. Instead, she focused on the rooms upstairs and what changes and improvements she wanted to make to them.

Meleri thought of the nursery and the small pieces of furniture she'd found in the attic, and she began to imagine the walls painted a creamy white with blue curtains on the windows and a tiny rug of blue, yellow and white. And she mustn't forget a small bed in the corner for Agnes—white, with a blue-and-yellow coverlet—for she would not even consider anyone but her own former nanny for her children.

The deep, rolling sound of a man's hoarse laughter came suddenly out of nowhere. Her heart leaped in terror. She turned quickly to give the gallery a good searching look. She saw nothing. Turning back around, she quickened her step as she continued up the stairs. She was so preoccupied, she did not at first pay much notice to the man she met descending.

As she passed him, she gave him a nod, much in the manner she would give the servants.

He nodded in return.

It did not strike her, until she reached the top of the landing, that she had passed someone—someone she had never seen before. He was dressed in a very peculiar manner. He was also hauntingly familiar.

That a stranger was coming down the stairs from the bedchambers was odd, but even more so was the fact that he was dressed in such a queer, old-fashioned manner. Was he some eccentric member of the family, with a penchant for quaint clothes, who was kept hidden away? A crazy cousin, perhaps? One confined to the unused servants' apartments next to the attic?

She turned and glanced behind her, but there was no one there. The man was gone, vanished.

So were the dogs.

Carefully, Meleri searched the dimly lit staircase and the length of the gallery. Nothing. "For the love of St. Valentine, what is going on here?" she whispered, deciding it was appropriate to call upon the name of the saint associated with lovers under conditions of duress. If this was not duress, she did not know what was.

How could he have disappeared so quickly? And the dogs? Had they decided to follow him, or had they been frightened away? She did not linger any longer, but hurried on to her room, thinking she would ask Robert about the bizarre happenings in the morning.

When she reached her bedchamber, Agnes was turning back her bed. "Good evening, milady."

Meleri shut the door and leaned against it, palms pressed behind her. "Did you happen to see a man come down the hall a moment ago?"

Agnes stopped smoothing the coverlet. "A man? No, milady. I haven't see anyone since I came up."

Meleri did not say anything further. While she removed her clothes, she was silent, reflecting upon what had just happened. She knew it was not something she'd imagined. She'd seen a man. She was certain.

While Agnes hung her dress on the door of the wardrobe, Meleri slipped into a gown of fine muslin, then sent Agnes to her room. Determined to have a good sleep this night, she went to bed, somewhat uplifted by the feel of clean bed linen and a good supply of blankets. There was nothing like a warm bed to charm away fatigue. Wearily, she closed her eyes and fell asleep almost immediately.

She did not sleep long before she was suddenly awakened. Eyes opened wide, she lay utterly still, afraid to breathe.

Someone was in her room....

She remained motionless, straining to listen for the slightest sound, but all was still and silent. There was a full moon tonight, and the places where the draperies did not come together afforded enough light to make out shadows.

Her gaze fell upon the open door of her wardrobe and the figure of a man standing before it. A cold shiver passed over her. It was not until she sat up in bed and saw only her dress hanging on the wardrobe door, that she dared to take a deep breath. She told herself she must stop this nonsense at once. Every bush was becoming a bear, every shadow a specter.

She lay back down and settled herself in a comfortable position for the second time that night. Soon, her brain wearied and she passed into a dark slumber of disturbed sleep.

The next morning, Agnes inquired, "How did you sleep, milady?"

Meleri took a moment to realize where she was. She put her hand to her head. "I…I don't know." Her head felt woolly and clogged with recollections of the past night. Blinking like a wood owl, she felt befuddled, her mind unclear. She saw the dress hanging on the wardrobe and she remembered the curious night she had passed.

"Are you feeling well, milady?"

Meleri shook her head, hoping to clear it. "I feel fine, Agnes, but I passed a frightful night. There were so many dreams…queer dreams that made no sense."

"Sometimes it helps to tell your dreams."

"Oh, I dare not tell anyone for fear they would think me insane. What tricks the mind can play upon us, what extraordinary imaginings."

"It would put your mind at ease to talk about it," Agnes said, sounding somewhat authoritative. "Others can sometimes make sense of things we cannot understand."

"I don't know that anyone could make sense of this. I only remember snippets of things…a gray-castled city that appeared out of a mist, the flutter of old flags, black sailing ships and fierce battles being fought by men with grim faces. Everything was a mixture of dim, shifting images—of soldiers, queens and treachery—all set to the haunting skirl of pipes."

Meleri rolled out of bed. "You see? None of it makes any sense."

"You've been hearing too many stories of Scotland. In truth, milady, it has a painful, tragic past, and just hearing of the tragedy that has befallen others brings out strange foreboding in many of us."

"Perhaps you are right."

"You remember nothing in particular?"

She shook her head. "It's all a blurred image in my mind now," she said. "Lay out my blue dress…or the yellow one. Quickly! I must find Robert."

Agnes began rummaging for a dress, as if some national emergency had been declared. "Do you feel you are in some sort of danger?"

"No, nothing like that. I simply want to ask him about the man…the one I saw last night. Remember, I asked you about him?"

"Yes, but I saw no one."

"I know, and my curiosity has gotten the best of me. I cannot fathom who it could have been."

Meleri dressed quickly, with Agnes fussing and clucking over her as if she were preparing for an audience with the king. "My hair is fine, Agnes. You need not do any more to it. No, I do not need any jewelry. I am not going out in public."

She was buttoning the cuff of her dress as she rushed out of the room and hurried downstairs, only to learn she was too late. Robert, she was informed, had gone to the stables only minutes before.

"It is his custom to ride each morning," Gowan said.

Meleri brought her palm against her forehead. "Yes, of course he does. I knew that, but I somehow let it slip my mind," she said, the words trailing behind her, for she was already rushing out the door. She prayed as she ran toward the stables that she would not be too late, that he had not yet ridden off.

In her great rush, she darted around the corner of the barn and collided with the horse Robert was leading. The high-strung animal shied and reared, then snorted and danced around, shaking his head nervously. Robert struggled to keep hold of the reins.

She let out a thankful gasp. "Oh, am I ever glad I found you," she said, almost hugging his horse with relief. "I was afraid you were already gone."

He smiled and brushed her startled lips with his own. She felt a tingling thrill of pleasure at the contact. "Dare I hope you are coming to care for me?" he asked teasingly. "I do believe this is the first time you've missed me enough to come searching, and so early in the morning."

"I didn't miss you…that is, that isn't the reason I was looking for you. I need to talk to you."

He stood there, as if patiently waiting for her to speak her piece. Unfortunately, her mind was a tangled jumble of thoughts. It would have been fine if he had not kissed her, unsettling man. She always had the strangest reactions to him—constriction of the throat, a stomach fluttering with a flotilla of butterflies, a racing heart and legs that would not support her. Was that love? She frowned. If it was, it was very different from what she'd expected, and certainly nothing like what the poets wrote about. Never, not once, had she read anything that related love to the malfunctioning of body parts.

"Are you certain there is nothing wrong?" Robert asked.

"Yes."

"Well then, I was about to go for a ride. If you are up to it, you are welcome to come with me."

She looked down at her blue dress. "I am not exactly dressed for riding."

"We won't be taking a turn about Hyde Park, if that is what concerns you. I doubt we will meet anyone, and if we should, they won't be of the sort who would know if you were properly attired for riding or not."

"Very well," she said, "I would like to join you."

A few minutes later, her horse was saddled and the two of them rode off.

Much to her delight, Corrie and Dram accompanied them. The dogs snuffed about the brush, jumping a rabbit now and then, but soon seemed content to lope just ahead. When they crested the hill, the dogs paused.

As Meleri reached them, she realized they were waiting to see which way to go, for the path forked, one way running along the crest of the hill, the other continuing down the other side, where the land fell away to spread out in the valley below.

Robert rode up next to her and stopped.

"It is so lovely here," Meleri said. "I had no idea there was such breathtaking scenery so close to your home."

"There is a special beauty here, although many don't realize it. The Highlands have been given the reputation for beauty. Because of that, the Lowlands are oft overlooked."

What he said was true, and she thought it a shame that such a place would go unnoticed or even overlooked. However, if the Lowlands were known for anything, it was for being the place where many of the Border families acquired their fortunes—fortunes made by robbery and violence—just like they did in Northumberland.

They rode on and she watched the graceful movement of the dogs loping ahead, wondering if they might jump one of the large red deer Iain told her about. "Iain mentioned that deerhounds were bred to hunt deer."

"Aye, that is why they are so large. It takes a big dog to bring down a large stag."

"Do you think we will come across a red deer?"

He smiled. "Iain should have told you we travel farther north when we want to hunt red deer. They have been gone from these parts for many years. Now they are found only in the Highlands. Here, we hunt mostly roe deer."

"I am sorry for Corrie and Dram as well as myself. I would have loved to see them hunt. I still cannot get over their being so huge. They are the largest dogs I've ever seen."

"The Irish wolfhound is larger."

Irish wolfhound... She thought it such a clever idea to name a thing after its purpose. It made it so much easier for one to appear knowledgeable. Which was better than sitting there with a blank, dazed look, waiting for an explanation. "I suppose it would take a very large animal, indeed, to bring down a wolf."

"Aye, like the deerhound, the breed was developed for that purpose."

She shuddered at the thought of hunting wolves, although she did not know why. Perhaps because they, unlike deer, were predators. "Are there any wolves here, or are the only ones left in the Highlands...with the red deer?"

He laughed and she knew it was not at her, but at her astuteness. "Aye, wolves in Scotland are diminishing in numbers. We do not see them here anymore. What few are left are in the Highlands."

She was relieved to hear that. "I'm glad you're a Lowlander."

The sudden eruption of his laughter caught her off guard, not because it surprised her, but because she was so distracted by the sound of it. She decided immediately that he had the most wonderful laugh she had ever heard. What a waste that he so rarely used it.

She was coming to understand Robert, for she realized he was a lot like the land—tempered by hardship and conflict. She was also coming to a better understanding of his home, of Scotland. After all its edification, after the legends, the past, the poetry and the passion, after the inherent sentiment of affinity, after the unwavering brotherhood of the clans—after each of these there resided a determined purpose, an unrelenting stubbornness born of the suffering and afflictions that came before.

She understood, now, that he was a product of that past.

Meleri was suddenly conscious of the fact that *she* was changing as much as her circumstances. She was coming to love this land as much as the man who rescued her from a horrible fate and brought her here to live with him as his wife. She owed him so much. The thought of it warmed her with a sense of gratitude and well-being.

It was this warmth of feeling, and the friendship that continued to develop between them as they rode, that caused them to ride much longer than originally planned. In her enthusiasm—born of her recently acknowledged feelings—she found that suddenly she wanted to see it all: every childhood haunt, every fellside and burn, every moor where black-faced sheep grazed.

Although parts of the border landscape were similar to her home in Northumberland, it was not a place of gentle valleys and sparkling streams. Here, the sea, which was never far away, was anything but indulgent.

Robert was quietly indulgent of her wants, which made her think that he enjoyed their newly developed closeness as much as she did. She recalled parts of her journey with him to Scotland and seeing the landscape along Solway Firth and the Irish Sea. There, the land was barren and austere, a place of low, flat, empty shores and sandy knolls, swept by wind and rain, where spindly seabirds poked about in mudflats and old wooden boats lay derelict when the tide went out.

Forlorn was the word that came to mind—forlorn and, somehow, sadly forgotten.

Here, it was different. Beyond the well-plowed hill ahead lay the country of open heaths—bare, exciting and often mysterious—with solitary upland lakes, spectacular waterfalls and evocative names, like the falls at Corrie Linn.

As they rode, she asked questions and learned he loved to talk of Bonnie Prince Charlie and the Stuarts, of Mary Queen of Scots, of Wallace, Rob Roy and Robert the Bruce. She was reminded of the tragic ends they all came to and realized part of his love and attachment to this place was because of the blood that had soaked into the land itself—the blood of all those who came before.

She was suddenly ashamed—ashamed of being English, ashamed of the part her country and her ancestors had played in the suffering of these stalwart people. She prayed with all her heart that it might be granted to her to find a way to make up, at least partly, for the terrible injustice of the past. Why did freedom always command such a high price?

She fell into a quiet sort of solitude as they rode through small wooded glens and over treeless sloping hills, sometimes hidden beneath shadows when the sun went behind a cloud. The road was narrow as it meandered along like a country stream. Farther over, the purple hills in the distance seemed austere and silent, and the cattle on the gently rolling slopes hardly seemed to move at all.

They rode for quite some time, until they came to a roofless fortress. A tree-lined stream ran in front, but behind its walls, a long slope of moorland rose, bleak and stormy. They stopped there for a while to rest the horses and dogs.

After dismounting, they led their mounts and walked for a while. Once, Robert stopped to pick a small purple flower and handed it to her. "What did you want to talk to me about?"

Goose bumps broke out along the flesh of her arms at the reminder. "I met a man last night. I was curious as to who he was."

He stopped. "A man? Where?"

"At Beloyn, of course."

"Where were you when you met him?"

"He was coming down the stairs as I was going up. He wasn't anyone I recognized, so I was curious."

"When was this?"

"Last night, after I left the hall to return to my chamber."

The concern on his face vanished as he dismissed it. "It was probably one of the servants."

"No, he wasn't a servant," she said with much conviction. "That much I am certain of. There was something aristocratic about him and his manner—not to mention his odd dress. Although it was quite peculiar, it was far too fine to have belonged to a servant."

"Peculiar?"

"Yes, very peculiar. Certainly not anything one would see every day. I would call it old-fashioned, perhaps, or maybe eccentric."

Or, perhaps, from another time… She shuddered at that thought and wondered where it had come from, but Robert laughed at that moment, and she found herself relaxing and thinking less about it.

"There are plenty of eccentric folk to be found in Scotland," he said. "It is a fey place."

"I know that, but what I do not understand is, who would be coming down the stairs from our private living quarters if he wasn't a member of the family or a servant?"

"I cannot fathom who it could have been. You know the members of my family. There have been no visitors or guests at Beloyn recently. You are absolutely certain it was not a servant?"

"More than certain. Besides, I told you, his clothes were quite fine. Strange, but fine."

He seemed to ponder that for a moment. "What do you mean by strange? What did they look like?"

She glanced off, trying to conjure up the memory of what she had seen. "Black. He wore all black, save for a bit of white, which reminded me of a ruff—you know, the old-fashioned kind they wore about the neck. He wore tights and there was a short cape attached to his doublet. There was some sort of medallion around his neck, hanging from a long gold chain. He wore a long saber at his side. A most peculiar man. Oh, he had a black cap on his head, with feathers."

"Bonnet. We call them bonnets, not caps."

"I see."

"Was he clean-shaven?"

"No. He had a pointed beard. It was short, dark and well groomed. Do you know who it was?"

"No. The description of clothing is definitely not of these times. It sounds more like the clothing from the times of Queen Mary, or before." He was quiet for a moment, almost pensive, as if troubled by something. "Did it look like any of the clothes in the portraits in the gallery?"

That sent a fresh supply of goose bumps rippling over her skin. If he tells me it was that earl who disappeared from his portrait, Meleri thought, I am going back to England. "Yes, now that you mention it, he did remind me of some of them."

"Hmm."

"Hmm? Is that all you are going to say? Just hmm?"

"For now."

He did not mention the portrait of the earl, however, so she asked him, "Do you have any idea who it was?"

His mood was jovial and his tone quite merry when he said, "I would say he had to be an eccentric, just as you said. He must have wandered in somehow, realized he was lost and wandered back out, without having been seen by anyone, save you. It is the only explanation."

She frowned, feeling he had purposefully forced a lighter mood. She could not help wondering if he was hiding something. "I don't think some stranger could have wandered in without being seen by anyone. Besides, Corrie and Dram would have surely barked."

He did not seem to buy that. "Do you have a better explanation? Perhaps you were seeing things? A ghost, perhaps?"

She had known he would get around to that, eventually. "I could not have seen a ghost," she said, taking great care to sound quite adamant.

"Why not?"

"For the simple reason—as I told you before—I do not believe in them. How can you see something you don't believe in?"

He laughed. "Perhaps seeing one will help your unbelief."

"Have you ever seen a ghost?"

"No, I've never seen one. Perhaps I believe in the myth but not the reality."

"Then why do you insist that I've seen a ghost?"

"Because you seem convinced that you've seen one, and on that basis, it seems the rational answer."

"Do you think this could have anything to do with the Douglas legend and the missing earl?"

He shrugged. "Anything is possible."

She shook her head. "No, it can't be that."

"Why not? You've heard the legend and how it is said that the earl will appear at some point in time."

"Yes, and he has certainly waited a long time. Now, ask yourself this question. Why would the ghost…a *Scottish* ghost, mind you, choose an *English* woman to be the first person he decides to show himself to?"

"*If* you saw him…*if* you have been truly chosen, you will have to ask your ghost that question. Whatever they are, I am certain he has his reasons."

If you have been chosen...

All of a sudden, Meleri seemed to swell with pride and she brightened, feeling rather privileged, as if she *had* been chosen, like Moses, to lead them out of their bondage to the past. "What do you suppose it means, then, if I have been chosen...if I am the first one to see the earl's ghost?"

Robert laughed and said in a teasing way, "It means you either dreamed it, or you had too much whisky before you went to bed."

She was not ready to water down this discussion with humor. Strange things were happening and the dogs knew it as well as she. She wanted to have some answers, not humor. "Don't make light of this. I did not dream it. I saw him. I nodded to him and he nodded back. Even the dogs were acting strange. I only wish you could ask them. It is my guess that they have seen him, and on more than one occasion. That is why they spend so much time in the gallery. It is probably the earl's favorite place to frolic."

He burst out laughing.

"What is so amusing, pray tell?"

"Do you really think a ghost would...frolic?"

"Well, why not? What else has a ghost got to do?"

That seemed to have sobered him up, for he said, "You mentioned the dogs. In what way were they acting strange?"

"When I first approached the stairs, they were sitting at the bottom like they always do, staring toward the gallery, but they were very agitated. I opened the gate and called them to come upstairs with me, but they would only come so far, then they would turn around and walk a few steps, then come back and stop. They did this, repeatedly, whining and turning this way and that, until I decided to go on up alone. I closed the gate and started up the stairs. As soon as I did, I met the man coming down. Immediately, I heard the dogs whine. I turned around to look. The man was gone, and so were the dogs. Yet, the gate was still locked. There was no way he could have opened the gate and closed it behind him and disappeared in that short amount of time. Explain also, while you are at it, why the dogs disappeared like that."

"I have no explanation. However, they are here now and looking none too worse for the wear," he said, and she followed the direction of his gaze to see Corrie and Dram running with their noses to the ground, hot on the trail of something.

She nodded. "I know, but there are other happenings, too. Remember I told you I sometimes hear bagpipes playing faintly? Well, last night, I heard them again. After leaving dinner, I stopped to look out at the ruined wing from one of the windows in the gallery. I heard the pipes, and the melody was so beautiful, almost sad. I saw something like a vision. A mist settled over the ruins and the piper was there, standing on the ruins, playing. Behind him, I saw a ship, with black sails hoisted, flying a flag of death. Does any of this make sense?"

"I'm not certain. Strange though it is, what you describe reminds me of the story about the MacCrimmons of Skye."

"Who were the MacCrimmons?"

"They were the pipers to the clan MacLeod. The MacCrimmons created many masterpieces known as *piobaireachd,* which is the big music of the pipes. One of the finest they ever did is called 'Cumha na Cloinne'… 'The Lament for the Children.'"

"'The Lament for the Children,'" she repeated. "It sounds so sad."

"Aye, it is that. Heartbreaking, some say. Padraig Mor MacCrimmon wrote the lament over a hundred years ago. He was the father of eight strapping sons, before a foreign ship dropped anchor in Dunvegan one fine day, with a deadly fever aboard. The fever spread throughout the land of the MacLeans and Padraig Mor lost all of his sons but one. In his grief, he composed a timeless *piobaireachd* for his sons who were lost."

She stopped and looked up at him, seeing the deeply etched pain of endless suffering upon his face.

"There is so much sadness in this land," she said. "It is everywhere you turn. I feel its intensity. Here." She placed her hand over her heart.

"Perhaps you are becoming a Scot in spite of yourself," he said, and took her hand in his. He brought it to his lips and kissed each finger in turn.

She felt positively molten, as if she'd swallowed a sunbeam and it broke out in warmth. How could a simple act produce so many reactions? She was suffused with slow-penetrating heat. She was trembling as if cold. Her heart stopped beating one minute, and pounded with fury the next. She was light-headed with the nearness of him, with a yearning for him to do more than simply kiss her fingers.

"A Scot," she repeated.

"Aye, is it possible?"

His eyes shining, his lips turning up at the corners, he asked if she'd had any more encounters with his grandmother.

"Encounters? Who has time for encounters? I am too busy dodging specters and things that go bump in the night. Lord love Scotland! I have not had time to form an opinion, much less have a conversation with your grandmother. Too much has been happening."

"Now I know the secret to eternal wedded bliss."

The bubble of gaiety she had been floating in burst, and in its place, she could feel raw wounds in her pride. She felt unclean and used, and wondered if this was how all trollops felt in the beginning. "You are not married, so why should you have any knowledge of what the secret is?"

"Are you becoming maudlin because you are anxious to become my wife?"

She hid her hurt behind her words. "If anyone is anxious, your lordship, it should be you. I am not the one with a royal command hanging like a guillotine over my head."

"Are you certain that is the only cause of your concern?"

"I did not say I was concerned," she said, wanting to hurt him back. "I was merely making a point."

"Aye, and stabbed me with it. Now that I know your feelings…there is no reason to rush things."

Why had he spoken so? Although she knew she was falling

in love with him, his feelings must lie in the opposite direction. She tried to keep the hurt from showing on her face, but she had a feeling he could see it well enough. To prevent him from saying something apologetic, which would surely bring on the tears, she said quickly, "So, what is the secret to eternal wedded bliss?"

"It is difficult to explain, but I could show you."

"What do you mean sh—" Her voice suddenly deserted her, for he took her face in his hands and kissed her nose, her eyes, her forehead. He pulled her closer and she felt his warmth, the solid comfort of his body. She relaxed and leaned into him. His arms tightened around her, and his lips moved softly over the surface of her cheek. He kissed her mouth firmly, parting her lips beneath his. Her flesh hummed wherever he touched her.

Beneath her hand, which she rested against his chest, she could feel the steady rhythm of his heart and wondered how it could be so steadfast, when hers was hopping as erratically as a crow. Her wandering hand suddenly slipped between the buttons of his shirt and she touched bare skin.

She gasped and made a sudden move to withdraw her fingers. He countered quickly, covering her hand with his, and held it there. "My shy, kindhearted lass, who has a hard head and refuses to believe in specters."

"I believe in them now."

Robert was looking at her strangely. "What is it? You look like you've seen a ghost."

"Sh," Meleri said, slapping at his hands. "Don't say that!" she whispered. "He might hear you."

"Who?"

"The ghost! I see him! I'm seeing him right now! A ghost! Oh, my Lord, I am seeing a real, live ghost!" she said desperately.

"A live ghost? Interesting."

"All right, be scientific. If he's not a live ghost, then he is a walking dead one." She swallowed so audibly she was certain he could hear.

Robert looked around. "I don't see anyone."

"There!" she said, pointing down the lane. "He is walking toward us… It is the same man I saw last night, and he is wearing the same peculiar clothes."

Robert looked again. "I still don't see anything."

"What do you mean you don't see him? How can you miss something right in front of your nose? He is walking, bigger than Edinburgh, smack down the middle of the lane."

"Lass, I'm sorry…"

She did not understand any of this. For a Scot who did his best to persuade her to believe in legends and ghosts, it was obvious Robert did not believe what he preached. He did not believe her, either. Evidently, he thought she was playing a trick on him.

She knew he was not the kind to take that sort of thing lightly. He let her know he had had enough of her nonsense when he dropped his hands from her. "I think it is time to go back," he said, and called to the dogs.

Corrie and Dram came running toward them, but when they left the edge of the woods and started up the lane, they suddenly stopped.

She crossed her arms in front of her in a triumphant manner, nodding in their direction, and said, "Explain that."

He ignored her comment and called the dogs again. Their odd behavior was exactly as it had been the night before, for they were agitated and whining, behaving as if they wanted to come, but were afraid to. He called them once more, and they took a few tentative steps, then turned suddenly and bolted away from the lane.

She stood quietly, watching Corrie and Dram running across a plowed field. They reached the middle of the field, and she was certain they were heading for home, when they turned sharply and made a sweeping circle to come up behind the place where Meleri and Robert stood. They stopped a few feet away. They refused to come closer, even when Robert called them.

"You see?" she said. "Well, perhaps you don't see, but the dogs obviously do. You may not believe me, but I do not think you should have any qualms about believing them. What else could account for their strange behavior?"

He seemed thoughtful. "I honestly don't know."

"You still don't believe me, do you? You think I am making this up, that I am using it as a way to poke fun at you and your Scots ways."

"I thought so before, but I no longer do. I know I was wrong. I understand something is going on here, but I am not certain what you are seeing, or more rightly, who it is that you see."

"It must be him," she said, so matter-of-factly she surprised even herself.

"Him?"

"The old earl…the one missing from the portrait."

He did not answer her.

She took his silence to mean he rejected that idea. After all, she was a woman and English, both inferiors in his mind. "Well, don't answer me, then. You either believe me, or you do not. Faith! I grow weary of all of this. First, you try to convince me that ghosts exist, and when I come close to accepting it, you act as though it was all my idea. Do not be forgetting I am not the one who made up that preposterous story about an earl who abandoned his portrait, one hundred years after he died. That is *your* legend, not mine. Frankly, I do not care if you believe it or not. From now on, I won't say anything—even if I see a whole legion of ghosts."

She wondered at that moment if the ghost had heard her, for he stopped not more than ten feet away, seemingly content to simply look at her.

Let him look, she thought. She clapped her hands on her hips and stared straight at him. "I shan't be telling you any-thing, either, you vaporous visitant…you…you wandering wraith! I do not want to see you. I do not want to be a part of this. Go find someone else to haunt and harry, you pestiferous phantom."

Robert started to speak but she cut him off.

"Talk to *him!*" she said. "He is your relative, not mine! I per-sonally don't care for either of you." To prove her point, she made a grand move to ignore both of them and walked to her horse. "I find the two of you a perfect match...a pigheaded Scot and a stubborn specter! You deserve each other."

She mounted quickly and rode all the way back to Beloyn at a fast gallop.

Robert did not catch up to her until after she had dismounted. She opened the gate and started into the garden, when she heard him ride up behind her. She ignored him and continued on her way.

"Wait up a minute," he said. "I want a word with you."

"Go away. I have decided I don't like you as much as I thought."

"Meleri…"

"You are wasting your time. Today, I am not talking to any Douglases...dead or alive."

Corrie and Dram came ambling into the yard. She snapped her fingers, and the dogs loped past Robert, slowed their pace and came to a stop next to her. "Come," she said, and started up again. "Those of us who see visions are not welcome here."

Corrie and Dram followed her inside.

The moment she stepped into the house, she saw Gram wearing a black silk dress that was a bit old-fashioned in a way that made Meleri think it belonged in one of the portraits in the gallery.

Seeing her, Lady Margaret came bearing down on her as if she had been marked for prey. "Hout! You are fairly out of breath. Where are you going in such a hurry? You look like you've seen a ghost."

"That is becoming an overused phrase around here, and one I grow tired of hearing. If you came here to have an encounter, you are out of luck. I have just seen a ghost, and I am not in any mood to discuss it."

"You saw a ghost? Where?"

Meleri threw her hands up in the air. "In my dreams...on the stairs...in the middle of the lane. It does not seem to matter. He does not appear to have any manners or preferences as to when, or where, he appears. He simply pops up, unannounced. God only knows he may decide to visit me in my bath!"

"It was the old earl," said Lady Margaret.

"I am not saying anything, and I adamantly refuse to address that statement. I have been doubted once already, and one Doubting Thomas a day is enough. I have decided to make it a steadfast rule from here on out that I will not discuss ghosts with anyone who does not believe in them... What did you say?"

"I said it was the old earl."

"Thank you. You have just moved up on my list of people I might be persuaded to like."

"Why would you say that?"

"Because, if there is anything I have learned, it is that Scots believe in ghosts when they aren't around, but the minute they appear, you suddenly turn doubtful. You, apparently, are the exception."

"Tell me what you saw."

"Why should I tell you? It is obvious you wish I would leave."

"Leave? Why would I wish that? It makes no sense."

"It makes perfect sense to me...and about as much sense as anything I've seen since coming here."

Lady Margaret stepped close enough to reach out her long, elegant hands and take Meleri's face between them. "Child, child, why would I wish for you to leave, when I have waited so very, very long for you to come?"

If Lady Margaret had slapped her, it would have been impossible to be more stunned or surprised. To say she was not overwhelmed by what she said would be tinkering with the truth. In fact, Meleri was so shocked, she barely managed to ask, "What did you say?"

Lady Margaret did not remove her hands, but she did smile at her. "I said, I have waited a long time for you to come."

"You are trying to tell me you waited for me, that you knew I was coming? Piffle! You would say anything to get what you want."

"I knew one would come, but I did not know it was you, until the morning I met you. If I appeared unkind, it was because I had to be satisfied that you were the one, that you were strong enough to stand up to the task."

Meleri narrowed her eyes suspiciously. "What task?"

"The task of being Lady Douglas."

"That I could do with my eyes closed."

Lady Margaret smiled. "Aye, I ken you could. You remind me of myself at your age."

Meleri put her hand to her head. "None of this makes sense. I need to go lie down."

24

She hurried on up the stairs and was almost to her chamber when she saw Hugh leaning against a doorjamb watching her with a big grin on his face. "What are you doing?" she asked. "Snooping?"

He laughed. "When the volume is that loud, you don't have to snoop."

She kept on walking.

"Wait a minute. What's wrong between you and Robbie?"

"Nothing, except I don't understand the way his mind works. I doubt that I will ever understand. I don't think *he* understands."

As she thundered past, Hugh reached one arm out in a lazy manner and caught her. "Whoa there, lassie! I think we need to take a walk."

"I have just returned from a ride. The last thing I need is more exercise. You are just the type to offer a glass of water to a drowning person."

"Humor me, then. Come along."

He led her outside with him, ignoring her sputtering threats to run back the moment he released his hold. His eyes, she noticed, were as blue as cornflowers and brimming with playfulness, and even that irritated her.

After a bit, her resistance began to tire her. It was no use. He was too persistent. Sometimes surrender was the easy way out. She noticed they had already passed the barn and the stone stable, and now were heading toward the orchard.

Two kittens bounded out of the bushes. Meleri stopped to pick up the calico and left the yellow one to follow behind. They walked on in silence, while Meleri gave her attention to the kitten. After a few minutes, she put the kitten down and watched it join the other. "Are you going to lecture me?"

"No, I am going to tell you some things that should give you a deeper understanding about the man you are going to marry."

"I don't think I want to talk about Robert, and I think he's forgotten all about marriage."

"He hasn't forgotten. He is giving you time to settle in. However, since you don't want to talk about Robbie, you listen and I'll talk. It always helps to have new understanding. Things look better sometimes when seen in a different light."

"Vexing is vexing, in any light."

"If you want to be happy with a man, you must understand him a lot and love him a little. Women never understand this, because their needs are different. Consequently, they love a lot and understand very little."

She did not say anything, but she was thinking about what he said as they followed a narrow, winding path that ran down to the stream, where everything looked like a kaleidoscope of illusion and color, constantly changing at the whim of the sun. The air was cooler here and heavy with the scents of summer flowers and the humic richness of leaf mold. The shrill call of a bird overrode for a moment the low, continuous babble of swift-running water, bubbling over smooth stones. Meleri kicked a rock out of the path with the side of her foot.

"Has anyone told you about our sister?" Hugh asked.

"Only to rub in the fact that she was killed by the English."

"Aye, it happened ten years ago. Sorcha was sixteen when she died."

They reached a fence, made from stones gathered from the

turnip field and stacked along the perimeter as a border. Hugh took her elbow and indicated a place. "We can sit here."

She sat down, not bothering to hide her displeasure. She folded her hands in her lap and waited.

"When Sorcha was sixteen, she went to England with a friend. When it was time for her to return, Robert decided to go to England alone to escort her back to Beloyn. When they were close to the border, they stopped to rest the horses. Sorcha walked down to the river to watch the geese swim. On the way, she encountered four Oxford students traveling through the English Border country on their way to Scotland to hunt grouse.

"When they saw her, they decided to hunt a little two-legged game. They gave chase, and when they ran her down, they did not stop there. She was a real beauty and a virgin and too much for them to pass up, so they had their sport with her. After all, she was only a Scot."

Meleri felt a rueful quiet settle about her, a great silence that stretched like the narrow shafts of sunlight that stabbed through the trees. Shadows contrasting light. Man and woman. Good and evil. Life and death. Throughout it all, there was pain. So much pain that suddenly she knew what happened and said, "One of them raped her."

It was not a question, for she knew the truth already, but some things in life cannot be skipped over. Some things must saturate and bog you down until your only choice is to wallow in them. However, once done, you must get up, wash yourself off and go on as before. There is no forgiveness in wallowing. Forgiveness comes after. Perhaps that was what plagued Robert. He still wallowed in his grief. Until he put it behind him, he would be unable to forgive.

"Aye, one of them raped her. He was the oldest and he took her first, and when he finished, he gave her to the others. When Robbie heard her screams and came running to help, they overpowered him, taking turns holding him and making him watch, while they took her and took her and took her. It did not end until all four of them had raped her."

She did not say anything. She could not.

"When they finished having their sport, the leader hit Robbie in the head several times with his gun. I am certain he meant to kill him. They could not leave a witness, and a shot might have brought someone. When Robert came to, he found Sorcha's body floating in the stream."

"They drowned her," she said, unable to say anything more, for the air was too thick with feeling. Whenever she inhaled, it lodged in her throat.

"Perhaps, although we will never know for certain. Robert thinks they left her broken and bleeding, and she drowned herself."

"Either way they are responsible for her death." The words sounded wooden and detached, something one would say by rote, not from the heart. Her insides were all twisted, too tightly for any feeling to emerge. She would have to leave it alone, and in time, it would straighten itself out—just like a hibernating snake placed in the sun will eventually warm and slither away.

"That's the way Robbie saw it," Hugh continued. "He vowed he would find a way to get even, that he would make the whole of England pay if he had to."

She shuddered, mindful of Robert's intense hatred, but she wanted to be understanding and fair, and she told herself it was not uncommon for those who grieved to say and do things they normally would not consider.

"Robbie managed to pull Sorcha's body out of the stream, then he passed out from the blow to his head. Iain found them. At first, he thought they were both dead. Robbie was unconscious for over a month. The first thing he said, when he recovered, was he had to get up, to dress for her funeral. When we told him Sorcha had been buried almost four weeks, he went wild. I do not think he ever recovered from the fact that he did not get to see her one last time, to tell his twin goodbye.

"In his mind, he had double the reasons for wanting to get even. I tell you this only because I think it is important for you to understand what has made Robert the way he is. I hope that, by knowing, it will make things easier for both of you."

Silence came again and she breathed it into her lungs, feeling its heavy weight. She knew he was watching her, waiting to see her reaction. Did he expect her to say she was sorry for four animals who walked on two legs? For all the horrible things man is capable of doing to others?

Yes, she was sorry.

She was sorry for a life cut short and for the suffering that preceded it. She was sorry for the family that missed such a lovely young girl—would miss her until the day they died. She was sorry for England and the good people who lived there, scattered among the bad, who had to shoulder the blame for something done by someone else. Strange though it was, she was sorriest of all for the four men. She tried to imagine the rupture of spirit it would take to make human beings willfully destroy a life for sport. How could someone not care that they wrecked other lives along with it—slamming them into a pit of suffering, where the only thing they could feel was the pain of separation and the eternal hollowness of loss?

"Did you ever find out who did it?"

"No, but I'm quite certain Robert found out, although he has never admitted such to me."

"He probably does know. It doesn't sound like Robert—to let something like that go."

"No, it doesn't sound like him."

"I don't understand why he won't tell you…if he truly knows?"

"I don't know. Robert is a private man and he deals with things in his own way. And then, there is the fact that they were twins, and there is a bond there that the rest of us do not understand."

"Extract his own revenge, you mean."

"That, too."

"Does Iain know, or your grandmother?"

"I am quite certain they do not."

"So much suffering," she said.

After returning to the castle, she was mulling things over, unaware that she had passed the library, until she heard someone call out her name. She stopped and looked to see Lady Margaret sitting in a chair near the window, a book in her lap. She smiled at Meleri and motioned her inside.

Meleri entered quietly and took a seat beside her. Lady Margaret closed the book, but kept her fingers tucked inside to mark her place as she held the book up for Meleri to see. "Do you like him?"

Meleri glanced down at the book and saw the gilded word *Shakespeare.* "Yes, I like him very much, and I know you do, as well. Robert told me you thought he went beyond being English...if that is possible."

"His words are oft more soothing to me than some of our own Scots'. Take the works of Smollett, for instance. He could bore a dead man. Have you read him?"

Meleri repeated the name, thinking it sounded like the name of a fish. "Smollett? No, I don't think so—at least the name is not familiar to me."

"How fortunate for you. Believe me, you would remember, if you had read one of his novels, for how could anyone forget *Roderick Random, Humphrey Clinker* or *Peregrine Pickle?*"

Meleri could not hold back a smile. She had no idea Lady Margaret had a featherweight of humor in her.

"Just mention one of those titles and I go beyond bored." The older woman looked down at the book of Shakespeare. "He has never bored me. Not once! I find when I read his words, all is forgiven, including his place of birth."

"Have you forgiven me for being born in England?"

"My dear, I could not be unforgiving to you. You have given much of yourself since coming here. My granddaughters adore you, and you have provided them with something to look forward to each day. You have inspired the servants and given them a reason to take pride in what they do. Already, Beloyn sparkles amid the changes you have brought about." She stopped and sat back. "Och! Here I go, gabbling like a goose among swans. I am sure I am repeating what Robert has already told you."

"No, you are not. Robert does not speak about any of the things I have done."

Lady Margaret patted her hand. "Don't think that means he has not noticed. He has had much on his mind of late. He has hardly been himself these past few months. There is so much responsibility resting on his young shoulders, and that, along with the everpresent knowledge that we could lose Beloyn, has made him hard and cynical."

"You could lose Beloyn? It is your ancestral home. How could you lose it?"

"It was heavily mortgaged and somehow the papers fell into the hands of the Earl of Drummond."

She gasped. "Not the *English* Earl of Drummond."

Lady Margaret nodded. "Aye, do you know him?"

"Yes, unfortunately, I do. My father said Drummond is without equal. He is truly a despicable man—the most depraved creature…avaricious…coveting…dishonest."

"It would appear we speak of the same man, a rapacious miscreant."

"In Northumberland he was widely known for his unscrupulous ways. It is said that he will not be satisfied until he has all of the northern part of England in his grasp. I did not know his ravenous appetite extended as far as Scotland."

"It is the Borders he is after."

Meleri thought about the huge dowry she had, and could not help the pride she felt, knowing that it would prove to be the one thing that would save Beloyn. "How long do you have?"

"Drummond gave us three months. We have less than that now."

"Do not worry about Drummond. My dowry is more than enough to take care of that snake. I am surprised Robert did not tell you about my dowry."

"He is not aware I know about Drummond." She turned her gaze upon Meleri. "Who would have thought it would be a slip of an English lass who would be the salvation of the Douglases? You have the heart of a Scot."

"In truth, I am beginning to feel as though I do." Meleri caught herself just in time, but not soon enough to prevent the telltale sign of embarrassment that she knew left her cheeks as bright as the blood that warmed them.

There was understanding in Lady Margaret's eyes. "Do not be distressed by your claim. Having the heart of the truest Scot is more than being born here, or having a blood tie to those who were. It is more than frenzied outbursts of emotion. It is the steady and peaceful dedication of a lifetime. A true Scot loves with his heart, and not merely his lips. It is both loyalty and love—a feeling that will warm even the coldest of Presbyterian hearts. Those who have sacrificed part of themselves to their home or country understand what it is to be a true Scot. Only they, who fought to make it, struggled to keep it and stand together stoutly to preserve it, will understand the matter of oneness with the heart. Soon you will know you are a daughter of Scotland."

Meleri felt warmed down to her toes. "In the short time I have been here I have come to think of Scotland as my home."

"That is because you were destined to love your adopted land. It was all a matter of timing and readiness. Everything comes at its appointed hour, not by accident. What is inevitable is inescapable. We cannot forestall what must happen, even when we have a premonition that all is not well. Shakespeare said it best. 'There's a special providence in the fall of a sparrow. If it be now, 'tis not to come. If it be not to come, it will be now. If it be not now, yet it will come. The readiness is all.'"

After leaving Lady Margaret with Shakespeare, Meleri returned to the gallery. She felt restless and undecided—something that was apparent when she began to drum her fingers on a long table that had figures from mythology ornately carved along the sides and legs. She studied the figures, then named them, one by one.

It took some time, and once she identified all the legendary figures, she allowed her gaze to wander around the gallery.

Here, as elsewhere, there were signs of neglect. She stole a glance at the crumbling plaster ceiling Robert had pointed out.

She understood why no repairs had been made around the castle for years. Perturbed by its deplorable condition and the dilapidated state it was in, she was becoming more than a bit angry at that lackadaisical, unfeeling and totally unfair ghost. If he knew where the bloody riches were, why had he not shown some concern? After all, it had been, and still was, his home, too. She could only wonder where he would take up residence, once Beloyn had fallen into complete ruin.

She had more matters to keep her busy than worrying about a reclusive ghost, so she decided to spend the rest of the day occupying herself with some of them. In no time at all, she went after the castle as if it were spring and she was the most prudent of housewives, for soon the maids were airing out draperies and bed linens, while rugs were beaten free of their centuries of dust.

Stone floors were scrubbed, windows washed and light fixtures were dusted and cleaned. Before long, the fragrance of clean, fresh air mingled with the aroma of wax and lemon oil. Soon, every corridor and staircase, every room and cupboard, every nook and cranny would be inspected, scoured and rearranged, and the air heavy with the smell of furniture polish and soap. She planned to leave not one corner of Beloyn's entirety overlooked.

The kitchen was next to the hall in the other rear corner of what had been, at one time, the inner ward. It contained huge ovens for baking, a fireplace for cooking and another for smoking meat. Along one wall was a storage area for wine and ale barrels. On the opposite wall, a livery cupboard stored salt vessels, dishes, pickles and spices. Behind the livery was a large pantry, where barrels of grains, vegetables and some cooking utensils were stored. Water was piped into a large stone sink from the cistern, which was located at the top of the corner tower. The cook and the kitchen help resided in a small apartment next to the kitchen.

Besides Gowan, Fingal, Agnes and herself, the twins had asked to join her, and much to Meleri's surprise, Lady Margaret walked into the kitchen wearing an apron. At first, Fiona was sullen and uncooperative, but she soon warmed to the idea of having a clean place to work.

Meleri assigned everyone a task. "Gowan and Fingal can help me with the cleaning and setting the kitchen to order. Fiona, if you would work with Lady Margaret and the twins, perhaps you could take stock of the supplies and come up with a list of what we have and what we need."

A different mood settled over the kitchen after that, as well as a cloud of dust. Every cupboard and drawer was emptied. The maids, who were working in other parts of the castle, were called in to help with the scrubbing and scouring of pots and pans, as well as washing down the walls and floors.

When everything was clean, they began the monumental task of restocking the pantry and shelves. Most of what they found was unidentifiable, stale, rotten or simply too mysterious to identify.

Ciorstag laughed when they finished, stating, "Taking stock of what we have didn't take overlong, since we didn't have much to take stock of!"

"Aye," Lady Margaret said. "An empty larder is a clean larder."

"At least we have a point to start from," Meleri said. "I'll take Fingal to the gardens with me to see what we can find there."

Lady Margaret said she would work with Fiona on meal planning. Agnes, being a fair hand in the kitchen, stayed to work with them. Meleri and Fingal went into the kitchen garden, only to find what precious few vegetables there were had not been well tended. Weeds seemed to be both abundant and hearty. "Who is in charge of the gardens?" she asked.

"Finlay," Fingal said. "He is also in charge of the horses and dogs."

"That is too much for one man." She looked around her, observing the overgrown condition of the garden, the dead trees in the orchard, the sparse, wilted clumps of herbs in the herb garden. "He obviously prefers horses and dogs to gardening."

"Aye," Fingal said with a grin, "he isna too fond of gardening."

"Then it's little wonder the gardens are suffering. Do you know of anyone who enjoys this sort of thing?"

"Aye, that would be Artair," Fingal said.

"Who is Artair? What does he do?"

"He is in charge of livestock…cows, sheep and such."

"Well, I couldn't very well call him away from that."

"Oh, he would be most happy to come if you called him to care for the gardens. He is no happy to be working with animals. He is a man of the earth."

"But who would take care of the livestock?"

Fingal scratched his head. "Weel, the best man for that would be Lulach. He loves all the little beasties, you ken."

"Lulach. That seems simple enough, then. We will ask Lulach to care for the livestock, and Artair to care for the gardens, and that will leave Finlay to care for horses and dogs. That would work out nicely, don't you think?"

"Aye, save for one problem."

"What problem would that be?"

"If Lulach cares for the livestock, who will do the fishing?"

"Of course, Lulach is in charge of fishing," Meleri said, feeling as if she had been sucked into some sort of game that had no end.

"Aye, but he doesna care for fish, therefore he is no fond of fishing."

Meleri released a long sigh. "Who would you recommend for fishing, then?"

"Murchadh. His father was a fisherman, an' his father afoore him, an' his father afoore him, an'…"

"His father afoore him," Meleri finished.

"Aye."

"And what does Murchadh do?"

"He gets drunk, mostly."

"Drunk?"

"Aye, he's in charge of the bothy where whisky is brewed."

"He obviously loves that job."

"Aye, he loves it too much. He would fare better fishing."

"We'll move him to fishing, then. Of course, we will have to find someone for the bothy. Preferably someone who does not drink."

"Somerled is the most sober of Lord Douglas's men. He doesna drink anything but water and sheep's milk."

"And what job would we be pulling Somerled away from if we put him in charge of the bothy?"

"Flocks."

"Flocks?"

"Aye. Flocks."

"Flocks of what?"

"Fowl. He tends the geese, ducks, chickens and sometimes the swans, when they agree to it."

"Who would you suggest to tend flocks in his stead?"

"Old Torquil. He loves anything with feathers. I've heard he once fell in love with Lady Fleming's hat because it was trimmed with pheasant feathers."

"And of course old Torquil has a different job, one of great importance that we would have to find someone else to do. So, put me out of my misery and tell me what it is, exactly, that old Torquil does now?"

Fingal looked up at her with a gleam in his eye. "Nothing, milady. He mostly sits around making proposals to all the young, single lassies."

Meleri gasped. "Proposals? What kind of proposals?"

"Marriage," Fingal said. "I hear he's tired of being a bachelor."

She narrowed her eyes. "And just how *old* is old Torquil?"

"He admits to being ninety, but some folks say he is older than that."

"Thank God," Meleri said, "we have come to the end of that."

"When do you plan to make the changes, milady?"

"Immediately, but before we do, I want you to tell me something. How did it happen that everyone is doing a job he does not care for? Who was the numskull who assigned them their tasks?"

"The earl did, milady."

"Well," she huffed, "he certainly didn't know what he was doing."

"Aye, he said as much himself."

"He did?"

"Aye, when he first became earl, he didn't know any more about being the lord of a castle than he did being overseer. He rode through the crowd of people who came to welcome him and as he passed, picked out a person to handle each job."

"Without asking who had the most ability?"

"Aye."

Meleri sent Fingal to make the changes in responsibility, praying that giving the jobs to those who had some interest in them would make the castle more productive.

25

Meleri went into the garden and set about gathering some of the herbs, pulling many of them up by the roots, to be dried and stored for use during the coming winter. Others she would tie in bundles and hang from the overhead beams in the kitchen. She was so busy working she did not hear someone approach until Corrie and Dram, who had been lying nearby, sprang to their feet.

She turned around. The basket in her hand fell to the ground. "Philip!" she whispered, as if he were another apparition.

He stepped closer. "Don't look so surprised, fair Meleri. Surely, you did not think I would take your disappearance lightly. After all, we have been betrothed for many years. Did you think you could simply walk out of my life and I would have no feeling about it?"

She was stunned to see him, but that did not override her curiosity. "How did you find me?"

"It was not easy, I assure you, but let us not dwell upon the past."

"Why are you here?"

"You are my betrothed. I came to take you home."

"Oh please, at least tell me the truth. Do you truly think I could believe all of that poppycock? The truth is, you don't care for me, Philip. You never cared. You only tolerated me because I was your father's choice."

"You are wrong there. Losing you left me devastated, blind and wandering, begging with a bowl."

"I don't believe this. Now your words are dripping with sentimentality. What will you try next?"

"You wound me. Truly, I have suffered greatly. Just the thought that you had walked out of my life cut deeply. That you could do so without a backward glance was like a mortal blow."

"It was nothing more than you deserved."

"It pains me greatly to have to agree with you. I treated you abominably, simply because I was a fool. I had not the slightest inkling as to your value…."

"My dowry, you mean."

"That is not it at all. I simply had no idea of what you meant to me, until you were gone. I hope to God I never endure that kind of agony again."

She tilted her head to one side and studied his face—unreadable as it always was. He looked worse than death. Perhaps he was speaking the truth. Perhaps he, truly, did grieve over her loss. His face was haggard, his eyes red, and he was not clean-shaven like he always was. It was obvious, even to her, that he had lost weight. Yes, he certainly looked as though he had suffered. Was it because of her?

No, you ninny! It is not because of you. Don't you fall for any of this, she told herself. This is Lord Waverly, remember? Waverly the underhanded. Waverly the cruel. Waverly the cunning. Whatever you do, you cannot, must not, trust him. Be wise and shrewd in your own right.

"Why are you really here?" she demanded.

"I have come to take you back to England where you belong."

She almost laughed. "Oh, Philip, surely you jest…or are you simply mocking me? I remember it was a favorite pastime of yours."

"Sweetheart, don't remind me of my cruelty. I was wrong. I admit that now. All I am asking is for a chance to make it up to you. I have come for you because I cannot bear for us to be separated from each other. You cannot imagine what it has been like.

You have been a part of my life since we were children. You are my life, my future. How can I have a future if you are gone?"

She started to speak, but he cut her off.

"No! Don't say it cannot be. Don't tell me too much time has passed. For us, it can never be too late. Tell me what I can do to make you understand."

He sounded so contrite, so sorry, she almost felt compassion for him, but not quite. She had never felt he cared overmuch for her, so why now? She would have to handle this delicately, which meant she would have to be as cunning as he.

It was with a soft voice and a tone of kindness and regret that she said, "I am sorry to hear these things, Philip. If you had only spoken in such a manner before, it would have made a difference, but the die is cast. I have crossed the border from England and into a new life. My home is here now, in Scotland. We cannot go back. What is done cannot be undone."

"It is never too late for lovers."

"We were not lovers, Philip. We never even came close."

"But we can be lovers." He stepped closer and lifted his hand to stroke the side of her face. "So you see, sweet Meleri, it is really quite simple. You will come with me to England, and you will be my queen."

He was being very persistent. Had he really changed? No, he had not. Did it really matter, even if he had? No, she told herself. It did not matter. She belonged to Robert now, heart, soul and body. The question was, how would she explain that to Philip? Her mind raced as she looked for a way out of this. She had to rid herself of this man, without involving Robert. Vivid in her mind was the ease in which he could turn on her and others, the venom he was capable of using and the cruelty he was so comfortable with.

Don't be trusting and do not provoke him. Diplomacy and tact were the tools she should use, and while she was at it, a little subterfuge would not hurt. Without much time to think, she devised a plan, a ploy to make him believe her; a way for him to think she was as sincere as he. She needed to get him away from here, at least for the time being, so she could think clearly and decide how best to handle things. In the end, she decided her only choice was to go along with him—to convince him that she was ready to go away with him.

She softened her expression and took on a defeated pose. "A queen?" She released a tired sigh. "Oh, Philip, you make it all sound so enticing. I came here to marry an earl, but he is a very poor earl. I daresay I would never come close to being treated like a queen here." She looked down at her red hands. "Already my hands grow rough from work."

He took her hands in his. "Your hands used to be so lovely." He kissed each palm. "They can be that way again. You were never meant for this kind of life…not even wed, and already you work like a hand in the fields. You have been beyond foolish and your folly has caused me great distress, as well as considerable inconvenience. I hope you realize that."

"Oh Philip, you are right. I have been so very foolish. But I don't know what I can do about it now," she said, looking around in a hopeless manner.

"You can come with me, as I said."

Somewhere in the house, a door slammed. It gave her the perfect excuse.

She stepped closer to him and lowered her voice. "If we are to succeed at this, it must be well planned. Leaving now will not work to our advantage. The family and servants would see us and alert the earl. He is poor, but he is a Scot and a very proud one. He would never let me go. I need time to think about this, time to find a way to leave here without being missed for a while."

"Time is something I do not have. I need to return home. I left urgent business to come here."

She looked around her. "I understand, but we must be cautious. I should not be speaking with you now. Someone could come out here any minute. If I came with you now, we would not reach the stables before we were stopped. I will meet you later. Wait for me down where you turn off from the main road. When it is dark and everyone has gone to bed, I will come to you. We can be well away from this place before they discover I am gone."

"And your earl? Where will he be while you are slipping from his grasp?"

"The men have been harvesting turnips. Robert goes to the fields early. By night he is exhausted and retires to bed shortly after dinner."

Philip did not answer right away, but stood there, obviously thinking over her words as he searched her face. She knew he was looking for some sign of deception on her part. Her heart was pounding so hard, she feared he would hear it and know his suspicions were true.

She was on the verge of turning and bolting for the house, when from somewhere inside she heard Ciorstag's voice. "Has anyone seen Meleri?"

She almost fainted when he said, "All right, but if you should fail to come…"

The world increased in intensity. Her eyes were unable to absorb the sunlight without hurting and causing brilliant pinpricks of light to float along her line of vision. Each of her senses magnified, until she could hear the crackle of a leaf growing and the sound a spider makes spinning his web. The smell of grass crushed beneath her feet rose, sharp and pungent, as it passed through air passages and caused her lungs to hurt.

"I will come when the last light is out."

At sunset, Meleri was alone in the garden. She needed to escape the house, for fear that those inside would sense something was wrong. She had gotten herself into a fine mess—one she did not know how to extract herself from. All she'd done was buy herself a little time, but for what? Why had she promised Waverly she would meet him tonight? She could not go back with Philip, and yet, she could not remain here. To do so would put Robert in danger, for she knew he would find out and try to settle things in his own way. The thought that Philip might kill him was too great a chance to take. She had to find another way, and soon.

Time was running out.

She sighed deeply and looked about her, as if by doing so, she would see the answers to the questions crowding her mind. In the west, a slow-dying sun spun a golden net of pastel shades and cast it over the earth below, frosting the leaves with a pale wash of flaxen color. The late evening air was cool, the song coming from the stream sweet flowing, and all about her the steady droning of bees settled into her consciousness with a contented hum. Dew was already beginning to settle on the moor grasses, making it smell like night.

A tiny orange kitten, furry and round as a puffball, bounced out of the bushes, saw her and stopped. With a violent arching of its back, it hissed and Meleri smiled sadly. She spoke in a soft voice. "Such a fierce little kitty. You didn't expect to find anyone here, did you?" She stretched out her hand and ran it over the arched back, until the bristled fur settled back into place. "I didn't mean to frighten you. What are you doing out here? Chasing garden crickets?" The kitten paraded back and forth a time or two beneath her hand, before curiously inspecting the basket of gathered flowers that sat nearby. The animal took a couple of swipes at the basket with shiny black claws. Apparently satisfied, it settled in an orange lump beside it.

A long shadow came out of nowhere and covered her completely, blocking the setting sun. She gasped, knowing Philip had changed his mind, but when she looked up, it was Robert standing beside her.

Relief washed over her. "You startled me. I didn't hear you come up. For a moment, I thought it might be the ghost."

"Or another kitten."

She turned her head to look at the kitten, digging its claws into the soft earth next to the basket. "Yes, that's a possibility, too. If there is one, there are bound to be others about."

She felt his hand at her elbow as he drew her to her feet. He had not said why he had come, and she searched his face for some hint, but she saw nothing beyond the clear blue eyes that were watching her with inquiry. She felt a bit shaky from staring into those mesmerizing eyes. Her breathing was quick and shallow, his nearness unsettling.

He pulled a leaf or two out of her hair and ran the back of his hand across her cheek. She turned her head away.

"I think you've been avoiding me," he said.

She leaned forward and dropped the herbs she was clutching into the basket before dusting her hands. "I've been busy."

"Aye, I have noticed. I cannot remember seeing Beloyn look so good. It's amazing what a little ingenuity, a lot of work and no money will accomplish."

"Yes, it's truly amazing," she said, knowing he would soon ask what troubled her, and knowing full well she could not tell him how she was terrified of Philip doing him harm. She could only pray that she could solve this problem by herself, but seeing Robert in the flesh made her suddenly realize just how impossible that sounded. Her only choice was to go with Philip. She could not live like this. The uncertainty was too much. She had no choice but to push Robert away. For her to weaken could cost him his life.

His expression became suddenly concerned. "Something is troubling you. Can you tell me what it is?"

"No, as a matter of fact, I cannot."

"Why?"

"Because they are *my* troubles and *my* concerns. I prefer not to share them. I want to work them out in my own way."

He took her hands in his. "Your fingers are cold."

But not as cold as your heart will be when I return to England and marry Philip.

"Perhaps you should come inside before you catch a chill."

"I am not cold. My fingers are wet from the dew on the leaves."

He lifted her hands to his mouth, caressing them with the warmth from his breath, the pads of his thumbs making lazy circles against her wrists. She watched her hands, breathless, her lips slightly parted. Push him away, she told herself, but her muscles would not obey.

"You've cut yourself."

The soft jolt of his words jerked her back to consciousness. She looked down and saw a small cut on her thumb, crusted with dirt and dried blood. "It doesn't hurt."

He lifted it to his lips, and she closed her eyes against the contact, against the deep, penetrating warmth so hungrily absorbed by her skin. She watched in dazed curiosity, beset by the heat of his nearness, the fresh-air scent in his hair. Still holding both of her hands in one of his, he used the free hand to lift her chin. Her breath quickened in response to the sleepy, hypnotic reaction her body had to the slow descent of his mouth.

He kissed one cheek, then brushed the curve of the other. She was unprepared for the rush of feeling that spread over her, with the erotic sensations traveling from his lips to hers as his mouth sought, and found, hers with a gently questing pressure that fired her blood. Urgency hummed and vibrated through tightly coiled muscles, yet her joints had all turned to mush. If he had not been holding her, she would have fallen.

A sudden rattling of leathery shrub leaves, the rustling and scuffling sounds of some late-evening animal, pierced the dreamy lushness that enveloped her in the warm cocoon of desire. She looked toward the shrubs with perplexed confusion, just in time to see Dram and Corrie thrust their heads through the glossy leaves and come bounding out in a gentle lope.

They broke apart and Robert said, "Perfect timing, almost like they rehearsed it."

"They are my guardian angels."

"Do you need guarding?"

"Only from you."

Their gazes held. She saw so many questions in his eyes, which were hazy from confusion.

"I wonder if I will ever understand you." He looked down and spoke to Corrie and Dram, who sat between them, regarding their human benefactors in a curious manner, heads tilted to one side. "Why did you choose this particular moment to interrupt us?"

"You cannot question fate. Some things are meant to be." She

allowed the dismissing look in her eyes to tell him their talk was
over. Quickly, she snatched her basket from its place on the
ground and walked off, leaving a trail of footprints across dew-
sprinkled grass.

Inside the castle, it was almost dark, with only the palest haze
of smoky gray light coming through the windows. No light penetrated the dark sable interior as Meleri wandered through the
castle like a lost soul looking for a lamp. Even when she found
a candle, she was afraid to light it. She was worried that Philip
might change his mind and come back to confront her. Was he
out there now, watching?

She had been lonely many times in her life, but never had she
felt alone.

At dinner that night, Robert was preoccupied, weighing in his
mind with painstaking thoroughness and care the same things he
had been pondering all day; namely, Meleri and the ghost. He
only caught snatches of conversation or the occasional mention
of his name when someone directed a question at him.

"Hello, Robert," Gram said. "Would you care to join us, or
would you prefer to quit our company to meditate in private?"

"What?"

"There are times," she said with calm composure, "that you
are an inconsiderate and thoughtless bore, but I cannot remember you ever being nonexistent. Would it be too much to ask if
you cared to grace us with your presence? You are here in body,
but your mind seems to have wandered off by itself."

"You are right, and I do apologize."

"You think too much," Gram replied.

"Right again."

"Of course I am. I am always right. I thought you knew that."

"I do, but there are times when I let it slip my mind."

"You are forgiven, then. You can think too much after the meal
is over. There, you see, here comes Fiona with dessert, and you
are still staring at a cold first course. A terrible lapse of manners,
if you ask me." She took up her wineglass and took a sip. When

she finished, she put the glass down and regarded her younger grandson, who sat across from her, grinning widely. "Hugh is feeling left out," she said. "I must rectify that."

"Uh-oh," the twins said in unison.

Hugh gave his grandmother a smile that would have made a seraph envious and blew her a kiss. "Be nice to me, Gram. You know I have tender sensibilities."

"Posh! The only thing tender about you is your head. Now, behave yourself, you vexatious boy, so I can pester Robert."

Hugh grabbed his chest with feigned pain. "Reduced to a schoolboy by the only woman I'll ever love."

"Do be quiet, you shameless rapscallion." She turned to Meleri. "That one I cannot coax a word from, and that one," she said, indicating Hugh, "I cannot stop from talking."

"Have you tried silencing him at gunpoint?" Robert asked.

"No, but that is an idea I might try on you, if you continue this vexing silence."

"It won't work," Hugh said. "He eats bullets for breakfast."

"That explains why he isn't hungry," Iain said.

Gram pinned Meleri with a questioning gaze. "And speaking of silence, you are being overly quiet, my dear. Are you feeling well?"

"Yes, I'm fine…a bit tired, that's all."

"Small wonder! Has anyone noticed all the work that has been done around here?"

Robert looked at her, wondering if that was the cause of the change he sensed in her. "She is fair to wearing herself out. She works like three and takes the most difficult tasks for herself."

Once the cinnamon baked apples were served, with Fiona's outright command to "eat them hot," conversation died down to a trickle. While the others ate, Robert's mind went traipsing off again, in search of a deserving thought and wandering off, quite naturally, in Meleri's direction. He was worried about his lass.

26

Robert knew something was bothering Meleri, and he could only assume she was beginning to doubt his intentions regarding marriage. To put her mind at ease, he sent for Gowan.

"Take a message to Donald McDonald."

"The minister?"

"Aye, tell him that he is needed at Beloyn to perform a wedding as soon as possible."

After Gowan departed, Robert went searching for Gram. He wanted to talk to her about their resident—but heretofore unseen—ghost, since she was the most knowledgeable about the legend.

It took him a while to find her, and when he did, she was in the kitchen, almost standing on her head, leaning into a flour barrel, which she said she was cleaning.

"I didn't know you knew how to clean," he said.

"I never knew, either," she said with a laugh that blew puffs of flour from the smudges on her face. She dusted her hands by clapping them together.

As flour filtered through the air, Robert coughed and took a step back.

"Did you come to help or to observe what work looks like?" she asked.

"The turnip fields have shown me plenty of that," he replied. "I came because I want to talk to you."

"Can it wait until I'm finished?"

"How long will that take?"

"Two hours, perhaps three."

"This is of an urgent nature."

She leaned over and put her head back into the flour barrel, and when she spoke, she sounded as if she were in a cave. "What is so urgent that you need to talk right now?"

"Meleri thinks she has seen a ghost."

His grandmother remained headfirst in the barrel. "I don't find that strange," she said with great resonance. "She is in Scotland. You know it is a common enough occurrence around here."

"Aye, but this wasn't just any ghost."

Her head popped out of the barrel, and Robert winced at the giant cracking sound as it came in contact with the shelf overhead.

Rubbing her head, she said, "She told me."

"Do you think it was the old earl?"

She picked up the edge of her apron and began wiping her hands. "Aye, who else would it be?"

"Did she tell you about his clothes?"

"Aye. That was part of the reason I suspected it was the old earl."

"You don't seem surprised."

"I was expecting it. I don't know why, but I had an uncanny feeling she might be the one to see him."

"That makes no sense, but she is convinced she saw him. I wanted your opinion, since you are more familiar with the legend than anyone."

"It is not my familiarity with the legend that makes me recognize those clothes, but the miniature of his cousin, James the Good, that is in the library. He is wearing almost exactly what she described."

"Do you think she could be the one with the heart of the truest Scot that the legend says the ghost will reveal himself to?"

"Aye."

"But, Meleri is English to the core. How could she have the heart of the truest Scot?"

Gram looked a bit perplexed. "You will have to ask the old earl about that. I'm afraid I don't have an answer. However, if I were to venture a guess, I would say perhaps she has a heart more in line with a Scot than an Englishman. She certainly has tried to do everything in her power to prove she is a part of the family. No one can accuse her of expecting to be treated differently. She carries her weight and then some. Or it could be referring to some future event that has not yet occurred. Both explanations are possible, and then again, it could be something else entirely."

"Or it could be that we are mistaken, that she isn't the one."

"If she saw the earl, he will not appear to anyone else."

"Do you think he will talk to her at some point?"

"Perhaps, if she speaks to him first. Ghosts are like ladies. They never speak until spoken to."

"Charming, a ghost with manners. We should have nothing to worry about, as far as getting him to talk. Remaining silent is not one of Meleri's outstanding attributes."

"Let me know if she sees him again…or if he speaks to her."

The rising sun was barely making itself known when Philip cursed and walked back to his horse. He was angrier than he could ever remember being. He had waited for Meleri all night. What a fool he was, checking his watch in the moonlight, first at midnight, then at two o'clock and again at three.

She was not coming. She never intended to. He remembered the words of Demosthenes. "A man is his own easiest dupe, for what he wishes to be true he generally believes to be true." Well, he had wished, and he had been duped, but what made him so bitter about it was she thought herself more clever than he. She was clever, all right, and well he knew that the height of cleverness was the ability to conceal it; and as far as that went, she had done it well.

He had underestimated her. He would not do so again.

As he rode away, he wondered if she really thought herself

clever—more so than he? Well, she was wrong on that score, and he would prove it. Now he understood the game she played. He would not trust her again. She might try to give him an excuse for why she could not come, but he would not believe her.

Philip could not bear humiliation, or being played for a fool. It was something his father excelled at; something he did at regular intervals. He was powerless against the duke, and that left nothing for him to do but accept his father's treatment.

He did not have to do so with Meleri.

Poor foolish chit! She did not realize he would succeed simply because he *had* to. She might be desperate, but he was more so. His entire existence, his future were all contingent upon his marriage to her. Marriage at all costs, and once that was done, he had the rest of his life to make her regret it.

He did wonder why she had played along with him instead of telling him she was married, not that it would have done her any good. He had already inquired about that and learned there had been no wedding.

He mounted his horse and rode off. She had not come to him as she promised, but that was not the end of it. He could always go to her.

Oh, yes, he would go…when she least expected it.

27

It was half past eleven the next morning, when Fingal came running around the side of the barn and found Robert mounted on his horse, preparing to go into the fields.

"The clergyman is here!" Fingal called out as he ran the distance to where Robert stopped to wait for him.

"Donald McDonald is here? Now?"

"Aye, 'tis him in the flesh…come with his prayer book, he did. Said he was ready to perform a wedding."

Robert dismounted. "Take my horse," he said, and handed Fingal the reins.

Five minutes after he walked through the door, Robert had everyone running in a dozen directions. The servants were rushing to the kitchen to prepare food, while the members of the family all made a dash to change into appropriate clothes. Robert stopped by to have a word with Donald, then went to find Meleri.

Fingal was waiting for Robert with a bouquet of flowers.

"I picked these for you to give to your lady."

Robert thanked Fingal and took the flowers up to her room.

"Donald McDonald has come to perform our wedding," Robert said after she admitted him into her room. "He is waiting in the chapel." He offered her the flowers. "Fingal picked these for you."

Meleri did not take the flowers. "You waited long enough."

"Aye, I did, and I am sorry I did, but I will make it up to you, lass."

She turned around and began sorting through some fabric she had lying on the bed. "It doesn't matter."

"Aye, lass, it does matter. I would not have us start our wedding with your lips in a pucker."

Clutching the fabric to her middle, she turned to face him. "It does not matter, because we won't be getting married today."

"Is there a reason?"

"I always have a reason for everything I do." Meleri looked down at the bouquet of yellow-and-white daffodils he had placed on the desk. It didn't seem fair. Two days ago, she would have leaped into Robert's arms if he told her Donald McDonald was here. But that was before Philip had arrived. Meleri was afraid, not only for Robert, but for the rest of the family, as well. She thought about what could happen if she married Robert and Philip found out.

It did not take her long to realize Philip would not hesitate to kill Robert, in order to have her, even as a widow. Marry him and you put his life in jeopardy, she reminded herself. As long as she remained single, the only threat was to her, since she was the one Philip wanted. "Tell him to leave. This isn't the right day for me to get married."

"Pity, because it's exactly the day I want for my wedding."

He picked up the bouquet from the desk and swept her up into his arms and carried her from the room and down the hall.

"In about two seconds I am going to embarrass you," she said. "Take me back this instant."

"I can't do any physical labor today."

"Why not?"

"It's my wedding day."

"Interesting, because it isn't *my* wedding day."

"Aye, lass, it is."

"You can't force me. I won't marry you."

"Ah, but you are wrong on that one, lass."

"I would like to see you try forcing me."

"You will, in about three minutes." He carried her down the stairs.

"Why are you doing this? It won't work. When he asks me if I want to marry you, I will say no."

"When he gets to that part, you may say anything you like."

"From this moment on, I will not say one word. You cannot marry someone who will not talk, who will not answer, and I am not going to answer. Nothing, not one word will I utter."

"I have prayed for the day."

He carried her through the gallery and down the hall. She could see everyone was gathered there: Iain, Lady Margaret, Agnes, Hugh, the twins and all the servants, and a man, who must be Donald McDonald, wearing the proper vestments and holding a prayer book. They were all staring as if they had never seen her before.

Robert dropped her to her feet in front of Donald McDonald and shoved the bouquet into her hands, while the priest began with the usual matrimonial preliminaries, which she did not listen to. Instead, she clutched the bouquet against her and maintained her vow of silence.

She stood stiffly, listening to Donald McDonald, not understanding a word he spoke. What in God's name was he saying? She had never heard such gibberish. Was this Robert's idea of a joke? She cast a furtive look toward him. He looked serious enough, and she decided this was for real. If it was real, why wasn't this minister speaking English?

He must be speaking Gaelic.

She frowned, trying to reason why he should be performing the wedding in that tongue. It must have been for the Scots present, or perhaps it was some sort of old Douglas tradition. Perhaps the first earl had married in a Gaelic ceremony. Well, in a moment, she thought, he will get to the English part, and then I will not say a word.

She was still waiting for her shining moment, when she could remain silent in front of all and sundry, when Robert's arms came around her. He pulled her against him and kissed her soundly.

Those gathered in the hall began to clap and cheer, and great waves of embarrassment rippled across her. She had never known anyone to kiss so long when they were just married.

Married?

Meleri put her foot on top of Robert's and pressed hard. He kissed her more firmly and with more passion.

She was about to haul off and kick him, when he released her. Before she could say anything, everyone began to crowd around them, offering congratulations, slapping Robert on the back.

She was still reeling when Agnes rushed up and gave her a kiss on the cheek. "Oh, milady, this is such a happy day, which is precisely what a wedding day should be. Aren't you happy to have such a fine husband? How does it feel to be Lady Douglas?"

Lady Douglas? Meleri stared at Agnes, stunned.

"Close your mouth, sweetheart, or something might fly in it," Robert whispered.

Meleri was about to shout to the top of her lungs that there had been a grave mistake made, when Donald McDonald came up and kissed her on the cheek then shook Robert's hand. She held the bouquet up to cover her face and whispered to Robert, "I want to talk to you," through gritted teeth.

"I am sure you do, wife."

It was a good half hour before Meleri could get him away from the celebration going on in the great hall and into the library. At last, she managed to drag him away, and as soon as they were in the library, she shut the door. "I want to know what is going on here."

"We were just married. I thought you knew that."

She stomped her foot. "We were not married, you bloody idiot! He never asked me if I agreed to this marriage."

"Yes, he did."

"He did not! How could he? He never spoke a word of English."

"Well, I can explain that."

"Please do. I want to understand how you could be so mistaken as to think that gibberish spoken in there constituted a marriage ceremony."

"I told him it was all right to speak Gaelic."

"How could he agree when he obviously knew I don't understand it?"

"I explained it to him."

"What do you mean you explained it? You explained what? That I do not speak Gaelic?"

"No, I explained to him that you were out riding and a tree branch hit you in the throat, and you have not been able to speak for several days."

"Of all the… You tricked me, you bloody bastard! I'm surprised you didn't tell him I was a deaf mute!"

"I thought about it."

She threw her bouquet at him and it went hurling through the air, end over end, swifter than bullets thrown from Spanish slings.

He ducked and crossed the room in three short strides. His arms went around her. "Aye, I tricked you and gave us both what we want."

"Balderdash! You have no idea what I want, and if you did, you wouldn't give it to me because I am English."

"Aye, lass, I do know what you want, but even if I did not, it wouldn't matter. I have ways of finding out."

28

The morning after her wedding night, the sun had been up for some time before Meleri was able to move. When she finally did open her eyes, she saw Robert was gone. Then she saw the sprig of heather on the pillow next to her. A note attached to it read, *Last night my soul found peace, and today I have awakened like a newly opened flower.*

She smiled and stretched luxuriously, then threaded the heather through the button on her gown and went back to sleep.

Later, when she awoke again, she felt rested. She attempted to get up, but nothing felt the same as it had the day before. She stretched and smiled, remembering their night of lovemaking. The result of all that lovemaking was that today her body felt like it had aged a thousand years. It creaked and ached, and she moved like an old woman. It took her a while to even stand up straight.

Agnes opened the door and came into the room with a breakfast tray. "You are finally up. I was beginning to wonder if you had been drugged."

Meleri smiled to herself. She had been drugged with the elixir of love.

Elixir of love? she thought as she sat down to have her breakfast of scones and tea. The rather pathetic attempt at being the poet amused her and she could not help smiling.

By the time she bathed, dressed and made it down the stairs, her body had limbered up considerably. She was almost back to normal as she reached the gallery. Her body revived and her heart soaring, she walked by the painting of the missing earl and felt a cold, damp chill that made her hair stand on end.

The dogs must have felt it, too, for they began to whimper. She spoke to them and patted each of their heads as she passed, telling them not to worry, that it was only "the old earl making sport, because he was bored and had nothing better to do."

She did not tarry any longer, for there was much to be done, with more rooms on the east wing that needed to be cleaned. Lady Margaret and the twins announced they would like to help. Shortly after they set to work, Meleri heard Catriona and Ciorstag giggling. When she turned to see what amused them, her curious gaze fell upon the sleeping form of Lady Margaret, her hand draped over the arm of the chair, a feather duster dangling precariously from her hand. Meleri smiled and brought her finger up to her lips, signaling the twins to be quiet.

"She missed her afternoon nap," Catriona said, her eyes sparkling brightly with true affection as she gazed at her great-grandmother.

"No, she didn't" Ciorstag replied. "She's getting it now."

The three of them worked quietly after that, until Hugh walked into the room, his boots thudding against the stone floors with each step. They tried to signal Hugh to walk softly by pointing at Lady Margaret, but they were too late.

Without opening her eyes, Lady Margaret said, "Hugh, must you come into the room like your feet were chiseled from stone?"

Hugh stopped and gazed at her curiously. "How did you know who it was, Gram?"

"You have the heaviest tread of anyone in the family. There was never any doubt. Now that you've awakened me, come and give me a kiss."

Meleri watched Hugh dutifully kiss his grandmother's cheek.

"Have you seen Robbie?" Meleri asked. "Did he come back with you?"

"No. I left after we finished the harvesting. Robbie stayed to let the sheep out into the field, so they can eat what is left of the turnips."

Meleri turned to the twins. "I think we've done enough for today. You need to practice your music lessons."

"Ugh!" Catriona said. "I'd rather clean than practice."

"Me, too," agreed Ciorstag.

"Then you should be happy since you will have had a chance to do both today," Meleri said.

"Couldn't we practice tomorrow?" Catriona asked. "I wanted to embroider the last flowers on the nightgown Gram gave me for my birthday."

Catriona's comment reminded Meleri of something she had been meaning to ask. "That reminds me," she said. "The first night I was here, someone left a gown on my bed. Do you know who it was, or who the gown belongs to? I wanted to thank them and return it."

"It was mine," Ciorstag said. "Catriona and I overheard our uncle telling Gram that your trunks had not arrived, so we thought you would need something to sleep in."

Meleri gave them both a fond embrace. "Your thoughtfulness far exceeds your age. If I ever have daughters, I hope they are just like the two of you."

"Does that mean we don't have to practice our lessons?" Catriona asked.

Meleri laughed. "No, it means you will practice your lessons knowing I think the two of you are quite the loveliest people I know."

Reluctantly, the twins left to do their practicing, followed shortly after by Lady Margaret and Hugh.

Once everyone had gone, Meleri put away her cleaning supplies. She was on her way upstairs when she passed the front door and found herself drawn by some inexplicable reason toward it. She paused a moment in the open doorway and stared out at the beautiful day. She thought how nice it would be to spend the rest of such a day with Robert, when she remembered Hugh said he was still in the fields.

She decided she would walk out to meet him.

The sky was anthracite gray, streaked with white clouds and rays of sun, although she did not know how long that would last. There was thunder in the air, and she could see that in the distance, over the purple hills of Dumfries, the blue clouds had turned turbulent and dark gray—a color she dubbed Scots gray, for its dark, brooding intensity.

As she went in search of Robert, she discovered a second vegetable garden, smaller than the first, this one planted with carrots, onions and cabbage, most of it overgrown with brambles. She pulled a few succulent blackberries and ate them as she walked, but when she saw the scratches on her hands, she wished she had been a bit more careful of the sharp prickles on the stems.

She stopped for a moment in the middle of the garden to inspect several plants. Gathered around the weathered base of an ancient sundial were several herbs, some she recognized—parsley, dill, mint, rosemary, thyme, rue—and some she did not.

She scooped up a handful of soft, moist earth and let it sift through her fingers. God must have loved gardening, she thought, for He planted the first one. Truly, it was the purest of human pleasures. She smiled to herself, remembering what Lady Margaret had said earlier in the day, when Meleri had commented on how much she looked forward to planting more flowers and vegetables and how she enjoyed working with them.

"According to an old saying, the best thing about gardening is when you're finished. If God intended for us to till the earth, He should have given us better equipment."

"In what way do you mean?" Meleri asked.

"To be a gardener, one needs an iron back with hinges on it."

Meleri thought about her life since coming to Scotland, about how she was already feeling so much a part of everything. Memories were meant to be gathered, like flowers, and when she was old, she could take each memory, different from the others, and arrange them in a bouquet to enjoy all over again.

Already she could recall much with tender affection. Unbelievable as it sounded, she knew she was becoming devotedly attached, not only to Robert, but to the other members of this most special of families, all of whom she regarded with particular affection and admiration. It was like having her own special chair, a place she could always go to find comfort, support and rest. She could not believe her good fortune. How was it that she was blessed with what she had always wanted—a family and a sense of belonging?

She was uncertain as to which feeling overwhelmed her the most. Was it a thankful spirit, or the irrepressible urge to do everything possible for them in return? She was so happy.

She loved Robert. She loved this family.

She loved this day. Everything about it was perfect, and for a moment she believed there was nothing she could not do. She was Michelangelo painting the Sistine Chapel. She was Hannibal crossing the Alps. She paused and looked back at the castle, hearing the thunder in the distance. She walked on a bit farther and climbed up an embankment. The beauty and bounty of the earth was gathered about her feet. From where she stood, she could look out over the Borders, where heather-clad hills and emerald valleys were laced with silver streams and rivers that teemed with salmon. Everything existed peacefully. A baronial castle, tucked into a hillside, and the ruins of a Spartan stone tower were both reminders of a battle-filled past. She thought of the missing earl, and wondered if he had ever visited these ancient places she saw. How much they had changed since he was alive.

She was immediately glad not only that she had come here with Robert, but also that his home was in this place. Having grown up on the English side of the Borders, she knew the heartbreaking history of the area, where every stream seemed to sing out and each valley rang with the sound of battle. She could still recall a few bars of a Border ballad of derring-do that Agnes would sing to her when she was a small child. Even now, the magic of this place seemed tangible and reached out to her in such a way she almost felt she could touch the wild magic of its hills and ancient fortresses.

She brought her hand up to shield her eyes to make out the ruins of a distant peel tower where it had resided for centuries on a hill of commanding height. She remembered Robert pointing out such a place to her on their journey here. "Beacon hills," he called them, explaining they were once an integral part of the survival of the Borders: upon sighting the English, the fires were lit on the hills and the message got to Edinburgh in five minutes.

Thinking about Robert made her yearn to see him, so she walked faster. She was as in love with him as she could be in such a short time, and she knew it would be a love that would grow. Surely, no one had a right to be so happy. Her life had meaning and a purpose now. She had never been so gladdened, so full of contentment. She was Lady Douglas now, and nothing could rob her of her newfound joy.

29

Banks of clouds were forming in the distance. A cool wind began to blow, and the Scots-gray clouds Meleri had viewed in the distance were now overhead. She heard the approaching sound of a horse coming up behind her and she moved to the side of the narrow path to give the rider room to pass, hoping as she did it would be Robert.

When she caught a glimpse of the horse and rider, her heart froze in terror.

Philip...

Even from where she stood, she recognized the hard lines of his face and the black cloak that billowed out behind stiffly held shoulders. Even if she were unable to see his face, she would have known it was Philip, by the manner in which he rode his horse with no regard for the well-lathered beast.

Transfixed, she stood watching him until she realized he was not slowing down. Afraid he would try to run her down, she turned quickly and grabbed up her skirts so that she might run faster. It was both fear and desperation that propelled her forward over the rough ground, mindless of the sharp stones that pierced the soft soles of her shoes and the brambles that reached out of nowhere to scratch her arms and face.

She was almost to the top of the hill when she felt the burning sting as her hair was nearly pulled from her scalp. A split second later, she was lifted from her feet and jerked backward. She fell down…down…down…into a dark and fathomless abyss.

Before she opened her eyes, Meleri knew she was gagged and bound, just as she knew the name of the person who had done it. Thankful he had not bound her eyes, she looked around.

Overhead, a rainbow-hued ring encircled a full moon, where long gossamer clouds stretched away from it, like bony fingers pointing at the world below and curling through the trees. Silver-dusted moonshine stole the color from the earth, painting everything from a palette with varying shades of ghostly white, leaving everything etched in black and white, like the crisp, distinct outlines of a silhouette.

The temperature had been much higher earlier in the day. Now the warm gaiety of the sun had vanished, leaving only shadows and the somber coolness of spectral fingers, clammy and cold. Next to one of the crumbling walls, she could see Philip hunched down beside a fire, adding more wood. They were near an old priory, for behind him, firelight danced over old religious drawings, still visible on the walls.

She closed her eyes, hoping he would not realize she was awake, when suddenly the gag was ripped away and her mouth was flooded with a strong metallic taste. She opened her eyes and saw him standing over her. She looked past him, staring at the murals again, where golden light from the leaping flames cast huge demonic shapes that frolicked gleefully over the time-forgotten murals.

He glanced at the mural. "Evil triumphs over good."

"Perhaps, at least for the time being," she said, "but in the end, good will always triumph."

He said nothing more, but stood looking down at her, a nightmare presence in the midst of waiting shadows. Her skin pricked, and all her senses came acutely alive, waiting, watching in readiness.

"So, here we are, two young lovers, alone at last."

"Lovers!" she almost spat the words. "You mock the very word when you say it."

"I saw you leave Beloyn. Were you coming to find me?"

"Hardly." She almost told him she was looking for her husband, but realized he would surely kill Robert if she did.

"I regret having to hear that. It would have made everything ever so much nicer."

"For you, perhaps."

"He has turned you against me, not that I am surprised. You were always more susceptible to falsehood than the truth. Not that it matters. The important thing is, you are my future. My *entire* future, and that is why you are coming with me now."

"What are you going to do with me?"

"Dear, dear, was that stress in your voice? Let me see now, what *am* I going to do with you? I have asked myself that same question. Now that I have you, I must consider my choices. The way I see it, I have three alternatives. *First,* I could leave you here, bound to perdition, to rot in this holy place, unless something more benevolent happens and you are rescued. Of course, the likelihood of that happening is remote, since this priory is well hidden and known by relatively few. That would be such a shame, such a terrible waste. You truly are a lovely piece—not quite my taste, but I can recognize quality. *Second,* I could marry you on the spot. That would ultimately please my father and secure my inheritance. Although I fear you are not too receptive to the idea, at least not now…which would leave me with no choice but to take you somewhere private, where there are any number of items perfected to change a stubborn mind. *Third,* I could kill you now and have done with it, but that would be putting a bullet in my own back, because you are far, far more valuable to me alive…at least for the time being. Therefore, I think we will go with the second one. What say you to that?"

"I say you will never get away with it."

"I will leave you to the council of your own wisdom, as well as your inborn desire to remain alive no matter the cost. You do know you either marry me, or you will never leave here alive?"

He stuffed the dirty rag back in her mouth and tied it behind her head. "Sorry, love, but I can't leave you screaming at the four winds, now, can I?"

"Umpb...rumplsh...mmphm!"

He laughed. "Careful, sweetheart, you are going to choke yourself if you keep trying to talk."

Meleri leaned her head back against the tree where she was tied, while she tried to dislodge the cloth jammed into her mouth. She gagged. Closing her eyes, she willed the frantic beating of her heart to slow. It would not do to use all of her energy on a fluttering heart. Dismal though the prospects were that she would ever be rescued, she thought of Robert and wondered if he was looking for her. She dozed off, with thoughts of Robert on her mind.

When she awoke, she saw Philip's golden head bent in front of her. "You probably don't deserve it, but I have brought you some water."

He removed the gag and she nodded her appreciation, her mouth too dry to speak. He held a tin cup to her lips and she drank greedily.

"Don't drink it too fast or I won't give you any more."

When she drained the cup, she looked at him and said, "More."

He laughed. "If only you were so greedy for me," he said wistfully, then rose to his feet. "It is time we were off. It will be daybreak soon."

He must have seen the surprised look on he face, for he said, "Melli, my dear, surely you didn't think we would stay here indefinitely? We must be off to England, by way of Gretna Green, of course, where you and I will be married."

She had already decided not to rail against him, for she knew it would do her no good in the end, nor would it further her cause. It would only serve to keep him on guard. It was her hope that by being the model captive, he would relax enough to make a mistake or two. She would be ready when he did.

He untied the rope that bound her to the tree, but he left her hands tied behind her. "I cannot ride like this," she said.

"You don't think I'm going to put you on your own horse, do you?"

He retied her hands in front of her and helped her into the saddle on his horse. A moment later, he mounted behind her, and they rode away from the priory.

As they rode, she found herself dozing off a time or two. When she finally awoke, the sky on the horizon was beginning to get an edge of dull steel gray. Joy flooded her soul at the thought that morning was on its way. A lot of good it will do you, she admonished herself. Philip is not some vampire who will see the sun and slink away. The joy ebbed from her slowly.

Her eyes were wide open now and she watched the road ahead. Before long, she thought she caught the shadow of something moving near the edge of the trees that lined the road, but decided it was a large animal—probably a deer—or her imagination.

As they rode up a steep hill and crested the top, a green, shimmering mist seemed to come out of nowhere. It hovered in the air directly in front of them. The strange sight caused Philip's gelding to whinny and dance around nervously before he reared. When he came down and his hooves slammed against the hard ground, Meleri's teeth jarred painfully.

Philip cursed and she knew he was having difficulty controlling such a big horse with her in front of him. Eerie green mist or not, she knew her only chance was now, for there might not be another one.

Without a single thought to what she might do to herself, she took a deep breath and threw the entire weight of her body to the left, shooting out of the saddle like a projectile. She twisted sharply in midair and landed on her side; her shoulder slammed against the rock-hard ground with such force, she heard it crack, fearing she might have broken her arm.

His horse reared again, and the impact of his mighty hooves shook the ground beside her. She heard Philip utter another curse and knew she had only seconds. She prayed it would be enough time to get to her feet and run, before he brought his mount under control and came after her.

She struggled to her knees, jabbing one of them against a sharp rock. She ignored the pain and pulled herself to her feet. She held her throbbing arm, looked into the shadowy, early morning light and decided the best thing was to run, in any direction.

She plunged ahead, guided by instinct and the faint hint of coming morning. She ran, with blood running down her leg and a sharp, twisting pain stabbing into her chest. *Robert, Robert, Robert,* she kept repeating to herself, over and over.

Behind her, she could hear the sound of a horse, and she ran faster, but not fast enough, for the next instant, she felt Philip's body slam hard against her before he rolled over her and down a small embankment. The impact knocked her to her knees and she struggled to get up again. She did not want to waste time by looking back, so she kept on running, ignoring the pain. She had no way of knowing where he was until she was a few steps from the top of the hill and felt his hand close around the collar of her dress.

She only had time to think, *Please God, don't let it end this way,* before he jerked her back, while she was still fighting to go forward.

"Damn you! Hold still!" he shouted.

"Let me go! Don't you understand it's over and you've lost!"

"That is where you are wrong, you devil's spawn!"

Thrown off balance, his hands closed vicelike around her arms before he spun her around to face him and she stared up into a face that was barely human. Before she could take a breath, his hands, like the claws of a wild animal, closed around her throat.

He said her name and cursed her before he drew back his hand, and she knew he was going to drive his fist into her face to silence her. She tried to scream, but was never certain if she did or not, for she was only aware of opening her mouth and the feel of air rushing from her throat. He swore again, damning her name.

Before she could realize what was happening, she was released with such force, she dropped like a stone. She landed with an excruciating blow to her head, followed by a blinding light. When the pain passed, she opened her eyes to a world that was spinning. She was mindful only of the sharp hooves of Philip's horse as they raked the air and pawed the ground, dangerously close to her head. She shuddered at the sound of Philip's hate-filled voice as he said, "You aren't saved yet, you bitch! Not by a long shot! I'll be back, and I will find you!"

He spurred Neptune. The big horse leaped forward.

Not able to understand why he fled and left her behind, she looked around to see if something frightened him away.

She had never prayed so hard to see Robert coming to rescue her.

Through the fine morning mist that was moving swiftly across the fellside, she made out the darkly cloaked figure of a man dressed all in black. She blinked her eyes to clear her blurred vision, then realized it was her own blood that made it so difficult to see. He came toward her, a sword of enormous proportions held in his hand.

She recognized him as the same strangely dressed man she had seen before. She reached her hand out toward him. "Help me…"

She could feel the blood running down her leg and from her mouth. Her arm and head ached abominably, but she managed to crawl to her feet. She was about to call out to him, when he gave her a brilliant smile. Immediately, his figure began to radiate and grow dim.

Meleri was suddenly aware she could see the hillside behind him, as if his body was transparent, enabling her to see right through him. She wiped the blood from her eyes and watched as his image hovered only a moment longer, before it disappeared altogether.

Footfalls came up behind her. Her heart stilled. Philip was returning. That was why the ghost left. There was no one to help her now, save herself. She started limping, gradually increasing her pace until she was running down the side of the hill.

"Meleri, for the love of God, will you stop!"

She almost cried at the sound of Robert's beloved voice. But she lost her footing and went sprawling, rolling and sliding over sharp rocks that cut into her, until she came to a stop.

Before she knew what was happening, she was grabbed and hauled, without a hint of compassion, to her feet.

"Lord deliver me from a stupid woman! What in the name of hell did you think you were doing, shooting down the side of the hill on your belly looking like you thought you could fly? Didn't you hear me calling you? Here, give me your hand…did that bastard tie you up? Here, now! I know you are glad to see me, but you need to be still, and stop grinding your nose against my shirt, so I can untie this knot… Dammit! Hold still! You gave me the worst fright of my life, do you know that? Look at you, bleeding from a dozen holes, every ounce of visible skin scraped clean as a deer hide."

"It hurts."

"Well, you'd better be thankful about that, because that's the only thing that's keeping me from turning you over my knee and beating the drawers off of you."

He yanked his cape from his shoulders and wrapped it around her. "You're as cold as the Firth of Tay. You will probably catch a cold, and I'll have to nurse you out of that one, as well. Hugh! Bring me some whisky."

"Iain?" she whispered.

He turned back to her. "He's all right. He and two of the men went after Philip. Here, lean on me and drink some of this. Do you think you can ride?"

She opened her mouth to answer and swallowed a loch full of liquid fire. Coughing and sputtering, she looked up at him, just as he poured another burning river down her throat.

"Don't look at me like I'm feeding you poison. It's whisky. It will warm you, if it doesn't leak out all of the holes in your hide, first."

"What are you doing here?"

"Trying to be the noble hero and save the woman I love, but as always, you are too damn headstrong to let anyone help you, so you beat me to it and saved yourself."

"It wasn't me. It was the ghost," she said as darkness started to descend.

He gathered her close to him in his arms and said, "Easy love, I'm taking you home."

Robert stood over her, stroking her forehead and speaking softly, in an assuring tone, telling her she was safe and all would be well. God love him, he had never in his life prayed so hard that what he said would prove to be true. He could not lose her. Not now, before he had a chance to tell her what she meant to him, before they shared a lifetime together and raised the barins he hoped they would have. If she would only open her eyes; if she would speak; if she would move but one tiny finger—anything, to show him she was still with him, that she had not gone away and left him, as Sorcha had done.

The agony of waiting and not knowing…it was eating into the heart and soul of him. She was so pale, so still, so small. He had never felt so helpless.

Gram pushed a chair behind him and told him to sit down. "You won't be of any use to her when she wakes if you are too exhausted to speak. Whatever you can do standing up, you can do sitting down."

He sat, gathered her small, pale hand in his and brought it up to his lips. "Don't leave me."

Meleri made no indication that she had heard him, and he lay his head on the pillow beside her and closed his eyes. He did not open them until much later, when the rest of the family came into the room, and the sound of it woke him.

It was an hour after that, when he first noticed her eyes were moving beneath the paper-thin lids. He leaned his head closer and told her how much she meant to him, how much everyone here had come to love her—him most of all.

She began to stir, slightly at first, and he knew she could hear voices long before she could open her eyes. He kept on talking to her, identifying the others as they spoke, telling her Agnes and Lady Margaret were hemming a new dress for her, that Gowan and Fingal had arrived with a bouquet of heather for her.

She tried to speak, but no sound came forth. He put his hand on the side of her face and said, "It's all right, lass. You're safe at home. Rest now." He was surprised at the emotion he felt when he touched her, for no one had ever been able to elicit such an aching tenderness from a mere touch. He realized she was crying, and he brushed the tears from her cheek.

She turned her face and kissed the palm of his hand. It was not an expression of love, but one of gratitude. Poor lass, did she not know it was he who was grateful, who would be grateful until the day he died? He gathered her to him and held her in his arms, content for now to do nothing more than rub her back in a consoling way. "Don't cry, lass. You are home now. Nothing can harm you."

"You came," she said. She lifted his hand and brought it to her lips so she could kiss his palm again.

He would never forget the terrible feeling when he discovered she was missing. He wished with all his being that he had found that bastard, Waverly, but Iain and the men had returned, having lost his trail when it began to rain.

She opened her eyes. "You saved my life. I would have died if you had not come and frightened Philip away."

"No, lass, you saved yourself. Waverly was already gone by the time we arrived."

"But I saw you. I saw you coming up the hill in your cape, with a sword in your hand."

"Black Douglas," Lady Margaret said. "It must have been the ghost of William that she saw."

Robert lay her head back against the pillows and brought the blankets up to cover her. He was about to turn away when she clutched his hand. "Where are Corrie and Dram?"

"Downstairs. The gate at the stairs is closed. They won't bother you."

"Bother me," she whispered. "I want them here."

"Here? You want them in here, with you?"

"Feel safer…I want them here," she whispered.

"Then you shall have them." He sent the twins to bring the dogs. She had drifted to sleep again but awoke when Dram nuzzled her hand with his wet nose. She opened her eyes and smiled at Dram, before she placed her face against his wiry whiskers. "Corrie?"

"On the other side of the bed."

She turned her head to see Corrie resting on the bed next to her. Robert could not help noticing Corrie's great brown eyes were watching her, as if she understood what had happened. Meleri pulled her hand out from beneath the covers and stroked Corrie's head. "Stay with me," she said, and closed her eyes.

After she was asleep, Robert left her with the dogs and walked Gram from the room.

"Whatever you decide to do," she said, "don't let your concern for her override your good judgment."

"What do you mean?"

"It is a rare man who is not moved by the sight of a woman's tears."

Some time after Robert and Gram had gone and Meleri was alone, she had another visitor—one who came into her room, bringing the mist with him. He moved without a sound, a dark cape swirling about him, and at his side, he carried a great sword.

Even in her sleep, she felt a presence and knew she was not alone. She opened her eyes and saw him standing just a few feet away. Corrie and Dram began to whine. "Go away," she said. "You frighten the dogs. I do not want you to be real. I do not believe in ghosts."

In an instant, his image began to shimmer and he was gone. It was confirmation enough that he had only been a figment of her imagination, for he did not look like the sort to obey a woman's command, whether he was real or imagined.

She put her hand on Corrie's head and closed her eyes. The next time she opened them, the heat of the early morning sunlight bathed her face in warmth. Agnes was by the window, drawing back the drapes.

"How are you feeling, milady?"

"Like I've been beheaded," she whispered. "My throat hurts abominably."

"You have the beginnings of a nasty bruise. Did he choke you?"

"I don't remember."

The door opened and Robert walked in, followed by Iain and Lady Margaret. "We came to see if you were ready for visitors," Lady Margaret said. "You've been sleeping for so long, it is becoming harder and harder for all of us to stay away."

Meleri wrenched herself upright, remembering her cuts and scrapes as they began to throb. She frowned and looked around the room, remembering her other visitor. "He was here."

Robert tried soothing her. "No one has been here."

"No, he came back. He was here, in my room, dressed as he was before. He had a great sword. I thought at first I was dreaming, and I told him to leave, that I did not believe in ghosts."

"What did he say?" Robert asked.

"Nothing. He vanished."

Lady Margaret patted her hand. "You probably were dreaming, like you said."

Iain's voice broke in. "Robbie…"

Robert went on talking. "Thankfully, you are almost recovered and that should be the end of it. No more ghosts. No black cape. No big sword."

Iain's voice cut in again, stronger this time. "Robbie, look."

Meleri looked along with everyone else and saw it in the corner, propped up against a chair, the sword's long sliver blade catching a gleam of sunlight.

Hugh picked it up and held it with both hands. "St. Columba! It is as heavy as the devil."

"It probably belonged to the devil," Robert said.

"It is newly polished," Iain noted.

Hugh handed the sword to Robert, who took a moment to accustom himself to such size and weight. Soon, he wielded it with a reasonable amount of dexterity. "A beautifully balanced two-handed *claidheamb-mor*," he said, using the Gaelic term. "A true, honest-to-Scotland claymore." He glanced at Iain. "What do you make of it?"

"It's authentic…made before the sixteenth century, I would

say. See how the quillons are at an angle to the blade and how they are diamond shaped? And here…see how each quillon ends in an ornament made of four open circles of iron?"

"Aye," Robert said. "The claymores that came into use in the 1600s were basket-hilt, because the hand was no longer protected by a steel gauntlet."

Watching Robert swing the claymore, Iain began to sing softly the words of a satirical song from the turn of the century.

> The sword at thy arse was a great black blade
> With a great basket hilt of iron made;
> But a long rapier doth hang by his side,
> And huffing doth this bonny Scot ride.
> Bonny Scot, we all witness can
> That England hath made then a gentleman.

Robert rested the claymore, tip pointed to the floor. "Of course, the big question isn't what kind of claymore it is, but *whose* claymore, and *where* did it come from?" He turned to Iain. "Do you think *he* left it?"

"Of course he did," said Lady Margaret. "This sword proves we are dealing with the ghost of Black Douglas and not something Meleri dreamed."

"And here I thought *I* was Black Douglas," Robert said.

"You are the present one. I am speaking of the original."

Hugh laughed. "Robbie, you are only a copy."

Gram shot him a silencing glance. "According to the legend, Sir William had a great claymore. This one fits that description."

"A lot of claymores would fit that description," Iain said.

"There is one way to find out," she said. "Supposedly, the earl's claymore was inscribed."

Robert and Iain began to look the claymore over carefully. "Here it is," Iain said at last, "but the words are faint and difficult to read."

"Can you make out a name?" Robert asked.

Iain didn't answer right away. After a few seconds, he said,

"Yes, I can make out the name William, First Earl of Douglas. There is another inscription, but it is too worn to be legible. I can barely make out the word *better,* and perhaps this one is *mighty,* but I am not certain."

"At least we know it is William's sword," Robert said, "even if we aren't certain how it got here."

"*He* brought it," Meleri said.

"Well, if he did, I don't understand why he would leave it," Iain said.

"No one believed he existed," Gram said, and Meleri felt the truth of those words bite into her. "He left his claymore as proof. A child could figure that one out. The legend says the Douglases will be restored by the truest Scot, one with a stout heart."

"That's it!" Iain said.

"That's what?" Robert asked.

"The inscription on the claymore," he answered, searching the long blade for the faint inscription he could not make out before. "Here it is: *Better is a stout heart than a mighty blade.*"

The three of them turned to stare at Meleri.

"It isn't me!" she cried. "If you had only seen me out there, quivering like a bowl of jelly, knees knocking, whining and sniveling like a baby. The moment I got a chance, I bolted like a runaway sheep. I am a coward, through and through. I come from a long line of cowards. We always have at least one in every generation."

She paused, watching them, seeing they did not look convinced. "I'm such a coward, I'm too cowardly to stay a coward. I am ready to pass the gauntlet to someone else. I have been choked, chased, pushed, knocked down, tied up, gagged, cursed, propositioned, lied to, ignored, humiliated and embarrassed to the point that I quit. I withdraw my nomination from whomever it was that nominated me. I do not want to be the one with the truest heart or the stoutest heart, or a Scot's heart, either. I will keep my own *English* heart, if you please. I want to live the rest of my life being normal…and normal people do not cavort with ghosts." She crossed her arms in front of her. "Now, is there anything I said that anyone did not understand?"

"I think you just about covered everything," said Lady Margaret.

"Aye, I've never heard anything so tragic," Iain said without a hint of sympathy.

"Your point," Robert said, "but the game isn't over yet."

She tried again. "Why is everyone looking at me? Don't I have any say in this matter?"

"You've been clucking like an overfed hen since we walked in," Robert said.

"You should feel honored. The earl has never appeared to anyone before," Lady Margaret said.

"Then tell him to go honor someone else. Not that it matters. I was making the whole thing up. I wanted attention and I thought that would be a good way to get it."

"And you made this up, as well?" Robert asked, holding up the claymore.

She scoffed. "Anyone could have left that in here. It probably came from the armory."

"This is the claymore that belonged to the first Earl of Douglas. It hasn't been seen since his death," Lady Margaret said.

"I grow weary of all of this," said Meleri. "I have been through a lot. My brains have been addled. I have a vivid imagination, for goodness' sake! It could not be a ghost. I will not accept that. I refuse to believe in them."

"Apparently, that doesn't make any difference. He obviously believes in you," Iain said.

"Well, I don't want him to," Meleri said, so crossly that everyone laughed. "And I don't want his fusty old sword, either. I wish he would take it back and choose someone else to frighten."

"Don't say that," Iain teased. "You might hurt his feelings."

"I hope he heard me! I hope he is hurt enough to choose someone else. I am not a Scot. I will never be a Scot. My heart is anything but stout. I am as yellow as a kite's claw. I told you before, I come from a long line of faint hearts. One glance from Philip and I have all the fortitude of melting wax. I was everything you could possibly associate with being a coward—afraid, yellow, hen-hearted. I don't have the courage of a bloody chicken."

"Don't fash yourself, lass. This is nothing you should concern yourself with now," Robert said. "The most important thing is for you to feel better."

"I do feel better. I was just a little shaken up."

"I think I will see what the twins are up to," Lady Margaret said.

"I'll go with you," Iain said.

Meleri watched them file out of the room, and when they were all gone save Robert, she glared at the claymore leaning against the wall. She crossed her arms over her chest and glared harder. "I wish Iain had taken that bloody thing with him. I don't want it in here," she said, sounding as irritable as she felt.

Robert came to sit down on the bed beside her. He picked up her hand and smiled faintly. "Such small hands to have been through so much."

She lifted her chin and let go with a pathetic sob, happy that for once she had managed to arouse his rarely used sympathy. She was suddenly startled when he threw back his head and the room rolled with the sound of his laughter.

She had been right when she decided the most beautiful sound in the entire world was the sound of Robbie Douglas's laughter. She waited patiently for him to take her in his arms. When he did not, she said morosely, "I would think you would at least offer me some comfort."

"Do you now?"

"Yes. I have been sorely treated and my body aches abominably. A little tea and sympathy would go a long way toward restoring my good humor."

"I might be persuaded toward sympathy, lass, but I can't abide by your English way of loving something as abominable as tea."

He was still holding her hand, still stroking her fingers, and for quite some time he seemed content to do only that. Then, at last, he looked up and smiled at her, his face an odd mixture of amusement and compassion. "I suppose you, being a woman of high temperament, are having a difficult time with patience."

"No, what I am having a difficult time of is making a decision. I am fairly rendered asunder trying to decide which I want more, to pick up that basin there and break it over your head, or to throw my pride to the wind and ask you to hold me."

"Then let me take the choice away from you." He put his arms around her and drew her against him, cradling her head against his chest. "How's this?"

She sighed. "Better," she said. "Infinitely better."

That was true. It was better. Not as good as it had been before, for pain was still in her heart, softened somewhat by the knowledge that Robert had cared enough for her to come after her. He also made an effort to act as if he cared. Was it possible? Could he have come to care for her, in spite of his original intention to use her against the king? All this thinking made her head ache. Right now, she did not want to think about it anymore. She would think when she felt better.

They remained as they were for quite some time, neither of them talking, until at last, she asked, "What are you going to do?"

"About what?"

"Philip."

"It's my worry. I will take care of it."

"I know you will, but what do you plan to do?"

"Perhaps I will pay him a visit."

"In England?"

"Aye."

"You don't need to go there yourself. Can't you send someone?"

"If you want your eggs hatched, sit on them yourself."

She shook her head and said, "I speak of danger, and he answers me with eggs."

"Shh," he said, and kissed her on the nose. "Rest and let someone else do the cackling for a while."

"A cock may crow, but it's the hen who lays the eggs."

30

That night, Meleri fell asleep in Robert's arms. In the wee hours of the following morning, they were awakened by the clamorous sound of someone banging the brass knockers on the front door. Pulled from a deep sleep, Meleri could not imagine who was knocking at this hour.

She watched as Robert sat up. She knew he intended to hurry downstairs before the clanging noise awakened everyone in the household.

"Who could that be?" she asked. "Are you expecting anyone?"

"No. I have no idea who it is."

She rolled over and leaned toward the end of the bed, trying to reach her dressing gown.

"Don't get up," he said, and leaned over to kiss her shoulder. "I'll see who it is."

He was into his shirt and breeches quickly and blew her a kiss before he said, "Go back to sleep."

"Will you be gone long?" she asked, barely getting the words out before she yawned.

"Not with a lass like you waiting all soft and sleepy in my bed. Keep yourself warm, I'll be back soon."

"And if I find myself getting cold?"

"Don't worry. I am confident I can find a way or two to warm you when I return."

He disappeared around the door, and she stared at the place she had seen him last. She intended to stay awake until he returned.

She remembered Robert telling her the night before how much he loved her and luxuriated in the thought of it for a moment before she rolled over and nestled down into the warm, downy bed and closed her eyes.

He woke her with a kiss when he returned.

Her eyes flew open.

"I didn't mean to startle you."

She raised her shoulder and rubbed it against the cheek he kissed, as if the kiss were still there and she could feel it. She shivered. "Brrrr. Your nose is cold."

He chuckled. "So is the rest of me." He went to his wardrobe and removed his boots and a pair of socks. "I wish I had time to warm up a bit. A couple of rounds in the bed with you ought to do it."

"Are you going somewhere?"

"Aye."

"Where?"

"Down the road a bit."

That answer told her a great deal, she thought. She watched him pull his socks on. "Who was at the door?"

"A neighbor."

Robert certainly did not volunteer more information than he had to. Scots, she had learned, were not lavish with words, or anything else. A more frugal lot she had never seen. Only two days ago, Agnes reported that it was a well-known fact that Lady Margaret never put dots over her *i*'s to save ink.

"It's a bit early to be paying a social call. What did he want?" she insisted.

"He wants me to go with them."

"Why?"

"They found a body."

"Where?"

"Down the road, not too far from here."

Exasperated, she decided getting information from him was like gathering scattered pearls from a broken necklace...you could do it, but it would take some time. "Why do they need you to go?"

"He's not someone they recognized. They are hoping I might be able to identify him."

Two complete sentences in a row, she thought. Unbelievable.

Suddenly, she shot up in the bed. "If they found a dead man, do you think it was the ghost?"

He gave her a look that said he found her charming in spite of that mindless comment. "You're so idiotic, you're adorable."

She crossed her arms. "I am not your ordinary idiot."

"Interesting. Remind me to give that some more thought when I have the time. Until then, I shall simply wonder how one would go about killing a ghost. Unless you can enlighten me, of course."

If her face was not red, it should be. She had never felt more stupid. "I did not phrase that correctly...."

He pulled on a boot. "No, you did not. Care to try again?"

"What I meant to say was, could I have seen a real man and only thought it was a ghost, and if so, could he the dead man?"

He pulled on his other boot and stood up. "It's too early in the morning for me to decipher that. I'll think about it and give you an answer when I return."

"Perhaps I should come with you. If it is the man I saw, I will recognize him."

He came to the side of the bed and kissed her. "I have a better idea. Why don't you stay here and work on a list of more questions to ask me when I get back."

Before she could retort, he was gone.

Edwin Muir and some of his men were waiting for Robert. When he led his horse out of the stables, they were dousing their lanterns. It would be daylight soon, and over the tops of the hills in the distance, the sky was already beginning to lighten.

"Sorry to put you to all this bother," Edwin said.

"No bother," Robert said, putting his foot in the stirrup and swinging into the saddle. "Has anyone sent for the sheriff?"

"Aye, James Fergusson stopped by my place on his way to Dumfries. He was going after the sheriff."

Robert nodded and the men started off. They rode in silence down the pebbled lane that led to a single-track metaled road. Once they reached it, they turned in the direction James indicated. They then rode toward the low sloping hills where the fires of druid sacrifices once blazed.

The sun was on the horizon, coming through the trees in slender red shafts, the confusion of leaves striking the road with lace-patterned tracery. Robert studied them for a moment. "Was it James who found him?"

"No, it was one of his men coming home late from a tryst," Edwin said.

"The body is still where you found it?"

"Aye, we thought it best to leave it that way for the sheriff."

"Could you tell what happened?"

"Not exactly. Daniel Murray found him. He said it appeared that his horse had dragged the man to death. When Daniel found him, his foot was still caught in the stirrup."

Something about Edwin's voice made Robert wonder if Edwin was holding something back. "Is there anything else? Something you don't want me to know?"

"No, nothing I want to keep from you, exactly, but James did find something strange when he arrived."

"Strange? You mean he found something that might indicate the man was murdered?"

"He wouldn't say murder, exactly, but he did say there were some coins lying next to the body."

"Scots coins?"

"Aye."

"They probably came out of his pockets."

"Aye, that is what I thought, but James said the coins were old ones. Very old."

"Hmm. That is odd," said Robert. "Perhaps he was a collector, then. I wonder how old, or what kind they were."

"James said he didn't recognize them, although it was dark and he was using a lantern to see by. I asked him if they could have been doits, bodles or merks. He did not think so. He thought they might be older."

They arrived at the place where the body was found. Just as Edwin said, Daniel Murray was waiting for them in a small clearing. No one else was there. Not even a body.

Robert greeted Daniel with a nod as he dismounted. "It looks like the sheriff arrived ahead of us."

"No, James hasna arrived with the sheriff yet," Daniel said.

"Then where is the body?"

"Not far from here. Angus Beattie and Donald Mackie are waiting with the man's horse."

Robert nodded. He knew both Angus and Donald, who were in the employ of James Fergusson.

"I suppose we might as well get this over with," Edwin said.

"Aye," Murray said, "This way."

Edwin and Murray walked ahead, while Robert followed at a slower pace. When they reached the clearing, Edwin and Murray paused to speak with Angus and Donald.

When a bright shaft of light struck the clearing, Robert saw something sticking in a tree nearby. Closer investigation proved it to be a dirk, quite old and solidly wedged, deep in the bark. It took some doing, but he managed to extract it.

"Have a look at this," Edwin called to Robert.

Robert slipped the dirk in his belt and joined the three men, where they were standing next to a fine blood bay, his reins wrapped around a tree branch. Donald Mackie held the bridle and stroked the bay's head. The horse was of exceptional breeding and conformation—one that would belong to a wealthy man; or else, it was stolen.

Robert walked around the bay with Edwin. He saw the body lying facedown, the man's left foot still caught in the stirrup and horribly twisted.

Daniel Murray was now crouched down on his haunches near the body. He came to his feet when he saw Robert and Edwin approach.

"Is the body where you found it?" Robert asked. "It hasn't been moved?"

"Aye. I tied the horse as soon as I discovered the body and the coins, then I rode after Mr. Fergusson."

"After James and I arrived, we thought it best not to touch anything else," Edwin said. "We left Angus and Donald here with the horse, so he wouldn't break free and drag the body off."

"I have heard horses don't like to be around the dead," Robert said. He looked down at the body and saw the clothes were badly torn and muddy. He glanced at the saddle. "The saddle appears to be English."

"Aye," Edwin said.

"Anything in his saddlebag?" Robert asked.

"No identification, but there was a purse full of English pounds," Edwin said, then added, "He was a wealthy man, whoever he was."

Robert nodded in agreement. "Aye, I thought the same when I saw the horse. The wealth alone should brand him as English."

"Aye," Edwin said. "English, or a robber. The horse and the money we found in his pockets could have been stolen."

Robert looked at David. "What about the coins that were found? Where are they?"

"I have them," Angus said, and he handed Robert a kerchief he had tied around them. Robert untied the knot and looked down at five coins. They were old. Quite old.

"Where did you find them?"

"They were lying here," David said, indicating a place near the body. "Three of them were lying on the ground right here, the other two were near his head."

Robert picked up one of the coins and turned it over in his hand. It was inscribed, but he could not make out the words. He walked a few feet away from the dense foliage of the tree, so he could see the coins in the full sunlight. He recognized three of them immediately and knew they were gold. He read the inscription. *"Ihc Autem Transiens Per Medium Illorum Ibat."*

"Latin," Edwin said, "but I didn't like Latin as a boy. Now I can do little more than recognize it. Do you know what is says?"

Robert nodded. *"'But Jesus passing through the midst of them went his way.'* They are nobles, worth six shillings and eight pence, or half a Scottish mark. They are from the reign of David II."

Edwin whistled. "Rare as virgin's milk. I don't think I've ever seen one of them before. How did you know what they were?"

"My grandmother has two such coins, although hers are more worn and not all of the inscriptions can be read."

"Fourteenth-century coins," Daniel said. "That makes them very old."

"And too rare and valuable to be lying loose in the dirt," Edwin added.

"Do you suppose he stole them?" Daniel asked.

Robert didn't get to answer, for at that moment the sheriff, Walter Robertson, rode into the clearing with James Fergusson.

Walter didn't seem too interested in what kind of coins they were, only in the fact that they were quite old, and the significance of them being found with the dead man.

"Daniel was just asking Robert if he thought they were stolen when you rode up," Edwin said.

"Could be," Walter said, then he rolled the dead man over and looked down at his face. "Does anyone recognize him?"

No one did, and the sheriff busied himself with his routine investigation before he enlisted the help of Robert and James Fergusson. "You can take his foot out of the stirrup now," he said.

Once that was done, he told Angus and Donald to lead the horse away from the body. "Tie him over there, away from the other horses. He is acting a bit skittish. No need to agitate the others."

Robert glanced down at the body. It had been dragged for some distance, for the face was badly scratched and cut. It would make identification almost impossible for anyone, save those who knew the man well.

"Was anything in his pockets?" the sheriff asked.

"We didn't check his pockets," James said. "The coins were found in the saddlebag."

Walter searched the man's pockets and produced a few shillings and a small silver knife with the initials P.W.A. engraved upon it. He did not say anything, but went on about his investigation. When he was finished, he ordered the men to put the body over the back of his horse and secure it. Walter then scratched his head and said, "Well, I agree the man is probably English, but beyond that, I don't know. It sure would help things if we knew who he was or where he was from. If only someone could identify him."

Robert had been quietly thinking justice had at last been served, and the bastard was dead. "I think there is a possibility that he is an Englishman by the name of Philip Ashton."

"Philip Ashton," Walter repeated. "What were the initials on that knife?"

"P.W.A.," James said.

"Philip W. Ashton," he said. "It could be." Walter looked at Robert. "How is it you have a name, but you can't identify him?"

"I have never met Philip Ashton."

"Do you know anyone who has, anyone who could identify him?"

"Aye, my wife."

Walter looked as if he had some more questions he wanted to ask, but he checked himself and said, "We will take the body to Beloyn," Walter said. "I am anxious to have this done."

As they rode toward Beloyn, Robert explained the association between himself and Philip Ashton, telling them how Philip and his wife had once been betrothed and how Philip had suddenly appeared and approached her, twice in the last two days. Apparently satisfied, at least for the time being, Walter did not ask anything more.

Robert was thankful for that. It was damnably difficult to maintain a casual conversation when his insides were knotted with disbelief. Ten years he had wanted to get even with this man, and then, when it happened, it had all gone so quickly.

Robert thought about Meleri, worried about the strain it would put upon her to be asked to view a dead body. She had been through enough already with this man. He was not sure how she would react to all of this. He was certain about one thing, however, and that was the dead man's identity.

If it were up to Robert, he would have left the bastard's body out there to rot. However, Meleri would have to identify him, so the family could be notified and the body returned to his home. Robert was filled with iron resolve, knowing he had to maintain a passive sort of front, for he could not register even the slightest amount of hatred toward this man, save the ordinary hatred he would have for what he did to Meleri. As far as Sorcha's murder, he could not, would not, ever let Meleri know the truth about Philip. Not to protect that English pig, but for another reason entirely.

If Meleri ever found out, he would lose her.

When they reached Beloyn, Robert invited everyone inside, but they declined. "I think it best if we wait here, then we can be on our way after your wife has had a look," Walter said. "Once we have a positive identification, we will need to make arrangements to have the body sent to his family. You wouldn't know where the family of this Philip Ashton lives, would you?"

"Aye, they are in Northumberland. His father is the Duke of Heatherton."

Walter grimaced. "Another reason to make haste," he said.

Robert went to get Meleri. He found her in her room, sitting at her desk, her red hair touched by the sun coming through the window behind her, bursting with all the colors of fire. She looked up when he entered and gave him a welcoming smile. In spite of the circumstances, it was a smile that warmed him considerably.

"I'm glad you are back. Did you get everything taken care of?" she asked.

"Almost."

"Were you able to help?"

"Some."

"Did you recognize the man they found?"

"Not exactly."

"Could you be more explicit?"

"I think I know who he is, although I could not make positive identification."

"Why not?"

"If he is who I think he is, I have never met him."

"And you think I sound confused? Talking to you…I get cross-eyed from the effort. If you've never met the dead man, how could you know who he is?"

He searched for a way to break it to her, but in the end, he knew the only way was to be blunt. "Meleri, I am quite certain it is Waverly."

"Philip?" All the color seemed to vanish from her face at once. "Philip is dead? Oh, dear Lord, he'll be furious."

He gave her the same expression he had given her earlier, when she made a similar idiotic statement. "Meleri, have you taken leave of your senses? The man is dead. How can he be furious?"

"How do I know? You're the one with the haunted castle. You tell me." She put her hand to her head. "Well, I hate to say this, but I'm glad it's him and not one of us. Are you certain he's dead?"

"He is. Believe me, he is."

"Are you certain it's Philip?"

"Reasonably so, just as I told you."

"How did it happen? Was it an accident? Robbery?"

"It wasn't robbery. Other than that, all we know is that something caused him to fall from his horse. His foot caught in the stirrup. He was dragged to death."

She winced. "Oh, how awful. It is such a dreadful way to die."

"Do you know a good way?"

"No, but no one deserves to die so horribly."

He told her that the sheriff was waiting out front with the others, that they needed someone who could make positive identification. "Since you are the only one around here who knew him…"

"No!"

"Meleri, there isn't…"

"Please, Robert. Not me."

"Love, if there was any other way…"

"Don't make me to do this. You don't know what you are asking."

"You know I would not if there was another way."

"Can't you find something to identify him? Was there nothing to prove who he is? No identification?"

"Nothing other than a silver knife with initials on it."

Her face went white. "P.W.A.," she said, as if familiar with the knife.

"Aye, those were the initials. You have seen it?"

"Of course I've seen it. I was betrothed to him. In England, it is common practice to give your betrothed a gift on certain holidays. I gave the knife to him Christmas last. The initials are for Philip William Ashton." She stood up, walked to the window and looked down to the courtyard below. "Did you…" She paused, her voice breaking. He went to her and put his hands on her shoulders. She did not turn around. "Did you tell them about myself and Philip? About his abduction?"

"No. I only told them what I thought was necessary, that he was a lifelong friend, that you had been betrothed but had agreed mutually to call it off."

"Did you tell them he came to see me, here?"

"Aye, I told them he had been here twice. I did not tell them of the threats he made or the abduction. I felt there was no need. I wanted to spare you."

She sighed, turned back to him and lay her head against his chest. Her arms slipped around him. "I suppose this is something I will live through, although if I had a choice, I would rather do anything than this."

"If I had any other choice, I would not ask it of you."

He tilted her head up and kissed her soundly, as if it were possible to transfer his strength to her. "Are you ready?" he asked.

She inhaled deeply and then released her breath, and he knew she was composing herself. "I doubt anyone is ever ready for such as this, but I am resigned." She put her arm through his. "You are coming with me?"

"Aye, I would not have you go through this alone."

"As long as I have you, I can face anything, do anything, be anything."

"That's my lass," he said, and kissed her again.

They went down the stairs, but when they reached the bottom step, Robert stopped her. "Identification will be difficult."

"I understand. His face does not matter. I could identify him even without looking at his face. I have known Philip since I was a child. There is a scar on his right arm, where it went through a glass window. There is also a small nick on his left shoulder where Tony wounded him during fencing practice."

"Then it should be over quickly."

"I have prayed that would be so."

In the end, her prayers were answered, for she knew it was Philip even before they looked for the two scars she described. When they drew back the sheet, she put her hand over her mouth and closed her eyes. After she gained control, she looked down at the body again. "Yes," she whispered. "It's Philip. He always had such lovely blond hair. How I envied it as a child." She stared down at him solemnly. "How sorry I am you have come to this."

She turned away and buried her face against Robert's chest. Behind her, Walter instructed the others to remove Philip's body from his horse and lay it upon the ground. Once they found the two scars she described, the sheriff said, "If you would be so kind, Lady Douglas, as to look at these…just so we can be certain."

"It's almost over," he whispered. "You're a strong lass with a pure heart."

She looked at the body again and saw the scars. "It's Philip. Those are the scars I described," she said, and turned quickly away. She grabbed Robert's arm for support.

"Are you all right, lass?"

"I…I don't know. I'm sorry. I must go inside."

Before Robert could say anything, she ran up the steps and through the open door.

Agnes was waiting inside with a glass of water. "Here, drink this. You need to lie down a moment."

"I couldn't. Not now. I don't want to be alone." She glanced around. "Where is everyone?"

"I believe they all went to church. Lady Margaret came asking about whether you wanted to go. I told her I didn't know, since you did not sleep in your room last night. I offered to see if you wanted to go with them, but she said I was not to disturb you."

"It was a good thing I did not go." Meleri looked out the window and saw the sheriff and his men ride off. "The sheriff is leaving," she said, and hearing a noise behind her, she turned to see Lady Margaret come down the stairs.

"What is going on out there?" she asked.

"Robert is coming inside now. He will explain everything."

Agnes opened the door, just as Robert came off the last step.

"How do you feel?" he asked when he saw Meleri.

"Much better."

He looked at his grandmother. "Where are Iain and Hugh? I want to have a word with them."

"They are at church where all good Presbyterians should be. This is the Sabbath, or have you forgotten?"

He rubbed his eyes. "To tell you the truth, I haven't had much time to think about what day it was," he answered. "Whatever day it is, it is going to be a long one."

"Who was that man?" Gram asked. "Why did Meleri have to go out there with you?"

He glanced at Meleri, and she shrugged. "I told her *you* would explain everything when you came inside."

"How would I ever manage without you?"

"You wouldn't," she said, trying to lighten her mood by teasing with him. "I am amazed you got by this long."

"Aye, events of great consequence often spring from trifling circumstance."

"Trifling, is it?" She was thinking of a leveling comment when Lady Margaret stepped between them.

"You two can argue off your tensions later. I want to know what happened. What are you trying to do? Give me an attack of anxiety?"

Robert took his grandmother by the arm and his wife, too, then escorted the two of them down the hall and into the library. "It's a long story and what I have to tell you would be better received if you were sitting down."

Once they were comfortably seated, Robert told Gram about Philip, leaving nothing out. Once he finished, she did not say anything for a few moments, as if she were weighing his words. "In light of what you have said, I cannot help thinking how good a thing it is that his death was an accident."

"That is what I wanted to talk to you about," Robert said.

Lady Margaret's expression turned more serious. "There is something you haven't told me?"

Robert stole a quick glance at Meleri and her heartbeat suddenly escalated. She was so full of dread, she could only look at him with a helpless expression.

Robert went on. "Aye, there were several coins found near the body."

"They probably fell out of his pocket. I see nothing strange about that," Gram said.

"These were old coins…quite old…from the reign of David II."

"That would make them from the fourteenth century, the same as the coins I have."

"Aye, they were identical to the two gold coins you have, b these were in much better condition. I could even read the inscription. *'Ihc Autem Transiens Per Medium Illorum Ibat'*."

"*'But Jesus passing through them went his way,'*" Meleri said.

"*'But Jesus passing through* the midst of *them went his way,'*" Robert corrected her. "Your Latin is very good."

"Yours is better." The smile faded and her look turned serious. "What is it about the coins that troubles you?"

"It isn't just the coins that bother me. There was also a dirk with an ivory handle." He drew back his doublet and pulled an ivory-handled dirk from the waist of his breeches. He stared down at the intricate scrollwork on the blade, and the name inscribed there. "Douglas the Good," he read, and handed the dirk to his grandmother. "What do you make of it?"

"I have never seen it before." She turned it over and studied it from every angle. "It would appear to be authentic, for it is obviously quite old." She handed it back to Robert. "Where did they find it?"

"They didn't. I found it stuck in a tree as I was walking back to my horse. I am surprised no one else saw it."

Meleri gasped. "You didn't tell them you found it?"

"No."

"Why not?" she asked.

"When I saw the name Douglas, I thought it best to say nothing. I knew it wasn't my dirk, just as I knew it did not belong to Iain or Hugh. But I knew it could cause problems for us."

"Aye," Gram said, "it could be the source of tremendous problems."

"On top of that, I wasn't certain it had anything to do with what happened. It could have been sticking in that tree for hundreds of years and no one noticed it."

"Or it could have been left there as a sign," Gram said.

"That thought crossed my mind," Robert said.

"A sign?" Meleri scooted to the edge of her chair.

"A sign left there by the missing earl."

"That can't be right," she said. "You told me Douglas the Good was killed in Spain and it was his nephew, William, who was the first earl."

"That is correct," Robert said. "James Douglas was Douglas the Good."

"Then how did William have the knife that belonged to James?"

"It was probably inherited," Lady Margaret said, "something that was kept in the family. An heirloom. It is reasonable to expect William would have inherited these things."

"So, you are saying you think Philip might have been murdered by the missing earl?"

"It is the only explanation I can come up with," Robert said. "I know this sounds preposterous…"

Meleri leaped to her feet. "We must be getting somewhere! That is the first thing you've said that I agree with."

"All right," Robert said. "Let us practice a little supposition. Suppose the ghost you saw was, in fact, the ghost of William, the missing earl. Suppose by revealing himself to you, you are the one he has declared to be the one with the heart of the truest Scot. Suppose he was the man you saw that first day when Philip attacked you, the one who obviously frightened him off. Suppose he knew what a threat Philip was. Suppose he frightened Philip's horse, causing his death, and left the coins and the dirk as proof."

Meleri sat back down and put her hand to her forehead. "That is preposterous. Things like this do not happen," she said. "Ghosts don't go around leaving tokens scattered about and frightening horses and God knows what else."

"How do you know they don't?" he asked.

"I…"

Robert went on talking. "I understand how you could be skeptical. Lord knows I was, too, in the beginning, but now I don't think these things can be chalked up to mere coincidence. There are simply too many of them."

"Aye," Lady Margaret said. "I think the time has come. I think the old earl is tired…tired of haunting this castle, tired of waiting for the legend to come true. I don't think he would allow anything to stand in the way of bringing the legend to a close."

"But wouldn't the jewels have to be found before that can happen?" Meleri asked.

"They will be," Robert said.

"All in due time, child. All in due time," Lady Margaret said. "We must be still and wait with patience."

Meleri stared woefully out the window. "I hate waiting! Truly! Nothing at all happens. Nobody comes. Nobody goes. Nothing is learned. Nothing decided. You cannot imagine how much I hate standing around doing nothing. I don't know how anyone can tolerate it. I would take *anything* over this! Absolutely anything!"

"Be careful what you ask for," Lady Margaret said. "You might get it."

31

Robert, his grandmother and Meleri had been in the library about an hour when Hugh and Iain returned from church with the twins. The moment they walked into the room, they must have sensed something was wrong, for Iain stopped and told his daughters, "Run along and change your dresses."

"Can't we stay for a while?" Catriona asked.

"Do as I asked," Iain said.

Catriona and Ciorstag looked terribly disappointed, but they did as their father bid and left the room.

Meleri came to her feet. "I will go upstairs with them," she said. "I've had all the deaths and ghost stories I can take for one day."

Lady Margaret stood, as well. "I think it is time for a nap. This has been a trying day."

"I will walk both of you to your rooms," Robert said, rising.

"I will be fine," Lady Margaret said. "Save that offer for when I am old and really need it." She left the room.

"Very well." He watched his grandmother leave, then turned to look at Meleri. "Then I will walk *you* to your room."

She placed a hand on his arm. "No, I am all right. Truly. I'm just a little shaken and would like to lie down a bit." She noticed Iain and Hugh were looking quite baffled by her behavior and comments, neither of them having a clue as to what she was talking about. "Stay here and explain everything to them. I'll see if the twins want to join me in the garden."

"You're sure you don't mind being alone?" Robert asked.

"No, I'll be fine. Really." She started from the room, and as she was going through the door, she said rather flippantly, "After all, what could possibly happen to me now?"

Catriona and Ciorstag were waiting for her. "Where is Lady Margaret?" Meleri asked.

"Gram said she would go on up. She was tired," Ciorstag said.

"We told her we would wait here for you," Catriona added.

"I'm glad you waited."

They walked toward the gallery. As they went, Meleri spoke of the dresses she wanted Agnes to make for them. "I'll show you the fabrics. They would be perfect for you. Agnes is a fair hand with a needle, although not exceptional. I think you will be pleased."

"Gram is very good with a needle," Ciorstag said.

"She has made all of our clothes," Catriona said. "But her eyes are not as good as they once were."

"Perhaps they could work together," Meleri said.

They decided that would be the perfect solution and the three of them walked on until Catriona said, "I am hungry. Let's go to the kitchen before we go change."

"It would spoil our dinner, and Papa would be upset with us," Ciorstag said.

"But they will talk and talk, and I am famished," Catriona said. "I didn't have time for breakfast before we left for church."

"You spent too much time on your hair, hoping Alexander MacKinsey would notice."

"I did not!" Catriona denied.

"Aye, you did, and all for naught. Alex MacKinsey's mother said he stayed home to help his father. Everyone knows you fancy him."

"I do not, and everyone does not think that. One would think you fancied Alex, since you always seem to know of his whereabouts. You don't see me asking about him."

"No, you wait until I find out, then you ask me."

"It doesn't really matter why I was late, or where Alex was. Neither of those will do anything to make me get over being hungry."

"Why don't you go to the kitchen," Meleri suggested. "If you had a small bite of food, I don't think that would ruin your appetite for later. I agree that your father will probably be talking to the others for quite some time."

The twins looked at each other, then rose up on their toes, each of them kissing her on the cheek, before they turned and dashed off toward the kitchen. By the time they disappeared, they were laughing, and Meleri wondered if she would ever have daughters such as these.

She absently thought about the dogs as she approached the staircase, so accustomed she was to see them lying in their usual place, their attention riveted on the gallery of portraits. She came to the old earl's painting and stopped, her mind filled with a dozen questions that all seemed to ask, "Was it you that I saw?"

She continued on her way, and as she went up the stairs, she felt a presence that came with a cool, chilling draft of air that seemed to rush up the stairs ahead of her. But when she looked, there was no one there. Next time I will not look, she told herself. I don't care if it drops to freezing in here and he comes up behind me and taps me on the shoulder. I will not look.

She hurried to her room and closed the door. She turned the lock, then began to laugh. "I am changing right before my own eyes…changing from a simpleton to an idiot! Here I am, locking my door to keep out a ghost! I must be losing my mind. Yes, that is what is happening. I am either dreaming or I am losing my mind. None of this is really happening anywhere except in my head." She tapped her forehead for good measure. "This is getting ridiculous. I have allowed all those silly stories about images disappearing out of paintings and legends and ghosts and missing jewels to occupy my thoughts far too much. Well, I won't let it do so again."

She went to her bed and sat down. "Starting right now, I am not going to think about any of this again. I will not look at that painting. I will not think about the old earl. I will not dwell upon any of those stories or legends. I will not give any of it one minute of my time. I know that ghosts do not exist, not even *good* ones."

Suddenly the drapes at the window billowed out and a great wind blew into the room, stripping leaves from the trees outside and driving them inside. A lamp fell over, knocking a vase of flowers to the floor.

Okay. So, she was wrong. She was persuaded. She believed. "You should be ashamed of yourself," she said. "What kind of ghost are you…trying to frighten someone half your size, when you are supposed to be a good ghost?"

He did not answer, of course, but that didn't mean he wasn't around. He was in here, all right. She knew he was in here. But where? She began walking around the room, hoping she stepped on him. It would serve him right if she smashed his toes. She lifted the valance on the bedstead and peeped under it. Where would a ghost hide? she asked herself. Anywhere, she answered. She supposed a ghost, being without solid form, could fit himself into any location, any size or shape, even a snuffbox if he so pleased. She lifted a knitted shawl from the chair. Nothing there. She continued looking, but found nothing.

At last, she said, "I know you are in here. Why don't you do the honorable thing and show yourself?"

Meleri lifted several toilet articles from her dressing table and looked beneath them. She opened her letter box. Nothing. One by one, she searched the drawers and cabinets of the wardrobe. At last, she threw up her hands in defeat. "Oh, I give up. Come out or don't come out. I don't care anymore. However, I do think it is rather boorish of you to remain invisible in a lady's bedchamber. What if I want to change clothes? I don't know why you are picking on me. I don't want to believe in ghosts. It was never on my list of suppressed desires. I am not a Scot and I don't think you are very nice to be picking on me. I certainly don't know why anyone would call you good. You may have saved my life the other day, but then you turned around and canceled everything out when you killed Philip. And don't try to deny it. I *know* it was you and I know you left your mementos behind as proof."

Another gust of wind came into the room, one that was much stronger than the first, then it died down quite suddenly. Everything was still and quiet. The draperies dropped back into place. From somewhere behind her, a deep baritone voice seemed to rumble out of nowhere.

"I did not kill him."

"Yiii!" she shrieked, and leaped in fright. She could have sworn she turned around in midair, for when she landed she was facing the opposite direction.

The ghost bubbled up before her.

He was standing on the other side of her bed, at first nothing more than a vapor glowing with light, a shimmering green mist, and then at last, a solid shape taking form. She was so shocked at his sudden appearance and the manner in which he dressed, the features she had wondered about for so long and could now see up close, that she did not say anything.

"Ye are remarkably silent for a woman who only a moment ago had plenty to say. I take by yer silence that ye believe in ghosts."

"You have not converted a man because you have silenced him," she said, trying to sound smug. "You surprised me, that is all. I am, you understand, not in the habit of receiving ghosts in my bedchamber."

"'Tis yer own fault. Ghosts only come to those who look for them."

"I was not looking for you."

His eyes twinkled as he watched her and said, "Aye, lass, ye were."

He wasn't as old as she imagined he would be—a sturdy man of medium height, with dark hair and a stern countenance. But it was his eyes that mesmerized her, eyes that were blue, darkly, deeply, beautifully blue. They were Robert's eyes. "I know who you are. You are the old Earl of Douglas…"

"I am no that *old*."

"I don't know how you can say that. You've been dead more than three hundred years."

"A man doesna age after he dies. Ghosts are ageless."

"So are women," she said. "And we don't have to die to be that way." She thought for a moment and then asked, "Shall I refer to you as the missing earl?"

"I don't like that one, either," he said. "I am not missing. I know exactly where I am."

She studied him with mounting curiosity, suddenly realizing what an opportunity she had here. Just how many times did one find she had a real and true ghost at her disposal? One she could ask all sorts of questions? "Where do you stay, now that you are no longer in your portrait? Are you with the Countess of Sussex and the missing Van Dyck?"

He laughed. "That shrew!"

She bristled at his choice of words. "There are worse things than being a shrew," she said with utmost piety.

"Name one."

"Scots."

He laughed again. "Ye have a quick mind, lass. That was an interesting guess, abeit an incorrect one. The Countess and I dinna see eye to eye. If I couldna spend five minutes in the same room with her when I was alive, why would I want to spend three hundred years crammed on a small square of canvas with her?"

"What do you mean, you didn't kill Philip?"

"It was an accident."

"It was an accident you caused, therefore it was your fault."

"Studied to be a barrister at Edinburgh, did ye?"

"One does not have to be a barrister in order to add two and two together."

"An accident means no one is at fault. If I wanted to kill him, I could have finished the job with one swoop of my claymore."

"You left your claymore in my room that day, or did you forget? And you *are* the one who frightened his horse."

"Aye, but murdering him was no my intention. It was my desire to warn him away from ye and this place, to frighten him enough to send him back to England where he belonged. When his horse tried to run away, he spurred the puir beastie unmercifully. His horse reared. He was thrown. His foot caught in the stirrup. I ken ye know the rest."

"Did you try to save him?"

"Do you wish to have him back?"

"No, but that doesn't mean I wanted him dead."

"Lass, ye are as wavering as a weathercock. Ye canna be in Edinburgh and Glasgow at the same time, ye ken."

"You never did answer my question. Did you try to save him?"

"Of course not."

"Why not?"

"I am a ghost. I am not God. I canna interfere with destiny."

"But, you just said you could have killed him with your claymore."

"Aye, I could…*if* that was his destiny."

"How do you know when it is someone's destiny and when it is not?"

"I know."

"Could you be more vague?"

"It is the nature of greatness not to be exact."

Meleri drummed her fingers on a nearby tabletop. "It would be my luck. I'm haunted by a ghost that is as boastful as he is full of pride."

"Ye are outspoken, lass—not marked by meekness, modesty in behavior, attitude or spirit. Nor are ye prone to showing submissive respect."

She shrugged. "I've never had a propensity for humility. Whenever I dwell upon my own imperfections, they seem sweet and innocent…utterly charming little attributes, really. Nothing at all like the outrageous imperfections I see in others."

He seemed amused by that and she found herself thinking, *Here I am, talking to a ghost, mind you, like he was an old friend.* Truly, this was the opportunity of the century. Just how many people could say they conversed with a congenial ghost, who was both charming and witty? She should be terrified, but all she really felt was a strange sort of curiosity. "Do you like being a ghost?"

"It has its advantages."

"For instance?"

"Ye dinna have to open doors. Yer feet never hurt."

She burst out laughing. He was a Lowlander, through and through, so difficult and provocative in some ways, possessing of a piquant wit and a penchant for getting to the heart of the matter. He even looked the part, with a large imposing head, the manner of a bird of prey and the eyes of an eagle. His speech was odd, quite different from the way Robert and the other members of the family spoke, but she had no difficulty understanding what he said. Not that it mattered. This whole thing was preposterous. She was dreaming. This was all in her mind. Suddenly, she closed her eyes and put her fingers to her temples. "Oh, I don't know why I'm doing this."

"What are ye doing?"

She dropped her arms and looked at him. "I will tell you what I am doing. I am standing here like a moron, carrying on a conversation with someone who has been dead for over three hundred years." She began to pace the floor, talking to herself. "This isn't happening. It's impossible. I can't be talking to a ghost. Ghosts are not real. *You* are not real," she said. "You can't be. Tell me you aren't real."

He did not answer, and when she looked back at the place on the other side of the bed, he was not there.

The wind came rushing into her bedchamber once again, blowing leaves, just like before, only this time the wind seemed to suck the air from her lungs and she felt herself growing dizzy. She gasped for breath and made her way to the fourposter bed. She had no more than sat down when everything went black.

When she awoke, she was lying on her bed, staring up at the worn canopy overhead. She looked around the room. There were no leaves on the floor. The lamp was on the table by the bed. The flowers were in the vase on the table in front of the window, unbroken.

Everything was as it had been before.

And yet, it wasn't.

32

Robert was in the library talking to Hugh and Iain. He was in the middle of a sentence when Lady Margaret entered the room, looking as regal as ever, in spite of the hardship and sorrow she had experienced in life. He watched her take a seat, as he had done many times, and found himself thinking he had never admired anyone as he admired her. She was a remarkable woman, a true aristocrat and the backbone of the family. He thought of Hugh, Iain, the twins and himself. They all owed her so much, more than they could ever repay, and now they had to watch helplessly as she grew old.

However, she didn't appear to be growing old today, for the moment she sat down, she took one look at the three of them and said, "My, this must be a grave discussion, indeed. I have seen happier faces on gargoyles."

"I thought you were going to rest," Iain said.

"I tried. I have insomnia."

"What you need is sleep," Hugh said.

Lady Margaret raised a brow and looked at him. "Really? I don't know why I didn't think of that."

Everyone was laughing at Hugh's comment when Meleri rushed into the library as if she were fleeing the London fire. She shut the door behind her and leaned back against it and said between breaths, "Am I ever glad to see everyone here and breathing!"

"I am certain we all share your sentiments on the latter," Iain said.

"Bless me, child, but you look like you've seen a ghost," said Lady Margaret.

Meleri motioned for her to be quiet. "Don't say that!"

Lady Margaret sat back. "Why not?"

"Because I *have* seen a ghost. *And,* I talked to him."

The room instantly fell into discussion and clever conjecture, sprinkled with a few suppositions, a speculation and one or two hypotheses. That gave way and Meleri was quickly besieged with questions and requests to leave nothing out. She did her best, going at it with devout eagerness.

With her wide eyes and rapturous expression, Robert thought she appeared more excited than shaken, which was an odd reaction for someone who'd had a recent encounter with a ghost.

The room had grown quieter when Robert asked, "Did you mention your kidnapping?"

"He said he did not kill Philip."

Hugh's expression was puzzlement. "How could he say that? The coins and the dirk...they had to be his. How could he deny it?"

"He didn't deny it. He really is quite the most truthful ghost... although I have not known any that were not...that is, I haven't known any ghosts...well, everyone knows that. Oh, yes, he did not attempt to deny anything. Perhaps there is some honor system for ghosts that they must always tell the truth."

"Meleri, will you stick to the pertinent facts?" Robert asked.

She nodded and went on with the details of how he only intended to frighten Philip so he would leave, adding something about his horse being spooked. "Philip spurred him unmercifully, until the 'puir beastie' reared. Philip was thrown and his foot caught in the stirrup. You know the rest."

"So, there you have it," Lady Margaret said. "Our ancestor is cleared of any wrongdoing."

"No mention of the jewels?" Iain asked.

She shook her head. "No, I'm afraid we were too busy having our differences. He really is a bit opinionated and quite the most stubborn man that I have ever met. I don't know how he became a ghost. He's too stubborn to die."

"You never talked about anything else?" Hugh asked.

"Of course we talked. There isn't much else you can do with a ghost, you know."

Iain laughed. "That is true."

"Aye," Lady Margaret agreed. "One can't exactly ask them to dance, can one?" She turned to Meleri. "Anything else?"

Meleri stared at the ceiling, apparently thinking back over their conversation. "I asked him if he liked being a ghost."

Hugh laughed. "You didn't."

"Of course I did. I was curious. How else was I going to know?"

Hugh was laughing so hard he could barely move, but he managed to say, "Tell me this is not happening," before he went to sit down on the sofa that flanked the fireplace, across from the one where Meleri and Lady Margaret sat.

Robert continued to stand near the fireplace, thinking about Meleri's performance, and it was a performance. It hit him suddenly that she wasn't being droll by accident any more than she was speaking with idiotic whimsy to amuse herself. She was doing her best to keep a grave situation from becoming another Douglas tragedy, and he could not remember a time when he had enjoyed her more.

33

When Meleri went to bed that night, she went to her room alone after telling Robert, "If you are there, I am certain he will not come."

She lay in bed a long time before going to sleep, hoping the earl would put in an appearance. When she awoke the next morning, she was doubly disappointed. One, because she could have slept with her husband, which was infinitely better than sleeping alone. The other disappointment was the earl's absence. "You could have let me know you weren't coming," she said. "It was quite rude of you. I am certain that you knew I was expecting you. If your feelings are hurt because I did not believe in you, I am sorry. However, you must realize this hasn't been any easier for me than it is for you. It isn't every day I go skipping around the corner and encounter a ghost. And that is all I have to say on the matter."

She rang for Agnes and went to her dressing table to brush the tangles from her hair. That was when she noticed her silver-backed brush was not there—and it was there the night before. She was certain of it because she brushed her hair before retiring. Perhaps Agnes moved it, she thought, so she asked her as she picked up the comb.

"No, milady. I have no idea where the brush could be."

Still puzzled, Meleri went down to breakfast.

The next morning, the hairbrush was back in its usual place, on her dressing table. Upon further examination, the small miniature painting of her mother was gone. By the third day, the earl had still not appeared, but the miniature of her mother was back in its place, and a gentleman's shaving mug was sitting where her golden locket had been.

Something strange was going on, Meleri knew, so she went to find whom the mug belonged to. Iain and Hugh both said it was not theirs. That left Robert.

Reluctantly, she went in search of him and learned he was in the morning room—an odd place for him to be, since the room had not been in use for quite some time. However, she decided she should become accustomed to strange things, since they always seemed to be happening around this family. When she came to the door to the morning room, she knocked.

"Come in."

Clutching the mug, she stepped into the room and closed the door. He was standing near the window, next to a large table that was covered with papers. A nearby window was open, bringing the out-of-doors inside with a breeze that set the papers aflutter. All the furniture, save the table, was covered with white sheets. When he looked up and saw her, he seemed surprised. "Meleri, what are you doing here?"

"I was looking for you…they said you were here."

He put the papers he was holding down on the table. "Do you know, this is the first time you have come looking for me without needing something."

"I came to see if this belongs to you." She held the mug out.

He moved toward her and stopped just inches away. "Aye, where did you get it?"

She explained how things had been disappearing and reappearing in her room, and how today, her locket was gone and the mug was in its place.

He was wearing an immaculately tailored black coat that had seen some wear, but on him, even a worn coat was a magnificent sight. "A missing locket…" He put the mug down and reached inside his coat to withdraw her locket, holding it up by the chain. "Is this yours, by chance?"

She watched the locket spin and whirl for a moment. "Yes. I suppose you found it in place of your mug."

"Precisely." He reached up to take one bright red curl and rubbed it between his fingers. As he did, he allowed his gaze to wander leisurely over her body and then return to her warming face. His smile was slow, thought provoking and oh, so sensuous.

"Thank you for the locket. It was my mother's. I would have hated to lose it."

He dropped the curl he was holding. "Allow me." He took the locket from her hand. "Turn around."

She turned and felt the electric shock of his skin coming in contact with hers as he placed the locket around her neck. When he was done, he did not remove his hands, but let them drop to rest upon her shoulders. "I missed you last night."

"And I you. I suppose I had better be going, so you can finish what you were doing." She made a move to leave, but he tightened his hold on her.

"There's no hurry. I'm interested in hearing why your friend is collecting trinkets and returning them to the wrong room."

"I don't know, but I think he is letting me know he is still around, and by not appearing, that he is still upset with me."

He kissed her shoulder and kept on kissing his way across her neck to the other shoulder. "He is a bit petulant, isn't he?"

"Thankfully, he is *your* ancestor. What do you think I should do?"

"I never thought I would see the day I would be asked to devise a way to humor a disgruntled ghost."

"Oh, that is a wonderful idea!" she said, quite forgetting herself and turning around to fling her arms around his neck. She intended to give him a sisterly kiss on the cheek, to thank him for the idea he had given her. She learned he was quite deft at maneuvers, however, for the next thing she knew, she was in his arms. "I need to think and I can't when you are doing this."

"Then, don't think," he said. "Feel." His mouth came down on hers, his hands cradling her head and tangling into her hair. His kiss ravaged her mouth and left her hungry for more, yet even then, she tried to pull away from him. In response, the flat of his hand slid down to the small of her back and drew her even closer against him. Her eyes fluttered shut on the intention that if she did so, she could pretend he was not there. It didn't work. He had too many ways to prove that he was. His hands moved at will, roaming, lingering, pausing, learning, until she realized she had no idea she was composed of so many hills and valleys, mountains, plains and curves. Not to mention highly sensitive ones.

"Have you thought of anything yet?" he asked in a low, murmuring voice that fairly set her to humming.

"No, I need to go elsewhere to think. I cannot do it here. You are too distracting."

"Going isn't one of your choices. Right now, you should be telling me you like what I'm doing."

"And if I say I don't like it?"

"I would say your body tells me differently. I have caught a hint or two, the slightest response—" he pressed her against him, closer this time "—there, you felt it, too, didn't you?"

She was thinking of a clever response when he began kissing her face, as if he were blind and learning the location of everything by touch. Her body was aching, until she felt she was bursting into a rainbow prism. "You should let me go think about your contumacious ancestor. I'm trying to help you, you know."

"Let me thank you properly, then." His arms came around her lightly, his hands finding the place at the base of her head where the hair was fine and curled slightly. He kissed all the major points on her face, then kissed her deeply. As she shivered with the pleasure of it, a moan burned in her throat. She pressed against him, feeling him against her breasts.

"You feel good," he whispered, kissing the slope of her neck, just below her ear. "And you smell good." He kissed her cheek. "Let's see how good you taste."

The silken contact of his mouth on hers was her undoing.

She was thinking this was what she had wanted since they were married—a few moments alone, to touch and kiss, to learn about each other in an intimate way. She was eager. He was more so. From the moment they touched, she was aware of just how badly she wanted this, needed this time of sharing closeness. He made up for all the kisses she should have had, for all the tender touches and longing looks she had been deprived of.

Robert took her hand and led her to the sofa. He paused long enough to draw back the sheet, then he drew her down with him and the two of them reclined. "This is better," he said, his hand on her breast. "I could grow accustomed to this every afternoon." He kissed her again and again, until her lips were swollen. Still kissing her, he lifted his hands up to the buttons of her dress.

"Do you think we should be doing this in here?" she asked.

"Shh. I told you no one ever comes in here," he said, going after the buttons again.

He opened her dress and was kissing his way down the open front when they heard voices coming from outside the door. She gasped. "Oh, no!"

"It's all right," he said, and he pulled the sheet up over them, covering their heads as well. "It's just someone passing by."

A door creaked open and a voice she recognized as Gram's said, "That piece of linen will make perfect aprons, and it is large enough to make one for each of you."

Meleri turned into a statue. Beneath her, Robert was moving his leg. She pressed her mouth against his ear and whispered so low, she could barely hear it herself. "Be still! What are you doing?"

"Trying to get my foot under the sheet. It is sticking out." He moved again.

Meleri had never prayed so hard in her life.

"Gram! Look! Something is moving on the sofa." It was one of the twins, but Meleri wasn't certain which one, since they sounded as identical as they looked.

"Where, child?"

Robert stopped moving.

Meleri held her breath.

"Over there, on that sofa."

"I don't see anything moving. It was probably a draft."

"Drafts don't have feet."

"Saints above! Is that another dead body?"

The sheet was suddenly ripped back.

Meleri and Robert stared up into the face of his grandmother like two downy owls blinking against a bright light. The twins, who flanked her on either side, were staring back at them in the same wide-eyed fashion.

"Hello," Meleri said.

"Whatever are the two of you doing in here?" Lady Margaret asked.

"Do you really have to ask? Has it been that long?"

"Aye," she said, "'tis been too long, but I ken you have just given me back a memory. But, why are you in *here?*"

"We were trying to have some privacy," Robert replied.

"By putting a sheet over your head?"

"I heard you in the hall," he said, and came to his feet. "It seemed a good way to avoid detection."

"If you want to avoid detection, don't hide under sheets in the morning room."

"Why are you in here?" he asked.

"The twins need aprons. I was looking for an old linen tablecloth."

Meleri tried to indiscreetly shift her clothes into their proper position and realized she was clutching the sheet against her, just as Robert stood and pulled her up with him. She kept hold of the sheet with one hand after Robert took her other hand to lead her from the room. They hadn't walked very far before she tripped over it. The second time it happened, the two of them lost control. Unable to hold their mouths in a tight grimace any longer, the room was soon filled with laughter.

"I worry about you, Robert," Gram said. "Truly I do."

* * *

"At last!" Robert said when they reached his room.

By the time he put his hand on the door, Meleri's heart was pounding with vigorous expectancy. She trembled with excitement, happy that she was no longer inexperienced. She knew what to expect. She looked forward to it. When she saw he was holding the door open for her, she stepped into his room. He took her in his arms. "What were you thinking?"

She put her forehead against his chest. "I was anticipating."

He chuckled and lifted her chin until she was looking at him. "Nothing to be ashamed of. We are all creatures of desire. I've been tripping over my high hopes for days."

There's something wonderful about a man who can always make you laugh, Meleri thought.

They began to undress and she seemed to be all thumbs. He already had his boots off and she had yet to locate her buttons. He must have noticed, for he said, "What's wrong?"

She found a button and fiddled with it a minute. "I seem to have misplaced my buttonhole."

He laughed. "Come over here and I'll help you."

He had a steady hand as he began to undress her, but he soon became frustrated. The cause was the dozen tiny buttons against his large fingers. "One would need the patience of Job to put something like this on every day."

"Job or Agnes," she said.

"Saints be praised!" he said with enthusiasm when he finished the last button.

They both laughed and she began peeling his doublet from his shoulders. His shirt came next, and she took a moment to run her hands over his skin, learning the feel and texture of him. He was smoother and softer than she thought a man would be. She wondered about the rest of him and moved on, undoing the fastenings of his breeches, which she tugged down to the floor as he stepped out of them. While she was still hunkered down, she glanced up at him, but never made it as far as his face, for something just above her head caught her attention.

"A slight distraction," he said. "Do you find it frightening?"

"To the contrary. I am quite fascinated. It is simply that I have never met one, face-to-face."

He laughed again. Then he pulled her up and held her close against him. As curious as he, her hands slid downward. He made a small sound and searched for her mouth, content for some time just to kiss, allowing his hands free rein. She could feel the moment he was ready to move on to something else, and she thought them well matched, for she found that she was ready, too. She gave a surprised gasp when he suddenly lifted her into his arms and carried her to the bed, where he sat, still holding her. He leaned back until he was lying down and she lay on top of him. She lowered her head and kissed him, aware of the change in his breathing and the way hers seemed to follow in suit.

"I liked it better when you were on top," she said.

In reply, he rolled over, putting her beneath him. "So do I," he said. "Tell me if I am too heavy."

In answer, she pulled him down for a kiss. Soon then they were joined. Together at last, in unison, sharing, touching, knowing that there would be so many more times like this, and knowing it still would not be enough.

Later, when they slipped into a tranquil sense of togetherness, lying quietly, their bodies still entwined, she kissed his shoulder. He squeezed her hand. "Do you know something?" he asked.

"What?"

"I never expected to feel like this about anyone. I knew I would marry, and possibly fall in love. But to this degree and intensity, I never imagined."

"Love was something I heard about but never witnessed," she said. "I was beginning to doubt its existence."

"As did I. Now I know love is as wonderful as they say it is. It's not something you can be taught. It only comes by loving, and in the end, you will risk anything to have it. Everything looks more beautiful when seen through loving eyes. It is worth a king's ransom, worth waiting for, worth fighting for, even worth dying for. The best thing is, it's a gift. We are free to give it, to receive it, to wallow in it if we please. We can write about it, talk about it, think about it and sing about it. We can even give it away, but we cannot command it. Once it ceases to be free, it no longer exists."

"That was beautiful," she said. "Where did you learn so much about love?"

"From you."

Later in the day, the men took the dogs hunting. Shortly after, Lady Margaret left with the twins, for she had agreed to accompany them to pay a call on their friend, Jane Graham. Meleri was in her room, talking to Agnes about Robert's comment to humor the ghost. "That is precisely what I need to do…only, how does one go about humoring a ghost?"

"I haven't any idea, milady, but I have confidence you will find a way."

"Do you have any ideas?"

"Oh, no, milady. I haven't any notions about it at all. I only know one thing about ghosts, and that is to run if I should encounter one."

Agnes, with her clucking around, was a distraction, so Meleri decided since everyone was gone she would go have a cup of tea in the morning room and think upon it. What *would* appease the earl? she kept asking herself as she made her way there. What would he respect? What would impress him or any man?

Bravery.

The word simply popped into her head. She hurried into the room and took out a piece of paper and dipped the pen into the silver inkwell, then wrote the word *bravery.* Beneath it, she listed various things she could do to exhibit some sort of bravery:

1. Milk a cow. *Since she was afraid of cows, having been kicked by one as a child.*

2. Ride a horse astride, without a saddle. *She decided that was more absurd than brave.*

3. Spend the night in a graveyard. *Thankfully, Robert would never allow that.*

4. Walk along the parapets that surrounded the oldest wing of the castle.

She immediately crossed that one out. There were some things she would not even consider.

She read back over the list and decided these deeds did not sound very brave. She realized she wasn't getting anywhere, so she turned the paper over and began to list things she was not inclined to do, things that she found frightening, but all she could come up with was one thing. There was one place in the castle that she avoided, a place she had not the slightest desire to see, a place she was afraid of.

The dungeon.

"Oh, no," she said. "I won't do that. Never. Never. Never. I would rather stick needles in my eyes!"

She should have known.

A week passed and Meleri still had not seen the earl, although she knew he was about, for things were disappearing and reappearing in her room on a regular basis. She decided to stop thinking about a pouting ghost and get on with other things. On this particular day, she put Gowan and Fingal to work cleaning out the accumulation of a dozen years from the morning room. After her visit there when Lady Margaret and the twins surprised her and Robert, she wanted to open the room and put it to good use. It was simply too lovely to remain closed off.

The twins arrived eager to help. They were in the highest of spirits since the additions to their wardrobes. Meleri noticed today they were wearing their old dresses beneath the aprons Lady Margaret made for them, and she found that endearing, for she knew how badly they wanted to wear their new ones.

"We came to see if we could help," Ciorstag said.

"Oh, yes, may we please? We have always loved this room,"

Catriona said. "We asked Gram to open it up several times, but she said she was too old to oversee so much house."

Meleri looked at their bright, eager faces and agreed. How could she not? They were such a delight to be around. "Of course you may help. I was just wondering who could carry these linens to the kitchen."

"We can!" they said in unison, and Meleri hugged them both. "Tell Fiona to put them with the others in the linen cupboard. There is plenty of room for them now, since we set the kitchen to order."

Catriona and Ciorstag stood like porcelain mannequins, their expressions eager as they held out their arms, while Meleri stacked linens for them to carry. "That should be enough," she said. "No point in breaking your backs. You can always come back for another load. One more trip should do it, I think."

After they were gone, Meleri began pulling the sheets from the furniture, discovering many lovely pieces whose quality was superior to anything she had seen elsewhere in the castle. A little lacquered cabinet signed by Pierre Garnier was in excellent condition, and so were the pair of gilt-framed chairs, upholstered in yellow damask. A small desk with a silver inkwell and an elegantly gilded French lamp stood in front of the windows. The draperies were of a pale green silk—which turned out to be a darker shade once they were dusted. When she discovered numerous bronze statues and vases of chased silver, she put Gowan and Fingal to work polishing them.

Many of the other pieces in the room were quite nice and functional, although not of the fine quality of the lacquered cabinet and the gilt chairs. An old, glass-fronted china cabinet was shoved against a corner, and upon closer inspection, she discovered it to be filled with exquisite pieces of porcelain, while on top, an ornate footed bowl of silver was found hidden beneath a dusty cloth.

More silver was stuffed in a small closet, which was locked. That fact did not slow Meleri down, for she was an old hand at picking locks. She was just in the midst of picking the lock, when the twins returned with downcast faces. "Papa says we must attend to our studies now."

"Of course you must."

"But we want to help you."

"If you do an exceptional job on your studies, you may come back when you are done."

About that time, Catriona noticed what Meleri was doing. She looked at her sister and the two of them giggled. "Where did you learn to do that?" Catriona asked.

"One of my father's stable hands taught me."

"Why did you want to learn?" Ciorstag asked.

"I was nosy, I suppose. It is a good way to know what is going on around you," she said.

"Will you teach us?" Ciorstag asked.

"I don't know…"

"Oh, please do," Ciorstag pleaded. "No one ever tells us anything."

That was precisely why Meleri had learned, so she was happy to pass the talent on.

Once she finished picking the lock to the closet, she opened it. Inside were mugs, salvers, wine coasters, water pitchers, serving pieces, candlesticks and a set of silverware, so heavily tarnished they were black. Then she spent a few minutes instructing the twins on the finer points of lock picking. "Run along to your studies now. We can practice again, if you like."

"Oh, we would, we would!" Ciorstag said, and danced toward the door with her sister mimicking her every move.

After they left, Meleri arranged furniture and organized the china figurines in the vitrine. Fingal and Gowan finished their polishing and left to do other chores, since the room was almost finished. The last task remaining was to find the perfect place for the bronzes and pieces of chased silver. Once that was done, she sat in one of the yellow damask chairs and enjoyed the beauty of such a room. She closed her eyes and inhaled the odors that surrounded her—the wax on floors and furniture, fresh air let in through the open windows, the seductive aroma of old things—

all combined with a little bowl of aromatic cedar, which gave of
its subtle fragrance.

She found herself thinking how many things remained to be
done and how there would not be any money to do the rooms
within the castle, let alone the gardens, or the restoration of the
ruined wing. If only that most stubborn of all ghosts would ap
pear and tell her where the Douglas jewels were hidden.

Dungeon.

There that word was again, popping into her head as it had
dozen times over the past week. "I don't care how many times
you remind me of that word, I am not going down there. Fin
another place."

34

Immediately Meleri left the room and went upstairs to her bedchamber. She wanted to select a few of the fabrics she received from Robert to use for dresses for the twins. Agnes was nowhere around, so she opened the trunk at the foot of her bed and had just begun to remove a length of cream taffeta, when Lady Margaret poked her head through the door. "May I come in, or are you occupied with something important?"

"Oh, do come in," she said, and rose to her feet. "I was going through my trunk. Don't you think this would be a lovely color on one of the twins?"

Lady Margaret came into the room and sat on a long bench beneath the window. She looked the fabric over. "It's a perfect color. Is there enough, do you think, to make each of them a dress?"

"I will ask Agnes what she thinks."

"You have given them far too much. It was so generous and kind of you to make the dresses you gave them last week. I cannot tell you what it has meant to them. They have never had anything so lovely."

"I have received more joy from seeing them in those dresses than I ever would have if I made them for myself."

"Do you need any help with the sewing?"

Meleri was about to answer that when she heard a noise that sounded like someone scratching on the wall.

"What was that?" Lady Margaret asked. "Did you hear it?"

"Yes. Where do you suppose it was coming from?"

"It sounded like it was coming from over there," she said, indicating the opposite wall.

The scratching sound came again, and Meleri went to the wall and put her ear against it.

"Can you hear anything?"

"No."

Suddenly, there was a loud bang and the curtains billowed out and a wind blew into the room, but the window was closed.

"What was that?"

"It's him," Meleri said. "It's the ghost."

They heard a sound, as if someone was walking on the other side of the wall. Meleri put her ear to the wall again.

"Is it the ghost?"

"Yes."

"What's he saying?"

"Thump, thump, thump-ed-thump."

"Does this go on all the time?" Lady Margaret asked.

"No, this is something new. He's a bit put out with me, you see." Meleri went on to explain her brooding friend.

"He's a Douglas, all right. Sulking is a Douglas male-inherited trait."

They laughed, then finished sorting though the fabrics. When they finished, Lady Margaret went for her afternoon nap. Meleri busied herself in the room when she heard the word again.

Dungeon...dungeon...dungeon...

"Oh, all right!" she said, wondering if that meant the jewels were hidden there. "You win, you stubborn old ghost of a man."

She changed into something warmer, remembering that dungeons were cold and damp, still fuming about the earl's stubbornness. After she had changed into a dark blue dress with long sleeves, she tied a gray woolen shawl about her shoulders. "All right. I hope you're happy you've won. I am on my way, but am warning you. If I catch my death down there, it will be your fault. I don't know why you couldn't have chosen the gardens or at least something a trifle more sensible. I hope you are satisfied!" She left her room and went down the stairs.

She was walking down the long gallery, still unable to contain herself. "Of all the hardheaded, obstinate, headstrong, persistent, contumacious, unyielding, inflexible people I have ever known, you are at the top of the list."

Beside her, a picture fell to the floor. *Bam!*

"I don't care," she said. "Knock them all down and see if it bothers me."

Five of six portraits that were grouped together dropped to the floor, one after the other…*bam*…*bam*…*bam*…*bam*… *bam*…

"You missed one."

Bam!

She continued in silence, letting him know she wasn't too happy with him, either. As she passed the morning room, the crescent clock on the mantel chimed six o'clock and she glanced out the window. Already the sun was going down. She would have to hurry if she was going to be back in time for dinner. She passed a mirror and took one last look at herself before going on her way, like the doomed Marquis of Montrose, led shackled down the Royal Mile to his execution.

Thankfully, she was able to reach the thick oak door that led down a narrow circular stair to the dungeon without encountering any of the family along the way. The door was not designed for someone her size to open, and she found it quite difficult, but after a few tries, she succeeded. A waft of stale, chilled air rushed over her, and she stood very still and closed her eyes, hoping to regain her composure, paying no attention to the air that blew the wisps of hair back from her face. She whispered a prayer before descending the awesome steps that yawned open like gaping jaws waiting to consume her.

Dungeon.

There was something haunting about going into a place such as this, for it embodied all the dispassionateness of disembod-

ied souls, of human suffering and pain, of gruesome torture—
and all for some unknown gain, some reckoning, retaliation or
punishment. And for what? They were all dead now. Meleri
turned up the faint flame of the lamp she had brought, for she
knew she would need it to light the way through the dark depths
below. With one fortifying breath, she held the lamp aloft as she
looked down the steep row of stone steps that led down, deep into
the bowels of the castle.

With a slight shiver of dread, she began her descent, stepping
carefully, for the stones were damp and slick with moisture and
age. The passageway was dank and the air grew cooler as she
went lower, the light from the yellow flame of her lamp glisten-
ing upon the damp places in walls that were moist from seep-
age. Now she was really feeling the dungeon's coolness reaching
up to her, and she pulled the gray shawl higher to ward off the
creeping chill. Her feet were getting cold, as well, and she wished
she had changed into sturdier shoes.

And still she went ever downward, until she encountered the
lacelike tracery of numerous spiderwebs like veins of silver
spreading through stone. At first, they were nothing more than
thin gossamer threads, so pale and fine they gleamed where the
light struck them, but as she descended, they grew thicker, spun
across the passageway and catching in her hair and eyelashes,
like a warning for her to turn back. She swatted them away and
took yet another step. By now, her eyes were becoming more accustomed to the dark, and she could see she was almost to the
bottom of the stairwell. A skittering sound reached her ears as a
rat scrambled out of her way.

Dungeon.

She had left the world she knew behind. A feeling of despair
came over her, a sense of disconnection. She was alone, distressed by the feeling she was the only one alive in the entire
world. She was truly frightened now, not only from what the
darkness reminded her of, but also from the fear of being separate, of being absolutely and completely alone. It was a terrible
feeling—a sensation as dismal and terrifying as the nightmarish

memory of being locked in a dark closet by a demented maid when she was a child. She felt as desolate as she'd felt then, when she hugged her knees and cried, wanting her mother, afraid to go on without her, afraid to die, afraid to be left alone and forgotten.

She was afraid now, of the creaking, scuffling, scraping sounds that floated up from below, of the very darkness that reached all around her, of the gripping fear that some grisly terror awaited her at the bottom of these fateful steps. At last, she left the last step and found herself in a wider passageway that opened through a dark arch into a large room that could only be some sort of torture chamber, for she had never seen such a hideous and grisly sight.

Of the numerous methods for extracting information or inflicting punishment, she could identify only the press, where prisoners were crushed to a slow and agonizing death. In one corner lay a pile of broken swords and ax heads, rotting leather shields and battered steel bonnets. Hanging on the walls were numerous shackles, chains and torture devices, all too gruesome to give any further thought. She hurried past the awful display and stopped at a large door. It was locked, but a heavy, rusted key hung on a peg next to it, and she put the key into the keyhole and slowly turned it until she heard a click. She dropped the key into her pocket, in case the door closed behind her, then stepped inside.

She was now within a larger room that contained five or six small cells, each with a thick oak door and a heavy lock. Her fear seemed to come out of the darkness like a clawing hand to grab her. She was chilled to the very marrow of her bones. She heard behind her a creaking, scraping sound. *Oooo...* Howls like the voices of wolves cried out. Rats scampered away from the light, leaving her with nothing to listen to but the occasional drip of water and a never-ending silence. *Tip-tap. Creak, creak, creak. Tip-tap, squeak.* She stood motionless, listening, but everything fell silent.

Somewhere out of the vast, dark silence that lay behind her, she heard the clanking of a chain, then the faint strains of a tune being played on the pipes, and she knew her peevish ghost was making his presence known. She spied a long, weathered bench that lay along one wall, and she went to it and sat down. She placed the lamp beside her. She had no idea how long she would have to wait, having no knowledge of how long a Scottish ghost was wont to brood and glower before restitution was made.

As she waited, she thought about all the stories she had heard since coming here to Beloyn, stories that were told by Lady Margaret or Iain at night, when the family gathered after dinner. Some dealt with the ancient Vikings and the epic tales of giants, dwarfs and trolls they brought with them to the Orkneys. Other nights there would be stories of the black-clad fin men, or the handsome, gentle and sometime deceptive selkies. Around her, the stale, cold air closed in. Faith! What she wouldn't give for a puff of fresh air!

Meleri wasn't certain how long she sat there, but she began to worry that her lamp would run out of oil. She knew she could never find her way out of here in the dark. She was about to call out, to tell him again what she thought of his peevish manner, when suddenly a green mist came out of the darkness beyond the doorway. It swirled and twisted, growing lighter as it approached, until it began to form and she saw a human shape materialize from the cold glow.

She could see out of the lantern light that he was eyeing her with amused curiosity and she breathed a sigh of relief. "Am I glad to see you."

He spread his feet wide and crossed his arms over his massive chest. "Weel, lass, imagine finding ye sitting down here all by yerself."

"Yes," she said, shivering and rubbing her arms, "imagine my surprise at finding you here, as well."

"Were ye scared coming down here?"

"Yes, and you very will know it. It was enough to keep me on edge and jumping at my own heartbeat." She glanced around her. "It is a creepy place, haunted by too much death and suffering for my taste. Definitely not a place I would have chosen to visit."

"Then why are ye here?"

"It seemed like such a jolly place! What do you mean, why am I here? Are we playing guessing games? You know why I'm here. Because you pestered me with that bloody word...*dungeon...dungeon...dungeon*...night and day, until I was sick of hearing it. You wanted me down here because you knew I was afraid of the dark. Well, here I am."

"'Tis a brave lass ye are."

"Was this some sort of a test, then? Some challenge I had to meet?"

"Aye, 'twas a proving ground of sorts."

"So, did I meet your expectations, or must I prove myself further...scale a glass mountain, perhaps, or swim a monster-filled lake?"

"Ye are a lass like no other, always testing the point of courage. I ken ye have met the challenge. Ye can rest yerself for a while."

"Does that mean I can leave this horrible, creepy place?"

"If it is that harrowing, what made ye come in the first place?"

"Instinct, impulse, intuition."

"Not obedience?"

"No. I don't care for that word."

"Ye prefer the word *rebellion?*"

"Not all the time. You might be happy to know I am mellowing...somewhat. I have not lost my temper for some time now."

"Is that so?"

"Yes. I am sorry, by the way, for hurting your feelings the other day. I did not realize it would anger a ghost to doubt his existence."

"I ken ye harbor no such doubts now?"

"No, I am convinced."

"I suppose ye think I will give you the Douglas jewels now."

"I don't know. I thought that might be the purpose of my coming down here, but now I am not so certain. Are you going to?"

"No."

"Do they really exist, or is it only a tale?"

"What do ye think?"

She remembered what happened when she doubted him. She would not be so foolish again. "I believe they exist."

"Do ye also believe I will show ye how to find them?"

"If you choose to do so, but I think you have not yet made up your mind." The lamp beside her flickered and she shuddered, feeling the cold had begun to seep into her bones. "My oil grows low. I must start back."

"It is already too low for ye to make it back."

A chill of despair crept over her, and she remembered again being afraid to die in the dark closet the maid put her in. Why was it happening? She had been told the earl was a good ghost, and good people did not entice others to their death. "Was that your plan, then? To lure me down here and leave me in the dark?"

"Is that what ye think?"

"No. I think you are a decent sort. I don't think you make war with women."

"And what will ye do, when yer lamp goes out?"

"I will sit here and wait for you to do something."

"So, ye have gone from not believing I exist to trusting I will save ye."

"That was the purpose of this test, was it not?"

"Yes and no."

"You speak in riddles."

"Aaah, riddles… 'Nothing is hidden that will not be made known, or secret that will not come to light.'"

"That is from the Bible."

"Of course. Did ye think I came from the *other* place?"

"No, and in spite of your not wanting to be called good, I think you are."

"Titles can be deceptive. Think of all those who called ye a shrew."

"How do you know about that?"

"A ghost must keep some facts to himself, lass."

"Do you ever grow weary of being a ghost?"

"Aye. The longer thou livest, the more fool thou art. I am the first of a long and noble line, and I have stood watch o'er it for a long, long time. But my candle burns low and I have no far to go."

"The end is near, you mean?"

"Aye," he said, "but for whom?"

She heard a shriek. The lamp flickered and went out. She had never been surrounded by such absolute blackness. Not a ray of light or one of hope could exist in such a place. The air was still, the dungeon strangely quiet. "Are you still here?"

No one answered.

She heard a scuffling sound and she lifted her feet off the floor, then drew them up beneath her and tucked her skirts around them. She was very cold and hungry, and she could not help thinking, what if? What if he did not return? What if no one thought to look for her down here? What if Robert never found her until it was too late? What if she died down here, unable to find her way out of the darkness?

She pushed those thoughts away, and to make certain they stayed away, she began to hum, occasionally singing a verse or two, then singing all the words, until she was so inspired, she was singing at the top of her lungs.

A sound, like wind blowing through a church belfry, swept through the dungeon. She stopped singing and the sound grew faint. A deep voice spoke out.

> O I forbid you, maidens a'
> That wear gown on your hair
> To come or gae by Caterhaugh,
> For young Tam Lynn is there.
> There's nane that gaes by Caterhaugh
> But they leave him a wad,
> Either their rings, or green mantles,
> Or else their maidenhead.

The sound of the rushing wind grew louder, then faded completely away. She was trembling as she sat there in silence, too afraid to move and holding her breath until she had to breathe.

"Are ye afraid, lass?"

She released a breath. "I am afraid of the unknown, but I'm not afraid I will be harmed. I have learned something today."

"What is that?"

"To never, ever doubt something you are sure about."

"Ye are sure I will see you safely from this place?"

"Yes, I am certain, because I have decided I like you and I know you would not be called the Good, if you were so bad."

"I ken I would fill yer lamp with oil if it were in my power, but it is not."

Another cold chill swept over her. "Then I must remain down here, in the dark?"

"No. I can give ye something else. Something that belongs to me."

The lamp flickered and came back on, illuminating the room brightly and burning with brilliance that was not there before. The light was so bright and glaring against her eyes that for a few moments, she could not see. When at last her vision returned she searched the room for a glimpse of him.

But the ghost of the earl of the clan of Black Douglas was gone.

She reached for her lamp and was stunned. There was no flame there, no burning light, but there was something that blazed in the center, like a flash of lightning, intense and blue-white.

It was a large, many-faceted stone, smooth and sparkling like polished glass. Brighter than silver, it glowed and lit up the room, but did not consume itself. She rose to her feet and lifted the lamp higher so she could better see it. It sparkled like star shine. Was it a diamond?

No, she told herself. It could not be. Diamonds were not this large, for in truth, it was as big as her fist. She would show it to Robert. He would know. At the reminder of her husband, she headed back the way she had come, passing through the rooms and passageways as she went toward the circular stairs.

When she reached the stairs, her feet moved with surefooted ease over the narrow steps until she burst through the heavy oak door and into the hallway of the castle. She paused only long enough to give the massive door a mighty shove and sent it clanging into place. Then, and only then, did she pause to take a deep breath, relieved at last to have fresh, living air, to be surrounded once more by the welcome of Beloyn's brooding peace.

Still clutching the lantern, Meleri walked quietly down the hall, then paused at the doorway that led into the gallery. There, she stopped long enough to think about what she should do. She looked at the stone in the lamp. It was as large and beautiful as before, but the brilliant light that guided her from the dungeon was gone. She must find Robert, but she did not want to encounter anyone else before she had a chance to talk to him. She removed her slippers, then opened the door slowly and listened. The sound of a piano came tinkling down from the music room, and she recognized a duet the twins loved to play. At the end of the gallery, Corrie and Dram had taken up their customary place to gaze at the grim-faced ancestors that lined the walls. Everything seemed to be going along as normal.

Shoes in hand, she went on silent, stocking feet until she reached the staircase. She gave the dogs her usual pat, opened the gate, closed it behind her and went up the stairs on tiptoe. Once she reached the top, she paused to listen again. She decided she would hide the lamp in her bedchamber, then go to find Robert.

She opened the door to her bedchamber and stepped inside, then turned to close it. She put the lamp on the table beside the door, then dropped into the chair next to it and leaned her head back until it rested against the wall. Safe at last, she closed her eyes and said, "Thank God, I made it back." She let out a long-held breath.

"I would not breathe that sigh of relief if I were you."

She jumped up from the chair so fast the slippers fell out of her hand. Robert was sitting on the trunk at the end of her bed. "Oh, am I ever so glad to see you," she said.

"You may not be in a minute, because I have been sitting here for the past hour, wondering if when I saw you I would kiss you senseless, or take you over my knee. Right now, I am leaning quite severely toward the latter. Where in the name of everything holy have you been? Did you not think I would be worried? Or did you even care?"

She rubbed her cold arms. There was a chill in her room, but thankfully the fireplace was lit, and the low-flickering light illuminated his handsome countenance in a way that made her want to rush into his arms. His linen shirt was open at the throat, and his hair was mussed, as if he had, a time or two, run his hands through it. There was something vibrant, alive and reassuring about him sitting there as he did, but she did not see any of the kind benevolence, or the gentle tolerance in his face, that she had grown accustomed to seeing.

She wished he were not angry with her, now of all times, when she so desperately wanted to feel the assurance of his arms around her, the warmth of his breath as he kissed her forehead. But she could tell there would be no such demonstrations coming from him this night, so with a sigh, she bent over and picked up her slippers, while she waited for him to fire the first shot.

"What's the matter, love? Can't you come up with an answer? Did you fall asleep in some corner of the stables? Did you take a long walk and lose your way? Perhaps you paid a neighbor a visit and did not realize you overstayed. Well, have I guessed it? I am waiting. What is the answer?" He looked down at the floor, where her slippers had been. "Surely you did not slip away to meet some unknown lover…."

"I have never been so insulted in all my life."

"Don't despair. The night is still young."

That he would even suggest such a thing was appalling. What did he think she was? She couldn't decide if she was more angry or hurt at his hateful words. She did not stop to think what might have prompted him to say what he did. She only knew she was so furious at his insinuation that she did not care if he had a reason or not. And when she spoke, she did not use her best judgment, either. "If that is all you have to ask after what I have been through, I have nothing to say to you. Not one single, solitary, isolated word."

"You have one second to tell me where you have been."

"Where have I been? I'll tell you where I've been! Freezing my arse in the dungeon with your ghostly ancestor!" she shouted, and threw her slippers at him, first one and then the other.

35

"You went where?"

Robert was furious. He could not believe what he heard. The dungeon was no place for anyone, let alone a woman, and certainly not a place for one to go alone. She had no idea what he had been through, or how he'd felt when he realized she was gone. For the past four hours, he had every available person, from Fiona to his grandmother, searching for her. No one had seen her. No one had a clue as to where she had gone. She had vanished. Without a trace, or a message. Without so much as a footprint.

He had ridden the countryside with Hugh and Iain, until it had grown too dark to see anything. As a last resort, he had come here, to wait in her room, wanting…no, needing to feel close to her. And now she came tiptoeing in here, prissy as you may be, acting as if he was the one in the wrong.

"I said I was in the dungeon with the ghost…you do remember him, don't you?"

"I don't know. I've never seen him, remember?"

"Well, I don't know why I was so privileged. I certainly never asked to see him. I don't know why you are being so difficult. Surely, you do not think I am having some torrid romance with a three-hundred-year-old ghost! And if I was, it wouldn't be in that horrid, creepy dungeon, I can tell you that."

"You have no idea what everyone here has been through. We searched for hours."

"You have no idea what I have been through."

"What if something had happened to you? Do you have any idea how long it might have been before we found you?"

"I thought about that."

"Apparently not long enough."

She stamped her foot. "I don't know why you are so angry with me. I didn't exactly go traipsing off to the dungeon because it was a favorite place of mine, you know. If I were you, I'd be careful. If you don't start being a bit nicer, your descendants will refer to you as Douglas the Rude."

"My descendants may never arrive if I stay this angry. Right now, the last thing on my mind is procreation."

"Well, we agree on something at last, because I wouldn't have your baby if you offered me the throne of England, Scotland and Wales!"

"You left out Ireland."

"Throw that one in, too," she said, kicking a small needlepoint footstool out of the way. "I am cold and tired and hungry and my head hurts. I feel like I have a headache over my entire body. I have been frightened out of my wits and scared to death, I've stumbled over rats and into spiderwebs bigger than an angler's net. I sat in the dark for what seemed an eternity after my lamp went out, hearing voices that recited creepy poetry until I was ready to sign myself into Bedlam. There is nothing you can do to me that I have not been through something far worse. I do not want to listen to any more of your hostility. This is my bedchamber and I will thank you to take yourself and your raving and leave."

"Why did you go to the dungeon?"

"Because the ghost let me know it was expected of me. He would not return if I did not go."

"And you went traipsing blindly off to follow him, without a word to anyone?"

"If I took half of Scotland with me, he would have never put in an appearance."

"You should have told me. I was worried beyond belief."

She went to him and put her arms around his neck and said, "I am sorry I worried you."

He kissed the top of her head. "You should be, but I was wrong to get angry at you. Perhaps they cancel each other out."

Too happy to say anything, she felt him put his mouth against her cheek, kissing her there before moving to take her mouth. She whimpered and pressed closer to him, feeling the unsteadiness of her feet and clinging tightly to him. He held her like that for some time, neither of them speaking.

At last she said, "You called me foolish. Is that what you think?"

"I did at the time."

"Your grandfather didn't think I was foolish."

"My grandfather? If you mean the ghost, he is not my grandfather."

"He certainly is…many times removed."

"It can't be removed enough to suit me." He released her and began to pace the room, back and forth, back and forth. "I don't understand what I am supposed to do, here. There are enough trials and tribulations to be surmounted when you are dealing with living mortals. Isn't that enough? Must I also deal with ancient relics who have nothing better to do than to clatter around in the dark and play hide-and-seek?"

"Shh! Don't talk so loud. He might hear you."

"I hope he does hear me!" Robert said in the loudest voice he could muster.

He stopped talking suddenly, for Meleri looked as if she might topple over. She was tired. He was tired. They were both upset and saying things they would regret tomorrow.

"Go to bed," he said. "We can discuss this tomorrow."

Meleri watched him go. Then she went to the door and looked down the hall. Robert was almost to his room. "I have something to show you."

He stopped and turned. He did not come back, but he did ask, "Is this another one of your antics?"

He would try the endurance of a stone. "The earl gave me something, but if you don't want to see it, fine!" She was about to duck back in her room and slam the door when he sighed and came toward her, walking as if he half expected her to throw a bucket of water in his face.

When he stepped into the room, she picked up the lamp and thrust it toward him. "Look at this, if you don't believe me."

He took the lamp and studied it for a moment. "How did you get this?"

"My lamp went out and I had to sit in that dungeon in the dark for an eternity. I wondered if he was going to leave me down there, and about the time I decided he was, he spoke to me. My lamp was out of oil. He said he could not fill it with oil, but he could give me something that belonged to him. The lamp came on again and when I looked, this stone was glowing so bright, it was like looking into the sun."

She saw he was staring at the stone, and she wondered if he had even heard a single word she said.

"The Templar's Diamond," he whispered.

She stared down at the stone. "The what diamond?"

"Templar. It has to be the Templar's Diamond. It is said that Sir James Douglas the Good acquired the stone when he was fighting in Spain, when he was trying to get to Jerusalem to bury the heart of Robert the Bruce. Before he died, he put the diamond in the box with Bruce's heart to be brought back to Scotland. It was given to his heirs. It disappeared with the rest of the Douglas jewels."

"Why is it called the Templar's Diamond?"

"Because it was first found by the Knights Templar during the Crusades."

"You are certain it is the Templar's Diamond?"

"Not positive, but I know who will know for certain."

"Who? Lady Margaret?"

"Aye. She saw a drawing of it when she was a young bride."

"What happened to the drawing?"

"She doesn't know. It was in the possession of my grandfather—my real grandfather. After he died, they could not find it. She never saw it again."

"Then we should take it to her."

"I'll take it to her. I want you to get in bed and rest before you fall over."

"But I…"

"You are weaving on your feet. Get into bed. I'll come back after I speak with Gram."

She was too weary to say anything more. He was right. She was tired and she was weaving—enough that he took her arm and guided her back to her bed. She sat down on the edge and looked up at him.

He kissed her lightly. "Go to sleep."

"I will," she said, staring down at her slippers.

"I'll be back later," he said, and left.

He had no more than shut the door behind him when the earl appeared.

He did not come with a draft of wind this time, but with the green mist that swirled until it took form. "If you have come to fuss at me, you can leave right now," said Meleri. "I limit myself to one tongue-lashing a day."

"No tongue-lashing, no more tests. This is a friendly visit, lass."

"Why?" She pulled off one slipper and dropped it to the floor.

"I wanted to see if ye were verra angry wi' me."

"I am not angry at anyone. Faith, I am too tired to even say the word."

"It didna sound that way to me."

"You heard?"

"Aye, lass, they heard ye in Brussels."

She dropped the other slipper. "He made me angry."

"That is as it should be. It is good for a man and his wife to have a brawl now and then."

"I cannot fathom what could be good about it."

His eyes twinkled. "Ye will understand better after ye have made up."

"I have made up with him…sort of."

"'Sort of' isn't good enough."

"I was nice first. Now it's his turn."

"Ye are stubborn."

"Only around tyrants. It is the only way to survive around pig-headed men."

"Ye will change yer mind after ye make up, and then ye will be glad ye had the argument."

"Humph! I doubt that."

"There canna be a reconciliation where there is no war. After a battle, where words have been fired and battle lines drawn, it is good between a man and a woman to kiss and make up."

"Bah!"

"Double bah!"

She could not help smiling. "I don't know why I like you," she said.

"For the same reason I like ye, I ken."

She sat there looking at him, unable to believe she was forming a friendship with a ghost. But she was. He was so likable, a real charmer, she thought, refusing to admit that it might run in the family. Her tiredness seemed to vanish and she rubbed her feet over the carpet by her bed. "Why did you want me to come to the dungeon?"

"I told ye. To prove ye were verra brave."

"You knew I would be frightened out of my wits. A true coward, I am."

"But ye went, in spite of yer fear. That isna cowardly. What ye did takes a lassie wi' courage."

"I don't feel very courageous."

"If it would make ye feel better, ye are the one wi' the bravest heart, because ye, of all the others, were the only one to go into the dungeon alone."

"There were others?"

"Aye."

"How many were there?"

"Three or four."

"And I am the only one who passed muster?"

"Aye, lass, 'tis certain that ye did."

"Well, fancy that," she said, then smiled. "You did make a good choice," she said.

"Aye. The best for last."

"I suppose you will be revealing the rest of it. When will it happen?"

"At the time of my choosing."

"Will it be very long?"

"I would like to say it would. Of all the times I have returned, I have enjoyed this time the most. 'Tis sorry I will be to see it end."

"Where will you go? What will happen to you…when it is all over?"

"What happens to anyone who dies?"

She felt overcome with sadness. "Perhaps we could find a way to make this go on a bit longer."

"Would that I could, but I cannot."

"I shall miss you terribly, I fear, for I have become quite accustomed to having you in my life."

A log popped and she glanced in the direction of the fire. She felt very close to crying. "Once you have gone back, will you ever be able to return again…even for just a little while? Just long enough to pay me a short visit?"

He did not answer, and when she looked back at the place where he had been, he was no longer there.

Meleri let out a long sigh and looked down at her hands in her lap. That is when she saw the ruby necklace lying on her bed, the deep color of pigeon blood, so vibrant in the glow from the firelight. She had seen it before, on one of Robert's ancestors the day he showed her their portraits. She picked it up, unable to believe its weight or its existence. This necklace alone was worth a fortune. Just how many bloody jewels were there in the ancient Douglas coffers?

Still in her gown and clutching the ruby necklace in her hand, she pulled the covers up under her neck and fell asleep.

When she awoke the next morning, she put the necklace in a safe place, then dressed and hurried downstairs. She was late to breakfast and found Lady Margaret eating alone. "Have you seen Robert?"

"He and Iain left early to ride into Dumfries."

"Why did they go there?"

"The sheriff sent word that he needed Robert to sign some papers related to the Englishman's death."

"So much has happened of late, I almost forgot about Philip," Meleri said.

"He left this for you."

She opened the note.

Meleri, my love,
I came back to see you last night, but you were sleeping soundly. It is my hope that the trip to Dumfries will be of short duration and I can return home soon. Keep a place warm beside you for me. Until then, I remain,

> Your loving husband,
> Robert

Robert returned shortly before dinner. Once the meal was over, they retired to the morning room to spend some time alone. He was sitting in a deep, comfortable chair Meleri called "his chair." He was reading the paper he brought from Dumfries, a rare luxury for him. In spite of how much he enjoyed the pleasure of reading a current newspaper, he would peer, from time to time over the top of it, just to look at her.

She was sitting across from him, in her chair, which was a smaller version of his. He thought about the girl he married and wondered at the woman who had taken her place. Although she supervised and cleaned and ran their home with a cheerful exuberance and determination, there was a secret quality about her—a calm reserve that had never been there before. It pleased him greatly to think he might have had something to do with that—although he knew the old earl deserved most of the credit. For it was he who gave her the assurance that she was not only accepted, but trusted and looked up to as the means of restoring the Douglases to their former prosperity. The earl had provided the means for her to feel needed, respected and loved. Surely the glow that came from her was one of contentment.

She stopped reading for a moment and looked up as she placed the book in her lap. "What are you going to do with the jewels? Are you going to sell them right away?"

"No. I want to wait to see if more turn up. I don't want to sell any more of our history than I have to."

"I'm glad. I, too, hate the thought of parting with something that has been in your family for so long. But I know you can't hold out forever. I received a letter from my sister, Elizabeth, in response to a letter I sent my father. She has spoken with his barrister, who is making the necessary arrangements to have my dowry transferred to you. Perhaps it will come in time."

"I don't want you to worry."

"Your worries are mine. When I see the earl again, I will mention it to him. Unfortunately, he can't be rushed. He comes and goes as it pleases him."

"Don't get too attached to him."

A sad expression settled over her face. "It is too late for that, I'm afraid. I have already begun to grieve for the time that I know is not far away, the time when he tells me I will see him no more. It is quite a difficult and heartfelt thing to lose a friend. I don't know if I can forgive him for leaving. I don't look upon that final vanishing act as something I can accept as easily as I accepted the fact that I had formed a close attachment to a ghost."

"Perhaps it is as difficult for him as it is for you."

"I think it might be even more difficult for him. He is the one who has to leave, the one who must go."

"Being left behind is not an easy thing to accept, either."

"No, but my life is full of the closeness of you and your family."

"Maybe he has someone waiting for him, as well."

She smiled sadly. "I would like to know that he did," she said. "If only there was some way to be assured of it." She picked up her book again and gave it her attention, and he knew the dis-

cussion of the earl was ended, not because she did not want to
continue it, but simply because she could not.

He saw the book of poetry in her hands and could not help
thinking of this wife who loved flowers, animals, Scotland and
books. Everywhere he looked, her saw her touches. Bowls of
roses scented the air, and soon they would be replaced by the
gleanings of approaching fall, which she was gathering on her
solitary walks with Corrie and Dram. Already, he had seen her
coming inside with a blast of fall air, great boughs of tawny-and-
gold leaves in her arms.

He glanced outside to see the sun setting, casting its golden
blessing on her immaculate garden, subdued with the last blush
of summer's fading flowers. Farther over, in the vegetable garden, early fall vegetables were maturing.

Meleri turned up the lamp beside her and he watched her
movement, as mesmerized by the sight of her as he had been the
first time he saw her. A moth fluttered about the lamp, thumping and tapping against it, but she did not seem to notice as she
went back to her book. About him, the quiet of the room seemed
to settle into his bones and he leaned back comfortably and released a sigh.

At the sound, she glanced up, and he could see the sadness
was gone from her eyes.

"It's nice having you back," he said. "I missed you."

"And I you. I find I can never stay very far away from you,
or gone for very long."

"That is because we are of one heart," he said, and thought of
no more perfect way to end another perfect day.

36

Meleri was troubled when she awoke. Not even the tender memory of a night in Robert's arms, or his loving support and concern for what she was experiencing, could erase the anxiety, the crowding of apprehension she felt.

She dressed quickly in a somber, dark blue dress with little embellishment other than a plain white collar and cuffs, for she was not taken with the more frivolous aspects of life this day, but with the premonition of something about to happen, something both sorrowful and grave. She walked downstairs, dreading even the rustling of her skirts against the cold stones of the floor.

Once outside, she thought herself on the way to the garden, but she was overcome with a sudden urge to go toward the small chapel that stood some distance away. She had not been there before, other than to pass by with a casual glance, for the chapel was no longer used, and she had not yet possessed any curiosity about the names inscribed in the family tomb, where generations of Douglases lay. Today, however, was different.

She walked toward the chapel, paying little attention to the scattering of old tombstones as she passed, until she came upon the perfectly symmetrical structure, Gothic by design, where the Douglases laid their dead. She stopped in front of a thick wooden door, studded with brass, beneath a Gothic arch. The door was partially open, and she could see a strong shaft of light that came from a stained glass window and scattered prisms of color over the stone floor.

She pushed the door open farther and stepped into the burial chamber, where the light seemed dazzling and bright. She walked along the perimeter of the walls, passing each crypt and reading the names inscribed. But there was one name she came upon that caused her to stop. Her entire being was suddenly overcome with a flood of aching, tender emotion, for the name she read. William Douglas.

"'Tis not my name ye be reading there, but that of a namesake."

She turned around quickly and saw the earl's ghost standing behind her, just a few feet away. She started to ask him where he was buried, but decided she did not want to know. "I am glad it is not yours," she said.

"Why?"

"It is sad enough, I think, to know you are dead. I do not need to be close to the place you are buried to remember you."

"'Tis a kindhearted lass, ye are. There are times when I regret my ghostly restrictions."

She smiled. "I have heard about your eye for the lassies and your sons by two women named Margaret."

His eyes sparkled. "Have ye now? And what did ye hear?"

"That you were married to Margaret, the sister of the Earl of Mar, and you had a son, James, by her. But I also heard you took your brother-in-law's widow as your mistress and had a son, George, by her, and from these two sons the Douglas lines continued—the Red Douglases through George, and through James, the Black."

"Ye are a well-informed lass."

"I try to be. It is true?"

"Aye. Does that alter yer kindred feeling for me?"

Their gazes caught and held, and for a moment, she was captured by the intensity of such deep blue eyes. "I do not base my friendships upon such shallow decisions. Besides, I knew of these indiscretions before I decided I liked you."

"Ah lass, would that I had more time. I wouldna choose to miss the years of your life."

"I wish you could remain, as well. I suppose there are rules and such, even for ghosts."

He laughed. "Aye, living or dead, we are always governed by rules."

"We are at the end of it, then?"

"Regrettably close."

"I wish there was some way to tell you, to express what I am feeling inside. We owe you so much. How can I ever thank you?"

"Weel, if it is a fitting tribute ye want, ye could name yer first-born William."

His image began to fade, and before she could say anything more, he vanished from sight. As she stood looking at the place he had been, she suddenly noticed a yellowed piece of parchment.

She picked up the parchment and read the words of an old rune.

Take no thought on the morrow,
For statues guarding murdered bones,
In a place of tears and sorrow,
Deep roots will reach beneath cold stones.
One must do all that is bidden,
Count if you can, five and fifty crosses,
And seek that which once was hidden,
Markers all of beloved losses.
Near a place where no color is lack,
Seek nothing of a babe's broken long gown,
First pass over the one that is black,
Or not stop not near a rider brown.
Continue toward sweet morning light,
And in the place of an ancient curse,
Golden steps leading to running white,
Lies the secret of overflowing purse.
Marks the place of what you seek,
Light from years of darkness now is taken
Wide angel's wings and great bird's beak,
From these ashes a fire shall awaken.
What was down shall rise in glory,

Do not weep as you pass by,
One's beginning ends another's story,
As you are now, so once was I.
Eternity will not hide a friend's regret,
Stairs go up and pass me by,
For one left behind most recent met,
I have returned, I did not lie.

Certain it was some sort of riddle that would lead her to the rest of the missing Douglas jewels, Meleri could only wonder at what it meant. She read it again, but when she finished, she was saddened to realize she did not understand it any more than she had the first time she read it through.

There was little doubt she would need help deciphering the riddle—from someone who had more knowledge of the area than she did. She had to find Robert.

He was easier to find than she anticipated, for she saw him riding into the stable yard about the same time she reached the grounds of the castle. Seeing her, he rode over to where she stood. "Were you looking for me?" he asked.

"Yes, I had another visit from the earl. He left me this." She handed him the parchment.

He dropped the reins against the neck of his horse and took the parchment. She waited quietly as he read, intrigued by the endless number of expressions one face could make all in the course of reading.

When he finished, he handed it back to her. "I make it to be a rhyme to lead us to the jewels."

"That is what I thought, but none of it makes sense to me. Is there anything that seems familiar to you?"

"Not at first glance. Go inside and find Gram. I'll see to my horse, and then meet you in the library. Perhaps the three of us can decipher at least enough of it to get us started."

Robert saw to his horse and then went straight to the library, arriving ahead of Meleri and Gram. By the time they walked into the room, he had cleared a place at the library table and pulled up three chairs.

He seated each of them, then took the place at the end of the table where Meleri laid the parchment. He read the riddle aloud for Lady Margaret to hear.

"It won't be easy to solve," Gram said.

"Perhaps we should work on one verse at a time," Meleri suggested, and Robert agreed.

"All right," he said, and read the first verse:

> "Take no thought on the morrow,
> For statues guarding murdered bones,
> In a place of tears and sorrow,
> Deep roots will reach beneath cold stones."

"Anyone make anything out of it?" he asked.

"Murdered bones. Have you ever heard of any references to murdered bones?" Gram asked.

Robert thought a moment. "No, not unless it could refer to the children of Gavin Douglas who were killed by English reivers."

"Aye," Gram said, "they are buried in the chapel yard."

"That would make sense," Meleri said, "for here it says 'in a place of tears and sorrows,' which makes sense for it to be a place of burial. And there are usually statues as grave markers, or found on top of the tombstones."

Robert read the next verse.

> "One must do all that is bidden,
> Count if you can, five and fifty crosses,
> And seek that which once was hidden,
> Markers all of beloved losses."

"The first line is clear," he said. "We are to do everything the riddle requires us to do."

"The meaning of the second line is apparent also," Meleri added, "for we should be able to find the place where that number of crosses can be found. And the third line tells us by doing what is required, we will seek what is hidden, which are the jewels. But the last one, 'markers of beloved losses'? What does that mean?"

"I think that line goes with the second line, 'Count if you can, five and fifty crosses, markers all of beloved losses,'" suggested Lady Margaret.

"Aye," Robert said, "that makes the most sense. So we know now we are looking in the chapel cemetery, and we must find a place where there are five and fifty crosses."

The third verse stumped him, and even after reading it a second time, it did not make sense.

> "Near a place where no color is lack,
> Seek nothing of a babe's broken long gown,
> First, pass over the one that is black,
> Or not stop not near a rider brown."

"I think we should go to the cemetery," he said finally. "Perhaps it will make more sense there."

The three of them walked to the cemetery. It did not take long to find the place where five and fifty crosses could be counted, for it was in the oldest part. The third verse, however, still had them guessing as to its meaning.

"Near a place where no color is lack," Meleri said. "What could that mean? There really isn't that much color here, for everything is mostly white and gray stones, green grass and brown dirt. Where no color is lack…it seems to me that would mean it would have to be near a place that had every color in order for none to be lacking."

"Aye, but where is that?" asked Lady Margaret.

"I've got it!" Meleri shouted so loud that Lady Margaret jumped. "When I was in the family crypt, the sun came through the stained glass windows and threw splashes of color all over the floor, *every* color imaginable."

"That couldn't be it," Robert said, "for that would mean we would have to dig up the floor, and there is nothing there to fit the description of the remaining verses."

"Perhaps it is near the window, but on the outside," Lady Margaret said. "That would put the place we are looking for between the chapel wall on the side where the stained glass window is and the place of five and fifty crosses."

Once they were in that part of the cemetery, they read the verse again. "I think the line 'First, pass over the one that is black' would come after the first verse, since the words rhyme," Robert said. "So we must pass over something black, and not seek a broken gown, and not stop near a rider brown…none of this makes sense," he said, throwing up his hands.

"Look over here!" Lady Margaret said. "Here is the grave of a child, and a statue of a babe in a gown, but the bottom is broken off. Perhaps it was a long gown at one time."

"That must be it," Robert said, "but now where do we go to find the rest?"

Meleri, he noticed, was looking at the paper with a serious frown. "What are you thinking?" he asked.

"The colors," she said, "black and brown, and here in the next verse is white. Why are those so familiar?"

Robert looked from Meleri to his grandmother and shrugged. "We may never know, just as we may never solve this riddle."

"All right," she said, "let's go to the next verse."

> "Continue toward sweet morning light,
> And in the place of an ancient curse,
> Golden steps leading to running white,
> Lies the secret of overflowing purse."

"What could it mean to continue toward morning light? Is it the sun?" Meleri asked.

"I think it is. Now we must find golden steps."

"I am telling you, this is a waste of time," Robert said. "There obviously are no golden steps here."

Meleri sighed. "I suppose you are right. If only he had given us some other clue, something to give us a hint as to what we are looking for besides these rhymes that don't mean anything to us."

"Was there anything he said to you that sticks out in your mind as being irrelevant, or something that did not make any sense at the time?" Robert asked.

"No, nothing except those verses that I asked Lady Margaret about."

"What verses?" Robert asked.

"They were from Tam Lin," Lady Margaret said, and she recited a verse.

> "O first let pass the black, lady,
> And then let pass the brown,
> But quickly run to the milk-white steed,
> Pull ye his rider down."

"That's it!" Meleri said. "That's why the colors were so familiar."

"What good are they to us?" Robert asked.

"Horses!" Meleri said. "There must be some graves marked with horses, and all we have to do is find a black, a brown and a white."

They walked around searching, until Robert was ready to give up. Suddenly Gram cried out. "Here it is! The black horse!"

Robert and Meleri rushed to where she stood, and there, on the grave of Sir Archibald Douglas, was a small bronze statue of a knight on a horse, the bronze having turned black over the years. "If this is the black, then there must be…"

"Over here!" Meleri called out. "Here is a brown granite headstone, with a horse carved near the name."

"Look at this," Robert said. "See these steps that lead down to the other graves? They are of the same brown granite, and the way the sun shines on them, they are a golden color." He walked down the steps and stopped by a grave. There, upon a white marble gravestone, was the statue of a white horse running with no rider.

"The running white," Meleri said.

"This is starting to come together now," Robert said, and read the next verse again. "So where is the place of an ancient curse?"

"Could that be the place where the children of Malcolm Douglas are buried? Remember, he lost all of his children to the plague."

"I don't know where they are buried," he said.

"I do." Lady Margaret led them to the place where five little graves were surrounded by a black iron fence.

They read the next verse.

> "Marks the place of what you seek,
> Light from years of darkness now is taken
> Wide angel's wings and great bird's beak,
> From these ashes a fire shall awaken."

"If we read the third line first, the place we seek will be marked by wide angel's wings and a great bird's beak," Meleri said.

"Which is this grave." Robert pointed to a grave. "The gravestone is an angel, and he is holding out his hand, where a big beaked bird is sitting."

"I think the jewels must be buried in that grave," Meleri said, "because the next verses simply tell us that a fire will awaken and light will come from the years of darkness. I take that to mean that we will find the jewels, the family will emerge out of the darkness and into the light. Read the next verse."

> "What was down shall rise in glory,
> Do not weep as you pass by,
> One's beginning ends another's story,
> As you are now, so once was I.

"What was down, is the Douglas name, and it shall rise in glory," said Lady Margaret.

Robert glanced at Meleri, who was suddenly quiet. "Lass, why are you crying?" Robert asked, and took her in his arms. "Are they tears of joy?"

"No, it is because I understand what he is saying in the rest of it. Those verses that remain are for me. He doesn't want me to be sad as I walk from this place. He reminds me that he was once alive."

Robert read the last verse.

> "Eternity will not hide a friend's regret,
> Stairs go up and pass me by,
> For one left behind most recent met,
> I have returned, I did not lie."

"Eternity will not erase his regret over leaving you behind," Robert said, holding her more tightly.

Suddenly, Meleri pulled away from him and wiped her eyes with the back of her hand. "Stairs go up," she said, running toward the steps they had come down a moment ago. "He is there! I am certain of it."

"Meleri, wait!"

"No! Don't come up here. I must see him alone!"

Meleri ran on, her feet flying up the steps until she reached the top. Breathing hard, she looked around, overcome with a feeling of melancholy. He was not here. Had she misinterpreted the verse, then? Was he not coming back? Was her final goodbye to be those words he spoke to her in the last lines of the rhyme?

She did not realize she was crying until she felt the warm path of hot tears running over her cheeks. She would not see him again. Ever.

"I ken I was a wee bit hasty branding ye a strong lassie. Why are ye are crying now, when it is all over?"

She blinked and wiped her eyes, unable to hold back the wide smile that stretched across her lips. "You are here," she whispered.

"Aye, did ye think I would not tell ye goodbye?"

"I was beginning to fear that was the way of it."

"Ah, are ye a lass of so little faith, then?"

"I have been known to have a weak moment or two. Will you be returning to the portrait now?"

"Ye have solved the riddle and my task is completed. I canna stay, once it is found."

"So, this is goodbye?"

"Aye, lass, I am afraid so."

"And I will never see you again? You will never come back?"

"'Tis done, lass."

"I shall miss you terribly, you know."

"Aye, lass, I ken it will be the same for me. Ye are a child of my heart, and it is not easy to leave ye behind, but I must go now."

"Why was it me? Why was I the one with the heart of the truest Scot? Why not Robert, or Iain, or even Hugh?"

"Och! Ye canna mean I would choose a man when I could have a lassie?"

She smiled at him, hoping he could feel all the love and warmth that came with it. "What was the real reason?"

"It was a good way to bring the two of ye together, was it not?"

"Yes, but that surely isn't all."

"No, and I ken ye willna let me rest in peace until I tell ye the way of it. It is a simple matter. Ye are the descendant of a Scot, a Knight Templar who saved my life and was killed doing it. It was my way of paying tribute to him. It was a fitting end to everything, ye ken, that our descendants would be together."

"I am a descendant of a Scot? But I am English," she said.

"English, Welsh, Irish…and Scot," said the ghost. "Yer Irish great-grandmother was the daughter of the Knight Templar. Now ye ken why you were destined to find happiness in a place of great sadness."

"You? It was you who came to me in those dreams from so long ago?"

"I always knew ye fer a smart lassie."

"Scot ancestors…treasures…I don't understand."

"Ye will, lass. Ye will before the day is over."

She looked at him, admiring as she always had his tall stature, the pride in his craggy face, the fire in his eyes. She wished she could have seen him as a mortal. He must have been an impressive sight.

"Tell me goodbye, lass, for I must go."

It couldn't be time for him to go. It couldn't be. She was so fond of him.

She was crying again, unable to stop the tears that bubbled up so freely. Truly, she felt her heart would break. "This is one time I really and truly hate the fact that you are a ghost. I have come to depend upon you and look forward to our exchanges. What shall I do when you are gone? Who will help me sharpen my wit?"

"I ken Robbie will be happy to help ye with that."

His image began to glimmer and she knew he was leaving. "I want to tell you goodbye, but how can I put my arms around a vapor? I don't suppose it would be possible to give you a hug…just one quick one before you go?"

He stood a short distance from her, his legs planted wide apart, his black cape billowing in the wind. His arms were crossed in front of him, and she could see the intense way he regarded her. "Ye are truly a bothersome lass."

She could not help smiling at that. "I know, but I was so overwhelmed with sadness, I had hoped…" She did not finish what she was going to say, for at that moment, she saw the transparency of his image was beginning to fill in. No longer could she see through him, for right before her very eyes he took a solid form.

And, oh, the sight of him was magnificent.

He was looking down at her in the same manner he always did, with his arms folded across his chest, when suddenly he opened them wide.

She ran to him, feeling the solid strength of his arms as they closed around her.

"'Tis quite a lass ye are, and ye have carved out a wee part of my heart for yerself."

"I shall miss you with all my being," she said, hugging him tightly. "A part of you will live on, for you will always be in my heart."

She felt the pressure of his kiss to the top of her head, then he pushed her back and she looked into his face. His form began to glimmer, then fade, and he was transparent once more. He gave her a salute, then turned and walked off, his image growing lighter with each step.

She called after him. "Don't go! I need you!"

"So does the Countess of Suffolk," he said. Then with a laugh and a wink, he vanished.

She remained where she was, attempting to resolve the feelings in her heart. The memory of her brief encounter with him was as wonderful to her as touching a star, and every bit as mysterious. Remembering their time together and focusing on the fact that she was fortunate that she had known him at all was cold consolation. A more comforting thought was that he existed still, somewhere beyond her realm to comprehend.

He did not disappear into nothingness. She knew now that at some point during her journey, she would see him again. And when she did, he would be standing as he had so many times before, with his arms crossed and his legs planted wide, his black cape billowing out behind him, as he smiled at her across endless generations, his face as fresh as it was during his days of battle.

Today, as it did during his time, the heather bloomed in the Lowlands, the grouse nested on the moors, and the salmon came in from the sea.

Some things never change.

37

In awed silence the family gathered inside the black iron fence. Only the twins were absent. Iain, having decided they were too young to be involved, had sent them to visit a friend. Agnes had accompanied them. Only Meleri and Lady Margaret stood quietly watching as Robert, Iain and Hugh dug into the soft earth beneath the wide spread of a marble angel's wings.

"I pray 'tis not the grave of a child," Lady Margaret said.

"'I have returned, I did not lie,'" Meleri said, reciting the last lines from the rhyme. "Everything will be as he said and 'from these ashes a fire shall awaken.' The jewels will be there." Wrapped in memory, she stood as still and silent as a tree. The grave was deep. It would not be long now.

The scraping sound of metal dragged against damp wood sent a cold shiver over her, and her heart stilled when Robert said, "We've found it. It is a casket."

"A grave," Lady Margaret said, her voice heavy with disappointment.

"No. It isn't a grave. Open it," she said to Robert. "Open it and see what is inside. You won't find a body…there will be nothing there except the jewels."

The men lifted the small wooden casket out of the ground. Meleri felt limp with a mixture of relief and anxiety. Her heart was beating suffocatingly fast. Robert turned to glance at his wife, then said something to Iain before he went to stand beside her. He gathered her to his side and stood with his arm around her as they watched together. The wood was soft and rotten in places, which enabled Hugh and Iain to break it apart easily. Inside, lay a smaller stone casket.

Iain and Hugh exchanged glances, then turned to look at Robert. Nothing stirred. Nothing moved. The moment was here at last, she thought. After almost three centuries, the wait would soon be over. At last, when no one could stand the tension any longer, Robert said, "Open it."

He pulled her more tightly against him and took her hand in his, to bring it to his lips, where he kissed her palm, then folded her fingers over it. "Hold on to that," he whispered.

She did as he asked, clutching her fist so tightly she could feel the bite of her nails digging into her skin. She glanced up once into his deep blue eyes and found not only the understanding, the patience that he had always shown her, but also love and reassurance. Together, they turned to watch.

Hugh let forth a jubilant cry. "A jewel casket! By the love of St. Andrew, we have found it."

Iain lifted it up so everyone could see. The lock was corroded and broke easily. Meleri held her breath.

With one swift movement, Iain threw back the lid of the casket and she heard him exclaim, "It's empty. There is nothing here but a small oiled pouch."

She stood there, weak kneed and feeling as if she had stared too long into the sun. She was certain it would be here. But it was not. *I have returned. I did not lie.* She clutched Robert's arm. "It is here. He wouldn't lie to us. I know it. We have to keep looking. It is here."

"See what is inside the pouch," Robert said

Iain unwrapped it and removed a ragged bit of linen. Inside that he found an aged piece of leather. He opened the leather and withdrew an old, yellowed piece of parchment, folded in half and in half again. He unfolded the parchment and spread it out on the top of a marble gravestone. Everyone gathered around. "What does it say?" Meleri asked.

"It's a map," Iain said.

"Of the crypts," Robert added, turning the map.

After studying it for several minutes, Robert said, "It looks like there is another burial chamber behind the crypt where Andrew Douglas is buried."

"Aye," Iain said. "We would have to remove Andrew's casket in order to get to the other chamber."

"The jewels are hidden there?" asked Lady Margaret.

"That is what we intend to find out," Robert said.

Soon, they had all gathered near the crypts. The stone that sealed the crypt of Andrew Douglas was removed. Stale, dead air rushed out into the room, and Meleri turned her head away, not watching, but listening to the scraping sound of Andrew's casket being pulled from the small chamber it occupied. Only when it was safely laid on the chapel floor did she turn to look at the empty crypt.

Robert looked inside. "Bring a lamp."

Hugh held one up for Robert, who climbed inside the crypt. "Here is the stone at the back, but I'm not certain how to open it." He crawled back out. "It seems solidly set in between the other stones. I don't know how we could move it, other than to tear into the wall." He began to look at the crypt again. "I wonder…"

"What are you thinking?" Iain asked.

"Look at the way these slabs are set. It would appear that the top, back and side stones were set first, with the bottom slab put in last, almost as if it were pushed into place."

Iain studied the crypt. "If that is the case, then we should be able to pull the slab out."

Iain, Hugh and Robert worked for more than an hour, trying to remove the slab, but could not. "There must be another way," Hugh said.

Meleri's curiosity got the better of her and she came closer and looked into the crypt. She studied the stone slabs and understood why Robert thought the bottom slab had to be removed, for it held the other slabs in place. "What if you didn't remove the slab, but lifted it up and stood it on its side?"

The three men stared at one another, then Iain laughed and slapped the other two on the back. "It takes a lass," he said.

The three of them tried for several minutes to push the right side of the stone upward, but it would not budge. Meleri couldn't understand why they persisted, but stubbornness seemed to be the way the mind of a man worked, especially if he was a Scot. "Why don't you try the other side?" she asked.

Robert gave her an irritated look that said he did not think that was going to do anything, either, but he followed Iain and Hugh's lead and began to put all his weight behind a mighty push. Suddenly, the slab moved, so quickly it seemed to have a power all its own. The moment it reached a position that was perpendicular to its former position, the other slabs began to move, folding and falling like toppled gravestones, one after the other, until Robert exclaimed, "There's a small stairway beneath here."

They removed one remaining slab that blocked their way. Meleri could see that now the crypt looked more like a small entry that led to the hidden stairs. Robert took the lamp and walked inside, ducking his head. Meleri fell in behind him, then Hugh and Lady Margaret, who was helped by Iain. They went down the staircase, which was circular and opened into a small chamber below the chapel floor. There in the chamber were five chests. A stone table stood in the middle of the room. The top of the table was a stone slab with hieroglyphic writing, which no one understood. Strange symbols and writings were etched in the stonework along the walls. "What do you make of it?" Hugh asked.

"These look remarkably like the symbols etched in the stonework of Rosslyn Chapel," Iain said.

"Where is that?" Meleri asked.

"It's near Hawthornden Castle, home of the Sinclairs," Robert replied.

"I was there once, many years ago," continued Iain. "The etchings are said to be Templar and Holy Grail symbols. Rosslyn was at one time spelled Roslin, which means Blood of Christ.

Legend has long had it that many of the Knights Templar settled in Scotland after they were forced out of France, where many of their numbers were burned at the stake. It was said they fought beside Robert the Bruce. Sir Henry St. Clair of Roslin also befriended them. Sir Henry's son, Sir William, accompanied our ancestor, Sir James Douglas, with the heart of Bruce, and died with him, fighting the Moors in Spain. Before long, they changed the spelling of their name from the Norman spelling to Sinclair."

"But why would there be Templar markings here, in this chapel?" Robert asked.

"I don't know," Iain said.

"Why don't you open some of the chests and see if there is anything in there to give you a clue," Lady Margaret said.

One by one, the chests were opened, and for some time, everyone was too stunned to speak. The chests were filled with far more than the Douglas jewels, which were found in a small chest. The family jewels were quite valuable, with a sapphire that was, as Lady Margaret said, "as big as hope." It also contained a gold crown set with rubies, a golden mermaid set with jewels and eyes of large emeralds. There was a heavy gold necklace with an Egyptian scarab, a large engraved amethyst, a very heavy bracelet with hieroglyphic markings, as well as pearl hat pins, emerald and diamond brooches, and rings set with stones of every color. But these jewels were minimal in comparison to what was found in the other chests, for inside those were vast amounts of silver and gold, mostly in the form of jewelry and coins. Two chests contained nothing but ingots.

"It can only be part of the Templar wealth," Iain said. "At one time, the Templars owned over nine thousand manors and castles all over Europe. Their wealth supported the largest banking systems. It also caused suspicion and jealousy among the European nobility, primarily, King Philip IV of France. He convinced the pope that the Knights Templar were not defenders of the faith, but were trying to destroy it. The pope ordered the king to arrest them, but when the king's men went to the castles, many of the manors were abandoned, and the large naval force anchored at

La Rochelle was gone. Where those eighteen vessels and all the wealth they carried went, no one knows."

"You think this might be part of it?" Robert asked.

"Aye, I think it must have come from the connection between William Sinclair and James Douglas, and that ties in some way with our ghost and Meleri's Templar ancestor."

"Perhaps we can delve into this more. We might start by going to Rosslyn," Robert said.

"Never explore a gift too critically," Lady Margaret said. "To do so might be a good way to lose it."

"There is more here than we can spend in a lifetime," Hugh said.

"I don't want to take it," Meleri said, and everyone turned to look at her.

"What do you mean?" Hugh asked.

"I don't want to remove any of it."

"You want to leave it here?" Robert asked.

"Some of it, yes. It is obvious we don't need all of this, just as Hugh said. It can only cause problems for us. Soon we would worry about being swindled, or robbed. It would change our lives. I don't know why, but I feel very strongly that we should take the Douglas jewels and leave the rest here."

"Don't you want to take a little of the other?" Hugh asked. "A few coins, a bar of gold?"

"No. I think we should take what is ours and leave the rest. Perhaps another Douglas living in another time will have need of it. I would like to think it would be here for him."

"She is right," Robert said, and he put his arm around her and hugged her tightly. "Our own family wealth is ample enough and will see us through the restoration of our home and lands. What would we do with so much wealth?"

"I can give you a list," Hugh said.

"I agree with Meleri," Lady Margaret said. "Too much money can ruin a family. I would not want the results of greed to destroy us."

"I think you are right," Iain said. "I think we will fare much better by taking what is rightfully ours."

Robert, Meleri, Lady Margaret and Iain all stared at Hugh, who laughed and said, "Don't look at me. When have I ever gone against anything this family did? Besides, I intend to marry a rich lassie."

Robert glanced at Meleri with a teasing look. "And where do you plan to find such a lassie?" he asked.

"England," Hugh said, and everyone laughed.

Epilogue

Later, after the Douglas jewels were locked safely away, Robert turned to Meleri. "Come lass, I will walk you upstairs."

"You must leave soon for England with the money for the Earl of Drummond."

"Aye, we haven't much time," he replied. "Less than a fortnight. How does it feel to be the lass who saved Beloyn?"

"It feels better to be the lass who married the present Black Douglas."

"What are you thinking?"

"I am trying to understand everything that has happened today and how my ancestor fits in with the picture."

He folded her in his arms and kissed her. "First we take the money to Drummond, then we find out more about your ancestor. It has been quite a day. Are you tired?"

"A little." If the truth were known, she could not think about being tired at a time like this, for she was so taken by his comforting presence, the way he had supported her, the patience and understanding that became his symbol as much as the Douglas plaid or the family crest. It was difficult to keep from crying over the sadness of losing the earl and the joy of having found such a man to love for the rest of her life.

His arms tightened around her, his lips moving softly over her cheek. "Remind me to tell you sometime how proud I am of you." He took her hand. "Come on. You should rest before dinner. We have a lot to celebrate tonight."

She walked with him, arm in arm, through the gallery toward the stairs, thinking how many times she had walked beneath this high ornamental ceiling to gaze upon the beautiful curving staircase. As always, the dogs were in their customary positions at the bottom of the stairs, but as they drew closer, she could see Corrie and Dram were not still and tense, or gazing along the row of pictures in the gallery. They were asleep.

As was her habit, Meleri gazed upon the sober and dignified faces of centuries of Douglas ancestors staring out at her as they passed. Only this time was different, although she was not certain why. Everything looked the same, from the ornate carvings of fruit and flowers that adorned the black wainscoting to the portraits lining the walls. But, unlike all the times before, she did not feel the oppressive mood that always hung over the gallery. Nor did she have the strange feeling, as she passed, that they were all watching her. It was as if everything had changed, as if they all knew and somehow approved.

"Hello, my loves," she said, stopping to pat Corrie and Dram, who'd heard them coming and leaped to their feet, eager to greet them.

Robert stopped beside her and she turned toward him, warming at the look on his face. Her heart was too full of happiness to speak and she hoped he could see all the love she felt in her eyes. *He will be the father of my children.*

The thought had no more than flashed through her mind, when she was filled with a comforting assurance, and suddenly she knew a son would soon come. A son they would name William.

She imagined the way the castle would look with its wing restored, and of the man she loved with all her being, the future they had ahead of them. She wondered how it came to be that a temperamental English lass had been so fortunate to become the bride of one man, who came from a long line of men known as Black Douglas.

A shaft of late afternoon sun broke through the window and Meleri felt the warmth of Robert's hand close around hers. From somewhere deep in the castle came the haunting skirl of bagpipes, reminding her that only one thing was missing to make her happiness complete.

They reached the portrait of the first earl. "I shall always treasure this picture," she said, and paused a moment to look at the place his image had once been.

Only now, he was there, looking as magnificent as he had when she saw him last. How lifelike he looked—almost alive—standing the way she had seen him so many times, with his legs planted far apart and his arms crossed in front of him, his great black cape swirling out behind him, a glimmer in his deep blue eyes, a smile upon his lips.

Tears gathered in her eyes. "You returned to the painting, just as you said." She put her hand on his image in the portrait and was surprised to discover it was warm. "I shall miss you forever," she said. "If only you could have stayed."

"Don't cry lass. He would not want to see you so sad." Robert drew her arm through his, and the two of them started up the stairs.

"I truly came to love him," she said, "to love living in a haunted castle. He was like a father. It is difficult to think I will never see him again, heartbreaking to realize it is over."

Then from below in the portrait gallery she heard it. *Bam!*

The final book in
the breathtaking
Bride's Necklace
trilogy by
New York Times
bestselling author

Kat Martin

Trying to win back the trust of his jilted love, Rafael,
Duke of Sheffield, presents her with a stunning necklace
rumored to hold great power. As much as Dani wants
to believe it can right the wrongs of the past, she fears
there is one truth it cannot conceal, a truth that could
cost her this second chance with Rafe, the only man she
has ever loved....

The Handmaiden's Necklace

"Kat Martin is one of the best authors around!
She has an incredible gift for writing."
—*Literary Times*

*Available the first week of January 2006
wherever paperbacks are sold!*

MIRA®

www.MIRABooks.com

MKM2207

New York Times bestselling author

JENNIFER BLAKE

Lisette Moisant is a widow, courtesy of the swordsmanship of Caid O'Neill. He bested her loathsome husband in a duel, but now she is a target for schemers who wish to steal her fortune and see her dead. It is Caid to whom she turns for protection, and guilt leaves him no recourse but to agree to Lisette's request.

But soon New Orleans is flooded with rumors, suggesting the two plotted to kill Lisette's husband all along. In a society where reputation is everything, the scandal threatens Lisette and Caid with ruin…and the person responsible will stop at nothing until they have paid with their lives.

Dawn Encounter

"The first in Blake's new series evokes everything alluring about New Orleans."
—*Romantic Times BOOKclub on Challenge to Honor*

Available the first week of January 2006 wherever paperbacks are sold!

LUANNE JONES

"No better than a pack of heathens." That's what their grandmother called Charma Deane, Bess and Minnie, three cousins growing up in rural Orla, Arkansas. To them, nothing could be better than being a heathen girl. But when Charma Deane is betrayed several times by her cousin Bess, she leaves Orla.

Now, years after leaving the "Aunt Farm" behind, Charma Deane's back to make peace with the past and repair the strained ties with Bess, and they remind each other of their old vow: live without limits, love without question, laugh without apologies and make sure that whoever dies first won't be sent to heaven looking like hell.

Heathen Girls

"Reading Luanne Jones is like an afternoon with a best friend. Lots of warmth, wicked wit and enough heart-wrenching honesty to keep things interesting."
—*New York Times* bestselling author Deborah Smith

*Available the first week of January 2006
wherever books are sold!*

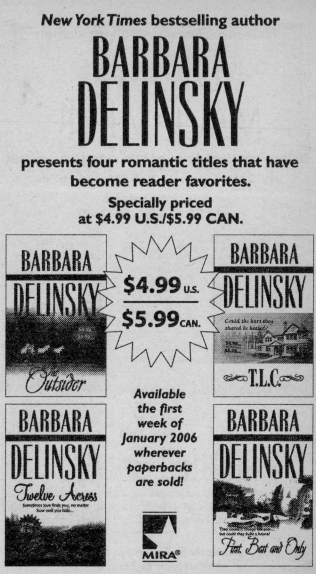

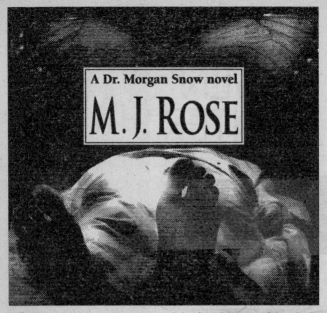

A Dr. Morgan Snow novel
M. J. ROSE

The Scarlet Society is a secret club of twelve powerful and sexually adventurous women. But when a photograph of the body of one of the men they've recruited to dominate—strapped to a gurney, the number 1 inked on the sole of his foot—is sent to the *New York Times,* they are shocked and frightened. Unable to cope with the tragedy, the women turn to Dr. Morgan Snow. But what starts out as grief counseling quickly becomes a murder investigation, with any one of the twelve women a potential suspect.

THE
DELILAH COMPLEX

"A creepily elegant and sophisticated novel, with keen psychological insights. M. J. Rose is a bold, unflinching writer and her resolute honesty puts her in a class by herself."
—Laura Lippman

Available the first week of January 2006
wherever paperbacks are sold!

MIRA®

www.MIRABooks.com   MMR2215